Elisabeth

Elisabeth

*Excerpts from the diary
of a Mennonite girl in the Gran Chaco*

By
Peter P. Klassen

Translated by
Jack Thiessen

Illustrated by
Mathew Staunton

evertype

2016

Published by Evertype, 73 Woodgrove, Portlaoise, R32 ENP6, Ireland. *www.evertype.com.*

Original title: *Elisabeth: Aus dem Tagebuch eines mennonitischen Mädchens im Gran Chaco.* Filadelfia: Verein für Geschichte und Kultur der Mennoniten in Paraguay, 2009. ISBN 978-3-7357-5702-9

Editor: Ernest N. Braun.

First edition February 2016.

ISBN-10 1-78201-150-1
ISBN-13 978-1-78201-150-7

Typeset in Minion Pro and Caslon Openface by Michael Everson.

Cover: Mathew Staunton.

Printed by: LightningSource.

Contents

About this book

*E*LISABETH—*EXCERPTS FROM THE DIARY OF A MENNONITE GIRL IN THE GRAN CHACO*—*is a novel. Accounts of this kind, selected from an isolated and relatively small settlement like a Mennonite colony in the Paraguayan Chaco, give eager rise to the temptation to identify individuals and their particulars.*

Such deliberations are futile because none of the people here depicted are literal; the village named is likewise fictitious. And yet, these fragments, sketched on a background which reveals a particular community, do constitute a reality and are therefore true to life, for in literature fiction can become fact. In this context, the short life of Elisabeth indeed assumes the contours of reality.

Elisabeth Unruh blooms in the time allotted her and within the religious, social and political norms of her community, her church and the world as it plays out at the time; she blooms, then fades like the Queen of the Night flower of the Chaco bush of her world. The life of a Mennonite girl in a Mennonite community integrated in and with a wider world, nolens volens, is the actual background of this novel. Elisabeth grows up in a world of friction in which a community of faith, Mennonitism, works out its distinctive facets of Christian faith within a societal tradition, daily impacting the early life of the protagonist. In spite of conflicts too numerous to count—the majority of which are intangible but distinctly pervasive—these conflicts are resolved by faith.

Choosing excerpts from a personal diary is a literary device to convey immediacy.

This work is actually similar to a testament, a legacy bequeathed. And while it is a monologue, it is on the lookout for an object, a compassionate opposite. I, personally, cannot very well be this opposite; the obvious discrepancy in age between Elisabeth and me rules out such possibility. And yet, the accompanying note attached to the diary, invited me as her conversational partner. While reading

1

the voluminous record, I found myself transported to a confessional, moved by the depth of soul and the loneliness of a fellow human in the search for a path in the labyrinth called life.

The diary consisting of four thick note pads has been sitting in a drawer of my writing desk for many years. The silverfish have eroded the silk paper which carefully encased the covering in numerous places. Only the picture with Dürers Praying Hands on the last of the notebooks has completely survived.

Some fragments of the paper, the ink, and the writing itself reveal the effects of the passage of time, even without any annotation. The first parts consist of fibrous paper. The keeper of the diary took care to prevent the home-made ink from blotching and the sharp steel pen point from spreading. The letters, in Gothic script, have been completely preserved in their original form and reveal curlicues and minor adornments as were common to school practices of the time. Those were lean times and writing wares were hard to come by. Gradually the quality of the paper improves, her writing gains confidence, and the final pages reveal the consistency of writing effected by a fountain pen. Without question, the thought patterns and emphases develop and mature in the course of time.

The year is frequently missing from the entries, and yet it is entirely possible to verify the chronology. Also, I established that the sheet lightning of world events, as revealed by the keeper of the diary, is accurately reflected by the young girl's sensitive soul. In so doing, she evokes the larger context. Any reader acquainted with the progression of historical events at the time will very quickly establish the necessary bearings.

The entire literary depictions which Elisabeth Unruh presented to her much younger counterpart shortly before her early death encompass less than twenty years. And yet twenty years, it appears to me, are quite sufficient to reveal everything life has to offer.

Although the accompanying note, as mentioned, was meant as a concluding statement to the entirety of the diary record, it is intended here to serve as an introduction.

My dear Luise!

By way of gratitude for all you have done for me with your dear and warm heart, I would like to bequeath to you my diary.

It was my intention to gift you my diary at Christmas. However, since we do not know where the lights of Christmas will burn for us this year, I will give it to you already now. You will probably read it with great discernment and possibly be too consternated by it all to do anything with such reading. If my diary were to have a title, it would probably be called "Mein zweites Gesicht" (My Other Face), which it will be for many.

All others, with the exception of you, know me only in one dimension, from one side: "Joy, a beautiful spark of the gods", and so on. But it is you who was allowed the occasional peak behind the obvious. This was of such help to me that I will never forget it. However, this other dimension is just as much part of me; in fact, it may well be that I am this other side. The known, my obvious side, is what I shared with people who were in my daily presence. I lived the other side only after I closed the door behind me.

Does it have to be this way? Why does it have to be like that? It is similar to a boil, a carbuncle which drains away at you, if you live as lonely as I did.

My brother David once said, he wished my eyes were windows through which he could see my heart. I told him that if that were the case I would draw the shades. Then we laughed and he again saw only the obvious side of me.

But now I open the windows wide and you can look into my heart. Some of what I have to say is known to you, since you shared some of my recent experiences. It is exactly this which gives me the courage to open the windows wide before you.

I now see how your good eyes look at me as they often did if words were of no avail. At such times you walked at my

side as if you were part of me. And now you are to receive a
part of me. Why did I not already give you this part of me
previously? Possibly because it was a dream, my deep
longing, my unfulfilled longing.

And now may God be with you.

Yours,

Elisabeth.

*Premonition of death? Before I let Elisabeth have a word—after her
words lodged quietly such a long while with her and even much longer
with me— it is time she had a word, and it surely would be in her
interest if I added a few words of explanation.*

*It was a long time ago that the pages of this diary were written.
Possibly much has changed in both the small circle, which had such
disastrous implications for the life of this individual, and in the larger
world as well. Much has likewise changed in all of our thinking and
our sensitivities. From that perspective it might be helpful if I were to
present a background and introduce some appurtenances from the
past to the stage on which the drama unfolds.*

*Elisabeth was sixteen when she arrived in the Chaco of Paraguay
with her family, together with a group of Mennonite immigrants. She
had been molded by the revolution and the civil war in Russia, then
by the flight from Moscow, Soviet Union, to Germany in 1929, and by
the brief stay in Germany from where she came to South America.*

*With her parents and five siblings, she shared the experience of
settling in a village in the Fernheim Colony located in the wilderness
of the Chaco; together they settled on a plot of land which they slowly
fashioned into a farm. This village then was her world, and it is this
world which she described and in which a reciprocal molding
transpired. This was the world of a community marked by a common
destiny, and determined by the principles of an ancient tradition of
faith. The forebears of this community of settlers were the Swiss
Anabaptists of the sixteenth century, known as Mennonites, who in
the course of time settled in common endeavour in the Netherlands,
and from there fled eastwards to Prussia, then to Russia. Their brand
of faith dominated not only their rigid tradition but asserted itself also*

in every detail of daily living. Various Mennonite splinter churches, resulting from many schisms, played a role in shaping the atmosphere in the small villages.

In Russia the stricter, pietistic Mennonite Brethren had separated from the main traditional Mennonite church body, and this divergence influenced and affected the life of these Paraguayan Anabaptists in the extreme. It was this age-old spiritual and clannish disposition which shaped and molded everything in the new community in this alien land, and it is here where Elisabeth blossomed, then bloomed with bright profusion, similar in my opinion to the Queen of the Night, a cactus flower, which comes alive briefly but splendidly in the bushes of the Chaco night.

It was always so: rare flowers swell to rare profusion in human society, poor as that society may be and as restrictively conventional as mankind tends to make it. The flower will bloom, since it is meant to; that is the mission of flowers: beauty, freedom. Such a flower surprises with its rich inner life, its sensitivity, its receptiveness which defies all odds and every chance of a restrictive community to provide adequate nurture.

Possibly this diary came to be precisely for this reason; it is the product of a soul which attempts to come to an understanding of its very self, its existence and its essence, which, it appears, is irretrievably intertwined with a community , intertwined or, possibly, captured by it.

Although I am obviously part of that very process of deciding what should remain of the diary, and what ought to be rejected, my intent is to deal with the inevitable gaps by inserting my understanding of this existential situation, so that reader can understand a little better.

I have divided the diary contents into four main categories and in categorizing the phases of her life in this progressive way, I have come to a better understanding of Elisabeth and how she developed. These phases obviously emerge due to the progression of time and the maturity of Elisabeth. Based on these developments, Elisabeth's diaries are not so much linear progressions as they are all part of a great sweep of a cycle that comes full circle. Or is it all the ancient vertical depiction of a human soul intertwined in its earthly life in all its drives, desires, longings, reservations and guilt while here below on earth, and subsequently facing a redemptive judgment in eternity? May the reader reach his/her own conclusions according to whichever criteria they apply to the case.

—Peter P. Klassen

THE QUEEN OF THE NIGHT

The Queen of the Night

20 October 1932

Mama is so dear and understanding. When she knows that I intend to write in my diary she makes the hurricane lantern available to me. I can then sit outside under the shadow roof of our house at the great table. And while the mosquitoes are a bit of a bother, they are not nearly the problem as they are farther outside, when we have to hoe the weeds in the cotton fields. Mama sits inside by the lamp with Jake. She is reading the *Bote* ("Messenger"), a German newspaper from Canada, while Jake is studying a book for school. Occasionally Mama also reads the *Mennonitische Rundschau* ("Mennonite Review") also published in Canada and which neighbours share with us. The "Messenger" is published by the Mennonite General Conference while the "Review" is a Mennonite Brethren paper. We belong to the Conference; our neighbours are M.B.'s.

Mama reads all evening long, page after page and later tells Papa about the many relatives and friends who migrated from Russia to Canada in the Twenties when things became constantly worse in our Old Home. I can still well remember how we left our village of Rosenthal by the Dnieper. Uncle Heinrich and his family were also part of that departing party.

"If only we would have joined them," says Mama, and then she sighs deeply. "Then we would also be in Canada now and not here in the Chaco, and our Maria would be with us as well."

Jake reads a great deal. He brings books along from the high school. While we are hoeing, he tells me what he has been reading. His favourite is *From Pole to Pole* by Sven Hedin. These are descriptions of foreign worlds. Jake is such an engaging narrator that sometimes I overlook the weeds while listening to him.

Papa is away at a village meeting, the village assembly. The settlers are deliberating as to whether they should be digging a third well in the village. The two wells on the Village Street do not provide sufficient water for all the people and the animals. Now frequently soldiers arrive with their horses and mules to water them at the village wells. The next well is far away. We girls have to fetch the water from the well in pails. The boys have no time to haul water since they look after the harder labour. They split the firewood, build fences and do municipal road work in the village. I put on a shoulder yoke and carry two pails of water at the same time. This yoke which fits my shoulders exactly was made by Papa and it is the nicest in the village.

Yesterday when I arrived at the well for water, Heinrich Friesen also happened to be there. The well has a wheel which has a pail attached at either end of a rope. When I pull up the full pail, the empty pail slides down into the well. Heinrich had to draw water before evening so that his cattle could arrive later to drink at a full trough. When I arrived at the well, he laughed and said, "I will help you, Lizzie" and then he filled my two pails. This has never happened before. No boy in the village ever helped me draw water. I thanked him while Heinrich hung the two full pails on my yoke. When I turned around again, I noticed that Heinrich was looking after me. Heinrich is no pious boy, the other people say. He is not converted, not born-again.

But what lot of confusion am I here putting to paper? A diary, after all, is meant to serve the purpose of self-reflection. However, I prefer to reflect on such matters which I cannot very well talk about, and I cannot speak about Heinrich to others either. That would lead to immediate gossip in the village.

I was the first to get up this morning. I started the fire in the stove which is located on the yard underneath a tree. We cook and fry everything there and do our baking in an oven adjacent, since we have no kitchen. When the fire was burning briskly and I set the water kettle on it, I looked to the East as if entranced. The skies were redder than red and the sun's rays fell on the *Urundey*, the tree on our yard and painted it red. And also the parrots which flew over our yard shimmered red in the sun, all the more surprising since they are green. They always fly as a couple and they alternatingly rasp while they fly. They are Amazon parrots, Jake tells me. I looked after the last couple until they disappeared behind the bushes.

"What are you dreaming about, Lizzy?" mother called from the window. "Get on with the coffee, we want to have breakfast." Was I really dreaming? Of what? Possibly about the parrot couple?

Now David and Abraham are returning from the fields. I had better stop writing since they would like to know what the diary has to offer.

21 October 1932

I intended to write about our work last night, but then when my big brothers returned I quickly shut my diary. David would surely mock me if he knew what I was writing.

We spend all day long hoeing weeds. Immediately after breakfast Abraham hitches an ox to the cultivator and then slowly tills the rows of cotton. We three, David, Lena and I then chop the weeds which the cultivator did not manage to kill. In the afternoon, when Jake returns from school he joins us in hoeing. We two then hold back a bit since we like to talk. Jake has much to tell about school and also about things in general. A war is raging in the Chaco, already as of September, and Jake has much to report on it.

Today something remarkable happened while hoeing. The hoe functions with a will of its own, almost, and the weeds, white-headed, wither. Then my hoe hit a weed which had a most peculiar scent to it. I rubbed this leaf in my hand and smelled it. Then I suddenly found myself on our churchyard in Rosenhof when our uncle was buried. Uncle Abraham. The Communists had shot him because his son, Hans, had served in the Mennonite Para-Military Unit. Many were shot dead at that time. The cemetery had the exact same smell to it as did the weed in my hand. I was seven or eight years old at that time and it is now more than ten years ago.

"Why do you remain standing?" asked Jake.

"Smell this," I said. "I have to think of the cemetery in Rosenthal; can you imagine that?"

"Yes," said Jake. "I can imagine that. Whenever I smell cow manure, that smell takes me right back to our cow barn in Russia," he said while laughing.

"Today I thought of the soldiers who marched through Rosenthal, first the Reds and then the Whites," said Jake. "Today we stood by the road fence at our school in Schönwiese and many soldiers marched past in a westerly direction. A great battle was fought to the south against the Bolivians who had advanced to the Chaco, our teachers said."

"Hopefully things will not be like in Russia, and hopefully they will have no canons," I said and Jake again laughed because I am so easily afraid. The Reds shot across the Dnieper with their canons and we had to lie flat to the floor in our rooms.

We had both remained standing, forgetting about our work. Lena and David were way ahead of us. We then busied ourselves to catch up with them. Lena and David like to work together. Then they talk about their Youth Meetings and their choir practices and about the weddings in the village and about the boys and girls.

And now I want to go to sleep. I am allowed to take the lantern to my bed. Then I read my Bible. When I was converted in June, I started reading the New Testament. Lena sleeps in the same room as I do. She fetches books from the teacher and then she tells these stories to her Sunday School kids. We both like to read and never get in each other's way.

7 November 1932

I will hide my diary because I do not want anyone to read what I am now writing. What happened the day before yesterday is something I will not likely forget, and certainly not now that I am writing about it. I do not know whether this incident made me sad, or whether it irritated me. And yet, deep down in my heart I experienced joy. I ask myself whether I am entitled to this happiness. Then, again, I think that I did nothing regarding this matter whatsoever. Even if this little item of joy is as minute as a droplet of dew on the grass when we enter the fields of cotton in the morning, the morning sun can take something so minute and render it golden. I feel similarly inclined.

It was Saturday, at eight in the evening. Mama and I were the only ones at home. All the others had gone to a Prayer Meeting. Possibly

Abraham had not gone either. He does not like to attend Prayer Meetings, even though he is already baptized.

I had washed my hair and wrapped a towel around my head. I had just taken a book to read. Lena brought it along from her teacher. It is called *Homeless*, and I find it engrossing. Then a clapping noise was to be heard. In Russia we knocked at the door when announcing ourselves while here we clap our hands when arriving on a yard; possibly because here the doors are generally opened wide, or, possibly, because initially we had no doors since we lived in tents. Now someone was clapping on our yard, and Mama went outside. Then I heard Heinrich Friesen's voice.

"Is Lizzie at home?" he asked. My heart beat so loudly that I heard its little thunder. Heinrich knew that I as at home and wanted to see me. Mama closed the door, and then she looked in my room. "Friesen's Heinrich was here and he asked for you. You have nothing going on with him, do you, my little child?" she asked. Mama's voice had a strict edge to it. I said no and continued reading.

Mama remained standing in the door. Then I looked up and said no once again. Possibly there was a trace of anger in my voice. And, of course, nothing was going on between Heinrich and me. The fact that he helped me at the well and cast a farewell look in my direction is something I cannot help or hinder.

"Watch out, my child, whatever you do," she said and sighed so deeply that I felt sorry for her. "Heinrich is not a pious person," she added.

These Friesens come from Sagradowka, and the girls claim that he already had had a bride there. He is already twenty five. I don't want to think of this incident any longer and would rather enjoy the droplet of dew or the Amazon parrot couple winging its happy way. At such times, Jake asks whether I am dreaming. Possibly I actually do dream and hopefully I will not dream about Heinrich.

Obviously Mama has informed Papa that Heinrich Friesen was here. I will not tell Jake about the matter. He would only laugh and crack jokes. Jake is fourteen and he says that the girls in school are stupid geese.

We had a hard day today. Jake and I went to the bush with Papa to saw posts for a fence. Papa cleared the trees of brush and cactus and then we two sawed them off with a draw saw. We were drenched in sweat and came home dead tired. I quickly wanted to record in my diary what happened this Saturday. Possibly I will rid myself of all thoughts by committing them to the written word. My diary is now headed for its spot below the mattress while I am heading straight for sleep.

15 November 1932

We had a very heavy rain, harder than ever before in my experience. I am again sitting outside by my dear, faithful lantern, and all around me wherever water stands there is chirping and croaking to be heard, like in a giant concert. The air is fresh and clean. Last night at nine, lightning flashed all over, followed by heavy thunder, and then rain fell all night by the bucket.

Mama got up, lit the lamp and sat down in the Middle Room and read the Bible. "That is how we also did it in Russia," she said, "when the lightning was so dangerous."

Papa was not about to be disturbed. "When the rain rushes, I can sleep all the better," he said, "and lightning strikes as God wills it."

The great masses of water brought to mind the soldiers who made their way through our village the day before yesterday, a whole regiment of cavalry. Their horses were emaciated and tired. Jake observed that the troop had no fodder for their horses and that they could not survive from the grass on the meadows. This regiment made its way to Toledo, said Jake, where they meant to build a fortification. How do these poor soldiers make do after such a heavy downpour? Presumably they do not even possess tents.

Today we simply enjoyed all the water after a long, dry winter. All of nature is celebrating, taking a day off. We could not manage any work on the fields because they were partially submerged by water. Behind the fields a thousand-voice choir of frogs droned. It was like a holiday, and we walked barefoot to the edge of the bush. Trees and thickets—all were under water. I covered my ears since the noisy choir of whistling and blowing, with nature's pipe organs at full blare, was too much for the human ear to bear. The boys rolled up their pant legs. Lena and I hiked up our skirts and waded to the next meadow pool, which stretched ahead of us like a great mirror.

Jake started splashing us and the others returned the wet favour and soon we were all wet. We slowly splashed our way back through a wet world. I was inattentive and sank up to my knees into a deserted mole hole. Abraham pulled me out, while remarking with a naughty grin, "Lizzie, Heinrich Friesen sends you his regards, and he asked whether you were ill two weeks ago, on a Saturday."

I was too taken aback to say a word of an answer.

"Yes, yes, she was sick" said Jake, while splashing water at me. "Sick of heart is what she was."

Everyone laughed and so did I, in order to hide my embarrassment. And now it is not only Mama who is in the know. Now the whole village will talk about a matter which I so much wanted to forget. Two weeks have passed and now the difference is that a droplet of dew has turned into a heavy downpour: from my knowing to an entire village's engaging in chewing of the cud of gossip.

2 December 1932

Our kitchen is now finished, ready. We did all the work ourselves. First we fashioned all the clay bricks on the water meadow because the clay there is good. Fortunately we managed that before the heavy downpour for otherwise the water would have torn it all away.

Abraham laid the wall like a professional mason. Papa built all the doors and windows on the carpenter's bench under the shadow roof. Then we laid the straw roof thatching. This was difficult work with everyone getting involved except Mama.

One of the boys dipped the reed bundles into the clay in the trough while two boys stood on the ladder and handed these bundles to

David, and Abraham glued them to the lathes. The reed roof is a thing of beauty. Then Jake took an axe and a wood mallet and straightened the lower side; this was done to perfection since he had spanned a taut string at a perfectly straight line.

"I am the kitchen's barber," he said. He is a joker.

Then Lena and I plastered the ceiling with clay and cow manure before we whitewashed it as a finishing touch. We fetched white ash from a burnt *quebracho* stump, which comes in handy for the whitewash. The ceiling and the walls are now snow white. And now I can occasionally sit down at the kitchen table when I want to write, or on Saturdays after the week's work is done, or on Sunday afternoons.

I have to write a bit about the war, for it scares me from time to time. Then invariably Russia comes to mind, where, while I was very young, I lived with daily fear like all the others. Once our village was in the hands of the Reds, then the Whites and then the marauding Machno bands. These burned, raped and murdered.

"This is nothing like in Russia," said Jake, "this is a real war with a real front." Jake speaks some Spanish, and whenever troops come marching into our village, he sidles up to them. When he then comes home he knows every detail about their weapons, their uniforms and their kitchen fare.

Papa was also in the school in which the commander has established his quarters. The entire school grounds were full of machine guns. "They have nothing but old weapons," he reported on his return. Possibly leftovers from the World War, which Paraguay purchased. Papa was an orderly in Russia in his time and claims to know his way around.

Recently Papa was in Trebol, which is now a military camp. When we came to this country, this town was our first tent camp. It was there that he met some Russian officers, named Belaieff and Ern. During the Civil War they had been officers under General Wrangel of the White Army, and then they fled like we did. And now Papa met them in the Chaco, where they are actively engaged in the Paraguayan Army. Papa was obviously moved since he had an opportunity to speak Russian again.

"The Russians know something about war," he said with a trace of pride. "Belaieff is constructing a defence unit in Toledo, which is meant to defeat the enemy. The Bolivians will attack here," said Papa, and Toledo is only twenty kilometres removed from our village. Jake calls this a real war. He takes joy in war while I am afraid.

15 December 1932

It was my intention to write a diary about myself but now I find myself writing about the war. The reason for this is that the war has come so close and because everyone talks about it with grave concern. Every day soldiers march or ride through our village and always in a westerly direction, towards Toledo.

Jake says the soldiers always ask about the girls in the village and whether he has any sisters. They know the words, "nice lady" and then they laugh. Jake believes the girls better be careful and keep away from the soldiers. How is one to live under these circumstances? Am I to constantly take cover just because I am a girl? And who will then fetch water from the village well?

We were much startled yesterday. Only Mama, Mena, and I were at home, working in the kitchen. Then we heard the street gate rattle, and when I looked through the window I saw two riders coming on our yard. They were soldiers; I recognized them by their ponchos which extended to their boots and also by the daggers which hung from their saddles.

"Soldiers are coming into our yard," I whispered.

"Hide yourselves, girls," whispered Mama very excitedly, while she crawled underneath the table. Lena and I ducked under the Dutch door which consists of two halves with the upper half standing open.

The riders remained standing close to the street gate. One of them clapped his hands while the other one called out. This sounded like a hello greeting. We hardly dared breathe and when I looked out of the window after a while, both riders had disappeared.

When Mama crawled from underneath the table it was so funny that I held my mouth shut so as not to burst out laughing. But Mama noticed this and she scolded me.

"Crazy child," she said while sobbing, "you have no idea what might yet come, when war and soldiers come marching along." And then she told about Russia, and how horrible things had been to the women and children when the roving bands devastated our villages. Many of the women and children then had to be taken to the hospital in Chortitz because the soldiers had infected them with dreaded diseases.

Lena looked down and said not one word while I was so startled because Mama started sobbing aloud, rendering her speechless.

What will become of us if constantly more soldiers arrive? Does Jake know what the business of women and diseases is all about? I cannot bring myself to ask him.

The two men on horses looked so serious, almost sad.

25 December 1932

I had hardly thought that Christmas Eve could be so beautiful. Mama had been very sad all day long before Christmas Eve. She simply could not get used to the heat at this time of year. For her it was not Christmas time when you sweated while baking cakes and the cicadas chirped so loud that you had to stop your ears.

Christmas and snow were so beautiful, and Christmas in Prenzlau in the refugee camp in Germany was the most beautiful of all. We had never before experienced a Christmas so festive and so fragrant. Everything had been prepared for us, the refugees: a Christmas tree that extended right to the ceiling and full of real candles, and glorious Christmas songs which we had never heard before. And here, of all places we sing "Softly the snow is falling."

And now Christmas Eve was so beautiful that I will never forget it. The military had departed and the teacher had practised songs, poetry and skits with the pupils. The men from our village had felled a tree in the bush which we girls decorated all afternoon. We had fashioned these decorations during the previous evenings. There were chains made from bright paper as well as stars and flowers. We wrapped fruits from the forest in silver paper to look like bells. One family had managed to bring along real wax candles from Germany. Unfortunately these candles soon bowed and bent since it was so humid.

And yet, everyone was so happy, probably because the entire village was assembled. The children were dressed in sparkling cleanliness. Their eyes radiated with pure joy. And also the village youth was all there, the girls in new dresses, the boys in white shirts.

We stood around on the school grounds for a while before we entered the school. The boys cracked jokes, led in that department by my brother, Jake, and the girls laughed. Then I noticed Heinrich. Our eyes met. Heinrich looked very serious. Greta, my best friend noticed this as well and she clasped my hand. "Heinrich Friesen is looking at you," she whispered. Fortunately no one noticed how the blood shot into my face and my heart thundered.

I want to be quite honest about this. Was Christmas Eve so beautiful for me because our eyes met, quietly and seriously? Hardly, it was on account of the great joy, that our Saviour was born. It was a great joy for me that Jesus was there for me, too. How joyful it would be if Heinrich was of similar opinion. However, Greta also knew that Heinrich was a non-believer.

When we then sang "*Lobt Gott, ihr Christen, allzugleich/In seinem höchsten Thron* (You Christians, altogether, praise God on his highest throne) with everyone from our village joining in, I knew that I was converted, and a child of God, saved through Jesus Christ my Saviour. For this reason Christmas was so special for me, and the heat was no deterrent.

The nicest part of the celebration came later that night when the youth of the entire village went carolling from door to door. We had practiced appropriate songs for the occasion during choir practice. However, the younger set too, which did not yet belong to the choir, also joined in the singing; Heinrich was part of our group as well. "Holy Night, Holy Night, you beam in holy stars so bright", is a song

I would like to sing all year long. The stars in the sky shone so brilliantly that you could almost read.

When we arrived at the Neufeld yard, we were served watermelon. Here we sang "The Prince of Peace" our finest song and then we ate that most precious of universal Mennonite fruit. Neufelds produce the finest watermelons far and wide, with some weighing twenty kilos.

Then our choir disbanded and we went home. Suddenly Heinrich was walking alongside of me. "You sang very beautifully, Lizzie," he said.

"Yes, it was most beautiful," is all I knew to say. "Good Night" I said, and then I ran until I reached the home gate. Was that stupid of me?

10 January 1933

The year of 1933 started with a storm. Christmas time was peaceful and serene and full of harmony, and then inclement weather set in. Everyday airplanes fly over our villages, sometimes three at a time. I did not know that planes of such size existed. They keep a fair distance away from the main village street, because the village is manned by the military. The school yard is also occupied and the soldiers have here constructed a bunker out of massive tree trunks. They store their ammunition here, so Jake reported.

Today a troop of mules arrived. The riders galloped through the village and whooped as they rode, as if for joy. Tomorrow they may well die but today they whoop and holler.

We also had to terminate our baptismal instructions. Reverend Reimer had already invited us to meet in the school. We had planned to meet there every Wednesday. But then the regiment came to our village, and the officers again occupied the school house. Now we have to wait for catechism instructions, possibly for weeks on end.

We had recently been studying the first question, and Reverend Reimer spent an entire evening addressing it. "What is meant to be your greatest and most constant concern?" The answer is: "My salvation!" We are meant to make this issue our life-long concern, the minister said. "Be mindful to be saved with fear and trembling" is how the verse goes which we are meant to learn.

When I told Greta about the catechism, she dismissed the issue with "If you are saved, learning the catechism is unnecessary."

Greta's parents belong to the Mennonite Brethren Church, where no catechism instruction is held prior to baptism. "In the General Conference Church the catechism is learned with baptism following, whether or not you are saved", she said arrogantly, "and that is totally wrong. The Mennonite Brethren have found the right way. First you are saved and received the forgiveness of sins, and then follows the assurance of salvation, and only then should you be baptized. Learning the catechism is of no consequence."

"However, I, too, am saved," I said.

"That is fine and good," she said, "but then the question of baptism emerges. In the Brethren Church we are immersed, backwards in deep water. This is what the Bible teaches. The General Conference Church pours a little water on your head, but that is no real baptism."

I was most unhappy. Greta is my best friend, but when she discusses baptism and the assurance of faith she strikes me as cold and unloving.

When I asked Papa about this matter, he reacted impatiently and angrily. "Who initiates this quarrel?" he demanded. "Possibly Reverend Reimer? This quarrel is caused by the itinerant minister Epp from the Brethren when he comes to town and denounces the General Conference."

I was more confused than ever. It was at the time that Preacher Epp came to town that I was saved in our school, as were others in my class. I do not know why this leads to quarreling. I would like to continue studying the catechism since the Reverend Reimer explains it in loving detail.

I would like to discuss this with David at some time. David read the Bible often and well. He is converted and studied the catechism and was baptized in the manner that the General Conference practises it. He often argues about conversion with Abraham. Conversion is superfluous, says Abraham.

Sometimes I believe that David may well transfer to the Mennonite Brethren Church. Mama says that in Russia many left the General Conference. If they were converted they were baptized yet again in the Mennonite Brethren Church and that by immersion. This led to much quarreling in many Mennonite families. Parents simply could not understand why their children switched to the Brethren Church. Occasionally the reverse was also true.

I am convinced that I am converted and I will stay in my church. Let Greta say what she will.

2 February 1933

I manage to write in my diary only rarely. I can do it only in the evening, but then I am so tired from the work of the day that all I want is to sleep. We are harvesting peanuts, and this is the hardest work imaginable. After a rain the earth is wet, and the peanut plants have to be pulled out of the ground by hand. This is most difficult, and sometimes Jake and I have to join forces and pull the plant out together. These plants are then placed with the fruit upwards so they can dry more readily. Then we heap them into piles with pitchforks. We sweat profusely in the hot sun. Then we sit in a circle and pull the peanuts from the plants.

And yet the work is pleasant. While pulling the little nuts from the roots we share experiences or tell stories. When the sun set today, we each placed a full bag of peanuts on our shoulders and carried the harvested peanuts home.

Since I am writing about peanuts anyway… Yesterday we stood on our yard after work and with five bags of freshly harvested peanuts, and all in one day. "And now we have our own peanut oil," said Papa proudly. Then soldiers came on our yard, possibly ten in number. Some of them were barefoot and they looked hungry. Each one then displayed something, either a pocket knife, or a small scissors or a small piece of soap while repeatedly saying "pan, pan" meaning bread.

Then Papa went to the kitchen and fetched a tin plate and opened a bag of peanuts. He filled the plate with nuts and approached the first soldier. He pulled his hat from his head and Papa filled it with peanuts. Then the second stepped forward and his hat was likewise filled. The others followed suit until they all had had their fill of peanuts. Then they laughed and all spoke at once, saying "gracias, gracias": thank you, thank you! They were left their little tokens of exchange. The peanut bag was half empty.

When the soldiers had departed, Mama came to the door. "That was the right thing to do, Papa," she said. Earlier in the morning she had complained about these very soldiers who at night had raided our watermelon patch. They had cut many green watermelons into pieces and ignored them. Now she praised Papa for his good deed.

During lunch Papa told a story about a Peters family originally from Kleefeld in Russia. This Peters kept watch in the watermelon patch with his shotgun. He kept well hidden in the kaffir field. When the soldiers appeared to steal his melons, Peters rushed forward, yelling, "Ruchi Werch!"—Hands Up!

The soldiers got the message as he paraded them with hands up to their commander at their camp. This anecdote made the rounds in all the Mennonite colonies of Paraguay and people had a good laugh, including the Russian officer Ern in Trebol. Paraguayan soldiers listened to Russian commands!

The commander in our village is very strict with his charges, said Jake. He had witnessed how soldiers had stood on a fencepost while holding the stolen watermelons aloft in their hands. Mama worries about Jake since he constantly hangs out with the soldiers.

20 February 1933

L ast night the dogs in the entire village were howling. One started howling and soon every dog joined in the mournful choir.

"In Russia it was always the same when so many soldiers fell at the front," said Mama. "First the Russians told us these things and we laughed. The men from the Russian villages were all fighting at the front. Mennonite men from our villages were not required to bear arms. They provided alternative services like working in the forest or working as orderlies or medics, like our Papa. Then when the war lasted for years on end and became constantly more dangerous we also started listening to the dogs lament." Mama is suggesting that things in Trebol were likewise unfolding.

Papa was again in Trebol. There military hospitals are being built. Papa had seen wounded soldiers and also captured Bolivians.

It is only our Jake who enjoys the war. He is constantly up and away and around now that the school is out. He is into something every day and invariably has a story to tell. Yesterday he had his pant pockets full of shells. He gathered these from a bottle tree which the soldiers used for target practice with their machine guns, said Jake. The entire tree trunk plus all the heavy branches had all been shot clean off by the shooters. We heard the rattle of guns all day long.

Now Jake has a fire going in which he melts the lead from the bullets. The rattle of the machine guns and the howling of the dogs does not bother Jake in the slightest. He finds life in its every form most interesting.

"That's the way boys are," said Mama. "Things were the same in 1918 when the Germans came marching into our settlements. Then it was Abraham who was constantly with the German troops, and he would have preferred to join them when they departed. But then when the German soldiers had left all hell broke loose." Then Mama told us about her brother Hans who had joined the para-military Mennonite Police force and had disappeared without a trace. He was not even baptized, that's how young he was. When Mama talks about Russia, I listen most attentively. She then constantly draws parallels and analogies between that life and the life we live here.

28 February 1933

Now it is really here, the war. We spent yesterday and the day before yesterday cutting our kaffir and all the while we heard the roar of cannons from Toledo.

We were all outside on the kaffir field. First we cut off the white panicles and place them in heaps between the kaffir rows. Jake and I then stuff them into bags, and the David and Abraham carry the bags to our yard. There we have a threshing floor fashioned out of stamped clay. Papa has built threshing flails and when the kaffir is dry we thresh it. Kaffir is highly important for us. It is ground to flour industrially in Filadelfia and we use it for baking as well as fodder for the chickens and pigs.

When Jake and I have filled two bags, we sit down on them and wait until our brothers arrive with empty bags. Yesterday we sat quietly on the full bags and we heard the thunder of war raging in Toledo. The Bolivians are attacking the fortress and, if they succeed, they will occupy our villages.

Then Jake resumed his telling, "The grenades rip everything apart. The soldiers who crossed our village were from Nanawa. There the Bolivians attacked them like they are now doing in Toledo. The grenades tear off the arms or the legs. Then the dung flies arrive and soon maggots wriggle in every wound, just like in our cattle when they suffer wounds."

I was so shocked at hearing this that I had to keep my mouth shut with my hands. Then even Jake was quiet as we were thinking about the soldiers in Toledo. When we sat at the dinner table tonight, there was more audible rumblings of war than during daytime.

"And now the soldiers will soon pass through our village," said mother, sobbing and sighing. "Just like in Russia, first the Whites and then the Reds following, with all taking along what was still left; our horses, our wagons, then the chickens and the pigs."

"The Bolivians will not manage to break through," said Jake determinedly. "They failed to take Nanawa, and they will not manage to take Toledo."

Things are unsettling. Today soldiers again moved through our village in a westerly direction, one military truck after another. Airplanes throbbed in the air, but I had thoughts altogether of a different kind. Why does Heinrich no longer come around? He will probably never return since he knows that Mama disapproves of him. Greta says that he is the most handsome fellow in our village. She prays that he will be converted. Heinrich's parents belong to the Brethren.

But what am I writing? I am far too young for Heinrich. He will find a different girl, one that is better suited to him, but then I would prefer not to be in the village.

5 March 1933

Two cars came to our village today driving very slowly. They brought injured soldiers. They were followed by five wagons. They brought food supplies and ammunition to Toledo, and now they are bringing injured soldiers as well.

I stood by the village street as one ox-cart after the other passed by our gate. I hear the injured groaning and moaning. One of these carts belongs to Friesens. When I recognized the oxen it was already too late for otherwise I would have quickly headed for our yard. Heinrich was sitting on that wagon. He greeted me warmly enough and I returned his gesture. The wagon proceeded to our village school. Jake, the invariable Johnny on the spot, made for the school where the wounded were laid out on straw. When he came home he said not one word, not even during lunch.

In the afternoon the women from our village went to the school. They took milk, bread and other edibles for the injured parties. We do not have enough milk from our one cow, but Mama took eggs which she had gathered and took them along for the soldiers. I much wanted to accompany Mama but she did not allow me to walk with her.

"Young girls ought not to show themselves," she said strictly, while again probably thinking of Russia and that dreadful legacy.

And yet, the two officers who appeared on our yard yesterday were most polite. One truck stopped on the village road. One of the officers spoke some German. He wanted to exchange canned meat for our watermelons. Papa agreed to the trade. One can of meat for a watermelon. We were in need of meat. "That was good business," he said. "The watermelons will do the soldiers good."

When the officers noticed Lena and me, they bowed gently and saluted us. I cannot imagine that such friendly and polite men would harm any lady.

And yet, bad stories circulate in the village. I prefer not to put in writing what Greta had to report. "That is the way these Paraguayans are," she said. There are girls who are not careful. She knew that some girls went to Puerto Casado or even to Asunción in order to earn money there. "They probably will all lose their way," she suggested.

26 March 1933

The battle of Toledo is over. It turned out to be a great victory for Paraguay. "The enemy has been vanquished," Jake reported. Some cavalry men brought this news to our village and to the school yard, which is teeming with military, who cheered wildly.

When Jake came home he was full of news. The Bolivians had laid siege on Toledo for twenty days with hundreds falling near the Paraguayan firing trenches and, given the dreadful heat, corpses had been counted by the hundreds. Jake is an animated narrator and loves telling gruesome tales.

I told Jake this but he merely laughed me to scorn. He knew exactly how many weapons, machine guns and artillery pieces and cars, the Paraguayans had seized and captured. The enemy had withdrawn all the way to Corrales. One side celebrated while the other lay dead in the heat of the sun like so many starved horses of the cavalry on our many meadows to be fed upon by the carrion vultures.

Peace has been restored to our village. The school has been declared soldier-free and instruction can again commence. We can again conduct choir practice and the teacher can resume his youth work. Hopefully catechism instruction will shortly start again as well. Our life is again free, and we can walk the street without any danger lurking.

Soon a wedding will be celebrated. Tina Neufeld is the bride and Peter Janzen the groom. Whenever a wedding is pending the girls are eager to know what the bride will look like. Greta is of the opinion that the evening before the wedding the young people will engage in fun and games and that such frolicking is every bit as bad as dancing. Anyone who is saved should not dance or frolic. However, the Neufelds are General Conference and not converted; such is Greta's opinion and judgment.

Whenever Greta speaks like this I am hurt since my parents belong to the Conference. Sometimes I think that Greta is arrogant because her parents belong to the Brethren. Greta intends to experience baptism shortly. There is something like spiritual arrogance, says Papa.

And yet on Sundays we all sit together and worship together in our school and no one takes note to which congregation anyone belongs. After the church service, something unusual happened. There was no longer any mention of the war but everyone spoke about Germany and Adolf Hitler.

After the sermon, the teacher read a letter which he had received from a pastor in Mölln, a refugee camp in Germany in which we stayed before departing for Paraguay. The great danger of Communism in Germany is over, the pastor wrote. Adolf Hitler had assumed power. President Hindenburg, much loved by us all, had called Hitler to power. There was relief and joy in all of Germany.

People in churches were thanking God that Germany now had a powerful leader.

"And that is what we also intend to do," said the teacher. "No one knows better than we do what Communism is all about. Now Hitler has put an end to them with a forceful hand and it may well be that all our brothers and sisters in Russia will someday experience freedom."

When I looked at Mama I noticed that she had put a handkerchief to her eyes and that she was sobbing, as did the other women. Mama was obviously thinking yet again of Maria who remained in Russia together with her family. They resided in Neuendorf and were not yet ready to join us when we took off for Moscow. Then it was too late and Maria was left behind with her husband and their two children in Russia. Now mother worries no end about her oldest daughter and her family. Letters from Russia are a thing of the past, if at all.

2 April 1933

Yesterday was Tina Neufeld's wedding and I am happy that I have a diary in which I can describe everything. I derive much joy from recording my sentiments.

It was the first time I participated in making flowers together with the other girls; one flower for each guest. The boys get white flowers with two little bows, while the girls get coloured ones with twirled crosses tied across the arrangement. We made these flowers for several evenings by the light of petroleum lamps at the Neufeld home.

Tina was so happy, and we sang song after song. Our favourite songs now are the songs of youth at times of war and we remember the soldiers at their many fronts. Tina has recorded all these songs in an album. "The sun sank behind the horizon, way down in farthest west and so did all battles sink." Or "Softly chimes the bell of evening, and all lie down to rest." These are sad songs about love and death. That is the theme of present Paraguay.

Everyone in the village assisted in the wedding preparations. The mother of the bride prepared the dough for the buns, and the groom then had to distribute a bowl of dough to each family in the village where buns were then baked. Tables and benches from the entire village were taken to the school as well as cups, plates and cutlery. Each item is marked so that the rightful owners get their contribution returned after the occasion.

I also helped in the decorations at the school. We wound garlands from the greenery of the jacaranda bushes. The decorated chairs for the bridal couple were placed underneath two thick garlands. Whenever I smell the fragrant jacaranda from now on, I will always be reminded of weddings, or funerals for that matter, for then the wreaths are similarly fashioned from the same foliage.

The pre-wedding program (*Polterabend*) was held on the Neufeld yard. The bridal couple sat at a table and each guest walked up to them and presented them with a gift. When all had come, the gifts were unpacked. Cups, plates, glasses, cutlery and whatever else is needed for and by a new family had been gifted.

Then the Young People sat down in a circle and the games started. Greta and I sat down at some distance and watched the fun. "Such games are a temptation for those converted," said Greta. I had nothing to say to that. Singing, while couples circle, is the most popular. Then comes Gentleman's Choice followed by Ladies' Choice. At such Choices an unmarried guest walks up to lady, and offers her his arm. Then they walk in a circle with everyone singing to their heart's content. These are identical songs to the ones Tina has in her collection.

Abraham plays along and is jovial. If I were to tell him Greta's commentary he would laugh me to scorn. David no longer attends these *Polter*-evenings since he became converted. He says that he intends God to assign him his bride, and not to pick a girl from a group of frolickers.

Suddenly Heinrich stood in front of me. "Lizzie", he said, "come and join us in the circle. It is all just a matter of pure fun." Had I listened to my heart I would have gotten up and joined him. But it is exactly the heart where temptations linger, so it is claimed. Greta had placed her arm around me.

"I am not permitted to," I said. Did I say this out of cowardice or did I really withstand temptation? Do I not want to or am I not allowed to. I believe Heinrich laughed as he bowed and went his way.

"When and if Heinrich gets saved, he will be your groom," said Greta.

My heart was very heavy when I later walked home alone. Mama and Papa were sitting by the lamp and reading.

"I have already been waiting for you," said Mama.

I said nothing and went to my room. Was I defiant? I did not manage to fall asleep for a long time, and I heard singing coming from the Neufeld home.

23 April 1933

The High School in Schönwiese has again started and Jake is already in the third grade. He enjoys school very much and I envy him. My time to attend school has passed, is over. In Russia I had just completed public school but during our flight no schooling was possible. Here in Paraguay it was clear from the outset that Papa would only afford to send Jake to a higher level school. Moreover, there are many who believe that girls and higher education are a poor mix. And yet I am highly interested in what Jake tells about school and I examine and read all his books: his geography text, natural history and now even his physics book. Jake is patient with me and he explains all the sketches and illustrations and he answers all my many questions in matters I do not understand. Jake is my favourite brother.

Several boys from our village attend this high school. Schönwiese is a distant way for them. Whenever a truck drives this route, the driver takes the boys along. The number of cars on our roads is constantly increasing. When Jake came home yesterday, he was very quiet which is untypical for him. Even at table he said not one word.

"What is the matter, Jake?" I later asked.

"Lizzie," he said, "I am unwell, sick. When we were on our way home a pick-up passed us and then stopped to offer us a ride. The driver grinned as he asked us to get aboard. Only after we had reached a fair speed did we notice that something was lying on the floor, covered with a tarpaulin. When a strong gust of wind blew over our vehicle the tarp flew off and we saw a corpse without a head, a Bolivian soldier. I was sick to my stomach as I leaned over the side of the truck and puked. At the edge of the village the truck stopped and we jumped off. The driver laughed when he saw our pale faces. We said not one word but ran home. I cannot manage to eat one morsel."

Whenever Jake experiences something like this his enthusiasm for war is over. But soon he will again be reading books about the World War and about the bravery of German soldiers and about the great battles and then his enthusiasm knows no limits. The victories of our local troops also cause him to celebrate long and often. Then every misery of his life is forgotten.

In addition to all this, the recent enthusiasm for Germany is great; teachers receive German newspapers and read them to their classes, as to how things are on the upswing under Hitler. Jake brought along an illustrated magazine from Berlin and we all made for it. Papa got to read it first and Jake had to explain what he knew. It contained pictures of Hitler, Göring and Göbbels.

Papa's greatest interest is Hindenburg. It was this federal president who came to our assistance when we left Soviet Russia.

Jake had to return this paper but I took a good look at the beautiful pictures and the soldiers in their uniforms and Göbbels with his wife and children. How beautiful must life now be in Germany! The people on the photos all appear so happy. They greet with raised hands, which Jake explains is the Hitler greeting. If only we could have experienced all that joy while in Germany. Or, better still, if we could only be there in person right now!

2 May 1933

A braham returned from the train station today. Late in the forenoon, we saw our team of oxen standing by our gate. Lena and I ran to the street to greet Abraham. He had a beard and his clothes were thickly covered with clay as was our wagon. His trip had taken him only one week. In previous times a trip to the train station, to fetch freight, could take two weeks or more. The village farmers took turns taking these trips.

Abraham was very tired. Mama made him some chicory drink and placed kaffir bread on the table. We also now regularly eat liverwurst and crackling lard after butchering pigs. Abraham claimed that the road to the railroad station has improved. The military has been working on the road for the necessities of their transport. The

previously swampy areas in which man and beast got stuck have now been filled with a series of logs, called a corduroy road, which is a great help. Abraham witnessed how prisoners of war were required to execute this labour. And while these roads are rough, they are now driveable, even in the wettest conditions. That is what is going on in the Chaco presently. When we arrived here, we assumed that only a few Indians lived in the land. Now automobiles, mainly called cars hum along, cannons thunder, airplanes drone and soldiers march.

Abraham has taken our cotton harvest to the rail station. We picked the cotton in March and April. This work is easy and clean even if your back starts to complain of pain, due to the routine. We picked like crazy, just to see who would have a full bag first. The cotton is picked into tin containers. These are gasoline cans and come from the military. Papa opened them with a chisel and then hammered the jagged edges of the cans into smooth surfaces. While picking cotton we sing our German Mennonite songs with me taking the contralto part, Lena soprano and David sings tenor while Abraham assumes the bass melody.

"While still with youthful heart we sing with happy voices steady, And for the Lord's service we are constant, always ready."

Lena would not join in singing songs like at the *Polter*-evening. She is very pious. I wonder if she has ever given marriage a thought. She is already twenty-two but has never had a boyfriend.

Come evenings, Jake and David stamp the cotton into bags with force of their feet. These large bags are tightly spanned in a large crate. When the bag is full, it assumes the form of the crate. Abraham then takes these bales of cotton to the train station. We are grateful for the cotton since it is our only source of much needed cash.

After Abraham has taken a shower and a shave, he slouches down into the hammock.

"Lizzie, come here, will you?" he called me.

I sat down next to him since I believed he had a story to tell about his recent trip, which generally is similar to an adventure.

"Lizzie," he said and he then spoke softly and confidentially, rather uncommon for him. "Lizzie, Heinrich Friesen was along on the trip. He joined me in my wagon while his ox-cart followed us. We spoke long and well and I can tell you that Heinrich is a very good boy. Of course he knows that our mother is concerned about him since you are converted and he is not. His opinion of you ranks in the superlative. In his mind you are the finest and most beautiful of women and not only in our village. Heinrich trusts me and that is why he told me, what he did.

I did not at all know how to answer him. I was totally confused and I believe I must have blushed furiously. Then, finally, after I had composed myself, I answered, "Nothing can come of a relationship in which one is converted and the other party not." My tongue was as dry as the midday sun.

Abraham noticed my excitement and, for once, he did not mock or make fun of me, as he said, "Do you know what Heinrich calls you? He calls you TUNA, which is Spanish for the Chaco cactus which blooms rarely but with magnificent profusion. TUNA is the word for this flower, the Queen of the Night."

My heart is so heavy, and I have no choice but to record all this. If only someone could and would help me in this deep, deep dilemma.

20 May 1933

It is Sunday and I am sitting in our small, dear kitchen and committing word to paper. Yesterday Jake and I went looking for our oxen, since our parents intended to hitch them to our wagon and go for a visit.

Jake has learned new songs in school and so we marched along and sang.

"Sing a song with happy lilt and trill.

It will through the landscape ring with joy, intent and will."

Now the students sing many songs from and about Germany and the German people. We are also part of the German people even though we live abroad.

The oxen were grazing on some distant meadow, and whenever we intended to hitch them up we had to search for them. Jake knows how to go about looking for them. He can even read their hoof prints and can tell from the prints whether the oxen are ours. Furthermore, each ox wears a bell around his neck and you can hear them from afar. We searched for the oxen and had a good time doing so while walking through the bush and the many meadows. In my memory I was in Mölln again walking through the German forest. One can hardly compare the Chaco with Mölln, but today the *Palo blanco* trees struck me as unusual as they grow on the edges of the many meadows. They are literally covered with ivory coloured blossoms and look like decorated evergreens. Jake broke off a branch of these blossoms which are wonderfully fragrant.

Jake also knows the names of the many bird varieties, like the *serima*, a roadrunner, which runs along the road, the bush hens which hop from branch to branch, and the cardinal with a red tuft on its neck, and which whistles happily in the bushes. Jake then sings "I had a comrade true" and we keep step to its easy lilt; Jake marches like a soldier. I wanted to discuss matters of faith with him, but I had better leave that be. Jake then cracks jokes and calls me "Pious Lizzie."

We would have long since celebrated our day of baptism had it not been for the war. In Russia baptism was done on Pentecost Day. We have to complete the catechism before we can be baptized. Now we have resumed regular baptismal instructions and I greatly enjoy Reverend Reimer's explanations and interpretations of the catechism.

Occasionally Mama claims that conversions are more important than baptisms but then Papa becomes agitated. He wants no changes even if the Brethren want nothing but. And yet, we all live in the same village, we attend a common church service and we sing in the same choir. Papa is of the opinion that the Conference in Russia had it right. All the young people attended baptismal instructions and all were baptized and all then were accepted into the church, where they belonged. Even though not all were equally steadfast in their faith, all were subjected to a common church order.

I then think of Heinrich. His parents are Brethren but he had no intentions of joining them by getting converted and baptized, Abraham informs me. He will obviously never belong to the church. He remains outside the fold like a lost sheep. I frequently wish that everything would be much simpler in matters of faith and baptism and belonging to a church, and that so much quarreling could be avoided.

"What is your understanding of being born again?" That is question # 62 in the catechism. The answer: "The change and renewal in me, the penitent believer, virtue of the power of the Holy Spirit which, through the Word of God, gives birth to a new being, a new creature, meaning that Christ lives in me and I in Him, and that I am entitled to partake of all spiritual fruits."

I know this answer by heart and will never forget it. Reverend Reimer then explained to us the meaning of daily renewal. We are sealed in the Holy Spirit and yet we must daily exercise renewal since we remain sinful humans.

Greta became seriously angry when I explained this to her, "That is the way you Conference people are. You simply lack assurance of faith." This is what the itinerant minister Epp explained in simple terms. To be converted means to be saved and as of that moment there are only the saved and the unsaved, the children of God or the children of this world; and such a decision is of the moment and the time and the place and the hour and the second of that very hour.

Is Heinrich a child of this world? If I had more confidence in Abraham I would ask simply ask him. However, this is impossible. Greta states that Abraham is a child of this world even though he is baptized.

We managed to find the oxen shortly before sunset and then we herded them home as fast as oxen decide to move. I suddenly cast a look at the bush and the cacti and I was shocked to find no Queen of the Night there. Why was I shocked? Does this matter of TUNA appear infantile?

22 May 1933

The day before yesterday I wrote about all the misgivings that surface in me when I think of conversion, baptism and the church. I am confronted by all these matters. In my deliberations I am greatly troubled by the differences in the churches, which amount to outright opposition to each other. And while such differences are covered by much commonality in the village, it remains fact. Greta is my best friend while Heinrich stands far removed on the bank of a stream in which he drifts. And there he stands, tall and sublime and I do not even know whether all this is of any consequence to him, including faith as well as the church, and even I.

The entire village was of one accord today during sadness and involvement in grief; possibly it is true that death is the common denominator, which attributes equality to all. A young woman, Mrs Töws, died and this forenoon was her funeral. By reason of the climate, funerals have to be conducted as soon as possible and we have all learned to get involved and participate with dispatch, irrespective of church membership.

A month ago malaria broke out in our villages. It is claimed that the military was infected with the disease. We had much rain in April and subsequently clouds of mosquitoes spread malaria quickly. It is claimed that in Toledo entire regiments fell victim to the disease. The military physicians and the orderlies fight the condition with quinine. They also make it available to us. They distribute it and also vaccinate the general public. We all had to assemble at the school where a Red Cross vehicle was parked. Abraham told of a young man from Kleefeld who had arrived deathly ill from the train trip. They had met in Pozo Azul before he went home to die.

If you ingest a great deal of quinine, malaria can be overcome. However, quinine affects the human heart, the doctors claim. This was the case with Mrs Töws. She was pregnant and her heart was weak. Her temperature rose to 41 C and she swallowed ever more quinine. She died yesterday afternoon; the baby remained in her body. Our choir is always ready to sing appropriate songs at a funeral. We are always ready for such emergencies because we have no resident doctor and the military physicians are not always available.

The entire congregation wept so heartbreakingly when we sang "Falling Leaves":

> *Falling Leaves, so tired of life,*
> *Fall from the trees, so weary of strife,*
> *While here below the fall winds swirl their ceaseless game,*
> *Naught and fleeting, uncaring, random and no aim.*

We hardly managed to sing, and I noticed the choir conductor's eyes were brimming with tears. What may Heinrich think when things are so serious? We are all so close to death. The choir stood to the side of an open coffin and we sang, "Angels, open wide the gate." While we sang, our men folk shovelled earth on the lowered coffin, the clods of earth rumbling on that dreary box. Heinrich stood opposite to me. He continued with his sad task, not releasing the shovel, and never raising his eyes although his shirt was drenched with sweat.

5 June 1933

It was Abraham's idea, and I had a hunch that he was up to something. He had invited some of the young people of our village to our home on Saturday night. Heinrich came with his two sisters, as did Greta and her brother. David and Lena also arrived. We sat in a circle by a clear moon and the evening was fresh, almost too cool.

I listened intently almost the entire evening long because I love to hear stories about Russia. I want to know more about Sagradowka because Heinrich comes from there. My childhood memories are intertwined with the dreadful experiences in Rosenthal although some of my recollections are hazy at best. Abraham was already fifteen at the time as was Heinrich.

The dogs barked in the village, otherwise all was still. We put on our jackets and moved closer to each other. I suggested we sing some songs but immediately there was disagreement about the choice of songs. Abraham and Heinrich do not like choral melodies while Lena and Greta object to folk songs. For Greta, "How beautiful is youth" is already too worldly.

Initially we had fun with our *tereré*. The boys hit upon the idea from the soldiers. The procedure is simple enough. You shed some yerba into a glass and stick in a *bombilla*, a thin tin tube. Then you fill the glass with water and sip it empty. Drinking yerba is done in turns. In the mornings when yerba is drunk with hot water the drink is called *mate*. We girls also tried the beverage but found it too bitter. Greta called it soldier fare.

During the drink, conversations commenced; it appeared as if the *tereré* eased the conversational flow. I would never have imagined that Heinrich was such a lively raconteur.

Our talk took a different direction when Abraham defended the para-military position the Mennonites assumed in Russia. The armed young Mennonites intended to protect their loved ones, women and girls, and the home villages against Machno and his roving bands. These men were armed and only did their duty. Unfortunately they were too ill-equipped in light of superior forces. They should have been better organized together with other villages as well as neighbouring German villages.

But then David came alive. "Everything terrible that happened to the Mennonites in Russia was a result of God's punishment for breaching His command of conscientious objection and love of enemy. Had we followed Jesus' teaching and offered the enemy to strike the left cheek when the right cheek was being hit and had we not used force, as taught by the early Anabaptists, things would not have turned out so badly."

Heinrich listened for a long time while Abraham and David were quarreling. Then he started talking about Sagradowka and the senseless murders and battles in the villages and of the things he had witnessed as a young boy, and also of what happened in Münsterberg where in a single night eighty-four people were murdered, of which eighteen were women and thirty-six children. Heinrich spoke about death and murder as a kind of senselessness, and as if it were totally immaterial whether you defended yourself or not.

"What does it matter if you defend yourself or not when you think of the children?" he asked. "When laws and limits all cease to be, no one asks such questions. If you then defend yourself you are right and if you do not you are also right. After it is all over, you can evaluate the situation and determine whether and what was wrong or right, and if a biblical principle was violated or not."

I was surprised that Heinrich kept on speaking in long and measured tones and I listened to him with total animation. "Then we talk about the wealth of Mennonites, and that God punished us for being rich." Heinrich spoke as one who has given such matters much thought. "In our village of Gnadenfeld lived the poorest people of the entire colony; poor suckers they were, and they fared no better than those in Münsterberg. What, then, is all this talk about punishment?"

I was surprised at what Heinrich said, and it almost seemed as if all that he had experienced there had to do with his faith or lack of it. But then I thought of his parents. These Friesens belonged to the most pious of our village and had obviously experienced everything that Heinrich did. Could it just be that the same experiences rendered some people pious while others lost their faith?

Then Abraham spoke up again and turned to David. "If you do not defend yourself as you demand, then such is your business. However, if you are required to defend someone and you fail to do so then you are wrong. And therein lies the entire Christian problem."

Then even David kept his peace.

I had never experienced such an interesting evening before. I would dearly like to know more about our past and our history and, I must admit it, Heinrich has awakened all this in me. I would like to know how he really is.

It seems that David has the easiest time of it all. No one will ever shake his faith. However, he will grant no one the right to vary from his faith.

We then did sing a song after all. Lena started singing, "Eventide has come again... Only the brook spills on to the pebbles much below as it flows forever on and on. And my heart tumbles right along in time's release. God alone can grant serenity and peace."

Heinrich did not join in the singing. Possibly he cannot sing at all?

22 June 1933

We had an abundance of rain in April, and Mama has planted vegetables in the garden. The garden looks good. We have carrots, radishes, cabbage and red beets. We are finally again able to cook real borscht like in Russia. Jake brought along meat from the military camp where butchering is daily done for the troops. If one takes milk or eggs to their camp, you are, in return, given a huge cut of fresh meat. Our food supplies are no longer as monotonous as in previous years. And so the war does have a positive side to it, at least for us.

The soldiers probably have a different take on the matter. Papa read in the "La Plata Post" that Bolivia is preparing a massive counter assault. A German general is in charge of this offensive, and he intends to attack similar to the World War, the German paper reports. Papa feels sorry for the Paraguayans since the Bolivians are much better equipped, he believes. They have airplanes, heavy artillery and even tanks.

Even we notice how the military is stepping up its efforts. The number of motorized vehicles passing through our village is constantly increasing and they are all full of soldiers. A few days ago a huge truck passed by, full of the wounded. I felt sorry for these bearded sick. What will become of them? They will probably have to do roadwork, as Abraham has witnessed.

However, in our village perfect peace reigns and yesterday we again had a Youth Program. The school was full of young people and the teacher conducted the evening meeting. We intend to stage a musical evening. There are guitars, violins, a mandolin and Neufelds have a foot-operated harmonium. Now we are meant to practice musical pieces and songs. Also, we intend to practice some poetry recitals and then the entire village will be invited.

Cold is seeping into my room and so I will stop writing and crawl under my warm blanket.

2 July 1933

And now I, too, have fallen sick with malaria. It is Sunday forenoon and everyone is at church. I feel dizzy but I grabbed some pillows and will attempt to write. Malaria first announces itself by a shivering cold followed by severe heat flashes as if you are afire. The fever attack lasts one day, with advance warning. Today I am free of fever and maybe I can manage to write.

Most families are severely affected. The colony administration demands a statistic of all villages for the military, which supplies us with quinine. Our village has a population counting 150 of whom 130 are sick. There are days in which the school is closed because more than half the pupils are sick abed.

I swallow the prescribed amount of quinine and then I have a humming in my head like a swarm of bees. Now Papa is the big man in our family.

"I was an orderly during the war," he says, "and I know how to deal with fever."

I had to undress and sit down on a short bench. Papa placed a bowl of water under the bench. Then he covered me with a quilt, and deposited glowing coals into the water. A hissing noise ensued until I screamed on account of the heat. Then Lena came and washed me down with ice-cold water. Then she took me to bed and covered me with a heavy quilt.

The malaria attack weakens me so much that I can hardly work at all even on a day free of fever. The Youth Meetings as well as our choir practices have been cancelled; I had so much looked forward to our musical evening.

Our baptismal arrangements have also been cancelled although we have almost completed our catechism instructions. We have already progressed to the third part, "The New Life of the Converted." Anyone comprehending all this and taking the matter seriously is free to lead the life of a Christian after experiencing baptism. And yet Mama—as previously mentioned, and as it appears to me—believes that the Brethren with their demands of conversion, have it even more right. Or, possibly, she has Abraham in mind, who appears indifferent to it all. Or she may be thinking of David, who after his conversion has become a different person. Or, so he claims. David got converted when the itinerant minister Epp launched a crusade in our village and explained the plan of salvation. Papa was very upset by all of this.

I often hear Mama praying aloud while crying and sobbing in her bedroom. Might it be that I am her concern? I then have a bad conscience, since in my thoughts I cannot let go of Heinrich.

However, most likely Mama is more concerned about Maria and her family. And while we receive no news at all, but we read in the Canadian German Mennonite papers *Der Bote* and *Die Rundschau* that things in Russia are growing ever more serious. Stalin is becoming ever more brutal against the landowners, the kulaks, and all Mennonite farmers in our villages back home are kulaks, for they are land owners. In 1932 many of these were arrested and not a word from them has been heard, so *Der Bote* reports. When Mama reads this she cries.

My hand is beginning to shake so I will put an end to my writing for now.

8 August 1933

The baptismal occasion transpired earlier than expected. Taking quinine vanquished the malaria attacks. I am very weak, still, but free of fever. The day before yesterday, early, we, together with some other families, made our way to a neighbouring village; altogether our caravan consisted of five ox-carts. When we baptismal candidates, fifteen in number, sat down in our dark dresses in solemn expectation I felt comfortable and happy in my faith.

Mama was also there and that caused me great inner joy, since she is often in doubt on account of all the new innovations by the Brethren. Saturday at the coffee table she was in a pensive mood as she remembered her own baptism. "Everything was so festive. At Pentecost the air was so fresh and clean. It was so warm that we ladies in our black dresses and white collars walked the street without coats and all in eager anticipation of the venerable Bishop Isaak Dyck, for he alone was the man of the hour. We were all sitting in church in Rosenthal when the stately carriage bearing him, the holy entity, arrived. Then the ministers and the precentors walked into church. Bishop Dyck stood still in the middle of the church and announced, 'Peace be unto you!' Then everyone walked to the front of the church, and the service could start. This solemnity is something I miss in these parts. We candidates then answered the catechism questions and recited the statement of faith. I felt the power of the Holy Spirit when the bishop poured the holy water over my head at baptism."

And even at our church, a new item of faith has been introduced because the ministers have decreed it so. Every one of us was required to go to the front of the congregation and deliver a declaration a personal testimony. Since some of our village boys did not want to do so or simply could not, they were not baptized.

Papa seems to have come to terms with all the innovations as well. He has been voted into the Church Council and has stopped smoking, because Reverend Reimer had a word with him. The Brethren strictly forbid smoking and so Reverend Reimer had a long and serious talk with Papa. We all had to represent a better testimony, particularly in the opinion of the Brethren.

When we assembled for family gatherings in Russia, all the men folk smoked their pipes in the great room and no one regarded smoking as a sin. Not one. Mama was only peeved when Papa failed to smoke a superior tobacco grade in public.

"I cannot stand cheap tobacco," she said, probably laughing all the while.

And now there is talk in the village about the men in our church who still smoke and Reverend Reimer now attempts to persuade them to lay off the sinful weed. I am happy Heinrich does not smoke because when everyone in the village talks about you such talk comes to my ears via Greta.

All fifteen baptismal candidates spoke about sin in our testimonies, and that our sins had been forgiven. Do we not often say this without giving the matter a second thought? During our catechism classes we discussed sins of an inherited nature and sins of committed deed. Inherited sin is the disposition towards evil, while "deed" sins are those committed based on such disposition.

I asked David what constituted sin in his opinion. "All youthful desires are sin." Then he recited a verse from the song which we are practicing for our Youth Occasion.

"And now, all youth rise up, fight every opposition,
And everything in your path, push to shameful end's perdition."

The melody to the song sounds like a battle song which we sing with enthusiasm. In spite of everything and all the questions raised, I have a feeling of security after my baptism. I now belong to our church and to the body of Jesus Christ.

Greta came around yesterday as well to wish me God's blessings, although she simply cannot let it be, but has to mention just how well she felt after being baptized by immersion, and to bury death by baptism according to biblical decree. And yet all this may be part of faith, namely, Greta's being so cutting when we speak about the church, and David's blushing fiercely whenever sin is mentioned.

And now I shall lay down my pen and walk to the village street. It is cool and the stars are shining brightly; there is even a tinge of frost in the nightly air. And yet the fresh air does me good as it cleanses me of all my difficult ponderings.

27 August 1933

I want to describe an experience. Greta and I walked arm in arm on the street when we heard music. The music came from Neufeld's yard. It attracted us and so we entered the yard where many people had gathered. Their oldest boy Jacob had returned from Casado, a port town where he works. From there he brought along a gramophone, a beautiful, big one with a huge horn. He had worked in Casado for over half a year and had earned sufficient money to buy the instrument.

Jacob Neufeld played record upon record with beautiful German songs we had never heard before. "There once was a handsome hussar" and "Adieu, you little officer on guard". More and more people arrived on the yard and it appeared as if Jacob Neufeld was proud of his new acquisition. He constantly turned the crank of the gramophone and a new song emanated from the funnel.

"And here comes 'Old Comrades!'" said Jacob and yet another march throbbed from the horn. Even the old people laughed and swayed to the melody.

"I remember this tune from Russia", said Old Man Neufeld, "we played it during the war," and his eyes beamed.

"And now", said Jacob Neufeld, when the march was over, "I will play you some Paraguayan songs. They are in Guarani, which is spoken and sung in all the land."

"Oh, I know this one", I heard a voice from behind me. I had not noticed that Heinrich stood right behind me. "The soldiers sang this song in their camp. A truly wonderful song."

I turned around and Heinrich was looking at me with a friendly disposition. He stepped to my side and we gently touched.

"I understand what they sing," he said. "*Campamento, campamento*. That is a song from the great war, of the last battle. The soldiers fashioned guitars from wooden crates and they sing most beautifully. I often sit by them at a fire, evenings, and listen to them. They sing this song often, probably because it is so sad."

His arm touched my shoulder and I let him do so. The song from the record was the most beautiful I had ever heard, although is described a terrible battle as Heinrich explained it to me. I hummed the melody for days on end.

Why is one immediately so ambivalent? I was so surprised and so happy to stand beside Heinrich, just so, as if naturally. And yet I worried that Heinrich was so often with, and so close to the, soldiers. They were rough fellows, said David, and he would keep his distance.

Darkness had already set in when Jacob Neufeld put an end to his music. "As a farewell, 'Old Comrades' once more" he said and then we broke up, tired from standing around.

When I walked back to the street, deliberately without Greta, Heinrich accompanied me. We walked together slowly and I noticed that everyone was looking at us. Suddenly I was indifferent to all their gawking; even Greta was of no matter to me. To the west, the red of late evening hung in the sky. There was not a cloud in the sky and yet the entire horizon gently beamed. Against it, the bush with black trees stood outlined.

"I will never forget the song *Campamento, campamento*," I said; "it was the most beautiful of all the records."

"I love the soldier's songs", said Heinrich. "They are all a bit sad, and all like a great longing or a lament about a misfortune. But they also have the most beautiful of love songs."

We walked a little piece on the road. The red of the evening quickly disappeared and soon only a violet strip was left on the horizon. Just like a great longing, I thought. If only I would have remained standing and had just listened a little longer. If only he would have embraced me! But then I suddenly had to think of Mama.

"Good night!" I quickly said, and ran for home. Heinrich stood still and I knew he was looking after me. Was he disappointed?

4 September 1933

It appears everything is locked away, no bridge and no path, with everything a hazy veil as the sun, now in September, before evening, disappears behind a curtain even though it is high noon.

And yet I have an indescribably happy feeling in my heart and I know exactly where it comes from. I know that Heinrich loves me. He did not say so because he is so reserved, and yet I am certain of his affection. I sometimes wish there would be no village, no church congregations, no faith and no commands, but only the two of us and above us the heavenly glow of evening and nothing but.

Everyone would be shocked to read these lines, and Mama would cry her heart out. I know that it would only add to all the sorrow she feels. She is so terribly sad because we received a letter from Maria in Russia yesterday and it is a sad one.

Papa brought it along; he had already read it en route. He was shocked and beside himself and knew that Mama would be unable to bear it. And so he discussed it with Lena and me before we broke the news to Mama.

"Bad news from Russia," he said and handed her the letter.

Mama slapped her hands to her face. "Is Maria dead?" she screamed and I thought she would be overcome by a paralysis of screaming. Lena embraced her and held her fast. "No, Mama," she said very serenely. "Maria is alive and so are her two children but Isaak has been arrested and sent off to Siberia, banned."

I do not know whether it was a cry, a sob or a prayer. Papa stroked her hair and said very peacefully, "We will now read the letter together. We all have to know, and then we will pray for Maria, and Isaak and the family." Mama collapsed into herself as if all her strength had departed. Lena held her in her arms and then we listened to what Maria had written. Jacob and David had also entered.

Maria wrote about the many arrests. All had entered the collective farms under the Soviet without resistance and yet these very men had now been detained, particularly in Neuendorf. They had been taken to Zaporozhje, but no one knew whether they were held captive there or sent on to the White Sea or to Workuta. The GPU (Secret Police) released no information although the women traveled to Zaporozhje every day to inquire. A great famine was feared, possibly worse than the one of 1920.

We all cried, even Jake and this seemed to lighten our grief a bit. I often hear Mama pray aloud when she is alone in her room. Sometimes she takes to the fields to weep so loud that the neighbours hear her sobbing.

The weather now makes things even worse. Often strong storms blow in from the north. These winds are hot and fatiguing and on our yard sand dunes literally drift up. The sand blows into our house through every crevice, even the smallest crack, and there is no escaping it. It penetrates the furniture and even the beds and there is no resisting it. Mama's soul is similarly violated.

And so I cannot very well turn to her with my worries and concerns, and I know full well that faith or lack of it run similar to fire and water. I then ask myself how so much pure joy can overwhelm my soul, considering all the storms in and outside and the calamitous news from Russia. It is a joy similar to a pristine lake, like the one in Mölln, Germany, into which we skipped stones and took so much joy in their expanding circles.

The human soul is a sealed book. You are meant to make do with the mysteries of life.

2 October 1933

Last night we traveled to Schönwiese for an evening program. Jake brought the news from school that a Hindenburg celebration was to be staged. The Youth Group from Schönwiese had prepared this event and invited all to attend. This was no simple matter. Jake had to take off on Sunday afternoon to look for our oxen. He managed to locate them in short order and soon all five siblings were perched on the cart. There were other vehicles en route but Heinrich was not part of the caravan. Did he prefer the company of the soldiers? At such moments my heart suffers from the jabs of uncertainty.

The program was very good. The old federal president, Hindenburg, was praised by various speakers at the occasion. He had advocated the Mennonite cause at the Moscow gates before the German parliament at the time when the German Communists refused to accept them. The Schönwieser Group sang beautiful homeland songs while others recited poems of the German Motherland. At the conclusion of the festive evening, everyone rose to their feet and sang "*Deutschland, Deutschland über alles!*" We had sung the same song on the train in 1929 when we passed the Red Gate to freedom.

The return trip on the ox cart, slow but very steady, was most beautiful. The moon rested in the sky and the birds of night sang their quaintly beautiful lullabies. "Almost like the nightingales in Russia," said Lena. The Queen of the Night beamed from the cacti on the edge of the road (TUNA was in my thoughts). We sang our lilting evening songs en route.

Abraham told a sad story about two soldiers who had died of thirst close to our village. Peter Fast and his brother Franz had traveled to a distant mossy hollow to mow some reeds. During their trip they had taken a slight detour in hope of shooting a deer. And there, underneath a tree, they had chanced upon the two soldiers. They had rolled their blankets together into a pillow and slept on them, with their rifles to the side. They appeared to be sleeping but had expired.

"It is obviously a sign that they died of thirst," Abraham noted. "If you are badly parched you are tired and all you want is sleep."

The Brauns, father and son, from our village almost died of thirst themselves a month ago. When they went looking for an errant cow in the Chaco bush, they lost their bearings; they had taken no water along to drink. Father Braun had had trouble keeping his son, Gerhard, from lying down to sleep. Towards late evening they had managed to find their way back to our village and Gerhard had consumed six glasses of milk, for fear he would die.

How many soldiers may already have died of thirst in the endless expanse of the Chaco bush? When we arrived home, the entire village had fallen asleep. We softly sang, "No nicer land in these old times" as we creaked our way home. There was still a light burning at the Friesen home. Then Abraham whistled and an unseen party whistled in return, while Abraham gently tapped my knee.

12 October 1933

Everyone was so tired that they all took to bed early. Jake and I share the light of the petroleum lamp. The first heavy rain of spring has fallen and everyone is in the fields ploughing and planting. I planted cotton all day long and now my legs are sore and tired. I have developed a routine in planting cotton by indenting the soil with my left heel, then throwing the seed into the little hollow and covering the little entirety of cotton hope with my right heel. In short order I am in planting rhythm, row upon row.

There are a few things I planned to record and Jake does not in any way deter me. When Jake is immersed in a book, he takes no further notice of what is going on around him. Moreover, he now has to study for his exams. And yet he is reading *Werewolf* by Hermann Löns, while studying. It deals with the Thirty Years War and I should also read it, says Jake. This is the way our farmers should also have defended themselves in Russia. Jake says the school library also has more books by Löns. Jake says he will bring me a book of German poetry along to read from school; knowing, as he does, how much I love poetry.

It was actually my intention to report on the huge Youth Meeting held in Waldesruh. The Youth Societies of all the villages arranged this meeting collectively. The Youth Leaders in the villages are generally also the teachers. There were some three hundred or even more young people assembled in Waldesruh. This larger group is now known as the German-Mennonite-Youth-Club. Addresses and songs comprised the major part of the event. The young people are to be properly raised, trained and educated to be well-mannered and competent, and to excel in things German while not neglecting their Mennonitism. The boys are meant to get involved in sports and do well. I was greatly pleased by it all and our songs broke forth in a fervent chorus, "On our Way with German Youth!"

Papa claims that some ministers are not at all pleased with this new kind of youth work. By that he means that all the young people are involved, whether baptized or not and therefore the distinctions between the church and the world are obscured. Nothing of the sort ever transpired in Russia. However, the teachers claim it is necessary to keep the young people away from congregating on the streets and committing mischief. Sometimes the street urchins in our own village were up to serious trouble. If only this were to improve.

Our great example now is Germany, said one of the speakers; there the youth is now properly educated and trained.

In all this I am overcome by a silent pain. Everyone is involved: Lena, David and even Abraham at times. There is one who remains outside and will probably never get involved. It appears as if he is standing on a far shore and is evaluating life from an altogether different perspective. I would so much like to understand him and I would even more like to pull him to my side.

If Heinrich remains offside, then everyone will judge him just like one of the teachers said in his talk about the ruffians loitering on the streets, or get involved with the soldiers. They have no interest in community. He believes that such are the remnants of Communist influence from Russia. With Henrich this does not at all apply. I rather believe that his childhood experiences are concerns not yet dealt with. Possibly there are conflicts among the adults, yet unresolved and which cause much tension.

However, I cannot very well resolve anything since we do not or cannot talk when there is no bridge and no path?

Jake snaps his *Werewolf* closed and I my diary. Early tomorrow morning our common lot and plot is the cotton field.

19 October 1933

School is almost over and I am happy. Soon Jake will be home all day and we will then work together on the fields. Jake is a suspenseful raconteur whenever he has read something or experienced mischief, an event, real or imagined. Now that he is reading *Werewolf,* he is re-experiencing the entire Thirty Years War, or so it appears to me. The fact that this material cannot at all be reconciled with conscientious objection and the doctrine of peace of the Mennonite faith completely escape him; he is simply too immersed in his book. I wonder if the contradiction is of any matter to him at all.

"I see our entire village armed and doing battle against the robbing bands," Jake pronounced enthusiastically.

"Now really, Jake," I said, "we are no longer in Russia."

Then he came to as if from a dream and we both had a good laugh.

Obviously Jake has much to deal with; his plate is full as the saying goes. Troops pass through our village daily, and we are happy at their victories. Jake knows Spanish well by now and he eagerly reports on the great battles fought to the west. At such times he whoops it up, and dances and sings, and we are happy for him. In addition, we now are eagerly happy and rejoice about what is going on in Germany. Jake sings patriotic songs about Germany, the Fatherland. Often we sing together and reflect on our stay in beautiful Mölln.

Jake also and finally brought me the book of Hermann Löns poetry. I copy my favourite poems into my own notebook. One of these poems really touched my heart.

"Do you know just how we are, and really of what kind?
Like the fields of grain which waft in wind,
Like the storms from raging north;
Raging round and back and forth,

While eye to eye so tender smile
But love is off our limits for the while."

If only someone were to come along and set these lines to melody. Then I would sing this song softly to myself at work.

"And the moon and starry hue
Your thoughts are mine, and mine with you,
Heart to heart with tender smile
But love is off our limits for the while."

If Jake were to hear this, he would say, "Lizzie, tear your chains of bondage and cast them off", while Lena would admonish me with a "Don't inflict shame on your Saviour!" and David would suggest, "Resist all temptation!" while Abraham would have a good laugh at my expense. And yet Mama's prayers and tears would hurt me most of all.

Reverend Reimer once claimed during our catechism instructions that he would not officiate at the marriage of a baptized and unbaptized party. This had never happened in Russia or, prior to that, during our sojourn in Prussia.

Oh yes, there is one other matter I must record. Greta Löwen has a boy-friend. She was very proud of him when she told me about her love. Aside from me, no one knows about Greta's pious secret. Recently after the Young Peoples' Hour was over, he, Isaak Dürksen, had asked for permission to accompany her home. Isaak also belongs to the Brethren. I have always had the impression that Isaak is not all that serious about life and David and Abraham claim that Isaak is the most jolly of the lot when they travel to the train station. And so I had assumed that pious Greta would never get involved with him. Greta claims he is an answer to her prayers and that in his heart he is a big boy, right with God. I fear that I will be even more lonely and lonesome.

22 October 1933

We finally managed to stage the Musical Evening Program. We had planned it for a long time but invariably something cropped up and forced delay. Now all malaria has been overcome. We took great amounts of quinine and the military medical staff warned us that a side effect was a weakened heart. But what is one to do? In Schönwiese a little boy succumbed to the disease. Many of the quinine tablets are very sweet and coated red, the easier to swallow. Generally quinine is dreadfully bitter to the taste. The little boy swallowed four of the sweet pills and died.

The Youth Hour is one of the most enjoyable of all diversions for me. We meet every Wednesday night in school and even Heinrich in involved, which both surprises and pleases me. The teacher manages to make these evenings both interesting and entertaining. David is in charge of the singing and he also practices spiritual songs with us. Occasionally a teacher from a neighbouring village arrives to present a talk. Our teacher has a book on good manners and appropriate behaviour. "What is lovely and appealing" is the title of the book. He reads this material to us, and it assists us in matters of table manners and acceptable conduct and behaviour.

Also, many magazines now arrive from Germany, and our teacher reads appropriate parts to us. It is wonderful to see Germany rising and shining.

Our school was filled for the Musical Evening. Jacob Löwen even had a balalaika. He built it himself from select wood panels and it produces a truly fine sound. One piece after another was featured on violins, guitars and mandolins. Even Russian melodies were played. During the latter, the balalaikas particularly came into their own. Then the older generation exchanged knowing glances while their eyes beamed with nostalgic knowing memory. Anna Löwen sang "Oh, where is my child tonight?" accompanied by the harmonium; this rendition was hauntingly beautiful. I noticed Mama wiping copious tears from her eyes.

When the beautiful evening was over we sauntered over the schoolyard and Greta was suddenly gone. Presumably Isaak had immediately made off with her. It was very dark and I walked home alone. After I have twice taken to my heels, Heinrich has made no attempt to walk with me. Suddenly Jake emerged and I was all the happier to see him at my side, cracking jokes and providing happy company.

He reported as follows, "I have been quarrelling with David. We are studying physics this year and machines are part of the study. The physicists, so the teachers reported, had attempted to build a machine which runs forever, the *perpetuum mobile*. However, such a construction is impossible, since friction is a constant."

And yet, David had refused to accept this. He was of the opinion and intended to prove it that it was possible to construct such a machine. David is forever on the lookout for ultimate perfection, for the absolutely flawless in physics as well as in matters of faith.

"Who knows, who is the happier, David with his faith or I in my reality?" asked Jake.

"I think you are," I said and took his hand.

Who then, is the happier? Greta, who in spite of all her piety does as she damn well pleases, or Lena who withdraws quietly into herself like a cactus blossom at early morning? Abraham, who appears to be above it all or Heinrich who appears to be immune to whatever comes along? Or might it be that he is unhappy when I flee from him? Is it possible to be happy if one is not converted and baptized?

Whenever Mama forgets herself and talks about her youth in Russia I have the impression that she was formerly happy. Once she gave herself away when talking about having danced in the living room of her parental home. And then she talks about Bishop Isaak Dyck and that there had been no contradiction to it all. Who knows what all lay buried in Mama? When did Mama become so unhappy? She bears so much grief and not only about Maria and her family. She suffers grief about her family, about the church, about our village, about our young people, about Jake, and about me and

Heinrich. Sometimes it appears to me that her faith has become stronger and her sorrow greater.

Does faith not make you happier and joyful? So it was said when I got converted and I truly believed it, and I want to believe it now and always.

19 December 1933

To celebrate a wedding during the time of Advent is normally forbidden; so it is decreed. And yet Tina Harms and Willy Janzen had to get married and so there was no alternative. It was a sad wedding.

Mama did not want me to attend the *Polter*-evening; she was of the opinion that one ought to show the girl, the bride, that one was not in agreement with her conduct, or lack of it. Tina had demonstrated no discipline and her parents had likewise failed in the rearing of their daughter. It was invariably all this extended flirtation before a wedding which led to such a debacle. This led to their having to get married, neck over head or ass over tea-kettle, and brought shame to the parents and the church, so went Mama's opinion.

And yet I know Tina well and I feel sorry for her. She has been punished enough by the gossip in the village. They call it a gallop-wedding, cause for derisive laughter. And yet, Tina was previously one of the reticent girls. As to how all this happens is beyond my knowledge but I wanted to show Tina that she was not inconsequential to me, in spite of everything and I wanted to give her a little gift and so I attended the *Polter*-evening.

The entire festivity was an occasion of confusion. Harms yard was full of military officers. Towards evening an entire car load of them arrived. Uncle Harms is a good friend of and to the officers. One of his friends is a high ranking officer, a colonel who speaks German well. Whenever they arrive at our village, Mrs Harms cooks them a good meal. The officers in turn gift them with canned meat goods and condensed milk. Greta suggests that the officers only come to the Harms on account of the girls. The village had much to talk about in this matter.

This time the military car arrived with much fanfare in the village. However, this fanfare was not only on account of the wedding. There was a further more important cause for all the happy noise as we shortly came to know. Paraguay had won a huge victory to the south, the most important victory to date. Two Bolivian divisions had been encircled, enclosed. Thousands of prisoners, two generals, weaponry, and ammunition had fallen into the hands of our troops.

Borscht by the pail full had been cooked for the visitors. After the meal, our teacher proposed a toast of salute to the brave Paraguayan army and especially to General Estigaribia and to the President Ayala. The officers applauded roundly and we all clapped our hands wildly.

Then a great deal of celebratory shooting broke out. The officers handed out weapons to our boys and they let fly volley after volley, enough to rid you of all hearing and seeing. Then the teacher announced that it was time for everyone present to provide food supplies to the army. Chickens, eggs, peanuts, marmalade… everything was to be provided to Isla Poí for the wounded in the military hospitals. Then the benches were placed in a circle and the nuptial program round commenced. The moon shone brightly and everyone laughed and made merry. Greta and I also sat in the celebratory circle. I was greatly surprised at Greta and her reactions to it all. Since she got involved with Isaak she has changed. Isaak has fewer reservations and she has followed suit. Presently Isaak appeared before us and offered her his arm. And then, surprise! Greta took his arm and they joined in the happy circle.

Heinrich must have seen all this and presently he stood before me. As in a dream I got up and accepted his arm and joined in song as we frolicked in a circle. Then it was Ladies Choice and I walked up to Heinrich as we sang "Softly peals the Evening Bell". I noticed how tense my inner being was in the expectation of things to come. David would claim that temptation is central to suspense and so I intend to resolve my uncertainty by speaking to the Reverend Reimer who is more liberal than the Reverend Wiebe of the Brethren. And let Greta resolve her issues in her own way.

Then Abraham surfaced. He grinned all over as if he were crediting himself with a little victory.

"Well, Lizzie," he said, "things finally are about the way I had long hoped for."

How can one forget so much in such little time? Mama, David, Lena… I was full of the game's delight and Heinrich often came to accompany me in singing while circling as the occasion offered. Heinrich held my arm firmly and affectionately. There was neither need nor occasion to talk; we sang and were happy beyond words.

Then I set off for home, alone. Mama was sitting by the lamp and reading the Bible. "My child, oh my child!" she said and sighed deeply which cut into my heart. Obviously she sensed everything and then some.

When I went to bed, I noticed that Lena was not yet asleep. She also sighed. Am I to suffer from a bad conscience? Tears rolled down my cheeks. I held my handkerchief to my eyes and must have fallen asleep. Oh my—all this ambivalence!

22 December 1933

Such a wedding is not all that nice, with the bride wearing neither veil nor wreath. From my location in the choir I could see Tina clearly and when our eyes met, I noticed that her eyes were brimming with tears. Willy sat stiffly by her side as if the situation left him indifferent. That is how their married life was launched!

We boys and girls served at the table. The girls had brought along white aprons for the occasion while the boys had clamped a towel over their chests. This is the custom here. The womenfolk prepared coffee in the school yard. Water is boiled on an open fire in a huge cauldron. Alongside on a table all the baked goods are on display.

When I went for a second cup of coffee, I heard Tante Harms speak to her neighbour. She was weeping.

"I would rather have buried my little Tina when she was little," she said. "Now all this shame! And to imagine what all yet lies before her? Poverty. So much hard work and arduous labour, and then all the little children yet to come. It is as if my heart will break!"

Is all of life nothing but weeping, sadness and tears? Is the *Polter*-evening only a mirage and for many nothing but wrong, yet again, and sin?

After we had washed the dishes, Greta and I walked to the Löwen yard. She has to milk their cow and I helped her. The calf was allowed to suck for a space and then tied to a post. Then the cow is "shackled" since the cows here are half-wild and kick like the deuces. Greta is very thorough and competent. While working, she laughs and talks as if she does not have a care in the world!

"And what about the *Polter*-evening?" I asked her.

"Oh well," she said. "Isaak believes the games are no sin. However, I am not all that accepting, because my church objects to it all. I will pay Reverend Wiebe a visit and tell him everything that went on. If he believes I fell into sin by joining in, I will beg for forgiveness."

I said nothing to all that. Some prefer it simple. I was envious of Greta and her ability to take life so handily.

7 January 1934

Our village has previously never experienced a New Year's Eve like last night and as for me? Not in my lifetime. There was so much noise, almost as if Toledo were again at stake.

At eight in the evening we all assembled in the school for an Evening of Worship. Our teacher presented a sermon and he reminisced on the year past. We have been in the Chaco for three and one half years and we have all experienced how God has helped us. The teacher mentioned the malaria epidemic, and the locust attacks which ravaged our fields. With God's help all this was overcome.

Then he spoke about the great victories of our troops. The battle front lies far to the west and hopefully the New Year will put an end to all the bloody struggles. And then the teacher took us to Germany, our Motherland, as it is now called, and the generous assistance it provided us when we lay at the gates of Moscow, full of fear and dread. And now Adolf Hitler is the *Führer*, and he is leading Germany out of all distress and need and constructing a bulwark against bolshevism.

Then I accompanied Greta to the Löwen home. Mama had given me permission to stay out till midnight, in order to ring in the New Year. Greta has paid Reverend Wiebe a visit and had asked for forgiveness for having joined the fun and games at the wedding. Now she is relieved, light of heart and happy again.

A group of young people of our age assembled at the Löwen home. Abraham was not present, neither was Heinrich. I have not seen Heinrich since the *Polter*-evening. I have seen him only once but I would like to describe this occasion since it so deeply cut into my heart.

Löwens grow the finest of watermelons and we were allowed to eat our fill. The night was so starry bright so that we could sit outside without a lamp.

Greta is so happy with her Isaak that one might well envy her. She gossips and laughs and spins around him while he smiles and says little. One could envy her except for Isaak.

Shortly before midnight the shooting began. A hundred rifles, if not more, were discharged. The soldiers from their camp supplied the weapons, but by now most almost every household has a rifle. Our boys and the soldiers had positioned themselves on each end of the village and they fired in volleys at cross purposes so that it seemed like so much lightning in the sky. They fired every minute for at least a quarter of an hour. Then their bullet supply ran short and there was silence, even though much shooting was also done in the neighbouring villages.

Abraham later reported, full of pride, that the barrel of his rifle had been so hot that he was unable to touch it. David considered all this inappropriate. This was no way to introduce the New Year; he would have preferred a Prayer Meeting.

And now I intend to write about the matter which so much depresses me. Who else am I to tell about it? Myself? I know what it is and it gnaws at my heart. I feel relieved by putting my sentiments to paper. It becomes ever clearer to me that there exists no bridge.

Sometimes in my dream I swim in a stream of water. While I am swimming, Heinrich stands on the shore, relaxed, almost serene. He smiles and looks at me but he does not even get his feet wet. And then I wake up, just before I submerge. "Yesterday around midnight I woke up crying and my most beautiful dream disintegrated like the foam of a wave…The heart speaks to the heart, but our love must stay apart." I have copied almost all of Löns poems into my note book. I can keep the book of poems until school starts. Jake tells me that many new books have again arrived from Germany. As soon as school starts again, he will bring some of them home for me.

It was shortly before Christmas when Mama sent me to the well to fetch water. When I was just ready to draw water, a military vehicle approached. As it came closer to the well, I noticed that it was not a soldier who manned the steering wheel. It was Heinrich who waved at me, as did the soldiers in the car. These soldiers asked Heinrich something but he shook his head. The vehicle then left the village and headed for Toledo.

Why did this so startle me and make me so sad? Heinrich has found a different world. He is now venturing into a different, a foreign world, and this is not only a different world from our church, but also from our village. And yet, the church is the most important institution on earth.

I fear that Heinrich is now deliberately divorcing himself, and that he is turning to something altogether different, as if everything here is too strict and restrictive and that he is searching for freedom and avoiding the life, previously lived. At times, I believe that he severed ties already in Russia and has failed to splice them together since then and while here. Is this possible? I carried the two buckets of water home.

"But my dear Lizzie," said Mama, "surely you have not been crying? Surely everything is well and good."

"Oh, Mama," I said. "I am sweating because it is so hot." Then I cracked a joke by singing, "Softly drops of sweat are falling from afar." Then Mama laughed; for once she really laughed.

9 February 1934

Yesterday Jake and I went to the bush to fetch fence posts which Papa and Abraham had chopped, together with the Indian chief Maito. The Indians know the location in the bush of good, straight *palo blanco* trees. They grow in the flats where water gathers during the rainy season, where it is presently dry. They have cut a hundred posts for a fence.

Papa is impressed by Maito. "He goes into the bush like an English tank," he says. "Without a care to the cacti and the thorns, he swings his axe as if he had done nothing else all his life long."

The posts are then carefully piled up so that we two can load them on our ox-cart. Jake has no fear of the bush. There are no soldiers on this corduroy road, he believes. It is really fun to work with Jake and to travel by ox-cart with him, which I prefer to working in the peanut or cotton fields. It is a nice diversion even though the work is strenuous.

Jake becomes confidential when we work alone, side by side. He told me the terrible story of a girl in Chortitz of the Menno Colony. Soldiers had raped a girl there one evening and when her father tried to intervene, they shot him dead. Jake gets animated and very excited when he tells me such gruesome tales and episodes. If anything of the sort were to happen in our village, he would fight and shoot and ravage to protect ours in our village, you betch'a!

I had goose and even gander bumps on my back when Jake waxed so brave, and I felt secure in his masculine company. Is it not a virtual contradiction that the same men who are capable of enforcement and rape are capable of lovingly protecting victims as well? My thoughts took me back to Russia and the self-protective unit on our own, Mennonite yard.

Jake felt mightily masculine and spoke disparagingly of the very soldiers whom he had previously worshipped for their heroic deeds. He has stories to tell about soldiers and what they have done with and to Indian girls. Wherever they find a girl, they simply take her and rape her, five or even more at a time. I freely permit Jake to tell me about such events since one is entitled to know about such matters. Had Lena been present, Jake would obviously have said nothing about violence of this kind.

German soldiers were different, says Jake. We had just received a new edition of an illustrated German magazine from Berlin, sent to our teacher. Our teacher receives a lot of mail from Germany these days. The magazine depicts German soldiers in rank and file wearing shiny helmets and Jake compares them to our soldiers who are often ragged and barefoot when returning from the Front.

I do not even want to think of Heinrich being with the army. If he is now being trained as a car driver, then he well might even be taken straight to the Front. A boy from Waldesruh, says Jake, is already a driver in the services of the army and is earning good money.

When Heinrich looked at me while sitting in the truck, his eyes were deep and friendly. He would never do what Jake tells about the soldiers. And yet, will that then not gradually become his world as well?

We loaded up the fence posts, twenty-five of them. It is difficult work although Jake always goes for the thick, heavy end; we did our work while having fun and laughing. Then the oxen slowly pulled the heavy load through the narrow bush roads. We remained quiet for a long while, for we were tired from all the heavy loading. I could hear the cooing of the wild doves and the chattering of the bush hens. In the midst of the cacti, the fire red of the cacti berries became suddenly visible. Jake stopped and we picked our hats full. It is a most delicious fruit which develops from the blossoms which we call the Queen of the Night, the TUNA.

Then we softly sang as we approached the village street, "On the Heaths of Lüneburg" and "A boy once saw a rosy stand". Jake knew that the former poem was by Löns, while the latter was a famous poem by Goethe.

It was noon when we came home. We had fritters and watermelon for lunch. Jake eats this meal as if there were no tomorrow. In the afternoon, we fetched another load of fence posts.

Today we picked cotton all day long and my back aches mightily.

27 February 1934

What a day we had today! As bad as in a war, so bad that Papa sits on an easy chair outside, all afternoon, sad and despairing. During the afternoon we were attacked by grasshoppers in their millions, swarms of them, and they ate and ravaged everything in their path. Anything and everything not yet harvested fell to their ravenous attack, cotton, kaffir, and even the watermelons and beans.

In the afternoon around four o'clock suddenly a grey cloud appeared to the south. We believed it to be smoke from a burning bitter grass patch. Then it came closer and as it approached we heard the very air harping and the rushing of their wings became apparent. Then the grasshoppers dropped like rain on all things green.

We took off for our fields; everyone from the entire village was on the move, even small children. Many drummed on tin cans, others rang cowbells, with everyone calling and screaming to disperse the hoppers.

I took an old pan to hand and drummed on it till the very enamel coating on it cracked and splintered. Then I ran through the cotton rows. In front of me the grasshoppers rose, attacked my face and landed behind me on the cotton. When I headed back in another row, all the leaves were already gone as if mown and shorn.

Everyone ran and drummed and cried until we were hoarse. Everyone fought lonely and forlorn on the expanses of the field and then we came to realize that we had no chance against a million hoppers. When the sun set the cotton plants were bare, the stalks bald and without bark and many of the cotton capsules, not yet opened lay on the ground.

Jake and David intended to save the kaffir. It was almost ripe and in wonderful stand, full of white pinnacles. They had taken a long rope with each one holding on to one end and running through the rows, screaming for their very life and drawing the rope over the plants.

I was dead tired by now and sat down at the edge of the kaffir field. This was to be our bread, the food and fodder for our chickens and pigs. I heard the milling of a million small teeth. Around me everything was still; the occasional cry and drumming from a neighbour's yard was still to be heard. The white field had turned black, every hope had dimmed.

We ate no supper, no evening meal. I have never seen Papa so dejected. No, I do not intend to speak about Russia, no longer. And yet here, he had always been courageous and hopeful, even if the rains failed to arrive and life appeared hopeless. And so it is when hope is crushed after showing so much promise just a short day ago. Our cotton looked better than ever before after adequate and timely moisture had fallen in January and then again in February. The kaffir looked better than in ages.

Mama also sits on an easy chair; she does not murmur. Possibly she feels pains of this sort only superficially. There are other matters which afflict her soul, as if it her soul has layer upon layers. I am very tired and yet I will not be able to sleep. Grasshoppers swarm before my eyes.

4 March 1934

Papa appeared to me like a general and I admire him. The grasshoppers, next morning, suddenly lifted off, as if upon orders. The entire, vast cloud of hoppers which had occupied our village swirled towards the skies and headed north, following the direction of the wind. From the vantage point of our yard, I could see all our arable fields, and they were all grey, as far as the eye could see.

Then suddenly Papa composed himself. With a voice bordering on the serene, he called us children, each one by name, and then we walked to the fields. Here, in a collective effort, we took stock of all that was left. Fortunately we had already harvested the peanuts and we had already picked the cotton once. Some stalks still had about one hundred bolls or capsules which were yet to burst, as cotton does.

"Possibly the cotton will produce yet another crop," said Papa, "if the frost will spare it, then we might yet have a harvest in May."

When we walked through the kaffir, we were silenced, subdued. It looked devastated. Then Papa said, "Look. The earth is still wet from the last rain. The kaffir will produce new pinnacles, small ones, granted, but many. There will be enough for fodder and bread."

We felt much lighter; much less sorrowful. When we inspected our watermelons we had a good laugh. The watermelons lay on the field without as much as leaf to them and resembled fat, little piglets.

"The watermelons will keep until the next military truck arrives, and then we will sell them all."

At lunch Papa drew up a plan. He had discussed the matter with Mama and now we listened to him in silence.

"The crop is insufficient to support our large family," he said very peacefully. "Abraham and Lena, will have to find gainful, paid employment. There are positions available for girls in Casado or in Pinasco. In the administrative offices of our colony there are employment opportunities posted and I will announce to them that

Lena is available if she agrees to it. Abraham will readily find
employment at the Cattle Station in Casados. Then there are two
fewer mouths to feed and you might even be able to send home some
of your earnings. David will take the trip to the train station from
now on. Jake will shortly resume his schooling. He must complete
Grade Four. We intend to have at least one of our children properly
educated."

Then Papa looked at me. "Lizzie", he said, "I know that much work
will now fall on your shoulders. If God will grant us health, we shall
make do and manage."

I looked at Papa and nodded. Papa then looked at each one in turn.
Abraham nodded. Lena nodded. On all of us lay a tension, an
expectation, as if a new future was introduced. I was surprised at
Lena. She smiled, as if she looked forward to this new chapter in her
life. Obviously nothing of any consequence could happen to her.
Nothing evil had ever beset her. And Mama, too, was peaceful, even
if previously she trembled when I as much as attended a *Polter-*
evening.

Am I in greater danger than Lena? Recently Greta observed, "You
are very much attracted to the boys; you better look out!" Then she
assured me that things between her and Isaak were very much in
proper order. She knew exactly how far she allowed boys to go with
her. Isaak was not at all forward. Some girls obviously did not know
that they got men folk all excited. Tina Harms had obviously not
known this either and now she had to bear the consequences.

Greta then reported that Tina and Willy had been excommunicated from their church. They did not even have to appear
before the congregation, since their situation was clear, a foregone
conclusion. Their church had simply cast their vote and the matter
was resolved.

"When their baby is born," Greta suggested, "then the two can ask
for forgiveness and then they will again be admitted to their church."

Reverend Reimer informed us similarly, during our catechism
classes. A sinner was not permitted to attend the Holy Communion
according to question number 83. This is the reason why sinners
ought to be excommunicated. "Whosoever partakes unworthily of

the eating of the bread or the drinking of the wine, such party is guilty of the body and blood of the Lord." So spoke Paul.

And Jesus said, "Whose sins you forgive, such sins are forgiven and whose sins you do not forgive, such sins are not forgiven."

When I think of Tina and that she ought to be happy for her baby I find all these strict measures hard, very harsh. However, Greta says, that's the way the scripture is: tough!

However, it was not really my intention of recording all this today. I know that Mama is full of concern, particularly for me, but the fact that she allows Lena to move on so passively concerns me.

Abraham will do as he pleases. I also believe that he will smoke when he is alone with the Paraguayans on their ranches.

It was my intention to write how close our family is in time of need. It is our intention to help our parents and not to add to their cares.

I am attractive, Greta claims. Actually I am rather glad to hear this. The soldiers whistle when they see me on the street. But then the girl in the Menno Colony comes to mind and I do not as much as turn around.

21 March 1934

It was like a migration all over again and our departure from Rosenthal came to mind. October 1929. There was much baking in the kitchen and buns were roasted for a long trip. Our ox-cart was laden to the very top with cotton and with Lena and Abraham's suitcases topping the load. After bidding farewell, they mounted the cart and David took the reins in his hands. In doing so, he had assumed his new responsibility as cart driver. They headed for the train station where the train took Lena and Abraham to the port of Casado on the Paraguay River. Then the ship will take Lena for a further stretch up river to Puerto Pinasco, where she will work as a domestic for a German family. It was a tearful farewell; mother could hardly contain herself.

I walked up to the village street and looked after the departing vehicle until it disappeared at the end of the street. In my day, we drove by horse and carriage from our yard to the train station is Saporozhje which Mama still calls Alexandrowsk. It was night time and our village lay back in darkness. Everything we owned was left behind. We were allowed to take only what fitted into our suitcases and baskets. And so I am surprised that Mama took along a little booklet, her catechism, and which was as important to her as the Bible. We also took along the large wall clock with the pendulum, although it was difficult to pack. It was a Kröger clock, a wedding present from Mama's parents. Now it ticks and tocks here in the Chaco just like it did in my earliest childhood days back home.

Ah yes, that booklet. It is astonishing! It was published in 1781 in Elbing, West Prussia and it contains the confession of faith "of those we call the united Flemish, Frisian, and High German Baptists—or Mennonites." It is a catechism like we have it here, although David claims the questions and answers are clearer and more concise. In it one can sense the faith of our fathers to which we must again find our way. Much has become too shallow nowadays. By this he means our General Conference Church. Papa will hear none of it, and so David takes care in his evaluations.

We now have a beautiful lawn on our yard. Papa visited a neighbouring colony and brought along Bermuda grass which grows very quickly. We siblings were resting on this lawn on Sunday night and discussed a church banning. An older man from a neighbouring village was banned on account of a sexual offence. That is the term Pastor Reimer used when he asked the young people of church to leave the church while married couples remained behind to witness the execution of the ban.

We were standing around our wagon when the guilty party appeared. He looked down, walked up to his wagon and departed.

"Now they have excommunicated him", said Lena. This will be a strict ban since the transgression involved a sexual offence. No one is to sit at table with him or have anything to do with him.

"How do you know that?" I asked.

"Such a measure is stipulated in our church regulations, and it is also biblical," she said.

When we were lying on our lawn in the evening, we got into a debate. I do not intend to defend such an offence and the measure taken was certainly appropriate. And yet, I find such a measure unduly harsh. I had to think of Tina Harms and how unhappy she now is in her early married life. She has been banned on account of an innocent child, soon to be born.

"Right you are, Lizzie!" said Abraham. "Such an excommunication serves no purpose. The ministry should rather help such people and counsel them. And, furthermore, if such a couple marries, than banning serves no purpose."

I was somewhat surprised while David and Lena defended the church. Where is one to draw the limits? The church has to rid itself of sin and can manage to do so only if it deals strictly with the sinners, suggested David. This is scriptural.

Next day David gave me Mama's booklet from Prussia. Then he showed me the answer. "The churches acted clearly on this issue as did the Anabaptists. Read it."

I read it, and I was overcome with respect when I read the very old script with an ancient alphabet. I here cite what I read, "I confess based on the teachings of Christ and his apostles that punishment and church discipline must be upheld and practised among believers so that the stubborn or those who have committed sins of the flesh by which they have separated themselves from God shall also not be tolerated in the community of the believers and be punished towards a return to righteousness and serve as an example to that end." One is to separate oneself from those duly punished and unrepentant sinners, and the text goes on, "for as long until the punished party returns, penitent and sorrowful for sins committed."

I had to think of the man who walked to his wagon alone and bent, and also of Tina. Is one now to distance oneself after they have been banned? Surely no one really does this, and I have to side with David who claims that we are no longer as strict as our forefathers were.

I do not agree with David on many subjects, but I enjoy listening to him because he is so sure of his views. On the trips to the railway station during which conversations frequently border on the frivolous no one can claim that David is given to loose talk as Mama often feared about Abraham. I would like to be so sure of myself as well, even though there are many things I simply do not understand. Is Tina therefore "stubborn" as the old catechism has it?

29 March 1934

I would never have set foot on the Friesen yard because that would have given rise to village gossip. However, this morning we went there, David and I did, since we wanted to see the jaguar which the soldiers shot last night.

All around the village, army mules and horses graze, some of them stemming from the time when the cavalry regiment was stationed in our village. One animal after the other had fallen prey to the jaguar and then, last night, the soldiers lay in wait and shot it. Then they took it to the Friesen yard for all to see. Many from the village had assembled there to admire the beautiful animal with its mighty paws and teeth and its spotted fur.

Heinrich came towards us and told us about the entire adventure in his carefree and interesting palaver, and I forgot all about existing tensions, real and imagined. I listened to him and asked questions and we conversed without reservations, like children; we exchanged pleasantries and laughed.

Then the teacher also came accompanied by his pupils. He had brought along a book in which all animals are described. He read to his pupils what the book had to report on the jaguar, the largest predatory cat in the Americas.

Heinrich told us how a jaguar kills mules. The jaguar sits in a tree and jumps on the unsuspecting mule and breaks its neck vertebrae by biting with its mighty teeth and strangling it with its powerful paws. The soldiers had mounted a tree and shot the jaguar from that vantage point. When a jaguar kills its prey, it invariably returns the next night.

In addition to the jaguar, the puma lives in the Chaco. The teacher also had a picture of it in his book and he now gave us a lesson about the predators, or beasts of prey. Then a girl from Grade VI was asked to recite the poem "Lion Riding" by Ferdinand Freiligrath. The soldiers applauded, even though they did not understand the poem. Heinrich then walked up to the soldiers and translated it for them as well as a song sung by the pupils, "Twilight time, twilight time, you guide by light my early death."

Then Heinrich came to David and me. "You know Spanish so well?" I said.

"I learned Spanish almost by accident," he said. "I have traveled to Camacho by truck twice by myself. In April I am to go even further right up to the Front. We haul ammunition there and transport the wounded back to Trebol."

"Is that not very dangerous?" I asked.

"Oh!" he remarked, "it is no more dangerous than Abraham working at a ranch. Also, I earn money which my parents need."

We spoke as if we talked about incidentals, like wind and weather, and yet what he reported made my very heart bleed. I remembered the song "*Campamento, campamento*" and the other songs Heinrich loves in another language. Are there girls with the soldiers? Only nurses. Does he take an interest in these foreign girls?

Everything was so free and candid, and yet so hopeless. "Like the grain fields and the wind, like the storm and the wild seas…" I believe David had no idea what went on in my heart.

7 April 1934

It was a difficult, a hard week. We are just back from a Prayer Meeting; these represent a fitting conclusion to the work of the week, in which almost the entire village gets involved. We are all tired from the hard work and it is as if everyone relaxes on the hard church benches.

On Saturdays much baking is done and the entire house is cleaned. We scrub the floors with a mixture of clay and cow manure. This hardens the floor and renders it dust free for a week. On Saturday evening an unusual smell pervades the house, which is simply part of Saturday: a blend of fresh baking, buns, crumble cake and the scent of the floors. The yard is raked and swept and the garbage is burned. The smoke of many little fires on many yards wafts through the village and even in the evenings after the Prayer Meeting, the aroma of it all lingers on. All this is part of Saturday.

One of the villagers—by turn—prepares the Prayer Meeting. He announces the songs and reads a scriptural passage. Then everyone rises and everyone is allowed to pray. First the men pray, then the women. When I intended to get baptized I also started to pray at these meetings. Obviously everyone notices who prays and who does not, and Mama claims that prayers are a form of testifying.

I have to admit that praying for me represents a certain surmounting, an overcoming of self, but later on I feel free and happily relieved since the women and girls around me pronounce a happy and audible Amen to my supplication efforts.

I noticed that even Papa prays publicly once in a while and that this represents an effort since it was not customary for the Conference to publicly pray in Russia. Gradually things in the Chaco become more and more Brethren and it seems that the Brethren here are gaining the upper hand.

Reverend Wiebe and Preacher Reimer preach alternately on Sundays. Only on communal Sundays, once a month, each minister preaches in his own church. Then the church members from several villages gather, each church to itself.

I am happy that we do not quarrel as much and as violently as in Russia, of which Papa occasionally speaks. And yet, on occasion he cannot contain himself. Members of the Brethren church had been so arrogant and self-righteous, as if they had an exclusive claim to heaven.

I get the same impression of Greta. She believes that the greatest danger exists in mixed marriages, meaning Conference members marrying Brethren and even, God forbid, the opposite. For this reason the Brethren accept no one who has not been baptized by immersion. Conference members have to be re-baptized in order to qualify for marriage. For this reason, says Greta, one ought to strictly marry in one's own church and she is so overjoyed that she and Isaak belong to the same, the only church, the Mennonite Brethren.

"With Heinrich the matter is doubly difficult," she informed me. "Firstly, he is not converted and baptized and secondly, even if he really were to be baptized, then such would transpire in the Brethren Church and he would be immersed, while you are merely sprinkled."

I let her ramble on as she pleases like birds twitter about still waters, or should I say like parrots scream, who have little inkling of how deep the water is.

What is to become of matters as in our village? We are sad together when someone dies and is buried and we are happy at weddings. I believe for Papa village community is more important than the differences between the churches and that is the reason he is prepared to compromise.

Last year an angry quarrel ensued when the itinerant minister Epp publicly attacked the Conference. This led to serious confrontations. Then Papa and other conference representatives compromised for the sake of peace and we had peace, once again, in our village.

8 April 1934

I was interrupted last night just as I was right in the middle of discussing church matters. Company arrived and I was unable to concentrate properly. Actually I had no intention of putting church matters to paper, but then again this topic seizes me like a raging torrent after a downpour.

It was my intention to write about the hard work, now that Abraham and Lena are no longer with us. We are dependent on the Indians who help us out during the harvest. Often I write about matters unrelated to what I set out to do. Then I let my feelings guide me.

It was already nine in the evening when Jake and his friends came to our yard. Two of them, Gerhard Braun and Peter Harms attend school with him and they are in the same grade. They arrived on our yard, singing. Their songs were so lively that I closed my diary and went out into the yard.

The air was fresh, as fresh as their singing, and my heart felt free. Is it really true that church matters and all that attendant baggage weigh so heavily on me? I constantly find myself contesting this very matter.

We took out our chairs since the lawn was wet with dew and then the boys sang one song after another. These new songs make my very happy. "Freedom is on my mind" is what the boys sang as well as some love songs.

> "In a cooling depth of water,
> A mill wheel utters sigh,
> My sweetheart has departed
> Who used to live hard by."

These are the songs they sing in school now; some are sad but they comfort me all the more. Jake has promised to write them down for me.

David later also entered upon the scene. He also enjoys singing these new German songs, even though the love songs are not for him. In Germany law and order is now the order of the day. High time, says David, because things had become a trifle suspect, particularly in literature.

The boys in our colony have organized a Pathfinder Circle, David reported to the boys. It is the intention of the club to take issue with matters lacking moral fibre. They reject smoking, alcohol and flirtation. Instead, they intend to get active in sports and encourage and nurture the good and the beautiful. "To that end, you also ought to get involved," he told the boys.

Jake and the other two boys had nothing to say to that. It may be that they were somewhat deflated in their enthusiasm. Jake and David invariably are of different opinions on many matters, which leads to quarrels. In my opinion Jake loves freedom while David tends to restrict.

The three boys soon rose and walked to the street. I remained behind, sitting with David. We often talk since we spend much time together working. It appears that his firm opinions numb my pain although we never speak about Heinrich. I allow his resolute demeanour to prevail.

However, I am quite capable of giving direction to conversations and so the topic of marriage was on the agenda. Marriages with unbelievers should not be allowed by the church under any circumstance, said David. This contravened the accepted order and flew in the face of the apostle decree. "Do not draw a common yolk with unbelievers" so it is written. "Even in the old Doctrines of Faith of 1781 this is explicitly stated," said David. "The two are to be like-minded, says Paul in his Letter to the Romans."

I felt challenged and so I told David what Greta had said about baptism and marriage. Only those baptized by immersion were allowed to marry each other. I said this with deliberate intent since I knew that David has his eye on one Sara Janzen from a neighbouring village and she is a member of the Brethren. David became conspicuously quiet since he had been baptized by sprinkling.

"I have to reflect some more on that matter," he said.

I said nothing further but I could not suppress a bit of *Schadenfreude*; let him stew and suffer a bit in his love! David takes his baptism very seriously. He had already previously observed that the form of baptism is not decisive; the heart's intent is.

Sometimes I believe that our Anabaptist fathers tended to over-complicate things. And yet, appropriate and well-chosen Bible verses are to be found in the catechism, substantiating every tenet and doctrine. This holds true for the Prussian Teachings of Faith as well. And whatever scripture teaches is binding!

14 April 1934

It is Saturday again, another hard week has passed, again an Hour of Prayer has come and gone and again I sit at home.

Papa is so happy that there will yet be cotton. The fields did turn green again and now the white cotton balls protrude from among the leaves. Also, his hopes for the kaffir comeback were justified. New pinnacles have sprouted. It is not yet ripe; the parrots fly screeching over the fields. Invariably someone has to play scarecrow in those fields for otherwise the pinnacles will turn black yet again.

We could never manage all the work if *Cacique* Maito and his family clan had not come. These Indians have built their grass huts about one kilometre distant on a water meadow and every morning they arrive to work.

I take joy every time these Lenguas come to our yard, and not only because they help in the labour, but because I delight in their uniqueness. They are as if they have sprung from nature. The men are powerfully framed and only wear a loin cloth around their hips. The women are also naked from navel to gable. They only wear a skirt made out of soft suede from deer hides. Their young girls virtually blossom in the freshness of their youth. They paint their cheeks a bright red. This means that they desire love, so claims Jake. They giggle and gossip and are always happy.

I watch them closely when they lounge around on our yard. We serve them watermelons for breakfast. Now in April, when the mornings are fresh with due, the watermelons have a glorious aroma. The Indians cut through the middle of the fruit and eat the flesh with their fingers and drink the juice out of the rinds.

Franz, as we call one of the boys, and Mary, as we call one of the girls, got married recently, it would appear. They act like children; laughing, chasing after each other and jumping into the cotton or they simply disappear in the kaffir field. Papa gets angry because these two pick so little cotton, but that leaves them unconcerned. I look at them with wonder and think to myself, how simple love can be. Nobody issues them orders; nothing interferes with their easy bearing. Or is this matter in accordance with Preacher Wiebe's claim in a recent sermon, that they are poor heathens, walking in darkness? He stated that we have been sent to the Chaco to take the gospel to the Indians.

The Lenguas have had a difficult past. When the war broke out, the soldiers persecuted them. The Commander-in-Chief ordered that every Indian should be shot dead. The claim was out that the Indians informed the enemy of the positioning and location of the troops and that they used the Indians for spying. We knew one Indian, Malvin very well. He had helped us in breaking our land, a strong, young man. Somewhere the Bolivian troops sighted him and shot him dead. The Lenguas had gotten involved between the fronts. Later his son, who had stayed with his clan, came to us with his mother. Their eyes were brimming with fear.

The order to kill them has been lifted and the Indians again dare to leave the bush to which they fled for fear. Abraham once paid them a visit, deep in the bush. He is a good friend of the Indians and the chief had taken him to their grass huts on secret paths. They had secured their camps with walls of bushes and in their huts they stored bundles of arrows.

But now the persecutions are over and Preacher Wiebe said that we were to reflect on how we could help these poor people. The Lenguas also should know about Jesus and that he died for them as well.

6 May 1934

"A mosquito, blade of grass, a man and a tree,
And each has a wish and a dream, big or wee,
And all crave a swig, but no one may drink
And all life is sadness, but not as bad as you think."

This is the reason why I have not written a single word in my diary for three weeks now. The verse is from a novel by Ludwig Ganghofer, which I have read. It is written in a dialect.

Jake brought me two books by Ganghofer from the library, one being *Edelweiß-King* and *Rush of the Forest* both of which I have read. I was so taken by them and so fascinated that I could think of nothing else. I told David during work all that I had read and I was surprised at how attentively he listened to me. The next day, he asked how things progressed in the novel.

Maybe Mama is right in claiming that reading novels is dangerous. In Russia it was said reading novels was a sin as was the theater. For that reason, she had never read a novel. When I now reflect on the fact that during the time I read the novels I hardly read the Bible because I kept on reading while already in bed and that, even during the Prayer Meetings my heart and soul were with Ambros and the duchess, who were so intertwined by such deep love and yet were forced to part, I can almost understand Mama and her concerns.

Possibly I am so strongly attached to such reading material because my heart beats for those in love, as does my longing. Then my thoughts find deep submergence and comfort in all the sorrow which love inflicts on mankind.

However, today in church we were rudely awakened to real life. A girl came before the church as we term it. I know Maria Falk who comes from a neighbouring village, an older girl, possibly thirty years old. She had been in Asunción working as a domestic. Other Mennonites who had been in Asunción brought home the news that Maria had been naughty. When she recently returned, two ministers had a word with her and she had confessed everything. Now she appeared before the congregation and asked for forgiveness.

When Maria Falk then left the room, Reverend Friesen explained what manner of sin had been committed and always lay in wait for young people in the big cities. Most of such sins were those of the lust of flesh, he said. For young Christians things were difficult when being alone in a big city. The colony and the church formed a protective fence, he claimed. He then recommended that we forgive the girl and we all raised our hands in favour. When Maria then returned and sat down with us, I noticed that she had tears in her eyes but that she appeared happy and free.

When we sat down for our evening meal, Papa praised our ministers. They knew how to maintain order, just like in Russia, he said. And things in the Conference simply were not as bad as the itinerant minister Epp had claimed; he had publicly stated our church lacked all discipline.

Indeed, this is the very matter I wanted to record in my diary, meaning the great quarrel we had in our village last year when the evangelist Epp presented his Plan of Salvation. Evening after evening. One evening he claimed that things in the Conference were downright luke-warm and that our form of baptism was no baptism at all. Then Papa with some other men from our church got up and walked out of the church. Everyone was consternated and stunned, including Reverend Epp and this led to many negotiations until the matter was finally resolved. I have rarely seen my Papa so agitated.

I started my little epistle with Ganghofer and I have again landed in our village and in our church. That is the way things are. In the final analysis all things revolve around my life and my life is an integral part of the village and the church. Why did Maria Falk not simply stay in Asunción? What made her return, knowing as she did, what was awaiting her? She cried and her crying eyes appeared happy.

Ganghofer's books for me are like a good walk. I then walk into a different world and yet this world somehow becomes similar to the world I know. Jake has promised to bring me some more books.

Jake is now reading a book by Edwin Erich Dwinger, *The Army behind Barbed Wire*. Jake treats the book very secretively and I am not to tell Papa or David about it. When Jake intends to read it he climbs up to the loft of our stable. What can possibly be so dangerous about this book? Books dealing with the World War are common and even Papa likes reading them. The teacher has received more books from Germany and he lends these to Papa. Maybe Jake will someday tell me what the book has to say. He made fleeting reference to the book dealing with German soldiers and some girls; that bad! Previously he had not believed such things possible. The teachers had cautioned him not to read the book. However, he was of the opinion that it is better to know everything, even risky books. I was reminded of the things Jake told me about the local soldiers.

14 May 1934

We celebrated Mother's Day in our village yesterday. This custom was introduced here from Germany, our teacher said in his word of greeting, and it is the first time that we celebrated this occasion. In Germany Mother's Day is celebrated in the entire country; on this occasion all German mothers are honoured. In the new Germany the family is held in highest esteem.

Then our teacher reminded us of Russia where Communism systematically destroys families and free love prevails. Small wonder, then, that Russia is headed for disintegration and Germany blossoms. God blesses wherever mothers, marriages and families are honoured.

The occasion had been prepared by the Sunday School teachers. Lena Unger, Maria Braun, and Liese Fast had invested great pains in the effort for it. We younger girls also assisted as well as we could. The entire school had been decorated with flowers from the *palo blanco* trees. The aroma is beautiful, and even more powerful than the lilacs of Rosenthal. The weather in May is truly awesome. The sun has moved far south and shines mildly on all the land.

The Sunday School pupils had learned poems and Mother's Day songs. Our mothers had baked fresh buns and other goodies and coffee was served to all, just as at weddings. After the celebration, the children played happily on the school grounds. They crawled into the bunkers which the soldiers had dug a year ago, and then the kids mounted the rope ladder which led to a giant *quebracho* tree on which the soldiers used to keep watch. The children played happily with hardly anyone remembering the war. And still, far to the west, fierce battles are still raging.

When all were so happily playing, I noticed Mama sitting in a corner with a handkerchief to her eyes. A letter had arrived on Saturday from Russia and Mother's Day reminded her of her children still there. Over there, in our former home, dreadful starvation ravages and times are unspeakably difficult. Maria writes that her legs are swollen and she does not know how to acquire adequate food for her children. She has no sewing thread to patch the family's clothes. Isaak is in banishment and she never hears from him at all. Work in the kolkhozes, the communal farms, is dreadfully hard. Whatever produce is realized has to be taken to central stations while the population starves. In the Russian villages things are even more desperate with many simply fainting and dying on the streets.

I walked up to Mama and sat with her and put my arm around her shoulders while she cried all the harder, but my gesture did her good. Then Greta also came to sit with us; she promised Mama that she would pray for Maria and Isaak.

When we joined the other girls who were already busily washing the dishes, Greta took my hand and whispered in my ear, "Lizzie, we intend to get married." A lengthy, drawn-out love-affair is simply too dangerous, her parents had said. Such lengthy affairs often lead to calamities as in the Tina Harms case.

When Greta gets married I will feel even lonelier. I know this even now, and then I shall get even more involved in reading beautiful books such as Ganghofer's novels. Jake says there are entire stacks of them available. Then I am far removed from my village and in a world which holds me captive.

1 June 1934

The beautiful month of May is past and now cooler and drier weather awaits us. I often watch the swarms of parrots in the sky. They are parakeets, says Jake, with black and blue heads. They swarm in entire clouds and are driven by the wind as they screech to high heaven. Then suddenly the entire swarm of birds falls into the weeds where they eat seeds so audibly that one can hear the cracking of their bites. The screech of parrots tells me that winter is coming.

I have parents and I have siblings as well as friends in the village. I can talk about books with Jake, and with David about matters of faith and the church, and with Greta about the people in the village, and yet I am totally empty at times when so much longing and loneliness befall me.

I felt deeply ashamed on account of my ingratitude yesterday. A truck full of prisoners of war stopped right in front of our yard gate. A smithy is located opposite to our yard and the truck was in need of repairs. I saw some bearded fellows dismount from the vehicle. When might they be returning to their families? Jake knows that the majority of the Bolivians are Indians and come from Altiplano in the Andes.

The prisoners walked back and forth in their ragged uniforms and were guarded by our troops. Our neighbour's children came eagerly running, curious as children are. One small fellow named Peter walked up to a prisoner and asked whether he had a pocket knife to barter. *Cortapluma* (pocket knife) and *pan* (bread) are words known to every child and bartered pocket knives are the kid's ultimate ideal. Then the bearded fellow took Peter by the shoulders and kissed his hair. Peter was totally confused. .

"He cried" said Peter fearfully when he came up to me. How many children may this fellow have at home?

There are again heavy battles raging in the distant Pilcomayo where our troops are winning one battle after another. On Easter Day we stood at the edge of the street and one truck after another loaded with prisoners from the Front passed us by. We counted fifty trucks.

The Youth Hour was conducted last night and when Jake and I walked home we interlocked our arms because the night air was so chilly. It was pitch black and we had to take great care not to stumble over the cattle which lie anywhere on the street and chew their cud.

Then Jake told me some of the things that went on in Dwinger's book which he had just read. The book tells about German POW's in Russia. The German prisoners had had a girl in their train compartment and Dwinger describes what they had done to and with her.

"I had never believed it possible that German soldiers would ever do any such thing," said Jake. For this reason he did not want to show the book to David and Papa, and that was also the reason the teacher was reluctant to lend it to him. There was another book by Dwinger *Between White and Red* which dealt with the Civil War in Russia. One of the teachers had finally consented for the boys of Grade IV to read it. After all, they had a right to know what transpires in times of war.

I was very happy that Jake told me all this, including the episode about the girl. Jake said she was a whore. I did not at all know that whores are so bad. When I read in the Bible about the whore Rahab, who rescued Josuas's messengers, I thought she had been a good girl. Now I intend to read that story once again.

When we arrived home to the warmth of the room, Papa sat reading *La Plata Post* from Argentina. "It contains a lot of news about Germany as well," he said. "Hitler should have come to power three years earlier and then we would all have stayed in Germany."

"Yes," said Jake, "then I would now by a member of Hitler's Youth and Lizzie would be in the BDM (*Bund Deutscher Mädchen*: Society of German Girls)".

Jake had already forgotten what he had told me about the German soldiers. We are all similarly inclined when we see the glorious pictures of the New Germany.

10 June 1934

I will probably let the story of the whore Rahab rest for a while. Who am I to question regarding such matters. Who can I ask? I know my Bible well and also secondary references. In the Book of Matthew I read that Rahab, as a mother, is mentioned in the genealogy of Jesus. If so, she obviously does not fit the pattern of the girl in Dwinger's book, of which Jake informed me. I do not intend to ask David about this matter because it embarrasses him and me as well.

And yet, all manner of thoughts circulate in my head. I intend to read the Bible to become a better person and not think about the German soldiers, or of the soldiers around here. This causes my head to spin and only further confuses me.

Heinrich has been gone for weeks now, and Jake knows that he has traveled by a military vehicle right up to the battle front. Word has it that severe battles are raging there with heavy artillery like in Verdun of a former day, says Papa. Where do these poor countries manage to acquire all the war material such as the many vehicles, the airplanes and all the ammunition for years on end?

Papa has just read the book *Verdun*. He borrowed it from the teacher, and I even had to let him have the reading lamp; he was so engrossed in the World War, where he had served in the middle of things in his capacity as an orderly.

And now Heinrich is in the middle of it all and far away; hundreds of kilometres which he travels with his military vehicle. Is it this distance which pacifies me and also because he appears to be the master of every situation? The word "impossible" invariably caused

me silent suffering. If only I knew if all this causes Heinrich inner pain. He always appeared so enlightened, so above it all. Or was he merely indifferent?

I have uncommon conversational partners. For example our bottle tree, which stands behind our house, close to the mighty *urundey*. I speak to it about life and death, and for me it is such an obvious symptom of change and transition, of the progress of the days and weeks of my life and years.

In April it was dark green and shadowy. In May it decorated itself with blossoms. I took a rake which extended to its branches and broke off some twigs with blossoms on them. They are like velvet and ivory in colour. I placed these on the table for Mama on Mother's Day.

Now in June the leaves are turning yellow and some are falling. In winter it turns completely bald. Then the north wind whistles through its thorny branches and scatters the white seed bearing cotton which have burst in their ripeness. Then the tree extends its empty branches empty and dead. And yet the tree has life and is full of life in its mighty trunk which resembles a fat stomach. Already in October the entire tree covers itself with bright green, even before any rain has fallen. I so much would like to write a poem or compose a song about the bottle tree, as Ganghofer has written about the grass and the mosquitoes, or Herman Löns about fire.

But I should rather confine myself to copying poems and songs. Now some more of Ganghofer's books were brought home by Jake as well as some poems by Mörike. However, the poems by Löns grab my heart like none other.

> *The red fire burns, the sparks are sent a-flying*
> *And then they scatter high and bright like life itself and fall…*
> > *for dying;*
> *My life immersed in nights and sorrow*
> *And I must weep my time away until tomorrow.*

Jake knows my literary taste by now and so he brings me books from school that suit my fancy. By way of thanks I read him my copied versions without admitting to myself or him how deeply they affect me.

8 July 1934

It is an icy cold Sunday. The south wind whistles around the corners of our house. The soldiers term this wind *Pampero*, because it blows in from the Argentinian pampas and, possibly from even further south, from Patagonia.

It is afternoon and very quiet in the house. Mama and Papa are enjoying their afternoon nap while Jake and David are visiting friends in the village. They probably are headed for the village swing as well despite the chill; this swing was built by the boys for Easter in front of the village close to an *urendey* tree, the highest tree in the village. Such a swing is an old tradition dating back to Russia and is truly a work of art. Close to the tree a high post is dug deeply into the earth. A mighty log is fitted into a branch fork of the tree on one end and the other end is secured on the beam. A long, heavy plank, secured by four mighty chains provides space for four swingers. Mostly it is the girls who swing. Some of our boys position themselves at the end of the swinging plank and set the plank in motion. I may just join in the fun later today.

It is dark in the kitchen, since we had to close the window shutters because of the cold wind. A fire crackles in the stove and the water on a pot boils with all providing cozy warmth.

When going to the swing I will probably become fully aware of my desperate loneliness. Greta got married a week ago. Fortunately the wedding was held before the weather turned, for otherwise Greta would have shivered in her thin wedding dress.

Löwens staged a huge wedding. They had butchered an ox and so there was meat a-plenty. Already Saturday at noon guests from the neighbouring villages were served borsch. Much cabbage was grown this year and the women brought it in quantity to the Löwen home. On the evening after the wedding, borsch was again served with much meat. A large tent had been erected since the school could not accommodate all the many guests who had arrived. Almost all of the Brethren from neighbouring villages had been invited. When after coffee the young people carried benches to the yard, Mr Löwen appeared on the scene. He declared in a loud and formidable voice that no games were to be played on his yard. Many of the boys and some of the girls then simply left and went away. They probably set off for the Neufeld yard where a gramophone is located, and games were in full swing as at most weddings. I noticed that Heinrich left the Löwen yard as well.

We formed a small circle. Neta and Liese Rempel had brought their guitars and so we sang songs from our Youth Hour. A sermon was presented for all guests and visitors. Our youth leader, the teacher, spoke about David who had vanquished first a lion and then Goliath. We as young people were to bravely follow his example and battle all sin in this depraved world. Whosoever stopped fighting sin was lost. This was followed by an hour of prayer in which the bridal couple participated.

When we sat at table the gramophone was filling the air They were playing the Paraguayan songs with sad songs which filled me with the ache of longing and nostalgia. Greta takes all this in stride with a *laissez faire* attitude even though she is married and has a husband at her side. She accepts life with ease and relaxation, like the rain and the sun and her daily bread, and talks to me about the things and events as if life bears no secrets.

"A man is such a wonderful thing to have, you can't believe it," she told me on Thursday when we departed the Bible Study. Isaak had remained behind with his friends and so we talked like in former times. Then she pressed my arm and said, "Lizzie, I am no longer a virgin." I was somewhat taken aback at so much candid palaver.

And so, for starters, I took the coat which Lena gave me, which she had brought along from Germany. It fits me perfectly. The cold air will do my face and my spirit good as I run over to the swing.

9 July 1934

Wednesday Night. It is actually an exceptionally fitting day to write. Generally I take time to write on Saturdays and Sundays. However, something transpired which I have to record. On Saturday I was totally confused and consternated, and Papa was the reason. He probably does not even know how he threw me off balance; balance, a state for which I strive with all my might.

We sat at home, all of us, which happens rarely. When sitting together in our warm kitchen, things became downright cozy and intimate. Since the south winds blew cold und un-abating, we sat closer still. Jake sat by the stove and served mate, a custom introduced by the village boys. He drew the water from the boiling water kettle on the stove. Generally, Papa does not drink either *mate* or *tereré* but today he downed a few gulps. "Does you good!" he said.

I no longer remember how the talk about the Löwen wedding came up. Whatever, we soon had a quarrel on our hands. Jake had also left when Mr Löwen forbade games on his yard. Jake is now seventeen and is of the opinion that the young people ought to pay such orders no heed. David took exception to this. He should have stayed there, said David, to lead by good example since he would shortly be leaving school and he ought to know what good behaviour in matters of discipline is all about. The Youth Leader's talk would have been good for him as well as for all the boys in the village who only intended to fool around and hang out in the streets.

Then, suddenly, Papa really got going, which really threw me for a loop since I was vacillating between my love for Jake and my admiration for David's piety.

"What Mr Löwen did was not right," Papa said in a huff. "That is no way to retain your young people. With such an attitude you really encourage the young people to take to the streets, since they have nothing useful to do and are bored in their leisure hours." Then Papa told us something about his youth about which I previously had no idea.

"In our village the young people danced, and danced well and they practiced these dances beforehand," he explained in a measured voice. "The parents sat in a circle, watching the dance and enjoying themselves. Certainly everything went as orderly and decently as here where playing at weddings is done."

Then Mama dropped her knitting and looked at Papa with total consternation. "Well now, do you want our children to dance? Surely we do not want again to live the luke-warm and shallow life of the Conference as formerly in Russia? Even Reverend Reimer no longer wants that."

"I am in agreement with the new measures introduced here," answered Papa after a pause. "But why do we have to pour out the baby with the bath water? To forbid our young people innocent fun and games is not only wrong, but it is also stupid and dangerous. Then the young people have no idea what they can do, and all the sad affairs we know about full well are bound to happen. Is that not the essence of real shallowness?"

"I want things to be as the teacher stated, and as we intend to have it in the German-Mennonite-Youth Society and in the Pathfinder Club," said David with deliberation. "We will not loiter in the streets and disappear in the dark. However, whatever causes laxity and leads to sin, we reject."

Papa then went on, in a soft persuasive language, as if he had not heard David's words at all. "Certainly matters in Russia were not all that luke-warm and as shallow as is now commonly stated in our village. Men like Mr Löwen became too powerful. They alone intended to stipulate what was good or bad and no one dared voice a word of opposition."

We all listened to what Papa told us about Russia and then, when a lull occurred, Jake suddenly burst out, "I want to get out of this village and out of this colony. I will suffocate here. Things in Germany are really beautiful right now! Friedrich Piehl writes me from Mölln in glowing terms, where he is a member of the Hitler Youth. There they march, sing, do gymnastics, practice athletics and are involved in sports. That is the kind of life I would like to lead. I want to wear a uniform like Fritz does on the picture he sent me."

"And our Mennonitism," David asked quite passively, "and our conscientious objector status and the faith of our fathers?"

"I want to go to bed now," said Jake. "Tomorrow I have to rise early and go to school!"

And so our confidential little round broke up, with everyone remaining alone and isolated with his thoughts, ideas and desires. As to whether Papa is unhappy within himself, considering how hard he tries for the village to conduct itself properly and peacefully? He certainly wants no quarrel with Mr Löwen and yet it seems to me that Mr Löwen in his sanctimony has the upper hand. Did people, like my father, have the upper hand in Rosenthal? And why does anyone have to have the upper hand in matters of faith?

I am concerned about Jake since he obviously feels unwell and restless in our society. What will become of him? I slipped into our house and bade Jake a good night and crawled under my warm comforter.

28 July 1934

This afternoon we carried Mrs Görzen to an early grave; she was mother to four children, the victim of a horrible accident.

"We stand silent and shocked," said the minister, "shaken and alarmed."

As deeply as the terrible accident affected me, I was just as impressed how such an event can wipe everything else clean off the slate of life: things that separate, annoy or cause pause. The entire village stood together, all ready to help, and all involved, until the men shovelled earth on the coffin of the lonely grave.

And again I saw Heinrich who never gave up his spade of duty, and it was as if he belonged there, here, part of us. The question for once was not if you were converted or not, baptized or not, whether you belonged to the Brethren or the Conference. All that mattered was community, participation, help. Whether Heinrich still has roots, tying him to us...?

We dressed the three little girls nicely with black bows in their hair. The smallest daughter is still in hospital with serious burn wounds. I could not but look constantly at the children by their mother's coffin, who appeared not to realize how their life had been so drastically changed with one sweep of fate's decree.

The choir sang, the congregation sang, with all looking at the minister with tear-veiled eyes, hoping to hear words of comfort. Not a single soul stood apart.

On the evening of the accident, on Tuesday, things were exactly the same as always. A strong north wind blew all day long and even late into the night, allowing no reprieve of fresh weather. It was exceptionally hot for a July day. Our village lay as if paralyzed by the heavy weather. Then we heard a clap of thunder, then another one.

We sat outside in front of our house. "Just like in Toledo," said Jake. We were looking for an explanation, when suddenly a pitiful cry filled the very space of air, followed by a fearful screech of wailing children. We were all on the street in a flash, we and many others, with all observing that the Görzen house was ablaze.

"Pails in hand!" yelled Papa, "and you, David, go for the ladder!" Papa took a long rope and then we all headed for the site of the accident in the middle of the village. The wheel of the village well was already busily squealing when we arrived with some men additionally drawing water by ropes and pails from the well. People formed a chain with the full pails being handed from man to man and the empty pails being returned. Other men folk were busily throwing spades full of sand on the burning reed roof.

Burning reeds emanate a horrible smell and I took sick from the stench. In addition, there was the woeful cry of the woman in the house and small Erna.

Gradually the fire was quenched and we learned just what had happened. Mrs Görzen had attempted to pour petroleum into a lit lantern. However, her jerry can contained gasoline. People in these parts exchange combustible fuels for edibles with the Görzens failing to notice that the soldiers had given them gasoline instead of petroleum, aka kerosene.

First the lantern had exploded and then the jerry can. Mrs Görzen caught fire like a torch, as well as her daughter Erna, who stood by her side and caught on fire as well. When bystanders tore off Mrs Görzen's clothes, her skin peeled off as well.

Just how quickly things transpire in spite of all advice and helplessness! Friesens own a riding horse, the only one in the village. Heinrich came galloping on the yard. "I am riding to the hospital in Filadelfia," he said to Mr Görzen, "so that adequate preparations can be made. Hopefully a military doctor is in attendance. If not, I shall ride to Isla Poí, the headquarters." And then he was gone.

Then things transpired more slowly. It took a long while until an ox-cart was readied, which transported mother and child. The cart with the whimpering mother and the crying child slowly departed. Many stood before the destroyed house and the wind drifted the acerbic smoke across the yard. Then one after another went home.

Then I observed the Sunday School teachers, Liese Fast and Lena Unger; they held the distraught Görzen daughters by their hands.

"Come along with us," Liese said to me, "you can help us."

We walked to the garden behind the yard. The late moon shone on the bright sand which the wind had heaped into little dunes. There, in the warm sand, we knelt down. Lena prayed first, then Liese and then I. We pleaded for the life of the mother and the child, for help and mercy. The little girls wept as they stammered forth their prayers. "Dear Lord Jesus make me whole, So I will make your heaven's scroll!" is what the littlest girl prayed.

Father Görzen had gone along to the hospital. Liese and Lena took the children along to their homes, where they found temporary custody until arrangements could be made for the family.

Pain and death can be so indescribably hard and incomprehensible. Now Mrs Görzen is dead. And small, little Erna has survived.

4 August 1934

On the 1st of August, Abraham came home for a visit but he will leave again soon. He had traveled very fast, at a speed previously unknown to us. It took him only two days to travel from Puerto Casado to our yard. A railed car on which officers ride had taken him along to our train station. There he had encountered Heinrich who was en route fetching military freight. Heinrich took him to our village, right to our door. Heinrich also got out of his truck to talk to us before departing.

There was no end to the conversations between Abraham and me, as if someone had arrived from a different world, a different star. Abraham had been employed at a cattle station, the Casado Company, all this while, where he had thoroughly acquainted himself with cattle breeding.

"We ought to do the same right here," he said. "It is a source of reliable income."

Papa was particularly interested in the war. Abraham now speaks Spanish well and had been engaged in conversations with the officers. Paraguay was preparing for a major offensive, he had been informed.

"I have seen the new trucks and new armaments, which are being hauled to the Front. It is hardly believable that such a poor country can manage all the means necessary for such a war. According to the officers, Bolivia has been roundly defeated."

Papa is sceptical about all this. He invariably draws comparisons with World War I. "We believed Russia was finished from all the blood-letting but it had the means to sustain a Civil War right up till 1920," he said. "And the Germans are also mobilizing yet again despite their serious defeats during the war."

Jake is all eyes and ears when Germany is discussed. In school the Versailles Treaty had been studied and he is of the opinion that Germany is right in objecting to this treaty. "Alsace-Lorraine has to become German again and the Poles have to return the corridor, as well as Upper Silesia. Hitler will manage all this in time, our history teacher informs us." Jake says all this with authority.

Abraham had a laugh. "You know what the officers told me? They said that we Paraguayans are the Germans of South America. Everyone against us but they cannot win against us. They referred to the great war which Paraguay waged against the Three Allies of the previous century."

Then Jake jumped up and clapped his hands and even David smiled. Then he turned serious and announced, "If Hitler maintains his faith in God, as he has said, and will do what Hindenburg advises him to do, then he will succeed in all things, just like King David."

I was much more interested in what Abraham had to say about Lena than in political discussions. He had visited Lena in Pinasco. She intends to stay at her job until Christmas. She is being well paid as a nanny by wealthy foreigners, who operate a tannin factory. She had sent along a fat envelope with money for Papa.

"There is enough money there so we can have a wagon built at the blacksmith," Papa happily announced.

It is hard to believe but Lena has had her hair cropped. Abraham brought along a recent photo of her on which she looks very stylish. Also she wears a modern dress with very short sleeves. She would never have worn such a dress in our village and would never have cropped her hair.

Mama was concerned when she saw the photo. "If Lena returns like this, then there will be much talk in our village." There is nothing Mama fears more than village gossip. That is why she is so concerned about me.

Then Papa became decisive in his tone and demeanour. "That is no bobbed haircut. Her hair is very prettily cut and some of the village girls now wear their hair the same way as well."

The Church Council has taken issue with bobbed hair, currently in vogue, and has decided to forbid such in church. Pastor Reimer then claimed at a Church Meeting that girls in Germany are back to wearing braids.

I also saw this very thing in German illustrated magazines and I like girls with long braids and boys with short pants. The fact that

Lena looks so stylish tickles my fancy enormously. Whether she ever entertains plans to marry? Why not? When looking at her long and hard on the photograph, I cannot help but entertain such thoughts.

5 August 1934

This afternoon Abraham invited me to go for a walk with him. We walked down the street and then to the end of the village to the swing. I was really proud of my brother, and who knows—he might even have been proud of me.

He has become more relaxed and more mature, way out in a far distance, as if he has gained an objective distance from things past. He acts a trifle superior, a bit above it all, and it did me a lot of good to talk to someone whose judgement is not dependent on the opinion of others.

The fact that he laughs at Mama who already now trembles if and when people will talk about Lena when she returns does not sit well with me. Mama is the way she is and I intend to love her as she is.

When we arrived at the swing, no one was there. The boys and girls generally congregate here a bit later in the evening. I sat down on the plank while Abraham stepped on one end and the swing commenced a swinging arc. Without any apparent reason, Abraham started talking about Heinrich.

"You never know what goes on within him," said Abraham. And he said this with such casual authority as if he had no intention of convincing me of anything. "Heinrich has lost all inner connections to our community. This probably happened already in Russia when the Civil War and then Soviet rule brought chaos and confusion into our way of life and nothing but. I believe that many young people at the time had similar experiences as he did. After the storm, they simply did not manage to find their way back to ship and they are still adrift on a plank. And Heinrich was not even in the self-Protective Unit; he was too young for that endeavour."

The tempo of the swing slowly became pronounced. I held fast to a chain and listened attentively. Abraham simply went on in his reverie as if he hardly took note of my presence. "For this reason, Heinrich has not managed to find his way in the church and not even to the Mennonite community."

Then Abraham was quiet for a moment as if reflecting how he could best explain this matter to me. "Do not believe, Lizzie, for one second that Heinrich is involved as a truck driver for the military for the money. I believe he is looking for an environment in which he can be what he is: a shipwrecked victim, a loner. And it is our perfect community which drives him and propels him to what he is: an OUTSIDER!"

The chains of the swing rattled softly and the irregular pace caused my hair to fall to one side of my face, then the other. Abraham expected no response from me even though he laid in pauses and gave the plank gentle pushes.

"Heinrich told me none of this nor in these words," he continued, "but these are my reflections on him. I can well empathize with him since I have been living with strangers for months on end now. But I have to admit that the forces that attract me home are more powerful than the forces that drive me away. With Heinrich such is not the case!"

Abraham then took a sweeping turn and sat down beside me on the plank and we simply let the swing come to rest.

"There is one thing of which I am certain, Lizzie," he then said, "you are the only one who could manage to keep Heinrich in our community, but I do not even know whether I should advise you to do so. I am convinced that in such event you would constantly be swimming upstream, into the current, and I do not know whether you are capable of it or even want to."

Abraham may have noticed that tears were dropping on my dress. He brought the swing to a standstill and then brushed my hair with infinite tenderness.

"Keep your chin up, Lizzie," he said softly, "you are as young and fresh as the morning dew and you have no reason to be the eternal outsider."

Then he laid his arm around me, shook me a little and I went for my handkerchief. We heard happy laughter which quickly approached and I quickly dried my eyes. A whole lot of boys and girls came running to the swing with Jake leading them all.

"Well, well, you two," called Jake, "almost like a couple in love!"

Abraham sat down on a tree trunk close by and we watched them all swing with the chains clanging and the girls squealing.

19 August 1934

Hindenburg is dead. Papa speaks of him like the grandfather of us all. He was our every help in time of need and we honour him as we did at a commemorative service last night in which the Youth Group of our village participated. We helped our teacher in preparing the event.

The Youth Leader had brought along a photograph of the General Field-Marshal in his stately uniform. We attached the photograph to the front wall and framed it with black flora. Above it we fastened a flag which we sewed from pieces of cloth. The German black-red-gold is no longer the flag of Germany, but the new swastika flag was not fitting for us Mennonites, said the teacher.

When speaking so much of Germany as we here do and celebrating it regularly, I wonder how the Germans, including Mennonites, conducted themselves in Russia. When the war broke out, all our men were conscripted, even if only to the medical staff, with Germany being the enemy. Now Papa enthusiastically talks about Hindenburg's defeating the Russians at Tannenberg in 1914. This is obviously a contradiction. However, everything may have changed, because the revolution, the civil war and Communism inflicted so much suffering on the Russians, and, above all, on the Germans in Russia. Obviously this led to considerable destruction.

I can still faintly remember the German soldiers who came to our village in 1918. How old was I then? Just four years old. At that time the Germans were our friends and the Bolsheviks our enemies. Mama cooked for the German soldiers when they came to our house.

Now I know that all that was not the reason for our celebration. We know that the former Federal President Hindenburg came to our assistance when the Soviet government in 1929 prevented us from leaving Russia. Our teacher last night explicitly said so in his speech. It was the intention of our local leadership here, to name the centre of our colony in Paraguay Hindenburg but Professor Unruh in Germany advised against it. He suggested Filadelfia because it means brotherly love. At that time, Papa was very angry about this, as I remember. Hindenburg would have been the proper term, he believed.

After the talk by the teacher, Jake and his friend Peter, both High School students, read poems about the German-French War in which war Hindenburg was an officer. They brought these poems home from school. Jake read "The Horses of Gravelotte" while Peter declaimed "The Trumpet of Vionville". They read so well that I had goose bumps all over my back. Heroism and death and sorrow are part of war. Foes and friends lie dead on the fields and then they mourn the dead like in the story of David and Jonathan in the Bible.

The teacher said, Hindenburg was a man of faith and so he died, believing in God. The boys in the High School sang "We advance for our prayer to God, who is just" which they had learned in school. Then the entire audience sang the German National Hymn, all three verses, with Jake holding forth in song like a *Heldentenor*.

Jake claims we foreign Germans are of equal value and standing as Germans proper in Germany, and so we ought to conduct ourselves in like manner. Jake's friend in Germany wrote him that the day will come when all Germans will go to Germany, where they belong.

The entire village was overjoyed that the teachers and the Young People had presented such a superb occasion last night.

9 September 1934

If only my heart and my blood were like my soul, as happy and peacefully balanced. Such is obviously Greta's lot. In her, physical fulfillment merges with her faith and her piety. At least, that is the impression I get. There are no apparent contradictions and no tensions, and I believe such is also the case with her now that she is pregnant. She is simply everything in one: wife, house-frau, mother and church member.

It seems as if I invariably start my entries by introducing my own person, which is probably a natural thing to do. And yet I intended to report on what transpired last week in our village. The itinerant minister was back at work in our village and he preached about Revelations every evening. He laid out the Plan of God, dating back to Creation right up to The End and the Rapture of the Church. I was so happy that I was already converted and baptized and had not fallen into sin. I was able to listen to it all with a degree of objectivity.

The minister spoke loudly and seriously and penetratingly, and our school was filled to the last man every evening. Many of our young people hung back after the sermon and were converted, as were children. Who would not be afraid when threats are made of the end of all things and that the rapture of the church is at hand? Jesus would soon come again, the minister threatened time and again. He spoke about the surprise and the terror which would come over mankind with so much fear and anxiety and vividness that I sat on my bench paralyzed with fear and constantly had Heinrich in mind. He failed to attend a single service even though he was home all week. Should I have walked over to his place and invited him to attend the service? He would not have come, not even to please me. I am sure of that and this is cause for my fear and distress.

And as for our Jake? I failed to recognize him and what he was up to. Already evening number three he stayed back and when he came home late that evening, he marched straight to our parent's bedroom to tell them about his conversion. Papa is very serious and reflective about it all but he does not talk about it. I was happy and relieved that Papa has overcome the serious confrontations with the Reverend Epp. Papa attended every evening's service.

The evangelizing minister spoke repeatedly about the contemporary peoples and nations, and how they fitted into the divine plan of salvation.

This forenoon, when leaving church, Jake and I walked home together. He told me that he had visited Reverend Reimer. He had confessed all his sins and asked to be baptized. While we were walking we softly sang the song "Oh, may it not be too late, too late to walk through the golden gate!"

Jake is constantly humming this song while at work or when alone. Obviously sermons and a conversion can affect the human condition a great deal. Mama is so happy about Jake's conversion. The school year is coming to a close and Jake intends to go to Asunción next year to attend university. How else could he withstand all the temptations in the big city? Papa does not yet know how we will manage the money to finance the university venture for our Jake. However, Abraham said he would return to work to earn sufficient money allowing Jake to attend university. And then he again started to engage in some mild blasphemy. "We need in our colony not only pious people but also clever ones," he said and laughed. His opinion of the Preaching Week is not stellar. This is sheer fear-mongering he says. He regards Christianity differently. In particular, he fails to understand why children are scared stiff by terror stories about the end of the world. Abraham told all this at lunch and everyone was quiet, even Papa. Obviously Jake had been scared into conversion. It was angst which did the trick.

2 October 1934

I am an angel swinging in the clouds. I am magically beautiful, clean and holy, but not flesh and blood, touchable.

Heinrich had said all that and even more, said Jake. All this and even more, Jake told me today all afternoon while at work planting beans. Yesterday a nice spring rain fell, the first of the year with lightning and thunder, and today in the forenoon Abraham and David plowed. Now we will have beans, watermelons and pumpkins. This morning Mama thanked God for the nice rain.

I let Jake talk while my breath ceased and my heart skipped a beat or two. I was as if numbed. Why is it that I am an angel, why am I not flesh and blood, why am I not of this earth, but swinging in the clouds?

Jake spent three days on the former Toledo battle field. Examinations were held at his school and so he had these days free. Heinrich took him to Toledo and also brought him back. During all this time, Jake melted the pewter from the lids of the canned meat products. There were whole piles of them available. Pewter fetches a good price. Jake poured many rods of pewter, which converted to cash, will in part finance his advanced studies in Asunción.

During their trip Heinrich and Jake had spoken about me and now I know everything. Jake explained Heinrich's thinking to me. To him I am an unapproachable being. He loves me like nothing and nobody else on earth but his love is like the love of the Virgin Maria, pure and immaculate, as the Catholics have it. He would never be worthy of my company; he being one who knows all about the dirt and evil of the human condition.

"But Jake, that is not the way things really are," I said repeatedly, barely being able to draw breath.

"No, that is not the way things are, Lizzie," said Jake with quiet deliberation. He had tried to rid Heinrich of his illusions but Heinrich had only smiled sadly and had had nothing to say.

Am I then really a Madonna? Am I really that much different from the other girls in the village? Is that the difference between Greta and me, which makes it so easy for her to be both flesh and blood and yet be more pious than I am?

"How do you perceive me, Jake?" I asked. "You are a man by now. Take a look at me, from top to bottom. Am I what Heinrich claims I am?"

We stood still, in the middle of the plowed field and Jake looked me over. He placed his pot with beans on the ground and smiled. Then he came up to me, embraced me and planted a kiss on my mouth. Then he picked up his seed beans and laughed uproariously.

"Lizzie, you are of flesh and blood, indeed," he then said, "and you are a very beautiful girl. The boys in school all agree. And yet there is a property of inapproachability in and to you and Heinrich knows this full well. He would never dare to get close to you."

I felt myself blushing all over the place. What do I want so that he will come near to me, approach me? It is my inner hope to be wanted but I know it is impossible. Heinrich is not a believer and I hardly believe that he would become a believer just on account of me. And now that Heinrich has said how I am, I am unhappy to death. I desire to be of flesh and blood, and I am of flesh and blood, and more so than anyone senses it. Not even Jake knows it, even though he embraced me and kissed me. Even Jake does not know what goes on in my inner being.

My flesh is burning and my blood is boiling while Heinrich claims I am swinging on a cloud.

4 November 1934

For more than a month, now, my dear diary, you have rested under my mattress, because I simply was incapable of writing. Now something has happened which is tantamount to a closure, like a decision of finality. I feel free, liberated and I can again write. Sometimes such liberation, even if painful, is similar to the death of a human being after a long and serious illness. Such was the case with our grandma in Russia who suffered from dropsy for a long while. When she finally died, we cried hard but we felt liberated from the lingering illness, as did grandma.

I am deeply consternated about what Heinrich said about me. It is both disturbing and bewildering to hear an observation of the kind he made. I wanted to gain a consciousness of my own identity, as to who I really am. Possibly I wanted verification that I am flesh and blood and not a heavenly creature floating on a cloud. If I am honest with myself, I must admit that this episode drove me to do something which a girl would probably never otherwise do.

Everything happened even faster than I had thought, unexpectedly and almost unwilled. What drives one to a decision which short weeks ago one would have deemed impossible?

It was during a battle against the locusts, a war on the hoppers. At the beginning of October a giant swarm of locusts came across our yard. However, they devoured practically nothing. Our beautiful beans which already stood in proud rows remained untouched, as did everything else.

The locusts were sluggish but we soon noticed that they were mating, sitting around as couples, male and female, almost becoming one, closely contacted. The entire grounds were covered with locust couples. Then the females bored little holes with their rear ends into the sand where they deposited their eggs. In places the soil resembled a sieve. Then the locusts simply disappeared.

After two weeks, the young brood hatched and they gathered into hopping swarms. They all hopped in one direction and laid bare everything in their path. Our green fields attracted them, like magnets, and all that remained were the bare stalks. However, by now we manage to vanquish them. We dig ditches opposite to the direction in which the locusts jump. Then we drive the locusts into the ditches until these are half full of hoppers. Then we simply cover them with soil and dirt. In the meanwhile, another ditch has been dug and locusts are driven into it as well and we continue doing this until the entire swarm has been buried, destroyed.

To this end the entire village is mobilized, for it takes everyone to dig and spade to win the battle against the millions of aggressive hoppers. Every yard in the village supplies whatever manpower is available to guide the hoppers into the ditch and to keep them from escaping. Everyone drives them and shoos them on: men, women and children armed with scarves, bags and rags, with the mayor supervising the battle by issuing orders and allotting the locust warriors. This transpired last Wednesday. During the locust hunt everyone is involved and the working of the earth is even fun for the younger set. When we had assumed our line of duty, I noticed Heinrich. He nodded at me and I was overcome with a heat flash which coursed through my flesh and blood; almost like a thrill.

The battle against the creepers transpired as usual, with the men digging ditches until their shirts were dark with perspiration while the women and children shooed. When the ditches had been dug, the men came along to assist in the shooing with Heinrich among them. It was almost midday. The men dispersed into long lines and Heinrich came towards me at the end of the swarm, there where the bushes form a thicket.

Whether Heinrich perceived the fire that was burning in me …? He retreated further behind the bushes and I followed him with my waving kerchief. Certainly no one took further notice of us. Suddenly we found ourselves standing opposite to each other, as if propelled by unseen forces. Heinrich remained mute as always. He just looked at me, quietly and friendly.

Then, suddenly, something exploded from within me into words, "Heinrich, I am no angel and I swing on no cloud, I am flesh and blood." It was flesh and blood that drove me, that much I know!

Heinrich looked at me with ever enlarging eyes and merely said, "Oh, dear Lizzie!"

Suddenly I lay at his breast, he held me close to his body and then our lips found each other and it was as if everything around me was turning in circles, the bushes, the clouds, the locusts, into confused bliss. Then, finally, we slowly separated from one another, only holding each other's hands; I retreated even further while our eyes remained attached.

And then I said, "Heinrich, it is not possible."

"I know, Lizzie," he said.

When we then again stood with the children and waved our weapons of cloth, no one noticed anything, not a thing. The children laughed and played again, bored by the monotony of it all while Heinrich and I gradually and slowly separated from each other, drifted apart as it were.

The last ditches were filled in with Heinrich assisting in the effort. I folded my kerchief together and walked home, alone.

My walk home took me past the edge of the bushes. It was the time of the Queen of the Night. An uncountable number of blossoms had bloomed that night. Now they had all closed up and hung grey and limp in the heat of midday.

Such things are possible. The pinnacle of happiness… An answer to a question received and a guilty conscience to have challenged fate in its decree of destiny. The two keep my heart in balanced tandem. Is it just that which makes me so free and relaxed?

I intend to go to our Youth Leader and simply tell him everything. I know that he guards secrets like a Catholic confessional. Ministers of the gospel invariably feel obligated to provide answers. Such is not the case with the teacher. All he is meant to do is to listen to me. That can help me; that can possibly help me.

"Free and relaxed". This entry of the 4th of November 1934 brings to a close the first part of the diary. This closure is arbitrary and possibly not as planned by Elisabeth, and yet it appears to me, in retrospect, as if a phase of her life has come to an end.

This girl has concluded an unavoidable reality which she labels free, relaxed. Her feeling of human worth is obviously every bit as important in its confirmation. The unusual step she takes, confirms that she indeed is a person of flesh and blood, a perfectly normal human being. This failed to separate her from the demands of her faith and society to which she has submitted herself by her rejection of Heinrich.

By consulting the teacher, she seeks out a second opinion by way of confirmation; he likewise acted on his conviction, of a mediator within church and community. She has little to say about the matter only that her decision was suffocated by her breaking out in tears, obviously a further indication that she had to inwardly force herself away from Heinrich and related potential. Her teacher's words and counsel meant to provide consolation and courage provided the necessary confirmation for her.

The diary entries now become less frequent, possibly because a powerful emotional motto in her life has finally been resolved. Greta is more fully occupied with her growing family while Heinrich entirely departs the scene. The Chaco War ended mid-1935. The victorious troops slowly depart the battle grounds and with them Heinrich also left for a different life and world. He probably found a new world somewhere in East Paraguay which suited his inner being. He remained missing and therewith became a lost son to the Mennonite world. One might ponder whether a society with its strict ethics failed to deal with people like Heinrich and forced him out or whether his love of freedom was such that it left him no choice but to move on.

The diary entries tell of the increasing existential difficulties of the Chaco settlers. Dry years and visitation of plagues rendered their hopes futile. Many chose to depart for East Paraguay where precipitation is more frequent and a brighter future invites. In 1937 one third of the Fernheim Colony departs and founds the Friesland Colony east of the Paraguay River. Less than one half of the settlers remain behind in

Elisabeth's village. This leads to a radical change in the social life of the village.

Things in Germany assume a constantly brighter light and future. And while that country is unattainably far away, it nevertheless stirs the hopes, ideals, and dreams, which appear all the rosier, the more difficult mastering the unforgiving wilderness is.

The return of the Saarland to the German Reich is celebrated enthusiastically. Hitler's birthday is occasion for Youth Meetings. For many, Hitler is the epitome of sobriety and high valour. He vigorously counters bolshevism, the trauma of all refugees. The German spirit, German creativity and thoroughness merge with the Mennonite churches, as a distant ideal, into one. The roll of Foreign Germans is elevated by and in the German Reich. This leads to a higher level of self-evaluation of a people, like the Mennonites, who led a subsistence lifestyle in bitter poverty with little self-esteem, in a foreign environment.

And as much as Elisabeth is interested in these developments, they remain peripheral to her; they fail to satisfy her expectations. Her primary search is the spiritual realm in which she can realize the object of her inner search. It is heart-rending to witness how a human being is subject to so many influences without having any idea as to the cause and effect of things over which she has no control, or awareness, for that matter. Centuries ago decisions were made and paths charted which appeared essential at the time and these are decisive even today for Elisabeth and her walk of and in life. The church reforms conceived as they were in Switzerland and in Holland four hundred years ago and the serious quarrels in Russia between the Conference and the Mennonite Brethren determine how Elisabeth Unruh in a village in the Chaco reacts to the language of her heart. She said no when her heart said yes and this was decisive for the further course and walk of her life.

The second part of her diary which I glean from the context, and in a sense render independent, starts in 1939. If the reader now assumes that the great world drama is decisive for this choice of date and year, he will be disappointed. Storms of an entirely different making touch Elisabeth's heart, storms to which she reacts by turning completely to faith as a fulfilment. While so doing, her longing for harmony between *body and soul, which she believes Greta possesses, remains paramount.*

In social terms Elisabeth has experienced change but she has remained even lonelier at age twenty five. In 1936 Jake transferred to Asunción for his university studies. David married Sara Janzen from a neighbouring village and switched to the Brethren Church. Abraham has likewise founded his own family. Even Lena left to the surprise of all when a village widower with a bunch of needy children asked her to marry him.

The family home has become empty, the village has become empty and her heart emptier than all.

MARANATHA

Maranatha

10 February 1939

This morning I climbed up to the attic to fetch my old peed, the water bucket yoke, which I formerly used to fetch water from the village well. I have not used it for ages since we have had a well on our yard for years now.

With that yoke I formerly carried two pails of milk to the Separating Room as we called the milk separating, or centrifuge hut, in our village. Everyone possessing sufficient number of cows takes their milk there to get it separated, meaning removing the cream from the milk. The cream is then taken to the creamery in Filadelfia by whatever farmer is free to transport it. We take the skim milk home.

My daily routine starts early with the milking. Mother and I head for the cow stable and we each milk three cows. We are very happy for this source of income which we have had ever since the colony has had a creamery. The mayor informs us that we will also soon be able to sell the milk since a cheese factory is in the works. To that end the colony offices have sent a young man to Argentina to learn the trade of cheese making.

Also, we will soon be able to sell eggs. They will be transported to the river ports and even up to Asunción. I have to look after the chickens, the calves and the pigs and I have to do this on my own and by myself. Mama looks after the household while Papa is mainly working the fields. He could not manage if the Indians failed to help. The Indians are not all that reliable, and Papa often complains when he needs them and they fail to show up. A week ago we were in the middle of harvesting the peanuts when Maito, the chief, simply took off with his family. Apparently they intended to celebrate some festival or another. What is one to do? Then it rained and a good part of the crop rotted on the fields. Then Maito remained for weeks close to the village. I enjoy this time of the year. I can help Mama and, come evenings, I still have enough energy to read a book or write in my diary.

Papa would like to convince Maito to work on a permanent basis like our servants in Russia did, but Maito, the chief, will have none of that. They are a free people, so my thinking goes. The Indians do as they please and what pleases them, and have no intentions of being forced into arrangements. Franz and Mary are also part of our operation. They have two children and Mary brings them along when coming to work. Mary was pregnant again and we were looking forward to her third child. Then she remained behind in her camp and when she returned, she still had only her two children with her. When we then asked her, curious as we were, she merely turned away. Franz and Maito also failed to explain as to what had occurred.

A missionary who gave a sermon in our village told us that Indians commonly kill a newly born child if the first two children are not yet strong enough to manage the long wanderings which the parents and the tribe undertake. We had also noticed that most Indian families restrict their family to two children. The Lenguas live in the terrible darkness of the heathens, said the missionary, and they can only be saved by the gospel yet to be brought to them.

Things with my dear Greta are much different. She has two children and is expecting a third. Whenever she arrives at the Separating Room with her milk, I feel sorry for her. We then have to wait our turn for the milk to be separated and have time to talk. Greta is tired and looks grieved and often sighs deeply. Her two children hang on to the milk pails as they slowly and laboriously drag their way through the sand of the village street.

"You are having a good time of it," she says, "you are free of worries." You ought to go and work with the Indians, she advises me. The Lord needs such clever and unmarried women. Already in Russia unmarried women occasionally went to the mission fields or to Java or Sumatra, wherever missionary stations operated.

Am I to regard this as God's beckoning? It may be that God has a special way for me, a field, a niche where He has purpose expressly for the likes of me. I so often ask for the sense of life, my life. Greta believes that the sense of life is children and children are of the Lord. For that reason she does not want to complain if one child follows another and life becomes constantly more difficult with each child. And yet Greta is angry with Mrs Görzen who constantly asks her whether a further child is not yet coming and she asks such questions with persistence whenever evidence is lacking after a year has expired. Mrs Görzen asks this of all young women and claims it is a sin not to have children when and if God so wills it.

I was greatly surprised that there was such a thing. But Greta tells me everything and also about her marriage. She very much hopes that she will not become pregnant so soon again and she fervently prays for a reprieve. But the Lord did not hear her prayer. It is simply so dreadfully difficult to look after the children and to be pregnant and to have to work in the fields if her husband needs her services.

"When it is evening and I am so tired and defeated, I simply lack the energy to resist Isaak and his advances," she tells me while sobbing. "However, Mrs Görzen claims that it is better to have a little bouncer on the pillow than on your conscience."

It seems to me that Greta sees the sense of life possibly in being heavy-laden, in her great fatigue, or, possibly, in her fear of Mrs Görzen.

25 February 1939

Last night I walked home alone after the Prayer Service, slowly and in thought. I thought of Jake and how we walked arm in arm when it was dark and I also thought of Heinrich. No one knows where he might be. Recently an acquaintance from Friesland wrote Greta that Heinrich had been briefly spotted there. He had looked after his parents and disappeared again.

And now I walk the street alone. The girls in the village are all younger than I am. In the choir I stand out in that I am older, or so it would appear to me.

At home, I re-read the letters from Jake in Asunción, one to our parents, the other to me. Mama worries a lot about Jake. In her letters she makes repeated reference to Joseph in Egypt, she says. May he remain resolute in his faith, and not forget his conversion and his baptism. I notice that Jake now lives in a different world. It is not that I fear for his faith like Mama does but he takes an entirely different view of our colony, our church and of Mennonitism.

Jake tells me that young people from Friesland now travel to Germany with a certain Mr Schröder arranging these trips. They are meant to become farmers in Germany. It is also Jake's dream to go to Germany. As soon as she has completed his studies in Asunción, he intends to go to Germany. He intends to attend university there and get involved in the German way of life, like in the Work Front, and also to be a soldier in the German *Wehrmacht*. It is simply glorious to hear on the radio what all is going on over there. A year ago Austria was incorporated into Germany with much fanfare, which Jake had heard on the radio. Now it is a certainty that Hitler will also win back the corridor to Danzig from Poland. Everything the Versailles Treaty destroyed will soon be restored. Then Germany will be powerful and there will be peace. Jake writes me all this and more.

Sometimes Abraham and David come home. Then we sit outside under the *Paraiso* trees and we have a lively time of it when discussing Germany and also world politics and everything else what is going on in Europe. Papa reads the *La Plata Post* more eagerly than ever before. I prefer not to mention Jake's intention of becoming a soldier and I also fear a bit for his faith, like Mama does. How would he ever manage to become part of our world again, now that he has assumed such a different perspective?

And as for me? I would so much like to become stronger in my faith, more assured. During a Prayer Meeting at the beginning of February it was announced that a Bible School is being planned. All the young people are invited to get involved, irrespective of church affiliation. Reverend Reimer said that nothing of the sort had ever happened in Russia because the churches were unable to come to a common accord on such matters.

Maybe all this is God's plan for me. Maybe Greta is right when claiming my life should be in mission work. It may well be that therein lies my niche in life. I hardly dare to write Jake about these matters, but I will have to do so. It may well be that he sees a warning for himself in my resolute position. David claims that God took us out of Russia and sent us to the Chaco in order to take the gospel to the Indians. He has assumed membership in the Missionary Society and claims that it is more important than anything else. His enthusiasm for Germany and for Hitler has been much dampened. He would never return to Germany as Jake would like to do.

"Germany represents a danger for us Mennonites in the Chaco," he claimed, when he and Abraham came to our place to discuss world events. "All this Germanism here is taking us in the wrong direction. Hitler demands the total man and Christ demands the total man and as for me? There is no question as to whom I will follow."

Abraham became mightily excited. "There is no problem in uniting both loyalties: Germanism and Christianity," he claimed. "Christians in Germany also make this very claim as do Mennonites over there. And also the Mennonite conscientious objector status is not of utmost importance either in life. All Mennonites in Germany serve in the military today for the Fatherland." I wonder if I ought to write Jake all this one of these days?

I will have a word with my parents and then I intend to enrol in the Bible School. That is my plan and my way.

12 March 1939

These Sunday nights hit you with a wallop. They bring my loneliness totally to the fore. Whenever married couples meet, I have the feeling that I am not part of them, that I am a poor fit. And yet, we were an integral part of each other only a few years ago, when we sang together at the Youth Hour or met at the common swing of the village. Now only the younger boys and girls hang out there and I also am not part of them. It is then that a strange feeling comes over me, something similar to fear.

Liese Fast and Lena Neufeld are now more than thirty years of age. Since Greta knows everything about and in the village, she informs me that Liese has a very difficult time of it. "She should marry the first best fellow who comes along," she claims. "The Bible terms this suffering unbridled sensuality, and Paul claims, it would be better if such people were to marry, but who is she to marry?"

Is it this which makes me afraid? I sit with Greta and she tells me such and related stories and of course, in the manner of her ilk, she knows everything about everybody, be it the trouble in the Rempel marriage, or old Mr Dürksen being jealous of his wife, since he believes she has an eye on a neighbour. Sometimes I think women have nothing else to talk about when they get together. If they then feel sorry for the unmarried girls, it is possibly because they need a cause to console themselves in their own misery? Obviously most of this is nothing but malicious gossip, and I do not want to expose myself to such a virus.

I would rather like to write about the afternoon of today since it provided me with so much material to ponder. The Indians yet again had a cause to celebrate. Whether they celebrate whenever they can brew beer, or whether they brew beer for a celebration, is difficult to say.

They call their festivities Ping-Ping because they beat and roll their drums during the entire party time. We heard the rhythm from far away and so we, David and Sara, Greta, Isaak and I agreed to visit the Indians. Their camp lay a good kilometre away on the narrow meadow. It is there where the Indians had built their grass huts. They had cleared a piece of ground for their festivity underneath the huge *urundey* trees.

There are still a lot of watermelons available and the Indians used these to brew a festive beverage. They had hollowed out a bottle tree and made a trough out of it into which they deposited honey, which together with the melon flesh fermented the brew. This drink produced quality alcohol and the men were all inebriated. They sat in a circle and drank the brew from large gourds with all talking and arguing with everyone else. The women displayed a circular dance. Then they walked in a long line while thrusting their staffs in unison into the ground. On the top end of their staffs the hooves of wild boar were fastened and while making a rhythmic noise, they sang a monotone melody.

I was captured and enraptured by the joyfulness of it all, as well as the dust, the smoke, the singing and dancing and the laughter of their girls who had rouged their cheeks scarlet red. I came to myself from my reverie only after Greta tugged at my dress. She was prepared to leave. Our coming and going did not disturb the Indians in the least. They were totally involved in the festivity, their festivity. We slowly withdrew and after a while their dogs barked after us.

Now it was David's turn and he launched into his favourite theme, that of mission. He spoke about the heathen ways of the Lenguas and the darkness in which they lived. He was acquainted with their fear of the spirits, and he spoke about the demons which rule their world. "A people in the claws of Satan," he said, and that sounded both bitter and unforgiving.

I cannot really come to terms with all this. David is cocksure about the ways which God directs for his children, and for him these are the Mennonites, our churches and our people. The various churches have reached accord to conduct missionary work among the Indians. "To take the light of the gospel to our brown people," said David.

If God has ways prepared, then why not for me as well, I reflected.

25 March 1939

Today is Monday and a heavy work day lies behind me. And yet, I must take a little time for my diary. Papa has a great deal of work with the kaffir. And while the Indians do the work on the field, Papa has to load the kaffir and transport it home where he forks the kaffir pinnacles onto the loft of the granary. I assisted him in this work and now my arms ache so much that I can hardly lift my pen to write.

What drives me to write is yesterday's Sunday. Last night a mission service was to be held in the large Colony Hall. David and Sara took me along. We manage the route to the hall by horse and wagon in an hour's time while two years ago it took us three hours by ox-cart.

Bright gas lamps illuminated the hall with the light being visible right to the village street.

At the door stood Anna Wall. We are acquainted since we attend Youth Meetings together here. She is my age and our greeting is invariably cordial. Her brother Peter, who is two years older, stood next to her. They had traveled from their village for the mission sermon. We sat down together on a bench and Anna told me that in August the Bible School was to start in her village. She and Peter had already enrolled. There is less work to do on the farms in winter and her parents are all in favour of them both attending the Bible School. It is to be a wandering Bible School, so to speak, which will be relocated every two weeks in a different village. People in respective villages will provide room and board to the students so that there will be no costs or expenses involved.

Peter sat in the Men's Section, opposite to us. I do not remember anything of the evening. I heard everything, I sang the songs: "Work for the night is coming!" which was meant to set the mission tone for the gathering. The missionary spoke about the Indians in the Chaco. He reported about an Anglican Mission Station to the south which he had visited. There parts of the Bible have already been translated into the Lengua language. I heard everything, but my thoughts were in and with the Bible School.

When Anna and I left the hall together, she whispered to me that I could stay with them if I intended to attend the Bible School. Her parents would also be accommodating Bible School students. To me all this was a dream, a stroke of divine guidance. The meeting with Anna and Peter and then the voice from above: Anna's invitation.

"The Lord is calling you, young man, The Lord is calling you, young woman!" That was the voice of the missionary from the pulpit, and I knew that this call was for me. By chance I glanced at Peter Wall and for a second it appeared as if his face beamed. Could it be that he was about to become a missionary, to place his life in the service of the Lord, this big blond fellow?

When we drove home, we spoke much about the missionary sermon.

At home Papa was still awake and he approached our wagon. David immediately reported on matters transpiring in Europe, which had been broadcast prior to the mission sermon on the radio in the colony hall, namely that the Germans had marched into Czechoslovakia. There is only one radio in the colony which was gifted us from Germany and many people assemble to listen to the news.

"And Poland is next," said Papa. "Stalin will not be sleeping all that well in the Kremlin"; it sounded almost as if Germany had also conquered Russia all in one sweep. During work today, Papa spoke only about the war. "The Germans are constantly becoming more powerful and this is our only salvation from Communism."

Mama got the drift of it all and at lunch she spoke only about Maria and Isaak. We have not received a single letter from them for a long time now, not since 1937. However, the newspaper reports that things in the Soviet Union are going very poorly.

All this is so exciting that I have had no opportunity to tell my parents about my plans. I dream about them, I dream about them although I am wide awake.

8 April 1939

We believed Papa would be returning from the train station today. Now travel by horses is so much faster than previously by ox-team. Mostly the transports now are back in four to five days.

It is difficult for Papa to undertake these long trips, but Abraham and David now travel with their own teams. They travel together so that the boys can help their father, particularly with the heavy bags.

It took longer this time around on account of the poor roads. We had much rain in March and in April and last night I saw lightning in the east. Possibly a heavy rain fell while they were en route. Then entire patches of road then become a swamp.

I have now discussed my plans regarding the winter months with my parents and they fully understand and support my endeavour. For Mama this will not be easy since she then will have to milk all the cows alone. It seems to me that she intends to make sacrifices.

"If you intend to serve the Lord, Lizzie," she said, "and if you even intend to serve in the mission, then such will also be my service."

Papa said very little to all of this. For him it is most important that the churches work in common accord and not with the Brethren, like in Russia, taking full control of the school.

Now Mama and I, for days on end, spend more times in the evenings, which grow longer by the day in conversation. Mama feels guilty for having rejected Heinrich. "Now you will become old and will not get married," she says.

Then I have to comfort her and I assured her that such, in part, was also my will, my decision. The cost of it all is no one's concern. Not even Mamas.

Mama tells me that her father, too, had been very strict. Two of her sisters never married for this reason. The men who were interested in them were members of the Mennonite Brethren. And grandpa feared that his daughters would have had to be re-baptized if they married staunch Brethren. He would never have allowed this and his daughters fell in line. Later he had had two old spinsters at home who were unhappy and disappointed in life.

It gives me pleasure to listen to Mama's stories of the past, and it makes me happy that the churches here get along better than they did in Russia. Anna and Peter belong to the Brethren and I notice no contradiction or friction. Nor do the two treat me condescendingly because I belong to the Conference. (The Conference, I might add, now calls itself the Mennonite Church).

I am eagerly looking forward to tomorrow. A Conference of Sunday School Teachers has been scheduled for Filadelfia and Lena and Liese have invited me to accompany them. While there, I will enroll in the Bible School. Anna and Peter will most certainly be there as well since they help out in the Sunday School. Peter is a man whose face radiates joy and faith. He is friendly and polite towards me and his sister.

Whenever I think that I will live with the Walls for two weeks in August, joy and anticipation overcome me. I will then escape the loneliness of my home village.

Jake wrote today that he intends to come home for Christmas. How will it be when we meet after such a lengthy separation? From his letters, I gather, that his interests now vary greatly from the ones that occupy my mind.

Could it be that faith is locally bound to groups of people and that faith changes depending on the environment? I am looking forward to discussing these matters candidly with Jake. But I am even more looking forward to what the morrow may bring.

19 April 1939

As if I had wings! As if I could fly! As if I could mount to great heights and regard all things below me as small and insignificant! I am carried by joy and I draw fresh air. This has nothing to do with Heinrich's remarks that I am carried by a cloud, unattainable. It is simply the joy of being alive, an inner feeling of giddy happiness. I milk the cows and I am happy; I carry the milk away and I am happy.

The fact that my joy is not even dampened by meeting Greta is a sure sign that my joy is a constant; I can take them all on, and I remain happy and joyful. Greta came plodding along the street with her two pails and a child hanging onto each pail. Her high pregnancy gave her obvious problems.

"You are beaming with joy, Lizzie," she said while sighing.

When I told her that I had enrolled in the Bible School and that the school would be a "movable entity", a despairing shadow fell over her face.

"Then I will be completely alone in my dreadful misery," she said while biting her lower lip to control her emotions.

I was terribly shocked. "Surely you are not living in abject circumstances, Greta," I said while looking into her tired, wet eyes.

"O, Lizzie!" she said despairingly, "I am not allowed to complain, but sometimes I feel that the waters of life swash over my head, with the children, and the Indians on the yard which I have to care for. And Isaak is depressed, when the caterpillars devour the cotton and there is not enough money to even buy shoes for the children. At such times I am envious of Liese Fast and of you. And now you, too, are leaving. With whom will I talk when you are gone? Possibly with Mrs Görzen who has a long moralizing finger wagging in the air? It took much too long for me to get pregnant, she claims, and the young Krökers have no child at all and that after having been married for two years."

Pious Greta had become a volcano of bitterness. I tried to console her. For me, Greta had always been the example of how a pious woman fulfills what the Creator has in store for His children and now she drags her heavy yoke through life. But then my sympathy mounted within me and I managed to console her from and with my heart. All that shall not reduce my joy and I will happily stand by her.

I had time in Filadelfia yesterday to enroll in the Bible School. The teacher was very friendly and he explained the courses we would be studying. "We will spend much time with Revelations," he said, "and with the End Times. The signs of these times are increasing with wars and rumours of wars. We have to prepare ourselves for such hard times, and I am happy that I am able to help the young people to that end. We shall always be greeting each other with "Maranatha"— the Lord is coming—just like the Early Christians had it.

In the forenoon we heard two talks for the Sunday School Teachers and then a group from Schönbrunn sang the song "And now the Ending Times are coming, and they are coming with full force!"

Surely a contradiction of some force is at play here. When I reflect on the fact that our people here happily throng to listen to the radio reporting on Germany, and its great ascent while paying no heed to the end of the world coming, I should be troubled. And yet, all this affects me not in the slightest in my inner being.

Every contradiction was wiped clean off my slate when Anna and Peter and I went for a walk after a common lunch. We walked a piece out of the village to the water meadow. Nature is at its most luxurious there with water everywhere after the last rain and with trees in full blossom now that autumn has arrived. The two were so jovial. Anna talks most animatedly of everything that goes on in her village. She laughs about the people but with no *Schadenfreude*. She has much fun with her Sunday School children. She embodies what one might term a happy heart.

And Peter is what one might term a dignified spirit. He has a deeply resonating and pacifying voice. His laughter is one of fun and humour. He evaluates all of life from the perspective of faith and yet his judgement in neither hard nor damning as is often the case with David. Peter claims that the church is the most important institution in life and that its commission is to missionize.

Then they talked about their parents. Their father was a man of courage who accepted every difficulty as from God's hand, including the locusts and the caterpillars.

In the afternoon, when we were back in the hall, the wind changed. It turned surprisingly cool and a misty rain started to fall enclosing all vistas. When we drove home, we pulled the tarps over our heads and allowed the horses free rein as they made their way home. In my heart the sun was shining. We sang the songs which the choir from Schönbrunn had sung and while singing my being was already residing at the Walls, while attending Bible School.

Papa returned from his lengthy trip yesterday in the late afternoon. The horses and the wagon looked like they formerly did when Abraham went for extended trips. Everything was covered with clay. When Papa sat on his easy chair late that evening, he appeared very tired. It was as if the courage, invariably his driving force, had departed him.

"If there will ever be a movement back to Germany, then I will be the first to go," he said. Again a contradiction to what the teacher had said about the impending end of the world. However, nothing could dampen my spirits.

21 April 1939

I believe all the young people of our colony were up and about yesterday. Everything came together so well and happily. After all the rainy weeks, the 20th of April arrived with bright sunshine and the birthday of the Führer, Adolf Hitler. The German-Mennonite Youth Club had planned a celebration in Filadelfia.

The young people of our village were also involved with the age difference playing no role. The boys of the village had organized three teams of horses pulling stately wagons, with the horses rounded and sleek from all the good kaffir they are being fed after a good crop. The horses trot, pointed ears, arched backs and blowing nostrils, pulling the carriage with the driver holding the reins proudly and professionally.

We were in Filadelfia already prior to seven in the morning. The hall was filled with young people. Then a radio announcement from Berlin was heard by all, announcing the birthday of Adolf Hitler.

I had done my utmost to dress up as well as I could. I had sewn a white skirt with a matching white blouse with a high collar, similar to a man's shirt. A red tie, similar to a cravat came in handy. Mama suggested that all this was a tad ostentatious but while saying so, she smiled—no kidding—Mama smiled.

"You want the boys to notice you, don't you?" she said while smiling. I like my Mama when she smiles.

In the hall I looked around for Anna and Peter, but they were not there. There are people in the Colony who regard Germany and Hitler as a danger. The Walls might belong to these. I could well imagine that Peter would be of such persuasion, similar to David who believes the matter now is simple but decisive: either Hitler or Christ. I would very much like to discuss this with Peter and attempt to understand his point of view in all of this. I was disappointed not to see them at the gathering.

The celebration in my view was most beautiful. It started with a service. Several ministers were in attendance. One of them delivered a short sermon, then prayed for the Führer, for the German people and for peace in the world. Two talks were then delivered. The first talk dealt with Bolshevism and the great danger it represented for the world, while the second dealt with the personal life of Adolf Hitler, who rose from a common soldier fighting in the trenches in the World War, to the saviour of the German people and then their saviour against Communism. Adolf Hitler represented positive Christianity and the churches in Germany supported him, said the speaker.

Then a boy, the son of the teacher, who had just returned from Germany recited a poem.

In closing, we all rose and sang the song of the Foreign Germans which is by now known to all.

"Far from the land of our forebears,
we drift through the land under a thousand flags as it pleases God.
And though we have parted from our former land,
we remain united by the blood of the bond."

This song has three stanzas and it seemed to me that everyone knew the entire song by heart. Then the German national hymn was sung. Jake probably was angry that we did not sing "Up with the banner high!" but our Youth Leaders do not approve of this ardent Nazi military song.

In any case, I intend to write Jake all about this evening's program. In his letters he seems to be of the opinion that the true and real Germans live only in Asunción, and that we in the Chaco are but feeble stragglers. Also I intend to write him about the Bible school, and about Peter Wall. I believe he may remember Peter from the high school even if Peter was in a higher class.

11 May 1939

Yesterday Mama told me, "Why don't you go help Lena in all her work? She has no easy time with all the work involved in her large family."

I happily did so. Mama and I had managed all the weekend cleaning of the house by noon and so I walked down the street that afternoon to the other end of our village where Lena and her large family resides. I like to walk the village street even though many of the farms now stand empty since so many neighbours moved away in 1937 when the Friesland Trek happened. Empty, vacated houses make me nostalgic and reflective. There stands the Neufeld yard, where the gramophone previously blared, then there is the Löwen yard where we often met on a previous day. The Friesen house is dilapidated and will soon be demolished. I walk through a stretch of memory even though I believe I am too young to do so.

Lena embraced me for pure joy when I suddenly stood in her kitchen door where she was baking for Sunday. Outside in the bake oven a fire was blazing. The kitchen table was covered with flour and the baking flats were standing on the chairs containing buns, crumble cake and meat busters. The aroma of fresh baking filled the air.

Lena is a total Hausfrau, a totally married woman and a devoted mother even though she has no children of her own. I believe my sister is doing a yeo-ladies service. She loves her husband, Franz Regier, and his five children, one after and like the other, and they love her. Our quiet pious Lena... I believe it was good for her to spend a year in Pinasco where she learned to know a different, an additional side of life. Had she not enlarged her horizon, she would probably have greatly suffered from the fact that Franz smokes. Prior to marrying, he had quit smoking. However, once they married, Franz started smoking again which she did not approve of but preferred to him smoking behind biffies and in secrecy. Franz is a church member in good standing but he will not allow the church a voice in his realm of nicotine intake.

I helped Lena in the baking. Then we cleaned the rooms and swept the yard. We did everything together and spoke about former times while working. We reflected on Russia and talked about the beginning times in the Chaco. I asked Lena, if she found all the work too much at times, thinking, obviously of Greta and her heavy groaning.

"Not at all," she said, "I am healthy and strong and where there is love, no burden is too great. I can make do with little and Franz values that a lot; moreover he is an industrious, competent farmer and he loves me much."

At three in the afternoon we were finished with our work. Then we sat down comfortably in the clean kitchen and enjoyed the fresh baking.

Lena looked at me happy and beaming. "If things get difficult I think of Liesa Fast and Lena Neufeld and their lonely longing. Or I then think of the Enns Family where the widower married a widow and they brought twelve children into their marriage and added another three and it is difficult to maintain harmony in such a family."

"And you do not compare your lot with mine at all?" I asked her a bit testily.

"Well, Lizzie," Lena said while laughing, "with yours? You are young and beautiful and full of life. When on Sundays you enter church wearing your white skirt, then even the young boys sit nice and erect and admire you. No, Lena, you are beyond compare!"

Oh, how much good such a natural flow of happy well-meant praise does. It is as if dust were blown from the soul or rain falling on parched land. I noticed tears welling up in my eyes; I was both happy and proud. And now I suddenly managed to talk about all my little and not so little woes, my loneliness, my disappointment in Heinrich and my longing to go to a different world, to enter a new environment. I spoke about my hope to go to Bible School and I talked about Anna and Peter and what good people they were.

Our pious Lena blinked her eyes and asked, "Is Peter a handsome fellow?"

"What are you talking about?" I said as we laughed. A happy joy arose from the depth of my heart while reflecting on our happy discourse.

Then Lena turned serious, "Lizzie, you are right with God and you are of good character. You have proven that in the Heinrich episode. You will find your way which God has for you!"

Just then Franz entered the yard with his two oldest boys. They brought with them a cow and her calf which Mossy, the mother had calved somewhere in a bush clearing. Everyone was overjoyed for now there would be more milk. Their other children returned as well and I left the large happy family to go home.

Faith in God, constancy and hope are the thoughts that bear me as I walk.

3 June 1939

Everyone appears to be filled with his or her needs, distresses, wishes and ideals. I gather this from a letter I just received from my brother Jake, and I also observe that the differences between us become ever greater because our wishes and our ideals vary, and do so with increasing rapidity. It is quite possible that I do not inform Jake of this often enough. It is possible that I now harbour reservations, because in former times when we together sang new songs daily, like

> *"Freedom is the fire,*
> *It is the brightest light*
> *And as long as it keeps glowing*
> *The world will be just right."*

Jake told me a joke from the village of his school. An old man, who opposed everything new, claimed the song went, "Fire is a hellish shine"—so be it.

I only hope that Jake has not forgotten about his conversion, by which I mean the glorious inner feeling which at one time so closely connected us, so much so, that his great enthusiasm for Germany even took second place for a short duration. It is highly likely that I did not tell him this often enough when writing him. I am now eagerly anticipating Christmas when Jake will come home. Then I will tell him where my enthusiasms lie and also my calling.

It is possible that I now am closer to David than to Jake, at least in some aspects of life. In stating that a human being is filled with ideas, I mean David. Last weekend he traveled to a Mission Camp together with some friends. The camp lies a good thirty kilometres from our village. He set out on a Saturday and returned on Monday. When I then visited David and Sara on Tuesday evening, David noticed my great interest in the Indian mission. David and Sara know that I have enrolled in the Bible School.

They were still at the supper table when I arrived. I joined them at their table and our conversation started. Sara is a good Hausfrau, marital partner and mother. She placed all the delicacies of their last hog butchering on the table, like liverwurst, smoked sausage, head cheese and onions, and I ate well and long and much.

The Dürksen family had no difficulties or reservations when David wanted to marry Sara, although he belonged to the Conference. They obviously recognized that David is a man of faith. Now he has transferred to the Mennonite Brethren Church, possibly out of his love for Sara, or possibly because he recognizes his ideals in their church. He did not even have to be re-baptized as was formerly the case when joining this elite club. This is obviously progress in the inter-church relationship.

At the Mission Camp which David attended, the first item on the agenda was the Indian mission. This is no simple matter, says David. The Lenguas are nomads with no permanent or physical address. If one now wants to take the gospel to them, these nomads will have to assume sedentary residency. This may be possible on the site of the mentioned mission camp. The missionaries are very busy in their efforts to that end. They are learning the Lengua language and are starting to translate the Bible into that language. Also, attempts have been made to preach to them, but just when the mission hopes mounted, the Indians simply disappeared; they took off into the bush for weeks and even months on end with the missionaries not having a clue where their potential crop of believers had disappeared to. Somewhere a new hunting area caught their fancy or there were wild fruits in the bush ready for the plucking, and off they went.

Death by illness also motivates their movements, as does their fear of spirits and demons, said David. If one of their tribe dies, they leave their last camp and they return, if at all, only after long periods of time. They are afraid of the spirit of the dead. David is convinced that only the gospel can help these people. The gospel will transform them, give them a new life, and enable them to make progress.

David then developed his theories for me. We are part of God's plan. Together with us, God wants to transform the Indians. In 1930 Canada closed its door to us. Germany could not accommodate us. Paraguay accepted us and we arrived in the Chaco. Now, is that not clear enough as to what we are meant to do?

When listening to David I could do no other than believe him, submit to his value and belief system and agree with him. Am I too easily convinced? Or is the thought and the plan of the Bible School so predominant in me that everything else pales in comparison?

When in 1937 so many of our neighbours left our village, and the Chaco for that matter, David frequently argued with them. However, the deserters chose not to listen to his belief that they were being disobedient to God by leaving the Chaco in favour of a more favourable address. That choice had nothing to do with faith was their claim. David remained totally intransigent in his position and the resulting wounds ran long, deep and unhealed.

If so much now comes to a head, like the possibility of the Bible school, the friendly invitation from the Walls, the interesting report by David about our duty here in the Chaco, is this not a sign of a divine purpose as well? Is there not a calling visible in all of this? The hour was late at David and Sara's home and their children had long since been taken to bed and David accompanied me for a stretch on my way home.

"You are so happily tuned, Lizzie," he said

"Yes, indeed," I said. "It may be the buzzing of all the things that await me and everything that will be so decisive for my life."

I ran the last stretch home, driven as I was by the strength and joy in my body. Papa was still awake, reading his paper. He looked over his glasses at me when I entered. I sat down next to him, out of breath from running. I laughed while Papa looked seriously about him and at me.

"There will be war, Lizzie," he said. "The English and French do not want Germany to rise. There will definitely be war. Things were just like this in 1914."

I barely heard what he said, since my heart was so full. Papa speaks about war, while my heart runs over for joy.

11 June 1939

Our bottle tree is losing its leaves. Our entire yard is full of leaves and I spent all day yesterday sweeping and raking, but to little avail. I raked and the leaves kept falling and when I carried my sweepings to a little fire where I burn the refuse, there were, again, leaves everywhere.

"Falling Leaves" I hummed, and which is the song we used to sing at the many funerals during our first years here in the Chaco. I hummed but I was not sad.

"You are singing burial songs while laughing," said Mama as she chanced by.

"I sing and I am happy!" I said.

The bare bottle tree reminds me that winter is coming and with it the Bible School will start. Oh, my dear diary, I can entrust everything to you. I intend to be honest with you and to try my heart and myself as well. I am happy not only on account of the Bible School and that I will then come to better understand the Word of God. I am also happily looking forward to meeting new friends and the new people I will encounter. It is obviously divine guidance that I met Anna and Peter. I did not seek out their friendship. It was our common way to the Bible School which led to our meeting before the school even started. Is this not God's guidance?

Sometimes things are like in a book, like in the stories, I so much like to read. After Jake departed, it was difficult for me to get books from the school. Then I simply went to the teacher and he gladly lends me the books he has. Books about the World War hold little interest for me even though he has a lot of these.

Goethe's *Hermann and Dorothea* impressed me deeply. This volume contained the most beautiful pictures. Initially the rhyming pattern presented difficulties but once I had mastered it, I derived great pleasure from the language. Strange, but I always saw Peter Wall in Hermann and I was Dorothea. This happens often when I read books. Even in reading the Bible I experienced a similar sensation. I believed I was Esther and had to dress up for King Ahasuerus. It is almost shameful how I get involved in the detail of things and in the smallest of details of life in the remote Persian lands. And yet, I was happy that all these things appear in the Bible. Hermann and Dorothea had an uplifting, ennobling effect on me.

I prefer not to discuss this with David; he would immediately castigate me and I would have a bad conscience. David is the kind

of person who imparts a bad conscience on his fellowmen. This may be his attempt to seek Christian perfection in all, just like he lives it. He calls it holiness and discipleship and sometimes I believe he is what he preaches. Hopefully he and Papa will never come to loggerheads in this matter because Papa cannot stand self-righteousness. He still levels this charge against the Brethren in Russia.

We now have a second teacher from Germany. Actually he is the third because one left the Colony after a quarrel. All who come from Germany impart enthusiasm in our midst. Papa believes these teachers will benefit our school. Our students will improve and also raise their "cut" by being physically more active since athleticism ranks high in Germany and in our schools now.

Unfortunately I am already too old for high school. Our schools here will shortly be receiving even more teaching material from Germany since much is being done for us, the Foreign Germans, by the mother country. The new teacher made reference to this and Papa is glad about this improvement.

The teacher also spoke about *Ostpolitik*, the German approach to Russia. Papa thinks about *Ostpolitik* in terms of Stalin, while Mama associates it with Maria and Isaak.

"Hitler will arrive too late," says Mama. "By that time our children will long be dead or banned and starved to death."

And yet Papa believes in Hitler and in his policies, while I am worried when I think of David's views. Papa hopes that Hitler will take all Foreign Germans home to his *Reich*. Papa believes we have no future here in the Chaco of Paraguay. I know David's thinking in these matters. He regards it a sin for us to leave the Chaco to which God has led us. Sometimes I believe that the quarrel will reach the pitch we experienced when the Frieslander left.

Anna and Peter share David's opinion and all those who attend the Bible School are like-minded. I hope all this will not result in a schism along family lines.

6 August 1939

It is almost unthinkable that I have not held my diary in my hands for two months now. Today is a quiet Sunday afternoon. It is a cool day and I sit in our little room at the Walls. The other occupants believe I am doing school work, and I am not about to be disturbed.

The great time for me started two weeks ago. Papa took me to this village already the evening prior. We stopped in Filadelfia en-route where an event was scheduled which Papa intended to attend. The teacher from Germany conducted the program. The program was organized by the Peoples Society at which the teacher spoke about Foreign Germans or Germans Abroad. After the program, Papa took me to the Walls, who reside in this village. We were welcomed most cordially, after which Papa drove home. My heart was a trifle heavy, considering that my parents would now be alone for six weeks on end. But I will return home for the spring and I will then work with redoubled effort. By then, I will also know what path God has allotted for me.

The evening in Filadelfia greatly impressed me. Germany is now invariably termed our Motherland. Germany is the mother who takes care of all her children. We Germans Abroad are meant to demonstrate our worthiness by remaining German. Walls were not present at the occasion since entry is gained by belonging to the Peoples Society, to which they do not belong. But such is hardly my concern.

However, all this merely constitutes a background for my present life. I have my hands completely full with the Bible School and what I am meant to learn. We are only a small group but we are aware of why we are here. The biblical subjects are demanding, as is German which is a required course and which will stand me in good stead for my diary entries.

We have enough time to discuss world events and evaluate them in the light of scriptural authority. Invariably someone has heard a news item on the radio, and we discuss the re-armament and the threat of war, and we talk about wars and rumours of war, as Jesus has it. The threatening signs are meant to encourage us to exercise mission work wherever we can, and for as long as we live in times of divine grace.

The Walls received me in such friendly terms, like a child of their family. The lodgings are sparse and modest at best but one feels that all is offered from a warm and loving heart. Anna shares her little room with me, which has barely room for two beds and a little table. Then there are four more siblings, and so the table at mealtime is fully occupied, and I am in the middle of it all. Mother Wall is most congenial and she supplies everything possible.

Things transpire very differently here from what I am accustomed to at home. This is a pious family. It is not that we at home are not god-fearing but our expressions to that end are not nearly as obvious. This may be due to the fact that Walls are Brethren. During breakfast a morning service is held here and evenings, before bedtime, the entire family gathers for a nightly devotional, where everyone, young children included, are meant to pray aloud. I am used to it by now but the transition to praying aloud for all to hear took some doing on my part. I reflect on what I ought to say but the others have no problem at all in repeating the same refrain evening after evening. I invariably look at Peter and believe that he is both genuine and honest. He is the oldest and so he occasionally conducts both the morning service and the nightly devotional. Off and on Anna takes over as well. She is so devoutly cordial in all this, so that a spark of her joy lands right on the plate of my heart.

When walking to classes in the morning the two take me in their midst. Always and again I am reminded of Hermann in Goethe's great drama, because Peter, too, is so helpful and serious. I would so much like to introduce this Goethe topic in our conversations but this is inopportune because the Walls do not know the work, and also because I might appear forward and that is the last thing I have in mind.

In former times, Heinrich stood on the shore and I swam in the stream, which constantly became wider. That was my perception. And now it appears to me that I am standing on the shore and viewing the stream. It flows past me and ever on. Am I to run alongside of the water as it bubbles on, and on?

But no, I do not intend to draw comparisons; neither do I intend to squirm or quibble. I intend to follow Lena's advice: believe, hope and trust. "No one can compare with you, Lizzie," she said and that gave me a jolt of up and on!

Unfortunately such impulses are of short duration. All too quickly I am then again the lonely girl who observes how others find their niche, willy-nilly, but they all do; Greta, Lena, David and also Abraham. Of what use is it to me that no one can compare with me?

It may well be that even Heinrich has found his niche, in a world in which I do not fit, and which is as distant from our village as is the moon or the starry skies.

13 August 1939

The "Wandering Bible School", as what they literally call it, has wandered, has changed location. For a whole week now we are in the next village. From Friedensfeld to Friedensruh, then to Schönwiese, then on to Schönbrunn and possibly even further. The names of these villages, admittedly, are pretty and consoling.

Peter Wall was required to give a talk to our class, "The Mennonites as Peace Bearers". Peter had researched the topic by reading up on the Anabaptists in Switzerland, the Mennonites in Holland and Prussia and also about Menno Simons. That was the first part, with the second part being about the Mennonites in Russia, their privileges regarding freedom from military service under the Czars, the introduction of universal military service, alternative services to be rendered, like in the forestry. Peter found it difficult to speak of the World War, the Civil War and the Mennonite Armed Self-Protective Units. In Peter's opinion and deliberations on this topic, this represented a serious, a grievous error. I was seriously reminded of David and of our discussion as well as of Jake and Abraham. In our discussion relative to his talk, Germany and our

Germanism, as it is now termed, was mentioned, and of the mounting enthusiasm for Germany.

This was the final point Peter made in his talk. Our privileges in Paraguay grant us freedom from bearing arms but Hitler and National Socialism teach military conscription. In our enthusiasm for Germany, we jeopardize our privileges with so many in our colony uncritically lending support for Germany and its policies, said Peter. The teacher praised the talk, claiming that it was good and timely.

If the truth be known, I am happy the time at the Walls is over. They were all so friendly and nice to me and Peter so polite, but the constant close proximity of everything and everybody became rather hellishly oppressive for me. I only hope that no one noticed my dislike of too much closeness. You get up in the morning, exchange politeness, walk to school together, discuss a thousand issues, sit down for lunch together, and I attempted to be and to look and to talk naturally and unrestricted. This goes on for day after day and becomes deadening in its routine; not an iota of change or variation.

This week represented a recovery for me, a reflection. I cannot and will not force anything into being, dare anything radical or new or initiate change. Peace, tranquility and happiness is expected of me and I am more and more afraid that everything is but a forced façade and noticed as such.

Anna at times looked at me with a strange composure, like a concerned question. However, our friendship lacks the depth for me to discuss such issues with her candidly. My fear at attempting to say my piece and express my true sentiments and thereby destroying everything by an open discussion, is probably all the greater. Anna's relaxed inner happiness is still there but I regard all this with mounting distance. The fact that I cannot laugh unconcernedly and immaturely, and that I am frequently absent in my thoughts might give Anna pause for concern.

"What is it with you, Lizzie? What is bothering you?" Anna then asks. "You are so good in school, you are one of the best and smartest."

The fact that she can pose such questions shows me that my thoughts and my longing are totally foreign to her and infinitely lost on her. At the same time, I believe that everything that concerns me is obvious, tangible and up front. The fact that Anna is totally oblivious to everything that goes on in my inner person is similar to looking in a blind mirror, and is a matter of depressive concern. This is all so bewildering that I am not even capable of recording my sentiments in my diary.

Well and good. I will respond by studying all the harder, taking my school work yet more seriously and asking God for peace and serenity. I pray to that end when I extinguish the lamp at night and in the morning when I read the Bible. While doing so, a poem by Goethe comes to mind and which I have recorded in my notebook, namely, "My peace is gone, my heart is sore, I'll find healing, nevermore." This is Gretchen's song in Goethe's *Faust* speaking, as I have recorded. But I do not intend to seek consolation in Goethe, knowing, as I do, that I am to find my strength in the New Testament. Is it a natural law to life or is it my personal lot that the streams are constantly widening, the shores gaining greater distance, even among people? All this has already happened to me previously.

So let me just crack open my Bible and take my chances with a random verse as Mama always does it whenever she is sad unto death. Here goes, and with it God's answer to my plight in Luke 6:48. "But then the floods came and the stream tore vehemently at the house but could not manage to shake it for it was built on a rock."

Well and good then! Whatever the floods are meant to be… Thank you, dear Lord! And now, I will go to sleep!

20 August 1939

I was so devastatingly shocked as if every drop of my blood had drained from my heart. We had a free weekend before our school would relocate in yet another village, and so I was able to go home. There are classes in two more villages, and then the twelve weeks will come to an end. I had looked forward to everything and, now that it is almost over and the end is near, a silent fear has overcome me and I also know the reason for this.

It is almost difficult to believe but I felt a feeling of liberation, of being freed when I returned to my home village. For anyone to attend Bible School is something special and during the church service on Sunday, I noticed people looking at me as if I had arrived from far away. Later on the churchyard, many came to shake my hand and bid me welcome home.

The shock hit me when I visited Greta that Sunday afternoon. Greta in her usual carefree demeanour, and coming and going straight to the issue, as is her way, asked me about Peter Wall and how far things had advanced. I was speechless and beside myself so I laughingly stammered a few incoherent words that there was nothing to it and how could anyone invent such preposterous nothings.

"Oh yes," Greta answered. Mrs Görzen had paid her a visit. Görzens have relatives in that village, who knew the Walls well, and at the last church meeting the women had spoken about it during the noon hour. They were of the opinion that Lizzie Unruh was after Peter but Peter already had a girlfriend. But who she might be, not even the all-knowing gossip Mrs Görzen and her M.B. clan knew.

I laughed and acted nonchalantly and yet was shocked to death. I was able to divert Greta from all her probing questionings but I felt my legs trembling. What can remain hidden in this world? Who has dragged the secrets of my heart into the exposure of the sun and into the wicked gossip of these women? And now, while sitting here and writing, I know nothing more than what Greta told me. And there is no one I can ask, Anna least of all.

Can something be torn from the heart which had not even taken root there? I believe this to be a thousand times more painful than a relationship of love gone wrong in which, previously, everything was clear, pristine. This is obviously similar to a miscarriage.

I most certainly did not attend the Bible School for Peter's sake but now it seems as if the last weeks in school will be nothing but sheer torment and I wish it were all over. And, of course, I will act as if nothing has transpired. I wanted to engage in a closer relationship with the word of God and wanted to know where God wanted me and what He wanted of me. That is all I wanted.

I walked over to Lena after my talk with Greta and feared I would face further questioning, wondering what she, also, had all heard or might have heard. It is possible that she perceived my anguish?... she asked nothing. She was friendly, balanced and even-tempered and casual as always, our good Lena was.

David and Abraham arrived at the parental home in the early evening. The main item of conversation was politics and I was relieved. This diverts me, and I admit I also take an interest in it. The world holds its collective breath. Once a week, a wagon with fresh meat arrives from Filadelfia. Animals are slaughtered there and anyone can order meat in advance. When the meat wagon arrives in the village, everyone is eager to hear from the driver what the latest news the radio has reported. The driver distributes the meat and reports what he has heard. The Germans in Poland are now suffering dreadfully, just as the Sudeten Germans did a year ago.

David was very quiet. It appears as if he is now at a complete loss, as speechless about it all as I am. For us in the Bible School all this is only "war and rumours of wars" as we read in Revelations about the terrors of the End Times and about Gog and Magog and the great battles at Armageddon.

And all the while my little heart trembles as if seized by cramps, but it does not tremble for fear of the End Times, nor for fear of the Great Battles but for fear of the great uncertainty. Or is it already the certainty that burns away at my inner being?

27 August 1939

The days drag on slowly, and I know how I perceive this progression because I live unchanged regarding the uncertainty of what is being said about me, with the exception of what Greta revealed in her chronic gossip. And yet, "My peace is gone, my heart is sore" drones unceasingly in my head. Nothing around me has changed, nothing has changed in interesting learning material in school, nothing has changed in the friendliness of Anna and Peter; nothing has changed in my cordial relationship to them or anyone else. And yet I have the distinct feeling that in all this unchanging rigidity, decisions are being made regarding my life and that everything regarding me is up for grabs with me being the last to know.

In Schönwiese I reside with a friendly older couple. Things in the house are very peaceful and this does me a lot of good. During this weekend the peaceful nature of it all has become so solidified that it buoys me up, like the rising of objects in water. (Obviously I have remembered quite a bit of what Jake used to tell me from his physics studies, right?)

I would have liked to go home after all the news that has transpired this week, but I lacked opportunity to do so. Anna and Peter left for home since their father came for them.

This morning we were all most excited, indeed agitated, and even our teacher claimed that "every measure and all values are now in a state of utter confusion." Last night the news that Hitler and Stalin have concluded a pact reached our village. This was the reason why I would have liked to go home. I would so much have liked to hear what Papa has to say about all this. This must have meant a hard blow for him. The boys in our school spoke about the devil and Beelzebub. Such talk makes me uncertain and drives me to the very edge of things, since Papa evaluates the world situation and the main players therein, Hitler and Germany, so differently from the position assumed in our school.

On the other hand, all this confusion gathering in the world fits rather well with my own feelings regarding this matter. Worse still, possibly, I regard all the general consternation as a satisfaction. It was all so simple when juxtaposing good and evil as Papa did it when speaking about Hitler and Stalin or, as they commonly do it here in Bible School, when speaking of Christ and the Antichrist. And now the dividing line suddenly runs diagonally, instead of vertically. I manage to make do quite well with this diagonal line by presenting a front of friendliness, politeness and equanimity, but knowing full well that below a volcano seethes while above a blue heaven beams.

"Lizzie, you are so strong, so balanced, so clever and so beautiful."
Who said this to me and when? Is it not discord what I now think
and write?

Anna and Peter will now be in their village and there they will have
heard what the gossipy busy-bodies have to tell about Lizzie Unruh
and with which intentions she attended Bible School, namely to find
a marriageable man, and that she is now living with a supreme
disappointment, and that it serves her just right. And then on
Monday Anna will give me the time of day, and she will know why
I acted rather strangely in her presence while I look at her with a
balanced composure.

Hardly. Anna and Peter will not lend their ear to crazy gossip. We
will be friendly and polite and well composed, unchanged.

4 September 1939

It has turned icy cold yet again, and we even had a frost one night
and that in September of the year. I sit in my little room and shake
from cold all over because lengthy cold periods cause the inside of
the house to be even colder than the outside. My little room is like
an ice-cellar.

The first sprigs of green have frozen, the sweet potato fields are
black, as are the bananas and the *mamoncillos*. Now nature awaits
the north storms which will blow everything bare, and with its heat,
burn what is left. The much awaited rain will probably follow in
October.

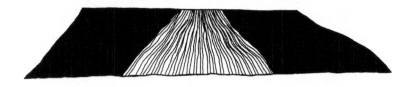

I was happy to be able to go home again on Saturday. There is only one topic on every agenda and that is the war. On Friday the Germans marched into Poland. For Papa this represents a salvation. Now Papa knows that Hitler had to keep his back free in the East since England and France failed to enter into any agreement with him. This forced Hitler to sign a pact with Stalin. Papa is now satisfied.

On Saturday evening we sat in our warm and cozy kitchen and drank *mate* and that in September! Abraham was also present and on such occasions nowhere in the world is there a more spirited discussion on politics than in our kitchen. Abraham claims to know exactly what will now happen.

On Sunday we had church and our church leader prayed for Germany and for peace. I was not able to speak to David since he and Sara had left for services at the Brethren church in Friedensruh, and I had to leave that afternoon. I wonder what David may be thinking of all that is going on.

At school we read interpretations about Revelations by theologians. Anna is invariably totally involved and excited about Jesus' Second Coming. She told me that her mother, still in Russia, had been just as excited at the time of terror during the Civil War, when she was a little girl. Her mother had told her that she had so much and so happily looked forward to the return of Christ. But then she got married and her great excitement had abated, and she had postponed her anticipations.

I laughed, "So marriage can become more important than Jesus' return?"

Anna looked at me, shocked. But then she also laughed. "Yes, indeed, that is the way things in life are. Human needs tend to be more important than heavenly matters."

We two have never discussed the matter of matrimony. Anna is younger than I am and it seems to me that, given her tender and innocent nature, she never gives these matters any thought. But maybe she is like Lena who is of such a silent nature that one never knows what goes on within them.

And what will become of me? The Bible School is heading for conclusion and I fear that everything will remain unresolved for me.

I have given thought to the mission and to the Indians but I do not even know if girls are needed for the mission, and, if so, to what end?

Anna tells me that Peter intends to be a missionary, and when there is talk about the mission in class, he expresses clear opinions on the matter just like David, and then I hear about our duty in the Chaco. Then a spasm seizes my heart and I experience pain, and yet my face displays no emotion. I participate in the discussions but remain peaceful and objective. Peter then looks at me as if I were a missionary, possibly a colleague with clever ideas. I do not believe it causes him any great effort to discuss these matters with me quite reasonably and with objectivity.

I dance high above it all on a tight high-wire, and am greatly admired with much fanfare while at the same time feeling that I have long since dropped, fallen. I, the beautiful dancing ballerina.

17 September 1939

The last weeks of Bible School in the last village… Is this now all that I have achieved? But I am not disappointed. The Bible School has given me what I expected, and I am deeply impressed by the hospitality of the people who took us in. When I told Mrs Martens, in whose house I am currently living, this today, she beamed and said, "It is a service to the Lord. And one should gladly render it. If it is not gladly done, it has no value."

I find the weather cooperating, at least as far as my heart is concerned, where everything has been swept clean. We are experiencing heavy north winds, the kind of weather which makes everyone groan. Already at nine in the morning when our studies commence, the wind starts blowing. We then have to close the window shutters for otherwise the wind blows right into the classroom. In spite of this, a layer of sand lies over everything: on the note books, books and desks. At the same time it is so dark in the room that we have difficulties in reading and writing. At noon, when we walk home, the wind envelopes us in its hot clouds of dust.

I hold my silk scarf to my face and inch my way through the sand dunes which mound the streets. When the north storms reach their apex, the wind howls all night long around the house. I then close all window shutters although it is hot and stuffy in the room.

And yet, to what end? I find the weather almost a comfort since the weather outside merely reflects my inner state. You cannot defend yourself against the outer elements, and even less against the inner emptiness and disappointments. To simply accept both is the best of all protective measures.

Anna and Peter have again gone home for the Sunday. Their father came for them. Anna acted a bit secretive, as if something important were to happen, but she had nothing to say. I would have preferred to go home even on foot, if need be. But it is simply too far and too dangerous for a girl. Military on horseback as well as cattle drivers abound in the villages. And at home I would have been greeted with surprise. How would I have been able to express myself as to what compels me? And yet, the way home would have been my proper diversion.

I will go outside and lie down on the hammock and watch the setting of the sun. The atmosphere of twilight is one of melancholy and I intend to expose myself to it. Everything is enveloped in a bluish-brown mist; the sun is a red ball which disappears even before it has reached the horizon.

"To bid farewell, the weather is just right, grey as the heavens is the world before me." When I copied this poem by Victor von Scheffel in my notebook years ago, I had no idea that the poem would one day apply to me. Scheffel obviously refers to rain showers, but the north wind appears even more applicable to me. Jake brought along books from school by Victor von Scheffel of a former day. *Ekkehard* and *The Trumpeter from Säckingen* remain in mind and memory. It has been so long. Löns, Ganghofer, Mörike…how far from my heart as they were and are. Now they resonate like muted strings of the lute.

24 September 1939

I went for my diary almost mechanically, similar to a life-saving device. That may be a slight exaggeration; however, it cannot buoy me up permanently. It is a straw, a life-saving straw. Whatever, I shall head for this very straw.

The whole week passed me by as a sleep walk. It has passed me by and I do not even know what I have done, what I have been up to, what I have said or how I have behaved or conducted myself. Most likely I have acted quite normally with no one noticing anything out of the ordinary. Only Mrs Martens occasionally smiled in her friendly manner when I forgot to eat, or probably sat day dreaming.

"Well," she asked, "are the examinations really so difficult?"

"Yes," I said, while also smiling.

Joy and laughter and joking everywhere and I am part of it all, at least I appear friendly enough, totally relaxed, as if I had expected nothing different, nothing more, nor less. During recess I extended my hand to Peter and congratulated him. He looked at me with great friendliness, beaming, while Anna embraced me and kissed me, all from, and with joy.

On Monday during the first class after the morning devotional, the teacher announced that he had an additional announcement to make, while cutting a bit of a mischievous face. Then he said, somewhat church-like, and in a jocund sub-tone. "I have the pleasure of informing the audience of the engagement of a bridal couple. The bride is Aganetha Harder and the groom is Peter Wall. We wish the couple God's blessings for their betrothal." Then he went on to talk about God's calling and the hope that the future wife would be an equal and willing partner in her husband's endeavours.

The entire class applauded happily while everything around and within me spun as if in a giant circle. I joined in clapping my hands as befitted the occasion.

I had an opportunity to go home yesterday but I declined the offer. It didn't pay to do so just a few days before school's completion. And what would I be doing at home anyway? Going to Greta would merely have intensified my torture. News of the engagement has obviously spread and Greta would only have insisted on every detail, blow by blow, high and low. I would even have had difficulty in accepting Lena's endearing approach.

Here at the Martens residence I am a blank, at best. No one knows anything about my inner conflicts. The Walls are hardly known to them and no mention is made of the engagement.

I did something this morning which I would previously not have dared to do. I did not attend the church service. I took my books and stated that I definitely had to study for my examinations. It was my intention to walk a little beyond the village. A most beautiful water pond is located there, probably three hundred metres from the main road with a narrow path leading to this idyllic location. This pond is surrounded by *algarrobo* growth which is sprouting tender green, and in the middle of the drink, *paratodo* trees spread luxurious, effusive blossoms. The sun just peeped over the trees inviting the yellow flower umbels and the tender green to sparkle with profusion.

I sat down under a tree, placed my books on the grass and then I managed to cry, finally, after a week. I let myself completely go, I let my world break down, go to hell, if you will, and myself as well, including my hopes, my resolutions, my dreams. The Bible School is coming to a close and before me lies the loneliness of our village and the void of my whole life.

It did me good that I let the entire relay of life's routine, of which I was an eager member for weeks, indeed months, simply break down, disintegrate. If only I perceived anger, rage at someone, but all I have, and have to face is a single, an infinite void, with me being a miserable, wretched rolled-up ball of dilapidation in the middle of it all. No wind in my sails, no air in my balloon.

Then I told Mrs Martens that I was unwell and that I wanted no lunch. I closed the window shutters and slept till sundown. My exhaustion was so total that it did me good and sleep was like a death. When I awoke I felt resurrected. I managed to open the shutters, breathe deeply and sit down with my diary. Martens were away visiting with neighbours; no one disturbed me, no one was there to ask, inquire.

Tomorrow I will again sit in class, interested and alert. We will be writing examinations. I will let the last few days glide past me and I will be the friendly, outgoing girl for them all.

There is one matter to which I seek clarity, if such is granted at all to mankind. Three months ago I spoke about God's guidance: I, Lena, Greta, David all spoke about it, and of my submission to His will, and of the path, I was prepared to walk.

The teacher in my village had presented me with a calendar featuring a daily tear off verse with scriptural guidance for the day, which he had received from Germany. I took this calendar along with me from village to village. The picture on the calendar displayed a cross at a parting of the ways, similar to a song which we as a choir loved to sing:

> *"The Cross by the Crossroads with the Golden Star*
> *Leads, surely, to the Saviour, though the path be far."*

It was the cross, the faith which led me all these years, which determined my decisions. It is for this reason that I had Heinrich go his way. I saw the parting of the ways before me and it was my intention to walk the right way towards a purposeful life. And all the while I dreamed about accord: A harmonious life, which has the intent and aim for faith, love, and fulfilment to merge into a purposeful life. I dreamt of the rapture of a stream which carries.

Now I will return to my village. There is no alternative. I will help Mama milk the cows, take the milk to the separator hut, I will clean the rooms, rake the yard. I will take joy in David and Abraham's children, help Lena on Saturdays, and I will separate myself another year from my youth. During the Youth Hour I will sit with young, giggling girls and the boys will be polite to me as they are to an older woman.

It now has to become clear to me that the cross and faith have not led me to that site in which my longing was located, and that accord, harmony and rapture have nothing at all to do with it all. Will I manage all that? Will Greta, Lena and David understand that everything, which we regarded as guidance, was no such thing in my understanding of it all?

We have spoken much about missions. How can I go to a mission station where Peter is a missionary? I cannot very well control myself a whole life long and pretend, and be part of a relay as I have now done for all of three months.

Am I now acting contrary to God's guidance or have I created a wrong image of God's guidance in my own inner being? It will be a sultry night but I will sleep. In any case, decisions have been arrived at and made, and that is a lot, much.

12 October 1939

My village again has me. When I came home three weeks ago, everyone greeted me, friendly, lovingly and interested. For them, I am still the god-fearing, pretty little darling. No one senses, or can imagine what has gone on within me during these three months. No one saw my dream picture, which shone so brightly before me and which then fragmented into total ruin. No one knows that within me, life became darker than ever before in all my life together; it is as if one has looked into a bright light for a long while and become blinded, and then tip toes uncertainly, at best, blindly into an unknown future.

Last Sunday a Church Hour was held and the lead minister asked me to present a brief report on the Bible School. I did this in keeping with what was expected of me. I spoke about the spiritual growth and about the rich blessings, without resorting to untruths. I spoke about the concluding celebration. "Maranatha" was the theme and topic: "Our Lord is coming!" Later many women and girls came to shake my hand. I had done very well and encouraged others also to attend Bible School.

The local church leader yesterday asked me to assume the leadership of the Sunday School in our village. I agreed to do so and I am sure I will enjoy the work. I will tell the children Bible, as well as other, stories and sing songs with them from the *Singvöglein* (Little Birds A-Singing) and in cooperation with Liese Fast and Lena Neufeld. We are now the older girls in the village. Girls is the term for such yet unmarried, old girls.

When I came home after school, a letter from Jake was awaiting me. His letter was as if from another world, so full of enthusiasm, so elated, so full of hope and full of future. Germany's victory over Poland caused boundless jubilation among the Germans in Asunción and Jake joined their every elation. Jake knows everything, every detail of that victory. Poland received its due punishment, Jake writes, and now it is France's and England's turn.

Papa also knows everything about the war and also that the Russians have advanced into Poland and into the Baltic States and into Bessarabia. This worries him a lot but he has unlimited confidence in the Führer. It seems as if I have spent the last weeks in a dream out of which I am only now slowly awaking.

Now the Baltic Germans will be re-settled in Germany, as well as the Bessarabians. Papa believes that such measures are the proper ones for politics on a large scale. The Germans will now all go home to the *Reich*.

The little boys in the village sing "We are on our way to Engeland." This song was played in Filadelfia on the radio and within days everyone is singing it in every village and I, too, am humming it. Recently this very song was published in *La Plata Post* and I could barely believe my eyes. It was composed by Herman Löns. Then I copied this song into my note book, and not because it is a war song but because it is by Löns, whose poetry I love. I leafed through my note book and read the poems which I copied years ago. The time frame from then to today seemed as great as the difference between the former love poems and this war poem by the same poet.

When I recently returned the Goethe volume to the teacher, he gave me a collection of Hermann Hesse poetry.

"I know that you like poetry," he said, "maybe you will like these. I do not like them all that much. You may keep the book."

Then we spoke about the Bible School and also about all the German folk movement in the colony as all things new are now called in our colony. This teacher, who formerly was so enthusiastic about all things transpiring in Germany, has become more and more reserved in such matters. The war may have caused this. If you are all in favour of Germany, you have to be in favour of war and that is a contradiction for many in light of the Mennonite faith and our rejection of bearing arms.

26 November 1939

Yesterday we celebrated November 25 in our village as we do every year. On that day we fled the Soviet Union but this year was special since it is the tenth anniversary of our escape.

Mama again was very sad even though she no longer cries as often as formerly. At the time we managed to leave Moscow and boarded the train for Germany, Mama suffered a nervous breakdown in her abject pain and despair. We had all so much hoped that Maria and Isaak would manage to join us in time, but that endeavour failed and was over, for all time. That curtain had dropped and was sealed. We were on our way to freedom while many remained behind in hell.

During the celebration, constant reference was made to the past ten years and how fast these years had come and gone. "It is as if it were yesterday that we left our yard," said Papa. His beautiful farmyard in Rosenthal... As if yesterday, but for me it seems like an eternity. For me it is an entire life. I was then not yet fifteen years old and now I belong to the older girls of the village. When we sailed on the ocean steamer from Hamburg to Buenos Aires, I did not really know with whom to associate: with the children and Jake, or with the youth and David. I was invited to sing in the choir which practised songs for the church service on board and then I joined Jake in his Sunday School class.

The sailors waved at me as I walked by the railing on board, with one repeatedly trying to engage me in conversation. His name was Fritz. I skipped away while the other girls laughed at me and the sailor.

Yesterday, when I stood in the ranks of the choir, I suddenly noticed that I was very tired, tired of everything, possibly even tired of praying. We sang the songs which we always practice for the 25th of November, like "Great are the things the Lord has wrought" and "We are a folk, drifted by the stream of time to the Island of this Earth" when suddenly I lost all verve as if I sang but only my mouth moved. It is the last ten years which have tired me out or is it the last three months?

Or is all this nothing but ingratitude? I am thankful for so much. For instance, for the book by Hermann Hesse, which the teacher gifted me. Also, I love reading the Bible, daily. I presently find nothing more consoling than the Psalms. Before I read anything in the New Testament, I start with a Psalm. At the same time I find that a poet like Hesse manages to formulate the heart's desires and troubles with a language beyond compare. After reading the Bible, I seek out a poem in Hesse's book, and while copying it into my note book, I soon commit it to memory. I recorded the following in my note book last night.

> *"The world falls from me, all pleasures,*
> *which once you loved, die away;*
> *how darkness looms in ashes."*

The conclusion reads:

> *"Hard and heavy is the way into solitude,*
> *Harder than you knew, the spring of dreams runs dry.*
> *Yet, trust! At the end of your path, home will be:*
> *Death and re-birth, grave and eternal mother."*

As if Löns to Hesse is but a single pace, not a pace further or higher but a step down, a step deeper.

If only I could talk about this with someone. But with whom am I to talk, if even my teacher says that he finds Hesse's poetry meaningless. I managed to discuss "The Cross at the Parting of the Ways" well with him. He understood the meaning and he provided counsel. The song and the picture were of help for the road ahead which I then believed to be mine.

And yet the parting of the ways now lies far behind me. Am I now really on the path into solitude, just as Hermann Hesse obviously experienced it?

3 December 1939

I always marvel at how courageously Papa sets out to do all his work when we finally have had a good rain. After months of parching weather, and everything is withered, he talks a lot about the Baltic Germans and Hitler's policies of a Greater Germany, and I have the impression that he would leave tomorrow if the way were clear. But when a heavy rain finally falls as it did at the beginning of December, then nothing holds him back; he then harnesses the horses and heads for the fields with the plough and hardly takes a break, even for lunch. Such renewed endeavour holds true for most in the Chaco.

A whole new chapter has been introduced in matters of hired hands. A new Indian tribe arrived two years ago from the south, allegedly from the Pilcomayo River Area, in our area. These are the Chulupis. It was a beautiful sight to behold an entire tribe of them under Chief Fultan entering our village. These Indians are totally different from the Lenguas. The men all bear rifles, probably from the Chaco War. Their loin girding extends all the way down to their feet and they wear long pearl strings around their necks. It appears that the men like ornamentation more than do their women.

I stood by the street and watched their long train enter the village. The women carried their entire household in giant carrier bags on their backs fastened to a headband, while alongside their little girls came traipsing along, naked on top, like their mothers, well-endowed and giggling. They drove a great herd of sheep and goats as well as some pack donkeys ahead of them. The entire train of them struck me as one living an unconcerned life.

The party, in its entirety, settled down at the end of the village, while the women immediately set about building their grass huts. Their little village was up and ready by the first evening. And now Papa has all the workers he needs. The Chulupis like to work and they are very skilful. There is no work which they do not master in short order.

"What manner of people they are!" said Papa. "Just look at how healthy they appear and how their women and girls are so vibrant."

I have to admit that when I observed these people and all the busyness of the village, I almost forget that very recently I had plans to prepare myself for mission work among the Indians. Plans and efforts to that end had the Lenguas in mind, who already resided here when we arrived in the Chaco. And now the Chulupis have arrived, and in such numbers that it is hardly feasible to include them all in the missionary effort. However David will probably feel confirmed in his notion that God has directed us to the Indians as our very own mission field. And now they are even forging their way here, he may well say, now they are coming even to us.

How may all this yet come to be, how will this be mastered, resolved? Our faith is based on a long tradition, centuries old. All the things that are part of this tradition like church services, weddings, funerals, the village life, all my youth, even my love comprise, indeed constitute, our life. Are we now meant to transfer all this accumulated load to these people, to these pearl-bedecked men and their rouged, giggling girls, and right into their grass huts? How can all this be realized? Not one reference to that end exists in the Bible except "Go and teach all people and baptize them!" David claims that we are meant to be obedient. While contemplating this, I sometimes wish that I could laugh so naturally as these girls do, so carefree, happily and so unconcernedly.

And yet, it may well be that all this is only one side of their life, the side which I see and which I envy. Behind this side, who knows, may lie everything the missionary termed the darkness, the misery of these subjugated people. He spoke about the terrible inner torments these heathens suffer, particularly their fear of demonic spirits.

And yet, we do have our faith, but what manner of inner torture do we suffer: Mama, Greta, Liese Fast, I, and possibly even Mrs

Görzen who bears suffering from one party to the next? How beautiful were the three months of the experience of faith but just how dreadfully did I suffer through it all!

I now hear the Chulupis singing by their grass huts. They have barely arrived and already they are celebrating some festival. They sing and dance every evening after work's end. They are round dances. The young men dance in a circle while the girls hang on to the men and dance and skip along. It is already ten o'clock, late evening, and they are still dancing. They will sing me to sleep.

18 December 1939

We had a difficult day today. We planted sweet potatoes today from early morning till sunset. Some Indian women helped and they are good at it since they also plant yams now and then in their tiny garden plots somewhere on an open field. When they are ripe, the Indians harvest their small crop. I dug little holes in the ground and the Indian women rolled the tendrils nicely into the openings and covered them with earth. We will need a good crop of yams since we pay the Indians with them.

In spite of my fatigue, I intend to write in my diary today. We are all very startled and excited. I walked to the street today when the meat transport arrived. A battle has taken place in the mouth of the Plata River which involved the German *Admiral Graf Spee* against three British war ships. Finally, when the Germans saw no way out, they sank their own ship.

This was a report of the first German defeat after their great victory in Poland. Papa believes that the British have superior naval power to the Germans, which they have now demonstrated and have done so right here on the coast of South America. But still, a two-front war is not a given yet, says Papa. Poland has been conquered and Hitler has concluded a pact with Russia. And now the French will get it and then the English. Abraham has just left. He was still around when news of the *Spee* arrived.

"If only we could manage to help," he said. "When the zeppelin "Hindenburg" burned, we collected money and peanuts as a donation." Papa laughed and suggested we would probably play little or no roll in Germany's winning or losing.

However, Abraham was not to be deterred. "Surely, one ought to find a way to help." I almost believe that Abraham would be a soldier, were he in Germany. What is he thinking? He does have a wife and children. Our men over here tend to completely forget that they are Mennonites. Discussions have never been conducted so animatedly in our village ever since Hitler has gone to war. Every victory is roundly celebrated over here, even more so than during the Chaco War.

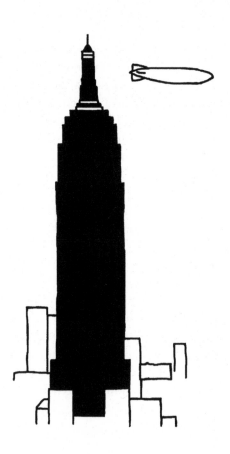

Hopefully Jake will be here by Christmas Eve. He wrote that he will depart in good time but if there will be rain, the road to the train station is often very poor. We have not seen each other for four years now. How will we appear to each other, how have we changed during all this time?

If things are like previously then I can talk freely to him, also about Peter. When Heinrich was on the scene, Jake was the only one who understood me. Jake having come to faith was probably the reason why we managed to talk so freely about everything. We had found common territory on which complete confidence was given. We unloaded everything that depressed or worried us and we even managed to talk about our feelings.

It is strange that love and faith are so tightly intermingled. In Greta's case, I found it almost kitschy how everything flowed together but in my case things transpired much the same. Even the songs which we sang at the time, even though they were hymns, assumed a longing for love and made me joyful of soul, and Jake experienced equal sentiments. "Oh, may it not be said 'Too late, too late, to march through that Golden Gate'." Strange!

These matters can possibly even be dangerous. A couple in love in a neighbouring village had just found the Lord and then fell into sin. That caused much excitement.

When Papa speaks about the Brethren in Russia and about the excesses among the "Free" and the "Rapturous" then such may have well been caused by effusiveness of spiritual ecstasy, spiritual confidence. Too bad, really, we should have discussed this very matter in Bible School. But I would have been much too inhibited at the time to ask questions about love.

Oh, but I am very tired and I write and I write and drift from sweet potatoes to the war and from war to love. And so this shall be enough for today.

25 December 1939

The fact that I am able to find a peaceful hour in my room is like peace after a storm. It was not a bad storm. Everything around me was is a state of whirlwind, as things tend to be when a family get-together is celebrated. On Christmas Day things transpired as they do in every large family. Abraham, Lena, David with their families were over, and even Jake had managed to arrive on the 22nd of December.

They all assembled at our family home for lunch and also for coffee. Mama and I had prepared everything on the 24th, and so everything was ready: chicken had been fried, the raisin stuffing made, the manioc and yams pealed, while buns and crumble cake had also been baked. Today, after the church service, we joined several tables together so that eighteen people could be accommodated.

The task of washing mountains of dishes after the huge meal is gigantic. Then the women and girls also get involved. Family gatherings with huge meals are a must, and that is well known even if it means cooking, baking and washing dishes and much work for the women. At Easter it is Lena's turn, and at Pentecost David and Sara will be in line to serve the family, with Abraham and Neta dishing it out and up next Christmas.

Fortunately we have the huge *Paraiso* trees on the yard so that the tables can be spread outside in the shade. It is fiercely hot outside but there is not enough room for all inside.

Now they are all gone. It is peaceful on the yard. Jake walks the village street, all alone. He does this every evening these days, once darkness has set in. "I wander through the past," he says. Sometimes he walks twice from one end of the village to the other, up to the village swing and back again. We have both not had time for each other, given the turbulent time Christmas brings with it. Jake will be staying here for all of January and will help with all the work at home; then we will opportunity to talk with each other, like in former times.

Jake has become a big man. He wears clothes like people do in the big city of Asunción and he has much to talk about. Last night after a celebration in school we two sat alone on the yard and he told me about a film he had seen in Asunción. There are several movie houses there and some of the films are most interesting, he says, particularly those dealing with the Wild West in North America.

When we went to church this forenoon, I wore my white dress with the red sash. "Oho!" said Jake, "you look splendid. You are ready for the Palma in Asunción. You have become even more beautiful, rounded out, more mature."

I gave him a gentle slap on the cheek for his jauntiness. Jake was dressed in a nice suit and he offered me his arm. We walked arm in arm to the street and then nice and modestly to the school. After the church service, we two walked to the teacher. Jake meant to thank him for the good Youth Hours which the teacher conducted at the time when many more young people still lived in our village. These lessons had given Jake much strength for his faith. The teacher was happy to hear this.

Then the two engaged in political discourse. Jake knows a great deal about the war. In Asunción the daily newspaper reports about everything, including the sea battle at Rio de la Plata. "The English are to blame for everything, for otherwise the German warship would not have had to depart the Montevideo port. It would have been able to repair all the damages from the battle to enable it to resume the battle. However, the English exerted pressure on Uruguay."

The teacher was highly interested. He asked many questions and Jake answered them as if he were delivering a report. The Captain, Langsdorf, was left with no option but to sink his own ship. The entire crew was then transported to Buenos Aires, since Argentina sided with the Germans. Langsdorf then committed suicide in accordance with the German code of honour for officers. The teacher was so impressed by this report that he asked Jake to give a talk about it in his Youth Hour.

Now I hear that Jake has returned from his walk into the past. He is not to see my diary. I will go outside now so that Jake can tell me more about Asunción. I have not yet told him anything about myself.

26 January 1940

A Sunday afternoon, the likes of which will probably come to haunt me frequently in the future. I am alone with my only real friend, my diary. The weeks with Jake will soon be over as well. After a few days he will leave. He can stay no longer because he works in a business in Asunción to finance his studies.

This afternoon Papa and Jake went to Filadelfia to attend a meeting of the German "Folk" Society. Many who want to remain Germans, as is the claim, have become members of this club. After the war is over, everyone who wants to will become German citizens and then they all intend to go to Germany.

There are some here in our village, like David, who oppose this German Folk Society. These are the ones who intend to stay in the Chaco because God has led us here. They also believe that we would lose our C. O. status if we went to Germany. When listening to David, but also Jake as of now, that might very well happen. They are in total agreement on this point. Abraham and David frequently get into heated quarrels about this matter, so much so that I fear for my brothers. Abraham then calls David an Englishman, who forgets that we are German.

All that lay so far removed from me when I was at Bible School, but now I am becoming constantly more involved in this matter. We hear ever more all about being Germanic. We as Foreign Germans will only survive and finally find peace, we are told, when we are incorporated into the large German Folk Community. In foreign countries we will all go under, meaning, lose our identity, and here in the Chaco we will finally dissipate altogether. We will soon be reduced to white Indians. Someone who visited us in the Chaco Bush allegedly said this and now these are Abraham's words as well. Jake speaks excitedly about Asunción. He brought along a picture book for Papa for Christmas *In Poland with Hitler* which depicts the entire war. The world is engulfed in flames and hatred and we are in the middle of it all. The great world out there is a rolling thunder and we are involved in little quarrels about it all, and who wants to go to Germany and who not.

Recently Mrs Görzen paid Mama a visit and she knew everything that is going on in the colony. In the high school the girls are now required to do gymnastics, just like the boys. That would never have been possible in Russia. And, as we all know, at the last school festival the girls performed their gymnastics in tune to music and that in gymnastic dress! It will not be long and they will surely be dancing as well. She is of the opinion that if the church now does not put an end to it all then worldliness will take over. And all this is being introduced by the new teacher from Germany.

When Mama told Jake and me all this, Jake could not contain his laughter. "Come with me to Asunción, Mama, and you will even see girls in swim gear," he said. Mrs Görzen is nothing but a pious old scandal-monger.

Then Mama got really huffy and mad. That is no way to talk about people, was her opinion.

"Humph, but Mrs Görzen is allowed to do so," said Jake and continued laughing. Such occurrences are now commonplace at our home, as if distant sheet lightning is visible up to here and we softly hear the thunder roll.

In spite of everything, I mustered the courage to speak to Jake about everything that truly troubles my heart, like matters of faith and of my great disappointment. Then all the sheet lightning and rolling thunder disappeared. I have a brother who listens to me and who understands. But that is an entry for another day.

I hear the rattling of a wagon. Our team is entering the yard, and Papa and Jake will be hungry, and at the table there will be much talk about the German Folk Society.

15 February 1940

Jake has left and I am alone. Obviously his departure was a foregone conclusion, and yet our togetherness gave me much inner assurance and strength, and I can now write about it all.

We sat together in the hammock, which we have suspended between the *Paraiso* trees. The moon shone clear and cast a deep shadow beneath the trees. Jake listened to me, he heard me out, and then he started talking.

"You have gone through a lot, Lizzie," he said. "However, I believe all that will amount to a saving grace for you." And then he started talking about himself. "My faith has rejected much, mainly that which we here associate with our life style. If the church is no longer there to protect and shield you and watch over you, and you are left to your own devices in the world, then only that which is true and genuine remains, and will stand the test of time and experience."

"What is true and genuine?" I asked. "Was what I looked for in the Bible school that not the real stuff, or what I regarded as such when I believed I had a calling for the mission? Surely it has not been invalidated just because Peter met me, because I was disappointed, and because I was catapulted from a dream world and my dreams into utter loneliness.

"It may well be, that this occurrence taught you what is genuine, Lizzie," Jake said after considerable reflection, "and if you have been unable to notice this, then you will experience it. And if you were catapulted into loneliness together with your faith, then you experienced a lesson every bit as hard as I did in Asunción, where I had to learn to live with a totally different value system from the one meted out by our community."

It did me good to be able to tell Jake everything. Just by being heard out without being immediately subjected to judgement, is like a healing hand. Still, I have received no answer whether faith lies deeper, at a deeper level from what we call church or even community. Does faith lie deeper than, for example, the quarrel about our German-ism and our Mennonitism, which probably is the case with Abraham and David? Does faith indeed lie deeper than my own disappointment? Does it lie deeper than Jake's present walk of life, by him no longer living as the church here teaches it, and as Mama so desperately wishes it to be?

Am I truly a person of faith in spite of not having mastered what I believed to be God's calling and what I regarded as His guidance and direction? Does faith in the final analysis exist in that deeper level, which we accepted as a gift, but which we cannot infinitely freely determine, or govern, or control, for that matter?

In listening to Jake, I reach that conclusion, and when looking into myself I take heart and I am consoled. "Nobody will snatch them from my hand," it is written. Possibly even Heinrich represented part of all this, at a much deeper level which he himself did not completely understand. There is also mention of a glimmering wick in the Bible.

I know that David would respond with a "No", followed by a threefold "no" to all of this. To him, only that applies which is visible in our deeds and in our walk. You will recognize them only by their fruits, he would say. Reverends Reimer and Wiebe and Epp are of similar persuasion and would evaluate church members by these standards.

Unfortunately we never entered into these questions in Bible School. And I myself was an open flower, and I regarded the petals and their fragrance and their receptiveness for that what I wanted to be, and which I possibly was not. I would probably never have understood Jake if my disappointment had not burned everything in me like the north winds burn the September blossoms.

Jake advises me to come to Asunción. "You will change there," he said, "but that is preferable to perishing here."

The die has been cast: Asunción. It is a different world, a life, a way of living which Jake has mastered and which has freed him and released him from an entanglement from which Elisabeth is increasingly beginning to suffer. It is an entanglement of faith with the social life of the village, in a Mennonite settlement. That, which for many years was her supporting lifeline, the relay as she once put it, has shattered, with nothing but fragmented shards of disappointments remaining. In comparison, Jake appears advantaged and self-assured and also more certain of himself in matters of faith.

It seems necessary to insert an explanatory note to the diary entries here. The entire year of 1940 can be eliminated, although it contains affirmations of the increasing loneliness, the loneliness in the village, but also in the normative life of a church which has inadequate counselling for individuals living on the borderline of established norms.

In her disappointments, Elisabeth no longer turns to pastors and not even to the teacher who formerly provided succor. Everything is too confining, too familiar, with all too much entanglement and being intertwined with a multitude of social and community relationships. Every revelation on her part would be tantamount to a public exposure. This then results in an ever increasing isolation, and a turn towards the inner self.

"Am I not like a plough, forgotten on the field, standing isolated, left to rust?" is one of Elisabeth's entries. "The horses which once pulled it have long gone elsewhere, frolicking, possibly on another more promising pasture."

The comparison to the black horses in Mörike's poem "Remember well, oh my soul" is obvious. Mörike is one of Elisabeth's favourite poets in her collection. This girl, not yet thirty, occupies herself, as Mörike did, with thoughts of death.

And also a further factor becomes ever more determining and fulfilling, diverting her, as it did countless others at the time. Influenced by Jake, Abraham and her father, she directs her attention during the Second World War to Foreign Germans, folk-Germanism and pan-Germanism. David's critical position to all this, and the Bible School drift into the background, evermore.

The German-Mennonite settlement in the forest primeval motivated by the hopelessness of a previously promising existence is drifting more and more into the world-wide confrontation, connected to the great hope of a home-coming to Germany after the war. The two looming fronts here identify themselves, on the one side as a German consciousness, in the sense of totally committed allegiance, and on the other as Mennonites, in equal consciousness of its faith tradition, combined with a will to remain in the Chaco.

The lingering disappointment and the appeal of enthusiasm for Germany, initially haltingly, then constantly more powerfully, streams into the vacuum of Elisabeth's consciousness and being. Loneliness and the inertia of lethargy find answer in hope for a Germany victory and a new life in another world.

The next chapter contains the historically significant years between 1941 till 1946. The diary entries are not always sequential, entered with occasional lengthy period lapses occurring. Otherwise they would exceed the limits of space available. A choice of material to be included during this time span had to be made in order to concentrate on those essentials which determine Elisabeth's life.

ALBATROSS

Albatross

Puerto Casado, 6 March 1941

When I woke up in our hotel room this morning, I heard water rushing, a whole stream of it as if it were never-ending. An employee, possibly a waiter, was watering the plants in the courtyard of the hotel. Water streamed out of a garden hose in a constant, powerful gush. Here at the river port of Casado water is not a scarce commodity as it is in the interior of the Chaco. The Paraguay River provides all the water wanted and the beautiful plants and flowers luxuriate in the clean air.

I lay underneath the mosquito netting which is stretched over the bed and enjoyed the unaccustomed noise of flowing water. Then I got up and got ready for breakfast. Some other parties from the colony were on their way to Asunción as well. We were served sweet coffee, gelato and each one was served a large beef steak which they here call *bife*, hot and served straight from the stove.

I now sit at the same table at which breakfast was served and after a long time I took my diary to hand. One Mrs Goosen, who is traveling with us to Asunción for medical aid, asked me if I were already writing a letter home. No, I am not writing a letter home yet, although my thoughts run back to the three-day trip, first from my village by horse team, then a very slow train ride, lasting a full day. The small locomotive pulled many cars loaded with *quebracho* trunks for the tannin factory, with two coaches at the back carrying passengers. The train ploughed ahead slowly and laboriously with its heavy load through the monotonous bush and by evening we reached the river port, the gateway to the Chaco as Papa terms it.

The farewell from home was easier than I had feared. Mama contained herself and wished me God's guidance into a foreign world. It was Papa who initiated my trip into a different world. He possibly knew more about my loneliness in the village than I had assumed. Moreover, girls travel to the capital city more often now to earn money to help out their parents in times of relative hardship.

"Just go to Asunción for a year," he already told me before Christmas. "Girls find employment there quite readily."

He had then written Mr Penner, who represents our colony there and who quickly arranged for my employment. I was to work there in the household of an employee of the German mission, meaning diplomatic service. I will then send home money as much as I can and that will compensate for the bad feeling I have in leaving my parents alone to manage the farm.

Abraham took me to the train station, together with four other passengers. When I was already onboard the train, he called, "Lizzie, we shall join you shortly, the war will soon be over."

This is our every hope. France has been defeated, and Belgium, Holland, Denmark and Norway occupied, and now it's England's turn to lose. Indeed, I feel like a precursor and I will even work at the German mission for a German family.

The new world has already accepted me: electric light in my room; you flick a switch and there is light. Tiles on the floor, showers to be taken, sturdy columns bear the roof thatched with roof tiles and there is water in abundance.

Last night was almost like a welcome party for us. After I had showered and had dinner I noticed that people were congregating close to a stage. We, the Chaco travelers, also walked up to the action and I was stirred by a beautiful evening. A group of Paraguayan singers and musicians had assembled with guitars and a harp. They all wore blue trousers, white shirts and a red neck scarf, the colours of their flag. They sang and played quite heavenly and I stood as if in a dream on Neufeld's yard in our village, where a gramophone played and behind me stood Heinrich, who said, "I so much love these songs." I was in a melancholy mood and the memory of it all suited me just fine.

The singers sang "*Campamento, campamento*" and the sound carried, full of sweet, heavy longing through the languid evening air. The people around me applauded after every song and I was part of the enthusiasm. Every people have such glorious characteristics and such marvellous songs. Papa often spoke of the heart-rending Russian songs, and when he considered himself alone at work, he sang of the Volga and the Taiga.

Now we are waiting for the ship here in Casado. On Friday we are to steam upstream for two days to Asunción. Jake will be at the port to receive me. My life is full of happy tension.

And now I will go down to the edge of the river. I cannot get enough of the water.

Toro, 8 March 1941

*T*oro is our steamer and comes with giant paddlewheels on both sides. I now make a second effort to write. I had been sitting on a bench by the railing of the ship, but I had barely sat down, when Mrs Goosen came by and sat down by my side. We are not acquainted at all, but she told me things as if we were from the same village and soon I knew about the quarrels of neighbours and the mischievous pranks the boys played on the streets. These tied a tin can to the tail of old Mr Penner's horse and had it dash down the village street. "The mayor has given up on these kids," she said. Then she told me about her ailment and why she had to attend a physician in Asunción. Whether I too had to see a doctor, she asked, while giving me a quizzical look-over.

"Well, you know," she said with grave concern, "the young Mrs Wiens went to Asunción three months after her wedding to a doctor, so she said. Suspicion then arose as to whether the matter concerned a baby since she had barely gotten married. That is the way they simply want to deceive you a bit. When Mrs Wiens returned, two ministers from the church were sent to the Wienses. A twofold suspicion was lurking. First her lifestyle before the wedding, and then having the baby evidence disappear. But then it was determined that the matter was only one of an operation due. None of all the talk in the village applied. It is really quite dreadful how quickly gossip in a village is hatched." I was quite happy that Mrs Goosen soon left. She suffers pain and cannot sit for long.

Yes, indeed, since yesterday afternoon, we are steaming on the "Toro" in the direction of Asunción. When the steward noticed that I placed my diary on my knees to write, he invited me to the dining room of the First Class. I was to write at a table there. I was a bit embarrassed to do so because, firstly I do not know Spanish, and secondly, I travel way below decks, Third Class. However, I followed the friendly fellow.

Classy people sit here. They drink beer and discuss. I managed to grasp that they are discussing the war and that two parties are involved. They become constantly louder but I act as if I hear nothing.

Things in Third Class are poor but everyone from the colony travels this class because first class travel is very expensive. There is no second class. We had a good dinner last night, starting with a bowl of soup. Then a stew of rice, noodles and meat followed. Hard gelatos are invariably served, also with the sweet coffee for breakfast.

Come evening, when the sun was setting, I stood in front by the ship's bow and enjoyed the fresh air blowing over the waters during a glorious sunset, reflecting off the river. I had the feeling that everything fell off me, the entire load of the last years and months. I am heading for an unknown world of which I know nothing and everything lies before me like the fog on the water of the early morning, and yet I feel free and almost hover and had to hold on to the railing to keep from gliding in air.

Tomorrow, shortly before noon, we are meant to arrive in Asunción. We shall be skirting Rosario, that very port were all the Frieslander, who left our colony in 1937, disembarked on a former day. Who knows, I might very well see acquaintances from our village.

I had better quit my writing. The men at the other table have become very loud and have become good and mad about differences of opinion. It may well be that beer plays into that mix. I constantly hear talk about Alemania (Germany), Hitler, Churchill. The two Paraguayan officers appear to side with Germany. The others are foreigners, probably Americans.

The stewards have started setting the table. The friendly one smiles at me and I had better be off.

Asunción, 10 April 1941

I just wrote a long letter home. Also, I am able to send my parents the first surplus of my earned money. I am being paid well is what the other girls who also work tell me. Before the day is over, I intend to take the letter to Penners; there are often people at the Penners who take mail to the Chaco.

I wrote them about a most engagingly beautiful film, which we saw a week ago in the theater. It was a German film "The Postmaster" with Heinrich George and Hilde Krahl. It was the first film I saw in my life. Jake came for me like the cavalier he is. He wore a nice suit and we walked arm in arm through the streets. The first film in my life and it was such a marvel. When we later walked home, we were still humming the haunting Russian melodies from the film and I still do, now that I am at work. The Mr Secretary of the Embassy is smiling by now!

This film was one of the reasons for my long letter because I know how much Papa is interested in everything having to do with Russia. I wrote in detail about the story of Dunja and the glorious Russian landscape. The film was based on a story by Pushkin with the best German actors chosen for the lead roles.

I am employed by the secretary of the German Embassy. Recently he took me along to the Embassy where a film was being shown. He told me how to dress and he was fully satisfied with me. He introduced me as his housekeeper. The film was called "Blitzkrieg in the West" and some senior officials from the Paraguayan government were also in attendance.

"This causes the English and the Americans here in Asunción grave concern," Mr Secretary claimed. After the film, he introduced me to the ambassador Dr. Büsing. The ambassador asked me various questions. He knew that we come from Russia and that we had been in Germany for a short while. He had paid the colonies a visit once and he praised the courage and diligence of the Germans settlers. I surprised even myself at how readily I answered the ambassador's questions, considering that the room was full of dignitaries, and I, a shy daisy, among them all.

Everyone spoke enthusiastically about the film, and how the soldiers marched and sang, the tanks rolled, and the *stukas* (dive bombers) bombed with the Führer invariably being with his troops. At the conclusion, the victor's parade march in Paris was shown. An employee of the embassy translated everything into Spanish.

And yet, everything that I have described is marginal. My life here is work and that is the reason I came here. I am in charge of the secretary's household and I had to learn so much that was new, that

I was quite bewildered for days on end. I am in charge of the meals and have to issue instructions as to what is to be cooked and prepared, and I am in charge of all the shopping as well as supervising the personnel, and I have not even managed the Spanish language. So I simply had to show and lead by example.

Fortunately Mr Secretary demonstrates understanding towards me. "We are patient with you, Miss Elisabeth," he said time and again during the first days. "You are quick to learn, that is obvious. You are intelligent and you will master it all."

I felt myself blushing all over when he encouraged me, which served me well. Now, after more than one month I really feel like a housekeeper and I even speak Spanish already. It is surprising how quickly one learns when being dumped into the water and has to learn how to swim.

It is good to know that Jake is here. I can always reach him by telephone. I simply dial his number and he is there. In the afternoon, he attends university classes. A further source of consolation is my faith; no, it is the primary source. My Bible is on my night table and I regularly read it. Also, I always pray in all hard times and also when joy overcomes me. When I pray it seems to me that my and Mama's prayers join forces in the universe.

Recently, on a Sunday morning I read my Bible on the veranda. Mr Secretary appeared and he asked me all manner of questions regarding my faith, about Mennonites and their teachings. It was then that I noticed how little I really knew. However, Mr Secretary was very serious and he continued questioning. "There is much you still have to tell me," he said.

When we recently parted in the embassy after the film, Dr. Büsing said that he would like to speak to me again at some time, later. I was so flustered that I curtsied when he extended his hand to me. What may the ambassador well want to talk to me about? Sometimes when I lie abed, tired, in my little room in the evening and read a book, which Mr Secretary loaned me from his library, by the light of a lamp, I believe that my life here is not really real.

And now I shall hastily take this letter to the Penners while it is yet daylight. Girls are not allowed to walk the streets after sundown, Jake informs me. He will always come for me when we are invited out in the evenings.

21 April 1941

A real "folkfest" was celebrated at the German diplomatic mission yesterday. Mr Secretary had also invited me but I had to make the trip on my own. The street car travels along the Avenida Colombia and I know my way by now.

The Führer's birthday was celebrated, and many Germans from Asunción were in attendance. Fortunately Jake was also there. He knows the head of the BDM (Bund Deutscher Mädchen: Society of German Girls) well from the German School and she had arranged his invitation. Dr. Büsing stood at the entrance and received the guests. When he shook my hand, he asked, "How are you doing in school, Little Lady?"

This was the reason why the ambassador spoke to me after the film recently. Earlier in the subsequent week I received a telephone call from the embassy. I was to appear the next day. My heart beat loudly as I sat in the reception room. After a short while I was received in his chambers.

"I have something for you," he said in a friendly manner. "We have a German Evening School here. Would you not like to attend it? It is free to you and the education will stand you in good stead. You may be able to use it someday, and we as well."

All that was rather enigmatic for me and I was so taken aback that I barely managed a word. And yet, what more could I wish for than further education? Furthermore, the school lies in my proximity, only a short stretch by street car.

I nodded, "Yes, I would like to learn more, to know more."

"You know, Miss Unruh," the ambassador said, "I immediately knew that you are most capable and highly intelligent. It may well be that are tasks awaiting you of which you still have no idea. Our times surely hold yet many surprises and it will depend on us if we are properly prepared to master them. For this reason I would like to introduce this possibility to you."

I was overcome by a feeling of great joy after all these pleasant words. I would have liked to talk about my short schooling in Russia and that I later had no possibility to attend school. But then the Mr Ambassador rose and my time was over.

"I will make inquiries about you," the ambassador said and extended his hand. At the reception I received a confirmation which I was to present at the school.

At the reception yesterday Dr. Büsing held on to my hand firmly and I had to tell him various things about the school. He appeared to be most satisfied. Then I meandered among the many strange guests until I managed to locate Jake. He greeted me stormily and introduced me to his friends. Everyone laughed and talked and cracked jokes with our Jake in the centre of it all.

Then we walked through the rooms. There were swastikas everywhere. A large picture of the Führer was framed with flowers. In front of it four Hitler boys were standing with flags, at attention and stock still.

Then the celebration started with the Paraguayan and the German hymn. During the German hymn we all stood at attention with raised hands. Then the German ambassador gave a speech in Spanish and German. I had never heard so much about the Führer. In this war, Hitler will reverse the injustices which have been heaped on Germany. "Germany is fighting for the repudiation of an injustice, while the others are fighting to maintain it," said the ambassador. That is exactly what I had heard on the radio in Filadelfia.

Then Jake took my arm and said, "Come, Lizzie, now the fun will begin."

On the yard wieners, buns, pea soup and beer and most everything thinkable was served. There was constant eating and humming and carousing. The more beer people consumed, the louder things became. Jake handed me a glass of beer but I did not like the bitter taste of it.

Then a band played and people started dancing. If a known melody was played, everyone joined in the singing. "There once was a true hussar," "Enjoy your life", "Rosamunde," and on and on. Then Jake approached me and wanted to dance with me but I resisted. Firstly, I do not know how to dance and secondly my village came much to mind as did our church and Greta, David and Mama.

And yet, I found it all very happy and beautiful and I could not really say whether any of it was sinful. Happiness is surely no sin. Jake obviously felt no complexes, nor scruples. He was part of the happy action and no one would have guessed that he bore any whiff of the colony to him.

When Jake took me home and stayed a while, he said, "Do nothing which goes against your conviction, Lizzie. Be that what you can be and want to be; just remain true to yourself!"

I was thankful to him for these words and we spoke for a long time about life in the Chaco. There are so many comparisons to be drawn and I find these most interesting. How is it with the measuring gauge which one applies when confronted with new situations, and then evaluates or judges?

David would say that there is only one gauge, one measuring stick, and that is the Word of God, the Bible. However, was not our village a gauge, our Mrs Görzen, our church with its rules and regulations, or the Brethren with even stricter laws? Was not the entire colony a gauge, which permitted the one to live there and how, and the other one to not do so? The girl who had an affair with an officer preferred to disappear in Asunción, and the German teacher who introduced new ideas but was sent packing?

Here everything is evaluated differently. Then David stands before me and I hear him declare in his measured and quiet manner that such is the way of the world and don't be surprised. You are not to get involved and that is that. All that is highly interesting and I have given yesterday's day much reflective thought.

8 June 1941

It is good that there is a fireplace in Mr Secretary's apartment. I have the personnel light a fire there in the early morning, and so we at least have one warm room available. While doing so, I think longingly of our little kitchen at home when we were still all together by the hot stove, drinking *maté*.

Sundays like these can become very lonely. I have moved a little table closer to the fireplace so I can write. In the afternoon I go to the Penners. Mennonites living in Asunción occasionally gather there for church services. There are not many and everything is kept very simple. We sing the songs from our hymnal and someone reads a sermon from a book.

Then there is much to talk about, particularly news from the colonies and even more importantly about the war, which is known about in every detail from the radio news. It was there that I recently met Liese Braun from our village, who in 1937, moved to Friesland together with her parents. We are of the same age. Liese has married in the interim and has two children. She told me about the young people from Friesland who in 1939 traveled to Germany, more than twenty of them. They were invited to do so by one Mr Schröder, to become farmers in Germany. They call these farms inheritance farmyards. But now the war has come and one after the other has joined the military. We counted the boys whom we knew from our village: Peter, Heinrich, Jacob and Franz, and Liese knew others as well.

"Are their parents not worried, now that there is war? I asked.

"No," said Liese. "They are proud of their boys, and once the war is over, we all intend to go to Germany, every one of the Frieslander. Home to our Greater Germany."

I had to think of Papa and Abraham and how life in the Chaco is now unsettled and that many in the German circles recognize the danger to our faith. This appears not to be the case in Friesland.

There is no quarrel about this matter with the majority being is favour of their boys going to war.

Liese says, "If a letter from one of our boys, who has fought at the Front in Germany arrives, everyone in the village reads it, as well as proudly looking at the photos of our boys in uniform."

Jake joined us and he was all eyes and ears. "If only I would have gone along at that time," he said. "After the war I would have immediately attended university there, either in Berlin or in Heidelberg." But then all the memories made us very sentimental. We spoke about the good old times when we were altogether, the many Youth Meetings, the beautiful Youth Hours, the weddings and the funerals. I am alone again but I cannot compare my loneliness to that of my village which became more and more restrictive, threatening to choke me.

The Evening School three times a week fully occupies my time. I eagerly learn German and Spanish, with both being highly necessary. We read German poetry and excerpts from German poets. The teacher is greatly surprised that I already know Goethe and Mörike and Hermann Hesse and so she addresses me frequently during her lessons.

The Evening School lends out books, and the library of Mr Secretary is available to me as well so that I hardly know where to start in so much happy profusion of reading material. Mr Secretary gave me some books to read from the war, unfolding, like *My Journey to Scapa Flow* by Günter Prien, a submarine commander, and also a book by Edwin Erich Dwinger, *Death in Poland*.

I asked Mr Secretary for permission to send this book to Papa. "Gladly," he said, "and extend my greetings to him; we are happy that there are people here and in the Chaco with a German consciousness."

I believe that I have become a bit proud. I am proud of belonging to these German people and that I am aware that I am of use. Recently Mr Secretary said to me, "Miss Elisabeth, the ambassador displays great interest in you. I would not want to lose you as my housekeeper, but you are born to higher things."

I believe I again blushed all over. I have become more confident of myself, since I am mastering both German and Spanish well and

I also find my dealings with people improving. To become proud, we were told in Sunday School, means drifting from the right path. Joseph did not become proud when he achieved high honour. When I say 'proud' I mean something different. I mean a feeling of happiness, joy and everything that lifts me out of my loneliness. If loneliness and depression is equivalent to humility, then I am happy that I am no longer humble.

The identical words remain: pride, humility, but they fill me with a different content. I intend to remain humble and retain the fear of God like Joseph did, even if, as Mr Secretary claims, I am born to higher things.

23 June 1941

After such a hectic day like yesterday, I have to withdraw into my little room. I have to document this experience because I believe that it was a stroke of fate which will be decisive for the future of all of us.

I already noticed the excitement of it all in the early morning. The telephone rang often and loud and I heard Mr Secretary speak excitedly. We generally laze about on Sunday mornings and I am required to serve coffee only at nine. However, yesterday everything was abuzz at seven, possibly even six. When I then appeared in the kitchen in my house coat, Mr Secretary was already in hat and overcoat. "I am underway to the embassy," he said excitedly. "Miss Elisabeth, war with Russia. This morning our troops attacked. Just at the last moment. Otherwise Stalin would have surprised us."

And then he was gone, without coffee or breakfast, and I was left alone, open-mouthed and a wildly beating heart. I was beside myself and ran from the dining room to the kitchen and back again. Russia. Stalin, and all our people, Isaak and Maria, what will become of us now? And then I thought of Papa and Abraham, and I suddenly felt an incredible distance to them all. It was Papa's dream that Hitler would settle a score with Stalin. It was the great disappointment when the two signed a pact. And now it had all come to this.

I see Mama crying for joy. Hope and fear, and I saw Papa full of pride that the political events were now finding fulfillment as he had wished it.

I had not yet composed myself when the telephone rang. It was Jake calling. "Hitler has attacked Russia!" he screamed with his voice doing summersaults. "Lizzie, I cannot believe it. Now Russia will fall as the Balkans fell and Crete." Then he became more subdued. "I will come around this afternoon. Dress up nicely and then we will go to the Vertua; you'll be my guest."

And there we sat in the elegant restaurant. Jake was wearing a stylish suit while I wore my dark jacket dress which I have purchased for special occasions. It was pleasantly warm in the locale with many elegant guests seated all around. The men had newspapers to hand with everyone talking about the war, about the unexpected, the great event, which would shortly change the world. You could feel the excitement in the air.

Strange, but Jake and I spoke about our village in Russia and about our childhood in Rosenthal, and the warm summer days when the grain was harvested and the hayracks with sheaves coming into the barn. We spoke about the peaceful years prior to our fleeing when Lenin introduced the NEP, the New Economic Policy, as it came to be known. Our farmers again seeded and harvested and everyone hoped that things would again improve, even under Communism. Jake spoke about our beautiful horses in the stable: Mischka and Halka and about our cows. But then Stalin put an end to everything. The Five Year Plan came like a frost over the land in 1928. Papa was entered in the Black List. Men were seized in the middle of the night by the GPU and we fled one midnight to Moscow. All that became clear to us children only much later.

"Jake, you would also go to war like the Frieslander boys?" I asked.

"Well, of course," he replied, "And now that Bolshevism is being attacked, for doubly sure. Who can then sit at home and watch idly by?"

"David would remain at home," I said. "For David neither Stalin nor Bolshevism would be reason enough to change his position and depart from the faith of our fathers and to give up our C. O. status of the Anabaptists and our Mennonitism."

"This faith of our fathers," said Jake. "I cannot any longer stand to hear this; I've had enough of all that. I cannot live with such conflict. It is not that my faith is gone and it is not as if all that has disappeared what I bear in my heart from my village days at home and our discussions to that end, Lizzie, but now my heart burns with excitement for our people, and for our Motherland and for the New Germany. I am ready to lay down my life for all this. Is it not a service to God to sacrifice one's life for others? If I think of Germany at night, my life knows fully what is right."

"That is a Heine quotation," I said.

When it turned dark, we went to a movie theatre. We watched an American film about Tarzan and animals in the jungle, a film in glorious colours. Prior to that we watched in the weekly show how the Germans attacked Crete. The soldiers jumped out of airplanes and glided in their parachutes down into the battle. So much discipline, so much heroism and then the victory. Sometimes I think that I have forgotten everything that happened two years ago and that was so important to me like what went on in the Bible School and the End Times and how we eagerly leafed around in the Bible to find documentation of the animal in the abyss and Armageddon.

I feel as if I glide in the air in a new world, in a world of enthusiasm in a hope for the future like the German soldiers in their parachutes. It is only that I intend to mount upwards and not downwards.

And still my heart trembles in the conflict of it all. I intend to read my Bible before I go to bed and I want to pray. I want to pray for Germany and her soldiers, who now will meet their death, and for Isaak and Maria in the uncertain fate of our villages in Russia. I want to pray for a world living in peace once it has been freed of Bolshevism.

22 July 1941

Death comes so unexpectedly, so suddenly. Three short months ago we celebrated the birthday of the Führer at the embassy and now Dr. Büsing is dead. The day before yesterday he died suddenly at age 61. All the glitter and the pomp at the occasion, the speech by the ambassador, his faith in a German victory is now all over and without meaning.

And as for me? I invariably had the feeling that the dignified gentleman regarded me as a father does his child. I associated hope with his kindly disposition towards me even though I did not know what kind. Mr Secretary repeatedly made suggestions, secretive in nature, and although I did not know what to make of them, my hopes and expectations were engaged. My attendance at the Evening School has not been affected and Mr Secretary informed me today that I should press on. "For you nothing has changed, Miss Elisabeth," he assured me.

Possibly nothing at all has changed. Death claims a human being with others assuming the role and life goes on as before. Such was the case with Mr Penner in our village whose wife died and after three months he married again, and such is also probably the case when high dignitaries die. But all this is probably superficial thinking.

The war progresses with victories reported, of a kind that no one had expected. I have written long letters to my parents about what we daily hear and read. The German troops destroy the enemy in giant battles of encirclement as they are called, and they are now advancing up to the Dnieper. Mama's heart will flutter. And oh, how they will all weep and pray!

All that is of no significance to Dr. Büsing any longer. "Come along to the German cemetery," Mr Secretary told me. It was quite simple. I simply boarded the street car and traveled many kilometres on the entirety of the Avendida Colombia up to the Cemetery Recoleta. I joined the many mourners, consisting of Paraguayans and Germans, and all being dignitaries. The small cemetery filled up, black with mourners.

A swastika lay on the coffin. A German pastor spoke the eulogy and told of a man who had placed his life at the service of others, and above all in the service of the *Reich*. Then the representative of the Paraguayan government spoke, followed by the Italian ambassador. Before the coffin was lowered into the grave, a band played very slowly, "I once had a true comrade."

This sad melody drove tears to my eyes and I became aware how much reason I had to be grateful to him. But then my thoughts were diverted. The melody suddenly took my every thought back to the Chaco. I walked with Jake along the narrow bush path in search of our oxen. It was a world so totally in order at the time, not even ten years ago. We walked barefoot in the sand and sang the song "I once had a true comrade" which Jake had learned in school and we dreamed about our happiness, lying before us.

These dreams have drifted apart like the clouds, barely formed already scattered by the wind. I suddenly felt how alone I was in the midst of many. When the clods of earth thundered on the coffin and

the most beautiful of wreaths were carried away, I departed the cemetery.

I had time for myself after the funeral since I had the afternoon free. And so I entered the church close by. At the entrance sat miserable human forms, crippled, dissipated people, wasted, begging. Then I entered the large cemetery from one mausoleum to the next. I read the names and looked at the coffins in the niches.

At one site many bronze tablets had been inserted in memory of the fallen in the Chaco War. Boquerón was there, Corrales, Toledo. That was ten years ago as well. I sat down on the stone bench alongside, closed my eyes and let the riders pass by my mind's eye, the troops in the sand and the trucks, which laboriously ploughed their way through the heavy sand of our village street. Heinrich sat in one of those trucks and smiled from his pilot seat. "It is impossible, Heinrich."—"I know, Lizzie."

Then I sat down in the street car and rattled back the long track down the Avenida.

10 August 1941

Jake took me home. We had both attended the church service at the Penners. We love to sing the songs, Jake as well. We prefer the songs from the Evangelical Hymnal with the more lively melodies. Since there are no hymnals, someone has to read the song texts. "Your gentle face looks at me, be it day or be it night" or "If life's storms beset you, and the strongest barely stand". Jake says he prefers the chorales. We sing along with great fervour and soon we are in spirit in our small school in our village in the Chaco with Papa and Mama. Then our faith envelopes us even if the sermon is often heavy and monotonous.

Mr Secretary happily allows Jake to come to our apartment and we sit around for a while. Today he even offered us a bottle of German wine, Mosel wine, and we were allowed to imbibe all by ourselves. Then Jake played the butler which he does with grace and aplomb. I drank a whole glass of the sweet wine. Jake laughed and said, "Careful, Lizzie, your eyes are already glistening." It was all very nice. We became happy and laughed a lot. Then I told Jake about the secretive intimations of the Mr Secretary, and he became most attentive. "Look out, Lizzie, what you may get involved with," he said.

But now I was the one who waxed courageous. "I would like to escape the confinement," was my answer. "I would like to experience something and sometimes I feel that I am sprouting wings. I would like to widen my wingspan like a white heron and glide over the trees and the waters, higher and higher. Do you remember our ponds at home and how we watched these glorious birds?"

Then Jake laughed and said, "Lizzie, before you know it, you'll be a poet. Why don't you write a poem about the white heron gliding over the water?" We both laughed, because the wine got us going.

But then Jake turned serious. Sometimes this happens very suddenly with him. "Or a poem about a black heron hovering over dead animals, carrion, which glide just as beautifully. Hopefully you will not get involved in the workings of this war in which you will be appointed, as clever and innocent girls are when needed."

Then he talked about the war and of the tensions also here in Asunción because the English and Americans are exerting ever mounting pressure on our government on account of our good relations with Germany.

Then Jake left and I slipped quickly into my room in order to pen these lines. Then a warm bed awaits me and a book on my bedside table lamp. Can anything be better?

I have discovered a real treasure in Mr Secretary's library; it is a volume of German poetry entitled *The German Heart*. It contains all my most beautiful poems by Mörike, Hesse, Goethe and Löns and many more. I discover something new all the time. I did not know Ricarda Huch at all. I find her love poem rather hard. "I long for you like the flood longs for the strand, like the swallow in fall for the southern land, like the Alpine son when at night thinks divine, of the mountains of snow in the bright sunny shine."

I thought that this longing had long since been quenched in me and only a spent black coal mound remained like after a bitter grass fire. But then it remains glimmering under the ashes.

If Ricarda Huch touches the strings of the lyre so tenderly, then my heart likewise vibrates, even though I know that these are words, wonderfully beautiful words. And why should I not allow them to softly resound, just softly resound like this evening after happy laughter with the Mosel wine? Ricarda Huch will now find space in my collection as well.

7 September 1941

I took a brisk walk to the Penners yesterday to check on letters from the Chaco. It is a good stretch to walk but during daylight I can manage it well. En route I like to take in the various parks where I sit on benches and watch the affairs of the day. The upper class walk the parks with their children, while the petty merchants sit on the sidewalks. These are salespeople who sell *chipa*, a pastry made from corn meal and sweet meats. In front of me the shoe shine boys bustle about chasing their glass marbles until someone comes along to have his shoes polished.

I had much hoped for mail and, indeed, a letter from my parents had arrived. I sat down in a quiet corner in the inner courtyard and read a lengthy letter from Papa, which amounted to a war report. The radio in Filadelfia obviously works overtime in reporting now that the war is raging in Russia. "Now the Dnieper is already in German hands," writes Papa, "and so are our German villages over there."

It is hardly conceivable that our people over there have been liberated. We know nothing more than that the Germans are there and that the names Dnepropetrovsk and Zaporozhe are mentioned.

"We hope and pray that Isaak and Maria are now free," Papa writes, "and all the others as well."

Papa often told us how the Germans in 1918 were greeted as saviours when they arrived in the colonies in Ukraine because the Civil War and the marauding bands had previously devastated everything so dreadfully. And now he reports about all this again with comparisons made to former times, as well as of now.

Papa also writes about the tensions in our colony and the various parties which have been organized. However, the war in Russia has shaken them all up to reality.

"And now the group intending to remain in the Chaco has become small," he writes, "and probably all will now realise that we finally need a permanent home after a hundred years of wandering around in foreign lands, in strange surroundings. Now all the Germans will be brought home to the *Reich* of Greater Germany."

But then I think of David and others from our Bible School, as well as Peter, and I am certain that they will not change their position. They will never allow anything beyond their faith of missionizing the Indians to prevail.

Papa's thinking in these matters is different. "God is everywhere, ubiquitous; not only in the Chaco and not only among us Mennonites. I believe He has led us here but also that He will lead us back again."

While reading my letter, I notice that for me all that what is happening in the Chaco now has disappeared in a past distance, as if it remains far distant from me. And yet, I did not really run away. It appears to me that I have been carried away, possibly even hurled away by a centrifugal force. And now I allow myself to be carried, to drift, and I hope that I will be carried away to new shores.

It is a Sunday afternoon. In the afternoon Jake will come along and then we will read Papa's letter together. We will discuss it and then attend a church service together after which we will see a movie.

The films *Festival of the People* and *Festival of Beauty*, documentaries with Leni Riefenstahl about the Olympics in Berlin are being shown. Jake claims Riefenstahl's films are superb. A year ago he saw *Triumph of Faith* and *Triumph of the Will*. Jake says that these films are running in Asunción much to the chagrin of the English and Americans.

The Americans here wanted to show the film "The Great Dictator" with Charlie Chaplin in which Hitler and Mussolini are ridiculed. Our government did not allow this, so as not to insult nations friendly to us.

8 September 1941

I am still completely dazed by the films I saw yesterday and I am equally as dazed by what Mr Secretary today told me. I still hear the cheering crowd on the bleachers and I still marvel at the athlete's achievements from around the world.

We slowly walked home, Jake and I did, overcome by a feeling of great joy. "I am so happy that I belong to this people," said Jake. I could not agree more.

This morning a surprise struck, which still haunts me. At breakfast, Mr Secretary asked me how I was doing and I excitedly told him about the films we had seen. But he did not allow me to go any further.

"Miss Elisabeth," he said. "Mr von Lewetzow has summoned you to the embassy. Would you go there tomorrow morning?"

My mouth probably stood agape. Mr Secretary laughed, "Have no fear, Miss Elisabeth," he said, "everything will be in your very best interest."

In spite of his reassurance, I am excited and an inner pulsation trembles within me. Mr Werner von Lewetzow is the successor to Dr. Büsing. He was dispatched here from Argentina after the death of the ambassador. He is a younger gentleman.

I am a bit uneasy. It appears that I am standing before a great body of water and I am to master it on my own. All others remain behind, even Jake. I would like to speak to Papa now. Jake is of two opinions in the matter. At times he warns me, and then again he sees no danger at all. If it were up to him he would have been off and to the Front a long time ago, if such an opportunity had presented itself.

He is envious of the Frieslander boys and maybe he will also envy me.

In any case, I will call him later today.

10 September 1941

Now I know everything and I know nothing. My heart jumps for joy and pride while at the same time I tremble all over. I feel elevated like from a wave, valued and respected and I float in uncertainty like in a starless night.

Mr von Lewetzow had me enter his room as soon as I arrived at the embassy. He asked me to sit in a comfortable chair while he sat opposite to me.

"Miss Elisabeth," he said in a measured voice. "You are a competent woman. I have the best of information on you and the highest recommendations. You are intelligent, and in the school which my predecessor recommended for you, you are the best. We also know that you have a heart full of love for Germany. All good Germans are ready today to render a service wherever the Fatherland might require them."

I must have beamed. I saw that in the friendly face of the ambassador as if in a mirror. Mr von Lewetzow then asked me many questions regarding my place of birth, my parents, the Mennonites in the Chaco, and I answered, constantly becoming freer and more candid. It was as if the friendliness and the interest of the ambassador released my tongue.

We also talked about the Mennonites in Russia and about our villages by the Dnieper, which are now in German hands, freed from the bolshevist yoke. While talking, I noticed that the ambassador's interest mounted. We entered into a proper dialogue, the kind of which I had never had with a person of such high order.

"Miss Elisabeth," Mr von Lewetzow then said, "it may well be that we will soon be in need of your services. Do not become flustered. We will not expose you to any danger. I am telling you this so that you can consider the matter fairly and in your own good time. Your cooperation will be totally voluntary. You will not be required to do anything which goes against your conviction. However, I do request that you conduct yourself with discretion. As you know, there is war and in times of war one has to expect enemies. Speak to no one whose confidence you doubt."

I mentioned my brother and my parents. I did not want to leave them out of the picture when it came to making decisions. Mr von Lewetzow nodded his agreement.

Then we clarified a practical question which was of great importance for me. This is the matter of my citizenship and my documents. I have nothing and I am nothing. When we fled Russia, we all lost our Russian citizenship and we traveled from Germany to Paraguay as stateless people. That has not changed. No one owns a passport. Many in the Chaco now want to acquire German citizenship. When I intended to travel to Asunción, the colony administration issued me a certificate that I was "Mennonita"; which is sufficient in Paraguay.

"We will issue you a German passport," said Mr Ambassador. "That is only a temporary measure, but assuming German citizenship during a war is impossible. After the war is over, we will resolve everything in an orderly fashion."

Then he took me to a different department and took his leave. Here I presented my personal information. I had to provide a photo. Then I would receive a German passport. Jake will burst with envy. I know well that Jake observes my every move with great interest.

"Lizzie," he said on Sunday when he took me home after the movies, "you are starting to blossom. You are becoming constantly more beautiful and more complete. I often think of how you looked in 1939 when I came home for Christmas. You were a wreck, cast about by the waves, every which way."

When I arrived home and was alone in my room I could not sleep for a long time, and even today it is as if the waves are really beating my every plank; the waves of joy about everything new and the waves of the past, my faith, by which I was still willing to let myself be borne unconditionally.

I intend to call Jake tomorrow because I have need to talk to someone. Also, I intend to write a letter to my parents although I do not want to unduly excite them. Mama has her plate full with what is going on in Russia. Ten o'clock has gone. On my night table lies my Bible and a volume of poetry. Lizzie, easy now, nice and slow!

13 October 1941

Yesterday was a holiday. Discovering America. It was as if Jake had taken my hand and led me into a whole new world. We spent the afternoon on the German athletic complex which the Germans in Asunción constructed from donations and voluntary labour. Jake and some other young men from the colonies, university students all, have diligently assisted in the endeavour, as if they were part of it all. They helped in the construction of the swimming pool with the sweat of their brows and the calluses of their hands. Jake told me that they had moved the earth by wheelbarrows on free weekends and sometimes even on Sundays.

And now Jake had invited me. "We will go swimming, Lizzie," he said, "and you will join in." I became unsteady, uncertain of myself… to go swimming with so many people? But then I got ready for it all. I bought a red swimsuit, a giant bath towel and a suitable swimming cap with all coming in an appropriate bag.

When I emerged from the changing room into the bright sun I was surprised at myself since I felt so comfortable and well and without a shred of hesitancy. This may be because no one stands out in the least. No one said a word; no one took the slightest notice.

But then I was reminded of how badly things went when a few girls went bathing with the boys at home, in another day. During an outing they had all jumped into a lagoon in their dresses because no one there owned a bathing suit. When that episode became known, the entire matter was dragged into church with many being highly excited, particularly the women. That would never have happened in Russia, or if, only if the girls had kept strictly to themselves, the women said.

"Have the young girl church members lost all shame?" a young man called out to the church assembly? "What kind of temptation is it for our young men to see girls in wet clothes?"

At the time I sat dreadfully embarrassed on my church bench, not knowing what to think. I felt horribly sorry for the three girls who had to go to the front of the assembled and ask for forgiveness. At the same time I asked myself why they had acted so imprudently. Surely they should have contained themselves and thought of the consequences. Those were my thoughts at that time. And now I walked into the bright light of the sun among hundreds of others and felt neither shy, nor shame.

Jake ran up to me and danced around me, calling, "Lizzie, you are beautiful, Lizzie, you are so beautiful!" We took each other's hands and ran across the green lawn with no one taking notice of us.

Jake dove head first into the water. I entered the pool from the shallow end because I cannot swim. I sank blissfully into the cool water. It was glorious. We frolicked in the water for a full hour.

At the refreshment area, a gramophone played German marches and songs, and some people started dancing. I wrapped my towel around myself and we sat down at a table. Jake had a beer and I enjoyed some ice cream. I was so free and relaxed and felt pure joy all around and within me. We spoke about the Leni Riefenstahl films and empathized with the athletes.

"In our villages, everything is so restrictive and confining," said Jake, "and they call that piety. You have shed all that, Lizzie, and now you are finally coming into full bloom, like the Queen of the Night in the Chaco bush."

Of course I felt much flattered; after all, which girl does not want to be beautiful? And if I draw a comparison between this sports complex and the three girls at home, who had to do penance before a full church congregation, I have to side with Jake's opinion. What has all that to do with piety? I did all that today and possibly even a bit more and I have no sinful feelings.

In the meantime I know that my faith is not only that what our village and my church has made out of me. Things go deeper, much deeper. More things and occurrences may yet freely drop from me and be rid of, and I will still retain that what gives me strength and keeps me balanced, maintains my equilibrium, while at work at Mr Secretary, during my conversations with the ambassador, or at the Penners, and when we sing the old songs, or yesterday's pleasure at the sports complex.

When I told Jake all this yesterday, he looked at me long and hard. Then he pronounced, "Lizzie, you also give me strength!"

It stirs me when I also find in the book *From the German Heart* beautiful passages about faith. It contains songs which we sang already in Sunday School like "Fairest Lord Jesus" as an example. Others again are totally new to me, deep and serious. I have already copied one by Novalis.

> *"If only I have Him.*
> *And only He is mine,*
> *When my heart onto the grave*
> *His loyalty, I'll not pine,*
> *Then sorrow is a stranger*
> *And I know nothing but devotion, love and joy, divine."*

2 November 1941

I had the day free as did Jake. He came for me in mid-morning and we then took the street car to Ricoleta, the large cemetery. On Michaelmas much action ensues there and we wanted to be part of it.

"We have to get to know the Paraguayan people better," said Jake. "They do things differently in so many areas and only after getting to know them, can one understand them better."

Jake had many good contacts to the soldiers during the Chaco War and his Spanish is so good by now that I barely detect differences between his use of the language and the Paraguayans. He also speaks Guarani as easily as we speak Low German at home.

In front of the large church, which is the entrance to the cemetery, sat many women selling flowers and candles. Jake spoke with them and had them explain the customs and habits of the Michaelmas holiday. I listened attentively since I know enough Spanish by now to understand.

Then we followed a funeral procession. The procession of carrying coffins into the church is never ending; these are the coffins of poor people. The priest sprinkles holy water on the coffins, murmurs a prayer, and then the group moves on to the cemetery, where far behind the beautiful family crypts of the wealthy, shallow ditches have been dug, long rows of them.

We followed the group and the wailing women mourners. I watched one woman who repeatedly cried in the same tone and called out the name of the deceased. As soon as the ditch had been filled in, there was dead silence, and then they were on their way, having done their duty.

We then meandered slowly through the streets between the beautiful mausoleums where the relatives sat ceremoniously on chairs. In front of the coffins, covered with nice artwork, candles were burning.

"They are praying for the souls of the dead," said Jake.

I was reminded of our miserable cemeteries back home. The sand mounds are dispersed by the wind and the rain and after a short while, one barely notices the location of the grave. No one gives a thought to the souls of the dead, for anyone who was not converted while alive and not saved, is also lost in death. Then no candle, no mass and no prayer before the mausoleum is of any use. I told Jake about my thoughts.

"Don't be so sure about that," he suggested, "Who can claim that what we were taught in Sunday School is alone valid?"

We engaged in a hefty quarrel. We have to depend on biblical evidence, was my opinion. However Jake stated that we have also to respect the faith of others and as to what transpires after death is something unknown, and not even known to the reverend ministers Reimer and Wiebe.

I left him to his thinking.

Then we again sat in the street car. "Is it not a contradiction, Jake?" I asked him. "You are euphoric about Germany as if it were the only and highest aim of your life while here people believe you are part of them. That is the way you speak to the people and about them as they do about you."

"Do you remember how Papa spoke about the Russians?" he answered, "about their workers, their customs, their songs? We will always live in this dilemma, for as long as we live abroad. And I find the tension resulting from the dilemma beautiful, certainly bearable and interesting."

"Would you love a Paraguayan girl?" I asked him.

Jake gave me no answer, but there are times when he hides a half-hidden smirk so that I do not know what he means or thinks.

Then we were quiet as the street car rattled along and passengers got on and off. Animated by the discussion about the Paraguayans, I let my thoughts roam in times of distant past. They also went looking for Heinrich but found him not.

13 December 1941

This week was full of excitement although things started so relaxed and peacefully. Now the entire world is at war, verily, the entire globe. I feel the tension in our house, and Mr Secretary believes, that in the very foreseeable future, Paraguay will sever diplomatic relations with the axis powers. The pressure exerted by the United States becomes ever greater and now, that the USA has also entered the war, the smaller countries in South America, which are basically friendly to, and with, Germany will not be allowed to prevail. Then much will change, says Mr Secretary. Some changes have already happened to me.

We had a great and promising plan for December 7, involving a large youth group from the colonies, which is working here or attending university.

December 8, the great festival of the Virgin Saint of Caacupé, the grandest festival of the Catholic Church in Paraguay, is celebrated and a holiday reigns over the entire land. On Sunday we all went by bus to Caacupé, and on Monday, on the holiday, we intended to relax.

We had a glorious trip by bus on a beautiful asphalt highway. Jake claimed that this road was built with American credit, which obviously obligated Paraguay to the donor, just as England had Uruquay in its pocket when the *Admiral Graf Spee* lay in port at Montevideo at the mouth of the La Plata River.

This new road leads over an elevation with a view far into the countryside, right up to Lake Ypacarai. In Caacupé many people had gathered; there was hectic activity everywhere with many pilgrims thronging, and all awaiting the wonder-working virgin and the forgiveness of sins. Once a year all sins are forgiven here, our group observed rather caustically.

It is a hard penance for the sinners when they have to ascend Mount Cristo Rey. Many carry heavy rocks in order to rid themselves of their sins. What might well be more difficult, I pondered, to carry a rock up the Cristo Rey or go before a church assembly and confess your sin?

We all climbed up the rock, and when we reached the summit, I was out of breath. My dress clung to me with sweat since the summer day was intensely hot. We sat down on the top rock and consumed our beverages and ate our lunch brought along for the occasion.

When I asked the question about the forgiveness of sins everyone laughed. No one had drawn the comparison between our churches and the Cristo Rey before.

"I would rather carry a stone up the rock," said Jake while again grinning with his usual touch of mild blasphemy.

But then the conversation took a serious turn. Anna from Friesland, and a quiet girl, asked, "How severe must the sin be in order for a sinner having to carry a rock up to the mountain, and what kind of sin is it?

"We can only draw comparisons," said Franz, a university student. "How severe must the sin be for the sinner to appear before the congregation and what kind of sin is it?"

"Ach," said Anna, "I believe all of us living in Asunción would have been called to confession; our merely living here constitutes sin and qualifies for confession. Whoever in the colonies lives like we live and does what we do, surely would have had to appear before the assembled congregation." Anna looked very sad, while saying this and no one laughed. And then she spoke again, the quiet Anna did. "I believe that all manner of things which constitute sinning in our villages is no sin at all. Sin is probably evaluated according to the environment and according to custom," Then she looked at me. "Lizzie, I recently saw you at the sports complex in your bathing suit and I knew that that was no sin, but at the same time I had our church in mind."

"If only things were that simple," said Franz "then one could pick the preferred spot in which to live and not commit sin. If you go to Germany, like the Frieslander boys do, you go to war and do not sin in doing so. And anyone who stays behind in the Chaco, has to remain a pacifist in order not to sin."

"And now," said Jake, "let's get up and going before we organise a new church in which we can carry stones for sins committed." Then he walked up to Anna and said, "You are right, my girl, things are just that complicated." Then a smile crossed Anna's pale face. When departing, everyone again became merry, and we commenced a happy descent.

When arriving home, the news of Japan having attacked the Unites States at Pearl Harbour surprised us. The very next day "America" declared war, and on the 11th of December, Germany and Italy declared war on the United States. And now the world's on fire.

That same day Mr Secretary summoned me. He explained the war situation to me and then he asked me, if I were prepared to go to Buenos Aires, if the shop here were to close. "You have a German passport and you have experienced a lot while here," he said. "They have need of you there."

I was surprised at myself, since I remained perfectly at ease. "Mr Secretary," I said, "may I consider the matter in peace? May I speak to my parents about the matter?"

"You may do that," said Mr Secretary, friendly as usual, "and if you have any questions or if you have reached a decision, come to see me. The ambassador extends his greetings to you."

I have not done anything as of yet, I have said nothing and I have written nothing. At night when my heart flutters, I seek refuge in prayer.

The reader will please permit me an insert here, for I have to condense parts of the pending third section. The reader is to be guided to what is decisive and determining in Elisabeth's life, and which then leads to the fourth and concluding chapter of her diary and of her life.

The third chapter obviously represents the pinnacle in Elisabeth's short life, at least as far as concerns the external part of her life. She frequently employs metaphors like water, storm and waves, which carry, drift apart, then again raise her: forces of destiny, which determine her life, and lift it into an unforeseen direction and into unforeseen circumstances...

It is explicitly in this third part where all this gains prominence as nowhere else. It is also noticeable in the length of actions described. It is also noticeable in the critical candidness of the author, now approaching thirty years of her life, and in her serene acceptance of it all. I also notice this in the writing style, in the penmanship of her ink pen. The earlier pointed and sharp-edged writing of a school girl has developed into rounded graphics from which a graphologist might conclude what Elisabeth only implies in a self-evaluation that seemingly borders on the curious.

The question arises as to what might have motivated the German ambassador to invest such measure of trust and confidence in her, and to which she responds, "These people obviously recognized my interest, my initiative and my honesty."

I will skip an entire year and will resume her entries dating December 1942. The political skies grow ever darker. Only in retrospect does this become obvious. At that time, faith in Germany remained unbroken. Propaganda, and possibly even more the wishful thinking of the Germans Abroad, as the Paraguayan Mennonites liked to call themselves led the way to that end.

The 15th of January 1942 represented a fateful day for South America. At a conference in Rio, the United States unmistakably demonstrated its hegemony on both American continents, with the Latin American Republics becoming dependent satellites of their powerful brother. The official word statement of that time read that Japan to the West, and the fascist states of Europe to the East, represented a threat to the continents.

On the 25th of January 1942 Paraguay broke its diplomatic relations with Germany, Italy, and Japan. On the evening of that very day, the secretary of the embassy summoned Elisabeth to a meeting. Her diary entry of the next day read, "The Honourable Secretary informed me that Paraguay had succumbed to the pressures exerted by the United States and Brazil. Now everything has changed, also for us. We were treated with great chivalry by Paraguay, he said, but the entire ambassadorial personnel will depart this country."

Elisabeth received an order to assume charge of the house, the furniture and the personal effects of the secretary, until such time as she would be issued further instructions. Her condition was that she be allowed to visit her parents in the Chaco one more time.

Elisabeth then describes the trip and her visit to her village. It is obvious that she has gained distance and independence from it all and her growing self-confidence is evident towards her parents, and also a certain independence, even towards her church. What is particularly apparent is her independence from societal pressure, which was previously so powerful for her, as well as for most others, especially her mother.

When she entered to attend the church service in her small school, with her modern hair style and Asunción dress, she mentions the atmosphere consisting of curiosity and rejection, which met her. However, she managed it without a dent to her composure. On the contrary, it was the gauge of her independence and her resilience which she had attained, and which now prevailed. These were the attributes which would stand her in ever better stead.

And yet Elisabeth never divorced herself from her community; she probably could not have managed to do so had she tried. This becomes particularly obvious in the fourth chapter. But she has attained distance from it all, and, in some measure, come to terms with her independence. It is explicitly this love of community to which she is fatefully connected and even seems to have become more secure.

It is above all her faith, the seed of which was laid in her childhood, which she now bears with her to a totally new world, a world with completely new standards and norms. In this new world no one asks about her background or whatever evaluative borders or barriers might exist, and which come into considered play. And yet the plant of her faith prevails—without confusing metaphors—against every force and flood, and appears even to have strengthened from the time her village milieu forced her to depart from Heinrich, or when she sought refuge in piety and ended disappointed.

When Elisabeth returned to Asunción in the middle of 1942, her landlord had already departed. He had left behind explicit instructions, as well as a carte blanche ticket for a voyage to Buenos Aires. As soon as she had resolved everything in Asunción, she was expected in Argentina, a cosmopolitan city with world events.

To act as the trustee for an entire inheritance as the secretary stipulated, in our day has an audacious ring to it, rather than one of inspiring confidence, and Elisabeth was overcome with insecurity. She called upon Mr Penner for advice.

"Oh my, oh my, my dear girl, what have you gotten yourself involved with?" he said, shaking his head. But he stood by her, and advised her and finally everything was satisfactorily resolved as per instructions issued her. The furniture was fetched, the expenses paid, and Elisabeth was free for the trip into the wide world, and to duties of which she had not the slightest notion.

At that time Argentina was regarded as the bastion for the Germans, despite the ever-mounting pressure of the Allies on South America. The Argentinean government made every effort to now retain its neutrality, which it had steadfastly maintained during the First World War. And while Argentina was forced to agree to the Rio resolution, it managed to determine independently when it would sever diplomatic relations.

Elisabeth boarded a river steamboat in December 1942, which took her downstream to Buenos Aires on a three day trip.

Ciudad de Corrientes,
12 December 1942

Yesterday a new chapter in my life started and I am eagerly looking forward to it. The time in Asunción and the contact with people there have given me much confidence. I have honoured the trust and the confidence of Mr Secretary and he repeatedly confirmed that he was happy to have met a person whom he could trust. In these times, he said, such trust is rare and therefore all the more necessary and valuable.

"Who in these times intends to live, better have a brave heart," the young people now sing in the colonies. As a result of the folkloristic work among the youth, many new songs are being sung, probably the same which are being sung in Germany as well, and particularly folk songs.

I felt the enthusiasm in various youth groups but I also sensed the reservations older people had, like ministers, and particularly in the evangelistic church which was called the Alliance Church in Russia. The conditions in the colony were very tense as a result and talks with Abraham and David sufficed to inform me.

I sit by the railing on a comfortable bench in First Class and have my diary on my knees. Glorious! I had a breakfast, not yet dreamed about, and my cabin has ventilators and every conceivable comfort. My ticket for the steamer *Ciudad de Corrientes*, an Argentinean ship, was issued for I Class.

I share a cabin with a girl, an employee of the embassy, who is also leaving Asunción. She comes from Germany and will attempt to travel back home from Buenos Aires. A passage on a Spanish ship, via Spain is still possible. It is a treat to hear her speak German and I am making every effort to learn from her. In Asunción my Mennonite German was ridiculed a bit. It is so flat and so wide, so East Prussian, they said.

Erika, for that is her name, stood by the railing when our ship left the port in Asunción and played the accordion. She played, "Must I now, must I now depart this little town." The people at the wharf waved and wiped tears from their cheeks. Jake was among them. He overcame his sadness by acting out. People looked at him and shook their heads but he seemed oblivious to it all.

Jake was very envious of me, as if I were heading straight for Germany. "Lizzie, you are one lucky person," he repeatedly said when we got together during the last few days before I set out. Fact is, I should tremble and be sore afraid. I know not a single soul in the giant city, neither did I know Erika previously. I regard it as a divine guidance that we were able to travel together. She knows the world and advises me well. When I told her that, she asked me what divine guidance was. I explained it and then she knew.

"The Führer also speaks about divine guidance," she said and I was surprised that she said it so disparagingly. Before we went to bed, Erika asked me about my faith. She is Catholic and she asked me such strange questions like whether we Mennonites believed in God, Jesus and the Holy Spirit. We then got engaged in a pleasant conversation and I have to admit that we share much with Catholics. Then we had a good and relaxing laugh since we had more in common than assumed or feared.

I then took my Bible to hand and read the portion I had had in mind, namely Galatians 5, about the law and freedom. Erika listened most attentively. Then she told me that her parents were practicing Catholics. This means that they take matters of the church very seriously. True Christians are having a very hard time of it in Germany now, she said. Some people are even being persecuted if they dared to express an opinion. There is much injustice in Germany now and she spoke about concentration camps for enemies of the state. At times she fears for her father when he speaks his mind so freely. He, too, could be arrested. He was a very steadfast man.

I was so shocked that I was unable to address the issue. We believe so devoutly that things are different in Germany than Russia, and that God is with the Germans and with Hitler. But I want very much to hear Erika out.

I have just watched the river for a long and thoughtful time. The water of the Parana foams at the bow of the ship. Since we have passed the Rio Bermejo the water is yellow, almost brown. At the confluence of the Paraguay and Parana Rivers, the water looked like a sea; it is seven kilometres wide there. One can barely see the shoreline. Erika and I stood by the bow sprite. At the juncture of the brown Paraguay River and the clear Parana a dividing line was clearly discernible in the water.

We then hummed the song by Lily Marlene, the new soldier song, which is sung by everyone now. First it was broadcast on the radio and now the song is sung on the streets of Asunción everywhere.

Erika said that her boyfriend is fighting in the East Front. He was a lieutenant in a tank division and she was often worried about him. They had intended to get married, but then the war broke out. She had then applied for a position in the Diplomatic Service and that is how she came to a foreign posting.

"Do you believe this war will end well?" she asked.

"Most certainly, Erika," I answered. "Communism has to be crushed and then the world will be saved."

She shook her head. It seems to me that Erika does not know what Communism is, or who Stalin is."

20 December 1942

I am in a huge city. Yesterday I walked the streets of Belgrano, that part of the city in which I now reside. I wanted to take a look at the display windows. Suddenly my imagination struck and took me back to Prenzlau in Germany, a memory which comes over me, just like previously in the Chaco, where we celebrated Christmas with paltry decorations and a tree from the bush. The luxury in the display windows here is probably even greater than in Germany, and yet it all appeared so artificial, so cold despite the great heat which vibrates in the narrow streets.

Maybe this happened because of the artificial Christmas trees, the artificial snow, which caused this sensation. But possibly it is my loneliness in this gigantic city with which I have not yet come to terms. It is odd that I am sweating on the outside and overcome with inner shivers, similar to malaria.

Mr Heyse, the head of the family where I reside, consoles me with patient friendliness. He explains much to me and prepares me for my tasks ahead. I am not to worry about anything, he says, since I am in good company. I am surprised at how much he knows about me, and even about Mennonitism and our colonies in Paraguay.

When our *Ciudad de Corrientes*, reached the La Plata River on the third day, we encountered rough seas with some of the passengers getting seasick. Erika and I again stood in front where the waves smashed high into the air and we sang songs into the raging waters which we both knew. "On the Golf of Biscay" and "Little Seagull, fly to Helgoland." Erica sensed my mounting tension, and she placed a comforting arm around me.

"Maybe I should tremble more than you do," she said. "Who knows, what awaits me at home? Kurt is in mortal danger every day. The aerial bombardments are getting more severe by the day."

Somewhat lost, we both looked into the distance and the future, when, suddenly, Buenos Aires loomed before us out of the fog, skyscraper upon skyscraper. The power and the force of it all struck me so bewilderingly, that I started shivering all the more. When in 1930 our ocean liner "Bavaria" arrived in Buenos Aires, I barely took note of it. But then Hamburg and Rio lay behind us, and I was a little girl in the lap of a large family and a familiar group. Now the golden city surfaced in the beaming sun out of the fog and it loomed larger and larger, like a monster alive, coming towards me and looking at me from a hundred thousand skyscraper windows.

And then everything transpired as smoothly as in a dream, so that I had to pinch my arm in order to determine my own consciousness. Erika did not leave my side. She pointed out the Heyse Family to me at the dock, who expected me and whom she knew. When we had disembarked, Erika introduced us. After a hearty welcome greeting, I was immediately deposited in a huge vehicle, and we were already gliding through the streets towards the gigantic city.

Erika was taken by another car straight to the embassy. I did not see her again. She called me to take her leave since she had to board her ship the next day. Adieu, Erika, you are such a good girl!

Heyses reside in Belgrano, a city quarter in which many Germans live, and in which one can even go shopping in German. I was shown my quarters which were even more commodious than my previous room in Asunción.

"First we will celebrate Christmas, Miss Elisabeth," said Mrs Heyse, "and then my husband will acquaint you with what you are to do."

Mrs Heyse is a very dear woman, such is my impression. The Heyses belong to the German Embassy and officially I am the custodian of their three children. "That is what you tell anyone if and when asked," said Mrs Heyse.

I know that I am engaged for the German cause, since Mr Secretary had already advised me to that effect. I had stated that I am prepared to do so, and I am ready.

27 December 1942

Mrs Heyse said that although she had lived in Argentina for several years now, she still had not managed to get accustomed to Christmas in summer. She did everything to convert their apartment into the Christmas spirit. She had decorated the rooms with *Thuja* (arborvitae) branches and lit candles, while Mr Heyse had brought home a huge cypress tree which they had decorated as a Christmas tree. It actually looked almost like a fir tree.

The Heyses took me in as a family member, and yet I remained a bystander, an observer. Heyses are Protestant. Mr Heyse read the Christmas story as depicted in the Gospel of Luke, and then we sang some Christmas songs. Some of these songs were completely new to me, like "Come all you shepherds, you men and you women!" or "Maria through a thorn wood went." Mrs Heyse played piano while two of the children played the flute. I found it all very beautiful and intimately cosy, but certainly very different from our celebration.

Mr Heyse said, "We celebrate Christmas like it is celebrated in churches. We do not go along with the new fad of its re-interpretation of Christmas as a Germanic celebration. "Holy Night of Brightest Stars" instead of "Silent Night, Holy Night" and so on is not for us.

Mr Heyse obviously noticed that I did not know what he was talking about. "Miss Elisabeth, you know," he said, "in today's Germany there are exaggerated and crazy tendencies and I only hope that all these aberrations and all this nonsense will never gain the upper hand."

I must have reacted rather startled, but I did remember what Erika had told me regarding her parents' worries. Mr Heyse then spoke

consolingly to me and said that one ought not to generalize in these matters. The church in Germany is still strong and the hotheads in the party could not do as they pleased. "Once the war is over, many matters will be resolved," was his opinion. Most of what one reads in the local newspapers or hears on the radio is subjective propaganda fostered by the enemies of Germany. You should not allow this to cloud your mind."

Mr Heyse then served champagne, a glorious bubbly beverage. A sip or two, and I felt part of the family. Under the Christmas tree there was also a present for me. The package contained a piece of jewellery encased in silver. It was rose quartz, said Mrs Heyse. "Rosa del Inca" it is called.

Actually I had already received my Christmas present, I thought, since Mrs Heyse had bought every conceivable item of clothing for me. When we came back laden with packages from our shopping spree, and I had tried on dress after dress, she said, "Now you can proudly walk Avenida de Florida." This is the grand shopping promenade which is full of shoppers and visitors till late at night. Even at midnight one can see whole families with their little children freely roaming this street, said Mrs Heyse.

No second holiday is celebrated at Christmas like we do, to say nothing about a third one, and so yesterday, Mr Heyse and I drove into the city in the direction of city centre and the port.

"You have to get to know the city," he said, "and in so doing, your work can start."

We then took the train to the Retiro-Train Terminal. This will be my route in the future. I had the feeling that the throngs of humanity, who here boarded or de-boarded the trains, literally swept me along with them. Everyone was running, bustling as if it were the last day on earth, and one could miss something dreadfully important were one to take it easy.

"Now then," said Mr Heyse, "open wide your eyes. Once you are sure of yourself in the city, I will assign you your duties."

Then we walked on foot to the port facilities and along the quay and Mr Heyse attempted to introduce me to this world port. He explained the partitioning of the port "the lay of the land, aka water" on a map. The passenger ships docked in one port, while the freighters in another. In addition to this port, the "Darsena Norte", further ports, are located in the south. They are accessible by street car.

"You will become acquainted with many names of ships," said Mr Heyse, "as well as the flags of the individual, respective countries." He showed me the English flag, the American flag, the Spanish, as well as many others which I was not capable of memorizing on the spot. I felt a bit bewildered when we walked past the forest of masts and cranes. On our return trip, we made a detour to Palermo, a further section of the city. "Here you can relax and take a break," said Mr Heyse. "You can take walks here unconcernedly when you are fed up with it all," said Mr Heyse. We walked through splendid park areas with arbours and rose gardens, marvellous ponds with sculptures and fountains. It seemed as if all the water, the fountains and the trees kept the air fresh and cool.

And then Mr Heyse introduced me to my duties with a casual deliberation. "You are to register the ships in port. You will ascertain when they arrive and when they depart. You are probably acquainted with submarine warfare. This is our most powerful weapon against England. We will bend the collective English knee with our U-boats. Now that America has joined the war, we no longer have to take any considerations."

Mr Heyse emphasized that I had to go about my duties inconspicuously. I was to record nothing at all in writing. My head was to be my notebook, since the port police could stop me at any time and subject me to scrutinizing control. Also, I was never to wear the same dress in the port area, a daily change of clothes was absolutely mandatory. I already have a bad conscience that I am recording all this in my diary. But nobody will ever get to see it. I will always keep it locked away in my suitcase.

What a life I am leading! I am Mennonite and will now get involved in war. I will be working for Germany. Am I without conflict? I have submitted to something and I know full well what can result from my actions, if, for example, a ship is sunk, the departure of which I have reported. But, with whom am I to talk about it? No one would understand me. However, it is war, would surely be the response. I now understand the conflict within our colony: to be or not to be: German or pacifist.

11 April 1943

M r Heyse may have noticed my inner conflict. "Do not worry about anything," he kept on repeating. "That which you are doing is but a cog in the wheel of a giant operation, of which you have no idea."

Not to worry? It is explicitly the worries which bother me and sometimes exhaust me. I know what is going on. I know full well that that our U-boats are lying in wait with their torpedoes as the German news weekly reports. And also in the evenings, we punctually hear by German shortwave from Berlin and prior to the news service, a tolling of bells announcing the number of sunken ships, sometimes ten, once more than twenty. Why does this tolling of the bells strike my heart?

12 April 1943

I t was the tolling of the bells which came via radio. Bell tolling for sunken ships which overcame me with doubts, then shook my conscience. Certainly, I want to render Germany a service, as Mr Heyse put it. He does it half-heartedly, I intended to do it with all my heart. And yet, I suddenly realized with terror that my service is the reason for hundreds of human deaths, and certainly totally innocent people and women with children who are on these ships sunken by U-boats.

In my desperation I went to Mr Heyse and informed him that I could no longer do it. Then I told him about my faith, about our Mennonite faith which we have held for centuries. I spoke about our pacifism and the many biblical passages which forbid killing and command love of enemy. I spoke until tears overcame me and could not go on talking for sobbing.

Then Mr Heyse got up and came towards me and stroked my hair. "Miss Unruh," he said very peacefully, "we neither want to nor intend to force you to do anything which runs contrary to your conscience. As of this moment, I absolve you from this burden. We will find a different service for you which may not be less responsible, but which will not bring you into such conflicts with your conscience."

Then he extended his hand to me. I went to my room. A heavy load has been lifted from my heart. And after I had prayed my evening prayer in which I thanked God for this change, I slept well and good.

16 April 1943

Papa sent me a letter of deep concern. He much wants to know what I am up to here in Buenos Aires. However, I can only tell him that I am engaged as a nanny; I have promised this to the Heyses. All mail is subject to censor during war and the North Americans are exerting ever greater pressure all about, including here. Espionage during war is well known.

I noticed great worries in Papa's letter. He compares the military campaign in Russia to the Napoleonic times and believes that the Germans will also lose in Africa, now that the USA has landed there.

However, when the Heyses take me along to social functions, I am constantly amazed at how confident the Germans here are of victory. Here in Argentina you can still speak freely and most of the statesmen here are of friendly disposition towards Germany, Mr Heyse tells me. But the others are also free to express their opinions. Many Jews live here with some of them having fled from Germany and they even have their own newspaper here.

I have become a real city girl, a lady. If people from our colony were to meet me on the street or in a park, they would most certainly not recognize me, and I notice that I feel rather good about the fact that nobody knows or recognizes me. I have submerged in the wider seas of this world.

Occasionally I have had to think of Heinrich. I wonder whether he, too, has felt the strong urge to slip under cover into a strange, a foreign sea. How far everything has been made to drift apart!

As of the day before yesterday I am enrolled in a training session upon the advice of Mr Heyse. This transpires in total secrecy, with the meeting address forever changing; sometimes we meet in the Heyse home. The instructor is an officer from the *Admiral Graf Spee*. He was a wireless operator on board of the cruiser and now he instructs his area of expertise. I have always imagined a German officer to be just like he is.

18 April 1943

In a few days, the birthday of the Führer will be highly celebrated at the ambassadorial residence. When we were having breakfast this morning, Mrs Heyse invited me to the event and I am eagerly looking forward to the occasion.

The Heyses inquired as to how things were going with my instructions and Mr Heyse implied that other duties might shortly be expected of me if I were prepared to do so. A wireless communication to Berlin was to be established. This could no longer be done by the embassy for reasons of neutrality.

We were able to take our time for conversations since it is Sunday. I have gradually become used to Sundays without a worship service. Sundays are meant for purposes of relaxation and I must freely admit that I have need for the peace of the day, although my thoughts then lead me to our little village, our small school, the sermon, the songs, the choir...

Mrs Heyse spoke about the officer who conducts the instructional classes. He belongs to the crew of the *Spee* as I have previously mentioned. He goes by an assumed name although this is no great secret in Argentina, where such people can freely come and go in the city. Officially all the sailors and officers are to remain interned, but the Argentineans quite happily shut an eye in such matters since they then do not have to guard them and provide room, board and incur further expenses. However, most of such accommodations are undertaken by other Germans. They invite these people in, give them jobs and look after them as well as they can. Some of them even managed to flee. They have disappeared to Chile, with some even managing to return to Germany.

Our officer is known to us only by his Christian name Erwin; he is protected by the embassy because he is being employed by the secret service.

"His talents cannot be paid for in money," said Mr Heyse. "He knows how to communicate with the simplest of gadgetry and we are dependent on him, given our limited means, as was Robinson Crusoe on his remote island."

"Just pay attention at the celebration at the embassy," said Mrs Heyse, "as to the number of *Spee* crew we will be meeting there. I will give you some inconspicuous tips to that end."

"Our officer as well?"

"Most certainly," answered Mrs Heyse, while grinning.

The officer has something serious, honest, confidence-inspiring about him. I was reminded of how enthusiastically Jake spoke about German soldiers whom he had seen in illustrated German magazines until he chanced upon the books by Davinger. Well, Jake would surely not have been disappointed in seeing these men, more explicitly this officer. I do not believe that I made any particular effort, but already at the second evening of instructions the officer praised me, and since then I have the impression that he addresses me specifically when teaching and when explaining the apparatus with which radio contact is to be made. The group which participates in these instructions is rather a colourful mix. We have been instructed to know as little as possible about each other. If someone is ever questioned by whatever authority, such party if not to reveal anything. We have all received instructions to that end and we have all agreed to it.

In the afternoon we all piled into the Heyse car, including me, and we took off to the Tigre-Delta. An over-abundance of fruit is available there: apples, pears, plums and even cherries. We brought fruit home for the entire week. When experiencing such an abundance of fresh fruit, my thoughts took me back to the poor villages in the Chaco. Fruits and vegetables there are a scarcity with many pale children to be seen on account of lack of vitamins. For them the return to Germany will be their salvation and I, too, fight for it. I, too, clamour for a German victory for all Germans in this world, and particularly the Germans in our colony.

When I once spoke to Mr Heyse about this, he smiled. "There is much talk about the return to the Reich," he said. "Such talk here in Argentina leads to tensions because here many Germans feel totally Argentinean and have no intentions of returning to Germany. We have to be careful here with such touchy slogans." So now I have become a bit wiser and have learned to hold my peace when talking is not in order. It seems to me that Mr Heyse feels like a German and he fights for a German victory but that he is no great friend of Hitler. Obviously there are such!

21 April 1943

Yesterday evening the Führer's birthday was celebrated. It seemed to me that fewer people were in attendance than in Asunción two years ago.

"We no longer make such a big to-do of these celebrations as previously," said Mrs Heyse. "The situation is becoming ever more tense and so we prefer to celebrate such events in private."

The ambassador gave a speech, and he spoke more about the severity of the battles and the necessity of the Germans to hold out than he did about victory. Two years ago the jubilation of the

German forces in their blitzkrieg victories throughout Europe was a cause for great jubilation in Asunción.

When the hymn, the speeches and the songs were over, we walked over to the cold buffet. I have developed many skills in matters of appropriate manners and etiquette so that I no longer stick out conspicuously. I no longer hang around lost like a dainty wall daisy, or, should I say, a dusty cactus flower in the Chaco bush. I move freely among the guests and I have learned to talk about inconsequential matters as if they were important.

Then Erwin came up to me, our officer, together with some of his comrades from the ship, along with some girls from Belgrano in tow. I took consolation in the fact that these girls certainly did not strike anyone as much smarter than I am. They laughed unconcernedly about the jokes cracked by the German sailors and I laughed along with them as if I were part of their party. Our maxim, which is to reveal as little as possible about one's identity, came to mind and I noticed that Erwin came to my full support in my discretion. I wonder if he knows who I am, from whence I come? He did not allow even the faintest glimmer of cognisance to enter the conversational scene, and whatever was said, skirted the issue masterfully. I am a nanny at the Heyse residence, and I come from somewhere in Paraguay. Then the band struck up a dance tune, and I fled to Mrs Heyse.

"But I can't dance." I whispered to her. "What will I do if somebody steps up and asks me to dance? Obviously I'll stick out like a stick in the mud."

"We'll manage that, Elisabeth," she said. By now she calls me by my first name and she has even dropped the formal "Sie"; all this has given me even more confidence. She disappeared for a moment and then she was back again at my side. "Erwin will be here shortly," she said, "he knows how things are and he will be your dancing instructor. You need only play along." Oh, that was simply glorious! The officer came along, bowed to me and I stood up as naturally as could be.

"Relax totally into my guidance," he said quietly. "However, I am not all that certain myself, Miss Elisabeth. Here in Argentina tangos are being danced a lot and the dance is new to me as well. But I am really hot to trot while guiding you in the dance."

And then the dancing strudel had already swallowed us up and no one as much as looked at us. Everyone sang "La Paloma" in Spanish and German. "I was called aboard, a cool wind is wafting…" and we danced, stepped on each other's toes, laughed, tried it all over again and then we charged ahead with mounting confidence until the dance was over.

The officer returned me to the Heyses. "A wonderful dancer," he said, and bowed to me. "I will soon return, but now you ought to dance the waltz with Mr Heyse, which will certainly be better," and then he bowed to Mrs Heyse and took her dancing.

Indeed, while waltzing, I floated in the air as if I had danced all my life long. Mr Heyse praised me and I learned to dance in one evening as quickly as I have learned everything here in Buenos Aires, have had to learn everything, be it espionage or radio communication.

When I lay in bed, the memories rolled over me, so that I was unable to sleep for the longest time although it was already three a. m. I had taken a hot shower, and now the cool night breeze streamed through the window. I lay on my back and breathed deeply. I thought of the terrors which I suffered when Greta and I played at the Harms wedding. What a strange piece of work the human conscience is!

All who had paid attention to me are beyond calling distance. Is anyone calling? Does anyone think of me, Greta, the Reverend Reimer, Mama, David? Am I the same girl with the same heart, the same faith under the same God?

And then I saw myself sitting under the *algarrobo* tree at the edge of the water pond, drenched in tears because a world had broken apart in and over me. For me these were worlds, and worlds apart. Am I now building a new world or is it being built within me? There is no other way for me to describe it. The devotion of the people around me, the esteem I feel developing within me a feeling of certainty, of self-confidence, an elation. These thoughts so much relaxed me that I fell into a pleasant sleep. I slept until ten in the morning since no duties were expected of me.

Only the melody of the night has remained with me, it resonates and vibrates on and on like a gentle distant thunder after a thunderstorm with pleasant, fresh rain. "I was called aboard, a gentle breeze is wafting…" The rhythm of "La Paloma" exhilarates me. Who am I? What has become of me?

4 May 1943

Again the die has been cast for me. Obviously I was asked for my consent but everything related to it is most enigmatic and secretive. Actually, I merely had to agree to work in a different sphere of operation which is connected to our radio activity.

Mr Heyse informed me that this initiative was no easy matter but that it did have appeal and adventure for young and competent people. Our security is not jeopardized since the Argentinean police issue no impediments unless they are provoked by foolhardiness. I have been informed that I will be part of a group for which I have the skills and the qualifications. These engagements will transpire far from Buenos Aires and will last for many months on end.

Are you prepared to be engaged to those ends? Mr Heyse asked of me. "Erwin, the officer and instructor, will be part of the team," he said, and I gained the impression that his presence would pacify or possibly even motivate me.

I have agreed to do so. Have I ever applied a Bible verse to my person or activity? "Whoever puts his hand to the plough and looks back is not suitable for the Kingdom of God." Was it at the time when I was at Bible School and I was filled with more and more trepidation, the closer the bottleneck approached? I now consulted Luke chapter 9 and read the entire passage again. I have agreed to it, and am persuaded that I have to fulfill an obligation, an obligation which will serve our people. Is it then wrong to assume that such obligation is of the Lord's Hand? And yet, I do not intend to misuse the word of God.

I cannot discuss this matter with anyone, not even with the Heyses. They might not even understand how such deliberations enter my mind. I have made this decision on my own and I will see it through to the end and on my own. I will follow my plough and not look back.

Possibly Mrs Heyse sensed that the things I am about to encounter make heavy demands on me, and that I have to make special efforts to maintain my inner equilibrium. Yesterday she brought me a small volume by way of a "Greeting of Farwell and Encouragement" as she put it. The title is "From the Other Shore" and it is a collection of German poems from Argentina, 1941, and published here.

I read excerpts from the collection last night. In doing so, a poem by Margit Hilleprandt caught my fancy and attention. It was written for me and my particular situation.

> *"This is the deeper sadness of our being*
> *We have to walk our way ourselves, and that alone,*
> *We often dream of harmonious togetherness*
> *And grope hungrily for loving hands to own;*
> *-and are like children, who in darkness fear*
> *That they will not find their way back home alone."*

I know that the verses of this poem apply to me and yet the observation that we are subject to the "horrible law", as the poet terms it unconditionally, appear too harsh. Are there not many people who are never lonely?

I intend to let the final lines apply to me and guide me at this time when I head out for uncertainty:

> *"Only occasionally bends through time and space*
> *God himself great and good as father's love to us,*
> *Let us forget His cruel law's decree*
> *In soul-like mystery: you and me."*

I will now lock away my diary. To take it along would be a risk all too great. It, at least, will wait for my return.

11 September 1943

The icy *Pampero* winds drove us to the north right up to the Argentinean Chaco and now the north storms drive us back south again. During the change of weather, which sometimes turns very suddenly, I watched the large birds like the caracara and the vultures as they are carried by the storm squalls without wing movement, as if will-less. I have become a storm bird myself, driven by the winds.

I have been away from Buenos Aires for months now, without a break and always at my job. My specialty was to assemble batteries, to provide the necessary electrical power and to connect the radio equipment –while a further activity was to cook. I have often been thankful that I learned cooking, already as a child, at my mother's side in the kitchen. To get a fire going so that it burns quickly and well is an art unto itself, and to do this with the simplest of means available, in order to cook a meal and as tasty as possible. This is something we learned in the Chaco during our early years.

I won the heart of the men with my meals quickly prepared, somewhere in the open pampas, or at a small ranch, and at any and all times when we were forced to change locations in short order. While the men laid out the antennas on a tree, if such was handy, or over bush and thickets in the treeless pampas, I fried eggs and bacon, cooked the noodles and prepared a sauce for which my Mama had praised me.

We returned from the Santa Fé province yesterday. We rarely ever surfaced in the city. We only occasionally traveled there by bus or by train to buy the bare essentials. We moved from place to place like restless migrating birds and at most barely skirted the settlements. Our sphere of activity could have been easily detected and so we were constantly on the lookout for new work sites. It was no easy matter to communicate with Berlin and to send them our coded messages and directives which we received from Buenos Aires.

Each and every time when we received confirmation by Morse code from Berlin that our communications had been received from our antenna, suspended as it was over a lemon tree or between two thickets, we broke out in thrilled applause. None of us was in the know about what was communicated since only Buenos Aires and Berlin knew the code.

When I again appeared in the Heyse apartment yesterday, "a weather-worn tired wanderer" sun burned in the extreme, and with tanned skin and unkempt hair, I was barely recognisable.

"Donnerwetter!" said Mr Heyse, "you look like someone who has been at the Eastern Front!"

I was cordially welcomed back by all and I enjoyed all the blessings of culture and civilization. I will spend a few weeks relaxing and unwinding like a soldier on furlough while the Heyses spoil me with love and attention. My comrades deposited me here and then they simply disappeared like the Arabs in the desert. I do not know a single address, not even Erwin's.

"Not to worry, Lizzie," he said when he left with all the others. "I will soon be in touch!"

I saluted him upon farewell, inconspicuously, impersonally, because I do not want the Heyses to know how close Erwin and I have become to each other. I was the only woman in the group, which obviously elevated my status, and particularly because I did the cooking. No one ever became suggestive, not one of the men, and I had the feeling from the outset, that Erwin was my personal protector even at an appropriate distance, with total respect, a model in courtesy, and possibly on account of his warmth and with an assurance which led to an ever deepening exchange of glances.

I am not yet in a position to put this in writing, at least not today. It seems to me that we have returned to port after a stormy voyage at sea and that I now have to re-orientate myself to find the girl which I really am.

Several letters awaited me on my return, from Jake and from home. Papa is much concerned. The Russians are again approaching the Dnieper. What will now become of our village which we thought was liberated? And we know only what we hear on the radio, as to what is transpiring there. No sign of life, no letter, not one word. "And now the Red Flood rolls back again," writes Papa. "It will roll right over the world."

Also the Heyses are deeply concerned, so much is obvious. The Allies have landed in Sicily. It appears to me that Mr Heyse is careful about what he says, but I gather that he has lost confidence. The fact that Erwin and the other comrades are more optimistic is probably due to the fact that they are younger. Erwin just recently turned thirty. Jake's letter is equally as optimistic; he, too, is full of high enthusiasm.

Mama's sentences are heavy with worry, as always. She was like this all her life. Now her last child, whom she worries about, is far away and about whose faith and future she trembles and I cannot even write her the truth. She probably senses that I am no nanny, as I tell her in my letters, and also Jake makes references to the effect that I am probably walking about in a magic hat like the dwarf in the Siegfried saga.

I had taken along the volume with the Argentinean poems in my luggage. I was surprised that Margit Hilleprandt, in addition to writing about the "cruel law of loneliness", was also capable of writing a tender poem on love. I found this poem so beautiful that I memorized it during the few breaks in our service. Here are a few lines from memory: "Now you are there, which my dreams suggest, the unique one, you, the wonderful, the stream, into which my entire being merges...you were subconscious—announced from the beginning. You lived already in my childhood weeping, and in the loneliness of my maiden years, deep and sweet and incomprehensible..."

19 September 1943

I have one week left in which to relax and rest, to look after myself and to enjoy the beautiful surroundings. In the Palermo Park the first signs of spring are obvious, and I experience these with particular intensity since the winter here is much harsher than at home. The trees stood bare, the lawns a dirty yellow, and everything was wet, cold and dark. I suffered greatly due to the harsh weather, more than I was prepared to admit in the southern pampas. I only now become fully cognisant of it all, now that it is all over and past. But now the trees are budding and the flowers blooming in the artistic display of many flower beds.

Our next line of duty will take us south. It will be summer there, in the proximity of Patagonia, but it will surely not be as unbearably hot as in the Chaco. And of what do I think when I now report on

the line of duty in Santa Fé, and the icy south winds which howled around our tents, and the eternal drizzle, and clothes, always damp in which I shivered like a young dog? What do I think of? Of what do I dream?

I think of Erwin's warm eyes, of his intelligent questions, his language which was music to my ears. If we managed to rent a rancho for several days, he looked for a secluded area for me, in which I could make place my camp bed. When he noticed that I read my bible by the light of my flashlight before falling asleep, he asked me about my faith the next day. His questions appeared to come from afar, from a person who had heard little in matters of faith from his family and in his upbringing.

What an incredible span my life has taken? There was a time when it was a sin not to say grace at the table or not to attend church on Sunday, and now all the way to the comrades right here, who have hardly had any connection to faith at all.

Erwin and I took walks during the icy winter evenings when the hoary pampas tinkled and glistened in the bright light of the moon. We conducted conversations which enabled me to realize new dimensions. Erwin is well educated. He concluded his high school senior matriculation and was then trained as an officer. And yet, I did not have to prove myself to him; I do not have to cover up my poor formal education. All these inhibiting factors which very quickly throw a relationship into imbalance, Erwin resolved with tactical skill, and our conversations invariably found a level on which we stood opposite to each other in a fair exchange of questions and answers, of give and take.

I noticed that Erwin was reading a small booklet. I rather jauntily took it out of his hands and noticed that it was *Der Steppenwolf* by Hermann Hesse. Then I showed off a bit and recited some of Hesse's poems, which I had recorded years ago in my notebook and memorized while doing so. Erwin was completely taken aback and that was my intention. I noticed that he took pleasure in all this and then he examined me as to my literary knowledge. Naturally Goethe and Schiller were mentioned but what really caught Erwin's attention was my knowledge of Löns, Mörike and Ricarda Huch.

Then I produced my Argentinean poems and read one after the other, including the one about loneliness.

"That is true quality," he said, "a very good choice."

I was tempted to also recite my favourite poem by Löns, about the grain field and the wind, the storm and the wild seas, but then I preferred to let it be. "But to love each other, may not be." Should I repeat that line?

Then I requested Erwin to give me *Steppenwolf* but he claimed it would bite me. I should rather look for other literature, and my bible also was not that bad of a choice either.

And yet, I will insist that he permit me to read this book.

24 September 1943

The day before yesterday Erwin called and invited me to go to a movie last night. A German film is being shown here with Kristine Söderbaum, "The golden City", a movie in colour.

It was a glorious film, a gift for me. Erwin assisted me in quickly coming to terms with this sad film.

"Kristine Söderbaum is being called the Imperial Water Corpse in Germany," he said laughingly, because she has to take her own life so often in the film. I regard this comment harsh since I found the film both very beautiful and gripping. A country girl in a big city. I was able to make a series of comparisons.

Then we drove to the centre of the Old City and walked arm in arm through the animated streets. We talked about the war, we spoke about our duties, and about the things that now await us, but our thoughts took different directions. I know that our thoughts went back a long way, mine to home in our village, and everything that had solidified and formed me, and, possibly, also kept me captive.

And as for his thoughts? Erwin wears a wedding band and I know that at his home his wife is waiting for him and a child, while I am here writing that it was a glorious evening. We walked into a café, laughed and exchanged glances, and spoke about matters which took us far distant from the reality which now burdens our hearts.

And now I am in my room and reflect on the weeks, possibly months which lie ahead of us. I tremble in happy anticipation of that what life possibly will grant us only once. And yet I know very well that it is not that for which I had longed, and what will explicitly be denied me. What is it that Margit Hilleprandt said in her love poem? "And remains with me but for a brief start, and greets me smilingly, only to depart."

I have never wished to be a storm bird, and I know that everything will wildly disperse me and that I am driven by storms like the vultures at the change of weather.

I borrowed an atlas from the Heyse book shelf and on the map of Argentina I trace a trip to the south in my thoughts. Even further south than the Bahia Blanca is where we will be operating. There are few disturbances lurking there and we cannot readily be located. I trace with my finger up to Patagonia and then back north, up the Parana and then the Paraguay River, skirting Asunción and into the Chaco. "Gran Chaco" is written in capital letters above the giant area before the Andes. How long can a life bear the tensions of these infinite dimensions until the containing strings sever? Infinite dimensions and yet thousands of kilometres are the shortest.

Erwin believes, that I have a strength in me and power and stability for which he envies me. He traces these back to my healthy breeding ground, the down-to-earth anchor of a community of faith, which grounds and guards, while I think at times of these as shackles, ballast, blocks on my legs, which hinder the storm bird from free and carefree flight.

When I applied for Bible School, I did not think of Peter and yet he became my fateful destiny. I did not come to Buenos Aires to meet Erwin, and now we stand opposite to each other and I know that he fills and fulfills my heart, my world of thought, and my longing. My service for the Fatherland, which is core, again now forms the frame of a picture—but only the frame.

1 October 1943

The preparations for our next venture took more time than we had planned. We had to take additional courses. Strange gentlemen were present, although they remained nameless. Technical improvements, updated gadgets and apparatuses were introduced, and we had to acquaint ourselves with this new technology.

Mr Heyse assured me that circumstances would be more welcoming and comfortable than in the Pampas winter. Some hundred kilometres from Bahia Blanca, German sheep farmers live, and we are meant to locate and establish our station and quarters there. We will find bases there and quarter postings. We will also have connections in Bahia Blanca.

The day before yesterday the Heyses invited me to a comfortable evening in their living room. Mr Heyse served an Argentinean Muskateller wine which in summer is drunk with ice-cold carbonated mineral water. It is a glorious mixture, refreshing and invigorating, and the Heyses wanted to know about our adventures. I got into conversational swing, possibly aided and abetted by the sweet wine. I spoke expectantly about our new initiatives, of my joy and dedication, and of our hope for victory.

Then Mr Heyse casually asked me a by-the-way question, as to what I intended to do after the war was over. My glass almost dropped from my hands.

Indeed, what did I intend to do?

And what happens, once the war is over? I had never doubted that once the war was over, our way is to Germany, just as Papa and many others in our colony hope for. Everything for which I had become engaged and involved in and done with happy sacrifice is linked and connected to this unequivocal aim. I remained quiet for a whileand Mr Heyse smiled. He has such a soft and kindly smile.

"I do not know, Mr Heyse," I finally stammered, and placed my glass on the table.

"I had no intentions of startling you," said Mr Heyse very tranquilly. "It may well be that you are more fortunate than we are. You have a home which is whole. We will return to a home completely devastated and destroyed. We have no idea what our cities look like today, and there is no end in sight. I daily listen to the BBC and if only half of what is reported is true regarding the aerial bombardments and carpet bombings, Germany will soon be a desert.

"Do you no longer believe in a victory?" I asked and noticed that my voice was completely hoarse.

"I am a realist," said Mr Heyse, "and a realist does not allow himself hopeful illusions. Even here in Argentina it is difficult to express things as hard and as clearly as a realist sees them. Furthermore, I am a diplomat and in that capacity I say that we believe in a victory."

Then Mr Heyse spoke about the U-boat weapon on which our warfare is essentially dependent. The Allies have developed new counter-measure weaponry, and then he spoke about the death of the U-boat as such, and about diminishing German successes in the battle of the Atlantic.

I was happy and relieved that Mr Heyse did not repeat the question regarding my future. It seemed to me that he had directed me to an abyss, which as of now, yawned at me darkly. I closed my eyes. I did not want to view the abyss. Must I now think of it? I turn away from the abyss. I intend to think only of that what lies immediately ahead of me, my duties, to which end I am preparing myself, of a sheep farm far south, and of a person full of warmth, goodness and understanding.

Yesterday was so beautiful, so very beautiful, and the memory of it all enables me to forget everything, including Mr Heyse's question. We walked through the twilight in the garden of Palermo, through the arbours and the rose galleries, and past the fountains in the ponds. And everywhere people walked, couples in love, behind the bushes. We were alone and hardly exchanged a word. We kept on walking as if with closed eyes. From an open-air restaurant tango music wafted. We sat down at a table and drank a spritzer and then Erwin took me to the dance floor. We glided over the dance floor, free of gravity. Only, after waking this morning, I again felt the weights on my soul and that I would never rid myself of them, never, ever!

The picture of the Youth Calendar, which the teacher gave me, appeared before my eyes again with the cross at the parting of the ways with the golden star. When did I change direction? When? At that time when Heinrich stood by the broad stream and smiled, or at the pond at the end of the village?

The day after tomorrow we will be on the train, and we will laugh unconcernedly and joke with no one knowing much about anyone else. "Strange, indeed, to walk in the fog..."

My diary is again headed for the suitcase. For how long? I wish forever. I would also like to lock my heart into the suitcase, forever.

The spontaneous question by Mr Heyse, as to what Elisabeth intended to do after the war, caused her bewilderment since she had previously never questioned a German victory, but also because she had never given her own future much thought.

What would indeed become of her and what would she do after the war was over? The fact that a German victory would bring about a radical change for her and all like-minded was a given, and regarded as such by her brother Jake and by her father in many letters over the years. This concept had become the solid basis of her thinking and all her decisions.

And now the question, posed so suddenly, gave her pause, for it opened the possibility that her thinking might not based on an absolute certainty. Indeed, that certainty might itself be in doubt. Elisabeth now faced the improbable spectre to which she reacted by shutting her eyes, the spectre of a return to the loneliness which she had so desperately and courageously managed to escape.

The diary was locked away with the year 1944 bouncing Elisabeth around every which way. The entries invariably made during the short breaks in her operations are sparse at best. They seem to intend to cover essentials by the entry of non-essentials.

Her espionage operations became more dangerous. The Argentinean government had to submit ever more to American pressure. This also meant increasing pressure on the activities of the Germans. In January 1944—Elisabeth was stationed in Patagonia with her troupe— Argentina broke diplomatic relations with Germany.

The radio activity was now even formally illegal and consequently downright dangerous, but for young people such danger became all the more alluring. "Now we're really going to go for it" comes through in Elisabeth's sparse writings of that time. Her activities are still commissioned. Berlin reacts and still is demanding. And yet, at least so it appears to me, Elisabeth's outreach for the human touch and relationship outweighs her political and patriotic commitments.

Her references to all this in her diary entries are sparse at best; suspiciously little is documented. Everything which had previously captured her, fulfilled her and given her wing can only be gleaned from excerpts, which I have labelled Part IV. It becomes obvious there that she is grasping for a straw, but in full consciousness that it was only a straw and that it would not carry her, not bear her up, not be her buoy.

And yet all this constituted no superficial surrender, much less dissipation by either side or party involved. Occasionally one gets the impression that she regards this experience which, through circumstance, transports her into isolation and exposes her to the most rigorous of demands, as a gift to which she believed she no longer had a right, a gift she holds in trembling hands.

And yet it is exactly her entitlement which causes her disastrous dilemma. Elisabeth did not allow herself to drift like a storm bird. And yet, it appears to me that her bitter disappointments, which life previously dealt her, have led her to believe that life owed her some degree of compensation, and that she had, simply put, some catching up to do in matters of the demands of her flesh, her "flesh and blood," as she wrote in a former day.

Inebriated by the ecstasy of bliss combined with the demands of the operations for an alleged bigger cause, she crosses the barriers which life and development had constructed all her life long. Elisabeth was well aware of violating the Sixth Commandment, even though it was clear to her that such trespassing was limited in time, due to circumstances.

This is probably also the reason she was so much startled and taken aback at Mr Heyse's question. What happens, when the war is over, irrespective of the outcome? She may well have wished that it would never end.

In March 1945, short weeks before the war was over, Argentina declared war on Germany. For Elisabeth and her comrades this meant that her underground engagements were impossible, over. The crew of the ADMIRAL GRAF SPEE, *which had been previously involved in every possible branch of espionage and endeavour, was left with no recourse but to return to internment and to await the end of the war. This was the most prudent measure, considering the pressure the North Americans exerted, headed by the hard-line ambassador Spruille Braden in Buenos Aires.*

This was also the time when Elisabeth had to part, to break up. She writes about a final trip in common with Erwin to Chacarita, the large cemetery in Buenos Aires. The objective of the visit was the grave of Captain Langsdorff of the GRAF SPEE, *whom Erwin intended to bade farewell. In actuality, it was the farewell of the two, the final Adieu from the storm-bird period, as she writes with a palpable harshness directed at herself.*

It was at this time—mid 1945 after the defeat of Germany—that she entered "The Winter Song" by Friedrich Nietzsche in her diary. "And now you stand there pale, condemned to Winter's Wanderings, just like the smoke, for colder heavens probes."

Again external circumstances, and not inner decisions, determine Elisabeth's return to Paraguay and to the Chaco. Heyses arranged a good position for her and she could have managed to lead a comfortable life there. The years "abroad" had proven to be a most beneficial school, which enabled her to master any situation.

Then in mid-1946 news arrives, that her mother has died and that her father is a lonely widower on his farmyard. Other factors now came calling. The SPEE *crew returned to Germany, and Heyses also departed for a destroyed homeland, as Mr Heyse put it. In the colony all hopes for a better future in the German Reich were dashed, destroyed as her father, now doubly sad, wrote.*

Elisabeth considered this a call for help. Who else would look after the father? And thus, at the end of 1946, she embarked on her journey home, a woman thirty-two years of age.

No wonder that she considers Asunción, after all the years of exposure to a more sophisticated world, "poorly." The country, based on the mounting isolation of an interior state, and under the rule of conflicting parties, had been driven to an existential minimum.

"We are facing another revolution," said Jake when he came to call for his sister at the port.

It was a comfort and consolation for Elisabeth that her brother was prepared to accompany her back to the Chaco in order to master the new situation with her lonely and neglected father, and to accompany her to their mother's grave.

REFLECT UPON IT,

O MY SOUL

Reflect upon it, O my soul

1 December 1946

And again I am sailing on the dear old "Toro", the side-wheeler steamboat, which stamps slowly against stream, northwards. And again I am sitting in the dining room of the First Class, but not as a tolerated non-entity. We are traveling first class. The cabins come equipped with ventilators, as does the dining room.

Jake has become an elegant gentleman who has mastered every social grace, irrespective of such company being business people, with whom we sit at table, or high officers, who are traveling to their garrisons in Conception or to the Chaco. Jake knows how to introduce me as a lady and to stand by me, look after me, and he is treated with respect as well. Obviously my hair style and my dress from Buenos Aires also play a role in it, as the saying goes, "Clothes make people!"

Jake and I probe each other in conversations during this voyage. Jake is to know everything about me, even if not here and now. He is the only person in the world in whose company I have no inhibitions and who accepts me exactly as I am, or, rather, who I have become. As to whether he will also encounter me with the same openness is something I do not know. But that hardly matters. I make no demands and neither does he. I will tell him what I intend to for my own sake and he knows that. He knows he is helping me in listening to me and he listens with full interest and attention.

We have time and we take our time. Jake will stay with us during Christmas and New Year, and I know that we will take a walk down memory's lane of our youth. Jake will assist me in preventing me from plunging into the abyss, into the abyss of my past, a past which has shaped me and which will now make demands on me.

"You will be startled, Lizzie," he said, "in observing how little has changed there, and how much you have changed."

We have much to come to terms with, and Jake no less than I do. When I boarded the ship in December 1942, which was to take me to a new world, Jake yelled "Heil Hitler" after me in boisterous volume. It seems to me that the breakdown of Germany, and everything associated with it, is a matter that he has not at all come to terms with, and that he lives far more powerfully in the disappointment of lost hopes than I do. Indeed, it appears to me that his faith in those pinnacle ideals remain unbroken.

But why have I sobered up more quickly than he has? Is the reason again to be found in human disappointments which placed demands on me, and having to sacrifice much, allowed my spirit to maintain a certain aloofness? Again, I am reminded of Mr Heyse's words.

When the news arrived of the destruction of Dresden and the deaths of tens of thousands, including women and children, everyone trembled. The city was full of refugees from the east. Mr Heyse became very quiet when there was talk about the Jews and the concentration camps.

"Miss Elisabeth, there will be a rude awakening," he once said during the fast days of war when I was sitting, tired of all the demands of my operation, with the family in their living room. Have I already awakened?

Evening approaches, and the sun is setting with a red glow behind the Chaco banks. The stewards are starting to set the tables. I would like to sit in the bow of the vessel where a breeze blows, since it is very humid. How often has a ship now borne me, upstream, downstream, with all being part of my life? I have the feeling that this is the final trip on a river, on the streams of my life, and it does not even sadden me.

15 December 1946

I should have much reason to be happy. I was greeted with love and interest wherever I went and where I met acquaintances. First of all it was Papa who held on to me like to his rock of salvation. At Abraham's, David's, and Lena's homes I was admired, the lady from the big city, above all by my nieces and nephews.

I have reason to take joy above all, in that Jake accompanies me, and that he is here and that he is helpful to me in my reorientation, in my coming to terms with home and myself, as the adjustment can be more accurately described. I want to value all that and gratefully accept it as such. Jake and I do much in common now and we have fun doing it, be it getting the fire started in the kitchen stove, lighting the petroleum lamps, or harnessing and hitching the horses. I have even started milking again.

The trip from Casado Port to our colony transpired exceptionally quickly. Jake had soon realized that the officers, who traveled with us, intended to use a rail car, and they took us along up to the Fred Engen station. There a truck was waiting to transport freight from the train station to our colony, a new convenience. And so we arrived the same day in Filadelfia which, incidentally, is now named Filadelfia, Spanish. There Papa was expecting us with his buggy and so we were home, on our yard, in half an hour.

"You claimed, not much would have changed," I told Jake. "There are all kinds of changes."

"I did not mean that, Lizzie, and you know it. I mean that what will affect you. I mean the air which you will again breathe, or, as you occasionally formulate it, the water in which you will again swim. I only hope that it will not strangle you, and that you will not go under. You will not have changed much and I would like to extend both of my hands to you."

Jake and I walked over to Mama's grave. We walked slowly at twilight across our schoolyard of old acquaintance, and then through the weeds and sand up to the small cemetery. And there lay the modest little mound of sand next to the others, not yet blown away as much, not yet washed away all that much. We stood there for a long time until it was dark, quiet and contemplative, and when we turned back step by step, I actually managed to find words which dissolved the sadness, the oppressing pain of memory.

"Here a sorrowful life has found its end," I said. "How happily it all started in Rosenthal by the Dnieper River. All we know is only the angst of the deportation in Russia. The worries during the flight and then the hard beginning over here, and the worry about her children remaining behind in much misery, and her constant concern about all their spiritual wellbeing. Mama has taken all this with her to the grave, even the final hopes which Papa and we carried towards a different ending of the war, and the hopes for a return and a reunion again. What might the preacher have said at the funeral? He will have spoken about salvation, of liberation, peace and eternal happiness. And everything will come to be."

Jake had remained behind, standing and looking up to the stars which shimmered in bluish brightness over us. "I find it consoling somehow," he said, "here below lie the mounds of sand, and there above arches the immense starry tent. And yet everything here below loses its meaning, collapses into itself like Mama's grave will in short order."

We held each other's hands like children, and all grief departed me. It was like a perfect harmony between the two of us that Mama's life had come to a close, and that peace surrounded her, like the soundless starry night of our village. We crossed the dark schoolyard and the trusted building looked after us through its black windows. I spoke Mörike's poem about the rosebush and the little pine and the black horses and death. "Reflect on it, oh my soul!"

What did I once write in my notebook? And why did I commit it to memory? Was there already then so much awareness of death in my soul?

"They have already been appointed,
reflect on it, oh my soul, to take root upon your grave and grow."

We both are inclined to sentimentality, Jake and I, and I freely admitted to it. And yet, it did me good tonight. When we walked through the sand of our village street towards our yard, we hummed the melody which at that time was so integral to our faith, "Oh, may it not be said, too late, too late, to walk through the Golden Gate."

26 December 1946

S cenes in which only the frame changes. The same yard, the same trees, the same house is the frame. The picture, however, has changed completely. Again, a family get-together with the customary turmoil. And Papa sitting there, tired, grey and absent-minded in his easy chair, with Mama's chair being empty. However, a crowd of youngsters frolicked on the yard, playing and laughing, unconcerned and ready to dive into life itself, the children lot of our families.

Not only has the frame has changed but also all the surroundings before which the picture hangs have changed. The entire political sky has changed. I remembered the conversations which formerly determined the tone and timbre when we previously got together, and I thought of the contrary ideas, which soon became confrontational.

Our settlement has experienced many quarrels and more schisms, and all on account of the question of the Germanism of Mennonitism, the return migration there, or whether to remain here. These wounds, it appears to me have not yet healed, and one does well in not picking at them. Otherwise surly moods ensue or injurious quietude. I notice this with Papa and Abraham on the one side, and David on the other. David is the most fortunate of the lot, it appears to me. He has remained true to his conviction and he shall remain right there. The events have proven him right. For him it was all a delusion, a wrong path, a disastrous course. His guiding pole of orientation was the faith of our fathers, Anabaptism, our Mennonitism.

And now we sat together like in former times. David was considerate. He did not boast that he had been right all along. Papa and Abraham, and particularly Jake, have not remotely managed to come to terms with it all, but that topic was not even introduced. I know that it is difficult for them to accept the fact that the dream of a Greater Germany is over and done with. But they still evaluate everything from the standpoint of the threatening danger of Communism. This danger is greater than ever. Germany was destroyed in fighting for Europe, while the Allies had aided and abetted the red flood. For them Germany is the sacrificial lamb and the world simply fails to recognise this sacrifice. The red monster will shortly stand by the Rhine and at the Atlantic, according to Papa and Abraham.

"Soon there will be talk about the last Germans, like Cooper spoke about the last Mohicans," Abraham once said bitterly.

However, our family get-together transpired peacefully, and that was good enough.

And as for me? I, being in the middle of all the turmoil, can keep my peace. I then think of Mr Heyse and how everything has turned out so differently from the way we wished and dreamed it to all end. No one knows what I was up to in all those years in Argentina. Even Jake makes no demands on me and I have the impression that he has decided to be tactful.

But in time he will know everything, all of it.

For all of them I am the nanny in Buenos Aires, who now and then sent money home and I leave them at it. For them all, I am an unwritten slate and a virgin, as the girl from our Youth Meetings and Sunday School. And yet I know, that by remaining quiet and protecting myself through isolation, I will again plunge myself into loneliness, just like after Bible School or, earlier still, after the fateful meeting while digging locust graves.

5 January 1947

Jake has again returned to Asunción which is his home, he claims. He departed, unconcerned and happy. "You are the only one I am worried about, Lizzie," he whispered into my ear when he left.

I believe that he has indeed cleared the decks here; our community, his church of faith, everything which in its time formed and formulated him is past, gone. A feeling of separation? Perhaps he became conscious at Mama's grave that for him more than just his mother had been buried. Possibly more than the last ties have been severed, dried up, like the umbilical cord of a calf.

Do I envy him? At times I do. I could have done the same, but I would never have managed to become as confident as he is. Or could I, possibly, have found the meaning of life, the longed for peace in the anonymity of a world city? With Jake things are obviously different. A man is capable of simply going about shaping his life, while a woman has to wait while she arranges herself in and on many levels. Heinrich and Erwin obviously did not suffer much, while Peter noticed nothing at all.

And yet I believe that Jake had to consciously jolt himself to break the ties and surmount the obstacles of retention. I noticed this from our discussions. Such ties are too deeply embedded in his blood; they are anchored in his spirit, in the character developed. Hundreds of years and many generations have forged an interconnection which an outsider is hardly capable of comprehending. Erwin looked at me full of astonishment and interested surprise each time when I told him about our community of faith and its established orders. When I told him that I would be banned from the community of faith on account of our intimate experiences, he was startled and wanted to protect me and "do without", abstain.

Jake had been forced to administer a jolt to himself and attempted to gloss over the toughness of divorce from his past by assuming jocund oblivion. He resorted to joking about the contradictions between that what was taught and the hard facts of reality. David then always became excited, since he could not bear the contradictions to his faith. Jake then had a good laugh as if he had scored a victory by justifying his divorce from his previous house of faith and order. "Our concept of faith is not the only valid one on this earth, David," he then said, "and not the only exclusively right one. Or do you truly believe in one church having exclusive claim in matters of salvation?"

On one occasion the two were quarrelling about Mennonite pacifism, with Jake introducing reference to all the wars and terror acts of the Israelites in the Old Testament. You shall not kill, so Moses taught, while Joshua slaughtered like a modern war criminal. And yet, David did not lose his composure. All this was part of God's plan and decree, and it was not up to us to contest such matters. Jake grinned: All that is nothing but a pious excuse.

Jake may be what he is. I know that his life is not in agreement with the "faith of our fathers." However, there is one matter which I sense deep in my heart. Jake has a wide and warm heart and I know that he has accepted me in it, even if my distress may be strange and foreign and bear an unacceptable name. With David I could expect no such thing.

Just prior to his departure, Jake and I again took a long walk on paths of old acquaintance, out of the village, through the bush and to homey pastures. It was a pleasant Sunday afternoon. The sky was clouded over after a recent rain. This walk became my confessional, and Jake accepted it into his world. Now Jake knows that I was involved in the war and he also knows that I am an adulteress. I spoke and he heard me out, almost as if he had expected it all.

It did me so good to finally speak freely about what transpired in Argentina over many years and to come clean, to give word to all the unspoken. Jake is no father confessor and is not capable of granting me absolution. Also, he did not attempt to console me or to pacify me. He listened to me and that did me good. It may be that he regards some of my confessions in a more conciliatory manner but he did not say so. He did not attempt to give me cheap consolation and I was grateful to him for not doing so.

"Do you know what, Jake?" I said when we sat down together on a tree trunk by the roadside. "I would like to pick up two large stones one in each arm and ascend Crista Rey, step by step, and unload them there with all the other stones. Do you remember?"

"I know, Lizzie," said Jake, "that you would walk the penitential pilgrimage and there would then be a few more stones lying on the Crista Rey. No, Lizzie, I am not mocking. You have done nothing more than I would have done, or Abraham, or the Friesland boys as far as the war is concerned. And as far as your love is concerned, with what measure would you like to have been measured?"

"With the measure the Bible dictates," I said resolutely. "Where else is our faith otherwise to find its measure?"

"I wish I had your certainty," said Jake while stroking my hair understandingly.

"It is because you do not possess this certainty, Jake, that I have the need to talk to you," I said. "For this reason I was able to speak to you and in doing so, I have already rid myself of some stones, even if not at Crista Rey. For this reason, my dear brother, Jake, I am most grateful to you. To whom else could I have talked? Not to Papa, for that would only have added to his pain, and not to David since it is difficult to speak to someone who has never been wrong. Lena would have been so shocked that I would have felt sorry for her."

We were already on our way home. The wagon tracks through the bitter grass, forced us to walk far apart, although parallel to each other, but we extended our hands to each other in mutual support.

A roadrunner traipsed ahead with his long red legs, always keeping the same distance from us. While running, he sometimes looked to the left, then to the right behind him at us so that I could see his beautiful eyes and the hair brush on his bill. The beautiful bird caused us to pay full attention to him, until he approached the village, whereupon he took flight in a long sweeping loop before slowly gliding to his home pasture.

19 January 1947

It is curious to note, that when conducting a conversation, thoughts and ideas enter into such realm of which the partner knows or feels nothing. It is then best to remain calm and continue in questioning and answering and act as if everything is perfectly right, proper and normal.

Liese Fast and I exchanged pleasantries, heartfelt words at our meeting after the church service; cordial, like in former times. Obviously I first have to come to terms with all the palaver about the elegant lady from the Big City, and whether she is still capable of talking to commoners, and whether she still speaks Mennonite Plautdietsch. I have by now learned to leap this hurdle, then the ice of time melts away, and conversations become more personal than I prefer.

And so I was immediately invited over for coffee at her home. I walked over in the afternoon. Years of hard work in the fields have dried up Liese, and she has by now become a typical old spinster. And yet, she is still a Sunday School teacher, as is Lena Neufeld, just like ten years ago. She asked me to teach again. Obviously it is time for the younger generation to serve in the vineyard of the Lord! You have gathered much experience and knowledge out there in the wide world and you could put all that to good use for our children was her opinion.

I was not prepared to deal with all that and I had to invent excuses. I asked for time out, a bit of time to reflect on her invitation, since everything was new again, and strange to me. I had to take time to come home again, I said.

That was just the right caption for Liese, for she connected the term "home" with the life of faith, and so with our heavenly home to which end we labour and to which we strive. That I was of the same opinion was a complete and total, unequivocal given to her.

"I now often think of my own death," Liese said, "for what is left to me but my death? When I go to bed at night, I see myself in my coffin, stretched out and beautifully ornamented. My hair is still beautiful, right, Lizzie? I have long thick braids and they are still almost black. I wonder how they will arrange my hair for the funeral? And then they will decorate me like a bride. All girls who are still virgins at death will be decorated like brides while in the coffin. Isn't that wonderfully beautiful? I dream of all this at night when my thoughts take me to sleep. These are such wonderful thoughts, now that I no longer have a sinful imagination as in younger years when my whole body burned in the inside, like a raging fire."

I probably looked at Liese with eyes, growing bigger and wider and stranger by the moment.

"Oh, Lizzie," she said, "you, too, will someday understand, and no longer fear death, and then you also can happily anticipate the wreath and veil as a reward for your virginity unto death."

Liese had baked crumble cake with red sorrel, crowning the pastry, as well as fresh buns. But my mouth became ever drier and I choked at every bite. And yet, I bravely munched and motored on; I can control myself. I am capable of carrying on a conversation even though my tongue is dry and my heart racing.

Liese wanted to walk with me for a space but I took my leave at the street gate. I was busy and in a hurry. Papa was alone and waiting for me. Then I ran out of the village right to the great *urundey* tree, where formerly the swing hung with its heavy chains suspended. Now all that remains is a deserted frame of former pleasures. I sat down on a tree trunk close to where I had formerly sat with Abraham. I felt so lonely, indeed lonesome, as a mother's soul alone.

I will obviously be punished even in my coffin and if I do not reveal myself, I will be decorated like an assumed bride. One wonders, as I do, how many girls have chosen a lie when wearing a wreath and veil at their wedding, in spite of their lost virginity? And I would lie with this lie in my coffin.

Tina Harms, the pale, came to my mind's eye, with a child under her heart, and with hair combed straight, and without wreath or veil, standing before the minister with her eyes brimming with tears. Happy Tina, I thought. Why do I now envy Tina? Possibly on account of the child under her heart, or because she was as honest as our village required her to be.

2 February 1947

W hen Papa and I returned from the church assembly, he let the horses walk slowly home. Since my return, we have not spoken together all that much, aside from discussing the daily necessities. Papa probably notices that I have much to digest. He does not probe.

"I have a feeling of guilt," he said, "that I had you come home. Perhaps you would have preferred to remain in Argentina instead of living here under impoverished conditions." He said that so softly, almost as if he were conducting a monologue.

I cannot very well tell him that even Buenos Aires had become a lonely and cold world for me. I may not speak about the difference between fulfillment, the warmth, the glowing joy of those years in the lonely pampas, and in the rawness of Patagonia and the horrible desertion when the war was over, with the decisive dice having been cast. I have to talk, I have to find many words, beautiful and harmless words, but I may not, and do not want to talk. I surround the most beautiful experience of my life with a wall of ice and scorn. I hide it from everyone and yet it burdens my soul in the extreme. I have spoken to Papa in friendly and dear terms, and I have consoled him and dispersed his misgivings.

The church was so cordial and open as I had not previously experienced it. I was called by name, a welcome extended; I was the sister who had spent much time away and whom the Lord had again brought home. Papa claims that in church much has indeed changed. The new leader is more open, cordial, more animated. He would very much like to speak to me, he had said, and to ask about my experiences during the time of war and to invite me to get involved.

I nodded and agreed to do so, while looking for words and wanting to withdraw into my snail's house; the crawl spaces, preferably, being as narrow as possible.

Papa allowed himself to be diverted and we spoke about matters which today affect us and also about the topic of today's church meeting. Thousands of Mennonite refugees are en route to Paraguay, a whole shipload full, with many more wanting to come. The churches and colonies have been requested to accept these poor people and to assist them in settling.

This topic is without end. Little is known, except that they are all Mennonites from Russia who fled to the west during the last years of the war from the colonies in Ukraine, from Chortitza and Molotschna and other areas.

"History plays topsy-turvy with everything," said Papa. "We want to depart from here because we see no possibility of building an acceptable life. We want to go to Germany, or possibly, even back to our old home by the Dnieper, and now the exact opposite is happening. Even more Mennonites are coming to the Chaco, and we are meant to help them."

The minister at the church service spoke about God's wonderful guidance, of His mighty arm. It had once again been confirmed that it had been God's plan all along to lead us to the Chaco of Paraguay in 1930. And now the way was open for other needy and suffering.

Papa has difficulty is regarding all this so simplistically and I admit, so do I. I was also a small cog in a bigger wheel. Which plan is God's and which is not? How many ruins remain behind on the wayside, how many wrecks, how much driftwood? Or is it possibly the rubbish of God's plan? Maybe I am such a little piece of rubbish?

The petroleum lamp crackles. The village is quiet, almost eerily still. Papa has gone to bed. In the distance, frogs are croaking, similar to drums rolling in a forest primeval, the old and familiar noise of a Chaco night in summer.

I wonder if I should persuade Papa that we, he and I, should move to Filadelfia? Papa can no longer master the work on the farmyard alone. I can cook, sew, earn a bit on the side; and, possibly, there is somewhere a bridge, a path, be it ever so narrow, that leads out of the loneliness out of the entombment here in this village now so empty.

17 March 1947

My life consists of encounters which can be so incisive as if a strudel had seized me or a whirlwind driven me. How often has this already happened that such meetings drive me into the deepest hopelessness and disappointment, or they appeared to lift me up to a crest of a wave to unfettered joy of great freedom? Everything then again came to an end, the depravity of the depth as well as the thrill of happiness. Are the Words of Solomon meant to console me when claiming, as he does, that everything has its time? To be born and to die, to plant and to be uprooted what has been planted, to break and to heal, to tear apart and to build, to mourn and to laugh, to complain and dance…?

But now I look back in gratitude on a meeting which transpired coincidentally the day before yesterday. Jake's friend from our village, Hans Wiebe, has become a teacher. He spent the summer in the capital city in order to improve his Spanish. Now he has returned because in March school will start.

Hans is an intelligent fellow, younger than Jake, but the two seemed to have gotten along well. He visited me to bring greetings from Jake, as well as a letter. Jake has probably told him about me for I observed a strong interest on his part as well as a cosmopolitan bearing, the likes of which I had rarely encountered here in our colony. I noticed that he was interested in my well-being and in my sensitivities.

He addressed me formally as Miss Unruh, and when I laughed and told him that I was still Lizzie in my village just like earlier, he laughingly accepted this form of address. He is probably ten years younger than I am, possibly fewer.

"We intend to meet tomorrow evening in Filadelfia," he said, "some of my friends and some girls. Luise, my lady friend, will also be there. Would you not like to come as well?

"Listen, Hans," I said while laughing, "In comparison to you I am an old woman, a girl left behind, as one would say here."

"Don't be so dramatic," he said quite seriously. "Age plays no roll with us. My good friend Hermann is ten years older than I am. And he is always part of our group. The main thing is that the spirit is alive and well as you are. You will see that we will have fun."

I agreed to go.

Yesterday in the late afternoon, Hans came calling for me with his father's wagon, drawn by a team of splendid horses, and so we arrived in Filadelfia in half an hour's time. Everyone assembled on the yard of Luise's parents. Luise is also a teacher in a village close by. It was a colourful group, comprised of young teachers, boys and girls of various ages and even a young married couple being part of the mix.

Hans introduced me. I was not totally unknown, but Hans in a deliberate voice of pathos declared, "This is Miss Elisabeth Unruh from Buenos Aires."

A lively welcome ensued with genuine friends, laughter, friendliness, and I was accepted into the circle. Naturally I was initially reserved, listening, and being buoyed by the element of conversation. Although a distinct tone and tenor with various turns of phrase, catchwords, and observations is soon a given in such circles, I as a newcomer did not feel at all out of place from the outset, and my initial keeping my peace was not at all embarrassing.

One of the teachers had a guitar and after animated discussions about world and colony politics, everyone started singing. I noticed that folk songs were a favourite; songs that are simple and of the heart, and which fitted this circle and the moonlit night. "A water man, wild, goes courting…" "There were two kingly children…" and then one evening canon after the next…: "The Stillness of the Evening everywhere."

Luise assumed charge of the singing; she appears to know an unlimited treasure of songs. At the conclusion of the meeting, she walked up to me, extending a cordial handshake and asked me to come again.

Is there consolation for my parched soul? We did not sing a single hymn and yet it all represented a gift from heaven for me.

31 March 1947

The waves of the Great War have now reached even us. I am no longer the only wreck over here which "spilled by the streams of time to the Island of this Earth" as the song goes and which we sang regularly in our "Home Song", the village choir.

We stood by the street and watched the wagons pulling past us, slowly and laboriously, with heavy loads of refugees. We waved, as did they. Wagons full of women, all wearing head scarves like in Russia, with handsome girls in the mix, and all pretty and healthy, wavy-haired, long out of style hereabouts, as well as many children. The refugees from Europe have arrived, from Russia, our old home. And now they come from Germany, destroyed. I really have the feeling that the pitches of the waves of history have now caught up to us.

Obviously, there is something to the Chaco. The first trek of our people was from Canada in 1927. Those were the descendants of immigrants from Russia who migrated to Canada in 1874 for reasons of the introduction of universal military service. They looked for refuge here in the Chaco from a world in Canada, deemed too encroaching, and they founded the Menno Colony with villages as we knew them from Russia. And then we arrived as refugees of 1929, and we have become neighbours.

And now the third large wave has arrived. The tensions overshadowing our colony shall remain unnamed. Relatives are being looked for and found. To say nothing of all the reports of those, already recounted or pending, who did not make it. These consisted mainly of men, fathers of families, predominantly, who disappeared without a trace during the great Stalin liquidations of 1937 and 1938. Many young men and sons also are missing, gone. The war swallowed them alive in the Russian and German armies. Then the Red Army rolled over the refugees in Poland and east of the Elbe River, and many of those fleeing were forcibly returned, including people of Mennonite persuasion, like those who were with us in 1929 when we were lying awaiting our fate at the gate of Moscow.

And all those, which the dreadful sieve did not manage to contain, are the rescued who managed to arrive in Western Germany, with many of these people now arriving in the Chaco. Many are still expected to arrive here, including those from the first ship. A civil war yet again rages in Paraguay for two weeks now. Connecting roads to Asunción have been cut. Not a single ship is now plying the Paraguay River, neither are news or postal communications functioning. Hopefully this soon will pass, like most of the revolutions in Paraguay. The remainder of the refugees from the first ship in Buenos Aires, and in part in Asunción, are forced to wait it out until the civil war is over.

Yesterday at the service, our church was full of new guests, women, more women and girls. The choir sang the song, "You ask the clouds far above, why they glow so rosy red, and why from East to West, from North to South, they head? …What a question! Because it must be so, the way they're meant to go."

At my side sat a young woman, of my age, but not acquainted with me. She held a handkerchief to her eyes, and wept heartrendingly. What might all have caught up to her and rolled over her after all the years of suppression and flight? I put my arm around her and held her close to me. Later she told me that she did not know where her husband was now, and that she had lost her only child during the flight. Now she has arrived, as lonesome as a mother's lonely heart, at the doorstep to the Chaco.

Outside in front of the church other women quickly assembled. They spoke much about their grief and sorrow. They are probably used to talking about it, and I gained the impression that talking about it was the best remedy for them to cope with their lamentations. And I stood there before them and listened, while they probably regarded me as a happy, well-kept flower in the protected remoteness of a place strange to the world. And yet, what does it all matter, at the end of the day? It is a consolation for me to hear about the sufferings of others. I am forced to, and also able to conceal my own grief.

Papa has questioned and probed the entire issue of the post-war confusion and its many players, and he is happy that Mama no longer lives to hear all the dreadful news. Maria with her children was en route to the west with all the others from Chortitza. Her husband already went missing in 1937. She arrived in the Warthegau, and then in 1945 she even managed to arrive in Thuringia. Then the entire group was sent back to Russia by the Americans as the Yalta Agreement stipulated. This news is according to the women from Rosenthal, who have also arrived here.

What is the cross I bear and what are all my disappointments when I now reflect on the afflictions which Maria had to suffer and which she probably still suffers, assuming she is still alive?

I have failed to report that we already reside in Filadelfia and that for a full week now. It was not easy for Papa to leave our farmyard, which he built up with our every effort over so many years. It almost broke my heart to witness him taking leave of his horses, and when he stroked their necks and walked away from them. His farewell from Rosenthal was probably not even quite as heart-rending, since we fled at night, choice-less, no recourse.

However, Papa realized that this re-location was the best solution for him, and not only for me.

12 May 1948

The evenings are long and it is pleasantly cool. We even have electric light here up till 10 p.m. every day, so that I enjoy sitting down to write. Sometimes I also sew in the evening by the light of a powerful lamp. Sewing is now my profession. I have learned sewing in short order and people trust my work. It makes me happy that I can ensure Papa and me of a steady income by cloth and the eye of a needle.

Further, there is considerable life in our house. We all had to accept refugees into our homes and we provided two rooms to that effect. It is a Falk family from the Borosenko villages. Papa knows all about this settlement. This settlement lay not far distant from our colony in Ukraine. The family consists of a mother and three children, two boys, aged 18 and 20 as well as a little girl of 12. The father went missing in 1937. The men from their villages were deported to some vicinity in the White Sea, Mrs Falk believes, or to Vorkuta. However, not even the remotest sign of life was ever heard from any one of those gone missing.

My life is everything else but monotonous since, aside from my sewing, there is much work to be done in the household. We have to become inventive while cooking, for the civil war drags on. And while we are not immediately affected here in the Chaco, everything has become scarce since the entire transportation system has been reduced. Flour and sugar are rationed.

Fortunately there is kaffir in abundance: kaffir flour, kaffir porridge. Meat, milk and lard are also available. Mrs Falk is happy in spite of all the frugality since the very products here mentioned were always in short supply is Russia, during the flight, and later in Germany. Everything was available only via food stamps, and in limited quantities.

Last evening Hans and Luise dropped by to take me along. The scary spectre of my loneliness has been reduced although it will probably never disappear totally from the depths of my innermost being. Yet, I have found an outer balance and the happy Hans has noticed this as well as his Luise, together with their colleagues and the other girls. The two embraced me, and the three of us then walked to the yard of Luise's parents, where everyone assembles under the beautiful *Paraiso* trees. It turned cooler and we edged closer to each other and again sang the fine songs accompanied by the guitar. "We are young and the world is open." I sang along and enjoyed it.

The conversations of the young people are highly critical. There is much talk about life in the community as well as that in the church, with all being highly aware of what is going on. They are all actively involved in school activities, at Youth Work and also in church. They question much of the accumulated tradition and would like to change things, thereby encountering resistance.

In all of this, the recent past in our settlement still plays a strong role. The young boys and girls were just as enthusiastic for Germany and its victory as I was in Asunción and Buenos Aires. For them everything German, the folk songs, all of literature, music, art, everything, was identical with and tantamount to the Third Reich.

I believe that now right here in the backwoods far removed it is more difficult to come to terms with reality than it is for the German people in Germany itself. However, with the arrival of the refugees much of the naked truth of recent times has been swept right over to our doorsteps and we have no choice but to deal with it. These people were immediate witnesses and saw things with eyes totally different from ours many thousands of kilometres away in the remoteness of Paraguay. It strikes me just how difficult it is to divorce oneself from ideals to which body, mind and soul were totally dedicated. The time has come to admit that serious errors were made, even if such were committed in good faith.

It probably became easier for me personally to do so because the breakdown of Germany also meant the end of my own personal life dreams. When the young people in our circle discuss these matters and even exchange heated arguments, I listen with bated breath and I tolerate their fire which in time will consume itself.

Luise must have observed this. "Something oppresses you, Lizzie," she said, and I know that in saying so, she meant more than the contestation of the past.

"Well, Luise," I said, "Do not worry about my soul. I have to come to terms with it. I observe your young happiness and I take joy in seeing that such is yours."

"I do not worry about your soul," she said while embracing me. "It is surely deeper than in many of us. And yet I am eager to catch a glimpse into the depth of your concern, particularly if I am in a position to help you."

I was happily relieved that it was dark and so I did not have to hide my tears. Possibly they were tears of joy.

I notice that these young people are in search of solutions, possibly even for salvation, and something on that wave-length stirs sympathetic reverberations within me. Reverberations and liberation, that is what I long for. Resistance and entrenchment are the cause of my fear.

17 May 1947

L uise wrote me a little letter, consisting of only a few lines. The reason for this was a poem by Hesse, his "Prayer." I was already acquainted with it, and it is contained in my collection. And yet, if someone else sends it along, it assumes a new effect. It then appears as if two souls are connected, like in a common bond.

Luise writes that she had read the poem together with Hans after a spirited discussion in which, yet again, the unresolved past experiences, specifically the contestation with Germanism and the Folk-Movement, as it has come to be known in our colony since 1933, came up for discussion.

> *"Let me despair, God, in me, but not in you!*
> *Let me savour the error of all misery,*
> *Let all the flames of suffering lick at me,*
> *Let me suffer every scorn, help me not in retaining me,*
> *Help not, in developing myself!*
> *—And yet when all the I in me destructs,*
> *That it was You..."*

Luise obviously senses that I am tortured by more than my former enthusiasm which I now believe it to be a mistake, and which appears like a fog lifting in the morning, exposing the true picture of the landscape. Luise has now attempted to help me with her tender empathy, in making the effort to come to my side, or, possibly, in coming closer to me.

I know that Hesse also was a seeker and that he probably remained one. Erwin gave me his *Steppenwolf* to read in a former time in Patagonia. I was deeply moved by it, by a *Mensch* who attempts to get to the bottom of the mysteries of being, shaken and rattled, torn back and forth, as if standing on a swaying, volcanic bottom floor.

"It is a tight-rope walk," Erwin said, when we spoke about the book, "and are we not also Steppenwolves?"

At that time, probably more than ever, I read my bible. Obviously, and certainly it was the search for security. On the one hand my blood, my desire to live, was grasping for a straw. On the other hand stood the norms, the demands, that which is valid as it had grown in me from childhood on, and had left their deposit of remnants, as it sometimes occurred to me—and all based on words of Holy Scripture.

Erwin did not seduce me. He was invariably considerate, full of respect for my belief structure, my sensitivities, my inhibitions. It was I who reached out for life, towards the straw of life, in full consciousness and awareness that the chalice poured me would contain bitter yeast below.

For this very reason Hesse's poem today proved so consoling, and, also, because Luise sent it to me. Even the ending is comforting: "for gladly will I go to ruin, will gladly die, but I can die only in You."

I believe with mounting steadfastness that the Bible has it right and is valid. It is, fundamentally, the foundation of our faith even if in our churches, in the course of centuries, layer upon layer has been deposited, thereby shifting priorities.

How often have I now read Psalm 32, "Regarding the Blessing of the Forgiveness of Sins." I know the entire story about, and of, David from my days in Sunday school. "For when I wanted to deny it, my spirit failed me... for your hand lay heavily on me both day and night, so that my moisture is turned to the drought of summer. Sela"

I have done a thousand times what the Psalm states. "I said: I will confess unto the Lord my transgressions." I have done this a thousand times, already in Bahia Blanca in Patagonia during my dilemma in which my distress was so great and my need so severe, and later after our military farewell at Langsdorff's grave in Chacarita, where, for me cross and swastika-cross, faith and realization was so fatefully intertwined, with all then coming crashing down, with only a heap of rubble remaining.

How light must the stones be which one carries up the mountain in Caacupe! And all who do it, do it according to a credo and carry the stones up the mountain. They believe in that credo and drag the stones, and are free!

And as for us? We believe in a different credo and this leads past the church community, before the church, in frontal exposure to the public. The church is our Cristo Rey, and you can interpret Psalm 32, as you will, and commit it to memory for- or backwards.

8 June 1947

The Borosenko Colony... the very name of which, has a dreadful ring to it as of yesterday evening. This Mennonite Colony was founded in 1856, as Papa knows. The village, Felsenbach, lies by the Basawluk Creek, just like Rosenthal lies by the Chortitza Stream.

Last night we all sat together in our warm kitchen, we and our refugees. It was rather cool outside and then Papa likes it when we sit inside with the Falks. He likes to listen to Mrs Falk telling us what transpired during the years after 1929 when all had to join the Kolkhoz; every village had to join, and she tells about the terrible famines of 1934 and about the repressions, as the deportations of men were called, and of 1937 and 1938 when the NKVD rampaged in the villages.

The two sons, Helmut, the older, and Siegfried were also present. When they were younger, they were called Abraham and Isaak. During the time of Germany occupation, they had to rid themselves of their Jewish names. Both were then also drafted into the German military service, with Helmut becoming a member of the SS, and Siegfried at the tail end of the war engaged in the "Folk-Storm" a very last ditch effort to stave off total defeat.

The boy's names were possibly the reason that in the conversation, an abyss suddenly opened for Papa and me, which we had not expected, and which we had previously regarded as unthinkable. We were again joking about their names. For jocund reasons Papa calls the boys Abraham and Isaak.

"We would not have liked to be Jews," said Mrs Falk, and she sounded a bit sad. "To be Jewish was very dangerous, perilously dangerous."

Papa had just blown off his anger by fuming against the Americans and the English who had supplied Stalin with weapons for a victory.

When Mrs Falk spoke about the Jews, Papa became highly agitated. "The Americans now try to blacken the German reputation by every means," he said, mad as a little Mennonite hell can allow it. "Now they talk about the destruction of the Jews, mass shootings and gas chambers. The Americans only have a bad conscience because they have helped the mass-murderer Stalin. And now they also have to make Hitler into a mass-murderer."

Mrs Falk and the two boys had become quiet when Papa got so excited. A lull of subdued silence ensued. Then Mrs Falk quietly asked, "But, Mr Unruh, do you not believe the matter with the Jews?"

"I cannot believe that," Papa said, emphatically.

Mrs Falk cleared her throat. It was obvious that she was having a difficult time of it. "Then we must tell you about an incident which happened in Felsenbach in the summer of 1943, some months before we fled. You should tell about the incident, Helmut, because you were a personal witness."

"I can speak to that," said Helmut. He had been a member of an SS Division, like most of the boys from our villages. He had his blood type under his arm, a tattooed sign. Now he laughed about the matter although he had had difficulties in Germany with it. The Americans did not want to release such people from captivity. However, Helmut was released simply because he was so young.

"Hitler clipped my wings," he now said and showed us his arm.

"But those in Felsenbach were no Jews," his brother interrupted, "those were gypsies. The matter with the Jews was told to us by the Sawatzky brothers from Nikolaital, when they were home on furlough, already in summer 1942. They were present in Charkow when Jews were shot there. In our village it was the gypsies.

"I know," said Mrs Falk, "but isn't that just as bad?"

Then Helmut spoke, "The entire group of gypsies had just passed us shortly before sunset. In summer we always worked until late in the evenings, much past twilight, in the fields, and we saw them coming along the Basawluk, with their wagons and horses, a long train of them. That night rain fell and no one was required to do field work in the morning. In the morning we heard that the mayor needed men for some work. The command, ordered by the police unit of the village, was that the hollow behind the gardens was to be dug deeper. This hollow was the collecting pit for liquid stable waste, collected there in winter. Soon everyone in the village knew that the gypsies were in line to be liquidated. That was the term in use at the time. Stalin also liquidated his enemies, the kulaks."

Helmut paused as if he found it difficult to recapitulate it all. "I was sixteen at the time. My friend Peter and I agreed that we wanted to see it all for ourselves, although it was forbidden to look and see. The cemetery, surrounded by a hedge, was located close to the waste pit. It was there that we hid, some one hundred metres from the pit. We saw how the first group of gypsies were driven to the pit, men, women and children. They all had to take off their clothes. Then the cracks from the salvos of the machine pistols were to be heard. We stoppered up our ears. Group upon group then followed until they were all dead. When the pit was shovelled full of earth, midday had come and gone, and we stole away."

Helmut was finished with his report and we all sat in subdued silence.

"Obviously all this is very difficult for you," said Helmut after a pause, "since you over here believed in Hitler."

"But why the gypsies," Papa asked. "what had the gypsies done to the Germans?" His voice was soft and hoarse.

"For the Germans all those were vermin," said Helmut, "weeds that had to be uprooted. They always talked about the pure race and the Germans were the pure race. Did you not know this?"

Papa was deeply troubled, and I hardly slept that night at all. Always and again the pictures passed by me, the large picture of the

Führer in Asunción, and then all our espionage missions over many years. Everything was noble and good, we believed. How did the song which Erwin and his comrades sang so often, go? "We belong to the best, for as long as loyalties last."

And then I thought of the circle of the young people right here, and that they still were believers in having fought for virtuous and higher aims and aspirations. I thought of Papa who was now totally confused because he cannot believe that Hitler and the Germans behaved just as badly as did Stalin and Communism.

And as for me? My own disappointment has become more complete as a result of this report and somewhat more conclusive than it already was. However, up to now I had held my peace and said nothing.

How am I to tell Luise about all this? I have to tell her. It may be that, based on this disappointment, we will become closer still.

21 June 1947

Yesterday was a cold Sunday with drizzle. Everything was grey, and the roads were muddy. Luise was determined to get to her village since she had to be at her school early this morning. She had no alternative but to walk. The distance is a mere three kilometres. I offered to walk with her and this morning I intended to walk back. However, I had barely left her village when the milk transfer truck passed me and offered me a ride.

When we arrived at the small teacherage on the school yard, Luise started a fire. She boiled tea and soon the small kitchen was cozy and warm. I told her the story about the gypsies. Luise was very shocked. I noticed that she struggled with tears. "How will your boys ever come to terms with all this?" she said.

Even before the Civil War started, Hans had subscribed to a daily paper *El Pais* from Asunción to improve his Spanish. He had reacted to all the reports of the elimination of the Jews just like Jake did. He simply did not believe the crimes. This was the worst form of slandering the German people. "Woe unto the vanquished." Such was already true of the Romans, and it has remained the toughest law of history.

However, Luise agreed with me. We have to confront the truth, and we have witnesses right before us. If we now look truth in the eye and do not deceive ourselves, we can more readily come to terms with our own past.

"This will be difficult for Hans," she said. "He and his friends were idealists in the extreme." She gave me a little page on which Hans had written some verses and presented to her. I took it along so that I could add them to my notebook. They render a proper documentation for the depth of error.

"That which we hoped for, happily longed for, has disappeared and the result has not met our expectations. We believed steadfastly in the victory of human rights. Smirking, the flag of victory now bears evil. Was not virtue our aim and our aspiration? It was a justifiable means of survival for our people."

Hans had written these lines in May 1945 just after the defeat, and his lines give hope that from somewhere a dawn after the darkness of the night must emerge. It is very tough to be disappointed by a fellow human. However, his lines express the sentiment that it is even harder when ideals fail to hold, and break down; ideals and hopes to which one has committed, only to realize then that reality is different, far different, and falls far short.

I then told Luise about Mr Heyse in Buenos Aires and of his reservations, and suddenly I was in the midst of a report. The report led to an admission, and the admission to a confession. Finally the lamp went dark since it lacked petroleum. The wick crackled and the stench of smoke startled Luise to life. I laid my hand on hers and she extinguished the lamp. Only the oven's glow emitted weak light. I continued my reverie into the darkness of the kitchen. The darkness became a confessional around us. I spoke softly and held nothing back. Nothing, not a thing.

Just as the dream structure of Germany, the high and lofty Fatherland collapsed into itself, I allowed myself to collapse unconditionally into the judgement of a friend. It did us good to talk to each other without having to look each other in the eyes, in the face. Luise listened, and I felt how she accepted me, and all I said. She took my hand and that was more than words.

And yet, I asked her a question, the age-old question by Martin Luther. How do I find a God of grace? I know that the question represents a demand, and inflicts pressure. A confession assuming absolution is based on a condition, on an imposed condition. I was prepared to take everything upon myself.

Stillness long prevailed in the room. Then Luise said, "You have a good and understanding Elder in your church. It may be that talking to him would be your freeing, the total release. We keep on looking for support in our churches, even though we are critical of it."

Should I, ought I look for this support? Would I find total release?

Then Luise placed some covers on the floor, and I had to lie in her bed. I slept well and good and deeply, lightened, as if I had unloaded rubble, rubble metres deep.

While having coffee at the breakfast table we looked at each other, free and freed. We had grown towards each other, matured on our road to the veracity of truthfulness, "Wahrhaftigkeit" as Kant has it, the supreme virtue.

Before Luise departed for her school and I left the yard, she said, "It is possible, Lizzie, that the gypsies and the Jew episodes for all their unspeakable horror, may someday help us in finding our way into the future, to plough a new furrow of future? It is dreadfully hard but we cannot, and may not, live with a lie, the lie. I am reminded of the parable of the chaff and the wheat. In our eagerness, we obviously accepted much uncritically and without review. It is good that truth can be found. And your veracity, Lizzie, remains in my heart."

They are all so young, all of them, so gloriously young: Luise, Hans, their colleagues and all the others. And they will all make their way and prevail. And I? Will I prevail, will I make it?

13 July 1947

Occasionally experiences are gifts, at least for me they are. That may well be on account of my age, since I no longer expect special experiences, and if they then come my way, they are gifts. Occasionally I catch myself singing emotionally goofy songs which only old people are entitled to sing:

> *"I set out with a thousand anticipations,*
> *And now return with much reduced aspirations...,*
> *I want to go home."*

And yet the week, now past, was indeed a gift, which I accepted with gratitude, like from a higher hand. The teachers had winter holidays, resulting in the sudden appearance of Luise and Hans in my room a week ago.

"You must come along, Lizzie," said Hans. "We are on our way to Hermann's cattle ranch for a full week. Hermann has a big rodeo and he has invited us. We will ride and rope and enjoy the life of camping far from our restrictive nest of trivial sticks and stones."

I hesitated since I had real inhibitions, but the two pushed and pulled me with jokes and laughter, so that I felt compelled to go and agreed to accompany them.

We set out on Sunday on two spring carriages, driving all day and into the night, taking breaks at campfires, sleeping in the open and arriving at the Estancia the next day. Hermann greeted us with exuberant joy. He welcomed us with a glass of red wine, sweet, like I had not previously known it, setting the stage and atmosphere for a week of which I admit that it was not only happy and relaxed, but amounted to a serious and reflective occasion. That constituted the inner beauty of it all.

Hermann is a single fellow of more than thirty, clever, powerful and wealthy. He belongs to those I call our group. We know each other well and the meeting of this week has revealed to me with stark clarity that my fate is sealed. I have clarified this with due sobriety in frank discussions with myself. Not even Luise has come to notice the slightest hint of my inner sleight of hand.

My deliberations, then: I could have imagined marriage with Hermann. That would have little to do with those flames which I had to subdue at age sixteen and which damn near subdued me. And nothing to do with the fire which I later let glow until I was almost consumed by that very fire myself. It would have been like a port with peaceful waters, possibly comparable to Lena's decision to marry a widower. All these were completely sober deliberations, factual, and in doing so, I measured my life in terms of length, height and depth with the result being, that I drew a final line, the signature of conclusion. I accepted it in due peace and accord, fully conscious that I represent the biggest hindrance to myself, I am my own impediment, my whole life long, with unresolved questions. I suffer no sorrow from it. I was able to be serene, happy and serious like all the others.

I would prefer to describe the rodeo. We, including the girls in our *bombachas*, the customary riding pants of cattle drivers, rode out

into the far spaces, to corral the cattle home. We sat on the fence of the corral built from palm logs and watched as the calves were lassoed, wrestled to the ground and branded. The air was heavy with dust and from the stench of manure and burnt cattle hide and hair. We were amazed at the skills of the cowboys and the other riders who went about their hard work all day long while whooping, howling and laughing.

Late in the evening we were served meat delicacies from the spit cooked over the embers of a *quebracho* fire, with the sparks flying into the night air. Hermann served beverages while Johann, a rider from the Menno Colony, played dance melodies on an accordion. He also played square dances and other funny games which these normally heavy of foot Mennonites had brought along from Canada. We even attempted to dance to new tunes but I held back so as not to have to explain where I had acquired considerable expertise in dancing.

But all that was obviously not the pinnacle, not the most important part of what was yet to come. The evenings out there on the yard by the camp fire turned out to be a baptism by fire, or, shall I say a purgatory. In any case it turned out to be something similar to a purification, like a painful rite of passage to a realization, as painful as it was. The fuse of ignition to it all was the story of the gypsies of Borosenko, with Luise initiating the discussion. Johann had generously stoked the campfire with *palosanto* wood. The fire was hot and heavy, reddening every face around. Possibly it was also the sweet wine served by Hermann which led from a talk to a heated discussion the very first evening. The discussion became so heated that Johann, not quite comprehending the topic, soon withdrew and lay down on his sheepskins. "You were probably all a bit drunk," he observed sarcastically the next morning.

No one was drunk. It was the desperate defence against a truth, which, like a house of a deck of cards, rather, an established pattern of thought that was to collapse and disintegrate. Hans and Hermann were besides themselves, screaming at Luise and me, talking about gullibility and handy condemnation. The refugees as well had succumbed to the sway of Allied propaganda, if they now told tales of atrocities.

I stated very calmly that I had no reason at all not to believe the reports by Mrs Falk and her sons. After all, the events transpired in their very village. Much of what we read in the newspapers may well be propaganda, just as much of what we believed was propaganda. But even if half of it were true, that would already be sufficient to destroy our innocent credulity.

I was already afraid that the entire venture would be spoiled by the explosive topic. During subsequent evenings, this topic was again and again discussed, with a turning point which I would term healing, coming about from an entirely different source, quite removed from what is true and what not. One of the girls, and a naïve one at that, posed an innocent enough question as to whether it was thinkable that even a Mennonite might have been involved in a scene such as in Felsenbach.

I said that the Falks had implied that also men from the Mennonite Protective Service, organized by the Germans, had been actively involved. "You can hardly imagine," said Mrs Falk, while making reference to acquaintances from her village, "what people are capable of if a concept, then a portrayal of an enemy, is presented with deliberate intent. This was certainly true of Communism as well. You would not believe the number of Mennonites who allowed themselves to be used or exploited by the Soviets, after they had been properly schooled to that end, or who believed that they would profit by so doing."

Then a deep silence set in with this silence leading to contemplation. The urge to fight was broken. What Hermann then said was material for a sermon. He spoke about Cain and Abel and that they represented an *Ur*-problem of mankind. There are Cains and Abels everywhere, and also among us.

Then Hans spoke about the deliberately stoked hatred as recorded in books and in German newspapers. "It is a hatred which seeks out the enemy and with intent to destroy such enemy. We sang, "The homeland strives to find peace, and to that end we seek out the fiend. No one shall bind sheaves among us, who is not meant for the job. And also we heard our share of the good German race and the bad Jews, even if all that was half a world and more away."

Everyone looked into the embers, reduced but crackling. Then Hans resumed his talk. "During these days of spirited discussions, I constantly reflected on what might well have become of me if I would have had to stay in Russia in 1929, in Felsenbach, possibly or in the Crimea, and I would have experienced everything which the years leading up to the war brought with them. Then the Germans would have come and shoved me into an SS uniform, which we so much admired on pictures for years on end. And then they would have explained to us as to whose fault all the misery of this world is, here and in the rest of the world. Would I have acted differently from the people in the Self-Protective-Unit, or the Sawatzky brothers and members of the SD?"

"Or they would have convinced the impressionable young men in the Soviet Union that the kulaks were bloodsuckers and guilty of the abject misery and distress of the population," Hermann added. "How many may well have cooperated in that effort?"

For all of us, as well as for me, this week represented a walk on the path to truth—or lack thereof.

17 August 1947

I re-read my latest entry. In the meantime more than a month has come and gone. We have later often discussed the problems, frankly and critically. It is not as if there is a past followed by a severance, to be followed by something else, an improvement. Everything is interrelated with the here and now having fewer problems which have to be resolved and which have to be confronted. I constantly notice this with my young friends and I notice it with me.

For this reason I intend to write about myself and to become aware, while writing, what I have to cope with. I have broken a marriage and if my deepest wishes would have been fulfilled, the war would never have ended and Erwin would never have returned to his wife and child. He had to tear his heart apart on my account.

It is this awareness which compelled me to follow Luise's advice. I visited the Elder and I confessed my guilt to him, my guilt with which I live in my church and which makes a mockery of the bridal decoration in my coffin and which Liese Fast is so much looking forward to.

The minister listened to me calmly and empathetically. The peace prevailing at the occasion appeared to me like an open door which caused me to become relaxed and uninhibited. I have withheld nothing, including my missions in Argentina. I soon noticed that the minister was less interested in my espionage than in the crucial issue, namely my sin of the flesh, as he termed it.

"There are sins," he explained to me, "which have to be announced to the church congregation. One minister by himself is not capable of dealing with such a load. It is not like in a Catholic Church and the confessional. It is only the church as such which is capable of granting forgiveness. Long centuries of practice and experience have revealed and proven that a complete release can only be attained if the entire church congregation hears the sin committed, and then rules on the issue. The public confession and open forgiveness also serve as a warning and a healing. We also find this in the letters by the apostles." He then read various Bible verses to that effect to me.

Did I not reflect on all this beforehand? Did I really expect a different response or outcome? Did I think of a confessional? Why was I then so thunderstruck by these explanations rendering me speechless? The Elder obviously noticed my mortification. He remained friendly and calm like a man with much experience in such matters.

"You do not have to make an instant decision in this matter," he said. "I know that all this sounds hard and that it is hard, and I want to grant you time. However, the way of release, the way of salvation with us leads via the congregation. I will honour your confession until such time as you return. Remember the Way of the Cross by Jesus. God is with you and He will lead you to the full truth."

What does all this now mean to me? It is not only the church which will now know everything about me, but also the entire colony. Everyone will know and talk about it; each in his or her own way will talk about it. And Papa will also hear about it, as well as my friends, all, everyone.

The next afternoon I ran to Luise in her village. She sat in her room and was correcting her pupil's essays. When she saw me at her door her face was like a mirror to me. I obviously looked shocked and consternated in the extreme.

"What in heaven's name is wrong with you, Lizzie?" she whispered. "You are dishevelled and green under the eyes."

She took me to her room, then went to the kitchen and made me a cup of tea, while I lay down on her bed. When she returned, I was again capable of speaking. I could tell her everything.

"I followed your advice, Luise," I said, "and the Elder says I have to go before the church to find real peace."

Luise had little to say, but she was with me, closer than ever, and I knew that she would stand by me and that I would not lose her.

"And neither will you lose Hans," she said while stroking me. "And neither will you lose anyone of our group."

The sun already stood above the bush and Luise walked with me for a space on my way home. I told her about our outing to Caacupe in 1941, "How much I would like to carry stones, many, many stones," I said.

"And I would help you do so," she said, "And I will also help you now." She would have accompanied me to Filadelfia, but I declined.

I ran alone through the dark bush as if through fog, and it did me good. "Truly, no one is wise, who does not know the darkness, which inescapably and softly separates us from all."

When I again sat in my room, I found some consolation in my poetry collection and again with Hesse. Should I not rather have read the Bible? But what would it have told me other than what the Elder had to say to me? Or should I interpret it differently, come to a different conclusion?

I have often thought of the age-old Statement of Faith which the Mennonites printed in Prussia and according to which they lived and conducted themselves. I thought of the time when David and I conducted such intensive discussions regarding the teachings of the church. It contained the strict ordinances, the way which leads to the church congregation and the way out for all those who continue to live a sinful life, without repentance. At that time it affected Tina Harms and the old man from a neighbouring village or the girls who had engaged in mixed swimming. The statement of faith came down hard and fast on them all.

And now it affects me, and I wish that someone would plunge me into the abyss which yawns before me and at the bottom of which I would prefer to remain.

23 August 1947

"It is strange to walk in the fog! Lonesome is every bush and stone, no tree sees the other. Everyone is alone." Hesse's poem accompanied me through the last week. It does me good to simply recite it as I walk along.

I do not whine, certainly not. Sometimes I simply reflect on the wealth of experiences of my years, even though it meant many a bitter chalice from which to drink, then and now. And I have so much consolation in, and from, our group of friends, true friends, possibly even friends for life. And all the while I feel that Luise in her tender way carries me, and that her knowledge protects and shields me with her hand and mine.

One is not to assume that one is the measure of all things. I was thoroughly tempted to judge life according to my own experiences. And now I see the pure happiness of love from Luise and Hans, unaffected, as it seems to me, certain and sure of the future and yet so strong, enabling others to be included in it as well. Such is also obviously possible. Life does not have to always go badly. Life is so totally different, so unpredictable, and I note with joy that I am involved in it without envy. Is this not proof that my fate is only one of many possibilities, one of a thousand, one of a hundred thousand?

And yet it has struck me specifically, and I ponder the reasons as to why I have not found fulfillment. Was it the restrictive atmosphere in our village, in our church, the pressures of the parental home, which were meant to provide me with direction? Were the inhibitions in my character which I failed to cope with?

Probably it was these and much more which I failed to comprehend and cannot even name or identify. The Elder spoke about God's ways in which we are to walk in obedience, or from which we err in disobedience. And yet, I looked for them, God's ways.

Tomorrow night we will again meet. We will again sing the beautiful songs with some of them made, it seems, just for me. "No blade on earth is growing, and all in heaven's sight, and no flowers are sprouting, without the sun's delight."

I am so much looking forward to it all. I will sing along, I will participate in the conversations. Hans has read a book which was already published after the war. It was written by Walter Küneth and is titled *The Great Fall*. Also someone sent him a speech addressed to the German youth by Ernst Wiechert, from Germany. We talk about it, critique it, look for salient points, look for a bond when everything about sways and crumbles.

I sing along and talk along without anyone noticing that my die has been cast, and that I feel compelled to walk through a ravine, through a dark valley.

I visited the Elder yesterday and informed him that I will walk the way he has shown me. I will confess my guilt before the church and ask for forgiveness. I will do everything expected of me. Is that the peace, which I feel in spite of the abyss, gaping before me, which I perceive, the reward for having given up every inner resistance?

I have passed the first test. I have told Papa everything. To my surprise, he remained perfectly calm. "We will walk the way of humility," he said. "We will bury our pride." Such is not Papa's normal vocabulary. Our pride, the pride of our family was always Papa's problem. Now they will talk about us, about his daughter of whom he always was so proud.

I no longer think of the burning of witches or burnings at the pyre. That was my great fear, the fear of the masses, which they jabbered, with their images and imagery. I would then have preferred to remain by myself, alone, as Hesse perceived the fog. But to remain alone with the likes of his faith does not fit our confession of faith. "All have to know it, as a warning and towards salvation," thus spoke the Elder.

I again read Psalm 32 today about the forgiveness of sins as prescribed by David. "And therefore I confess my sins; I did not hide my guilt." You, God, the Lord! I have done this always and again, time and again!

I had confessed my guilt to Jake; I confessed it to Luise; I confessed it to the Elder. According to the teaching of our church, this is not enough.

Am I again resisting? I do not want to do so and so be it! There are two weeks left until the church assembly. Prior to that, I am to meet with the church council. This means that I have to tell my story two times, two times in which I have to demonstrate my penance, two times that I have to ask forgiveness. I am already afraid that I am becoming dulled. Maybe it is that which scares me most, that everything will be dulled through the public nature of the exposure of our faith, our prayers, our confessions, our penance and our forgiveness. If only one would be alone in the fog, alone as Jesus was in Gethsemane, alone with the father, the Father!

8 September 1947

I stood in the sanctuary of our church, in front, and I saw all eyes directed at me, many eyes, large and serious, and I again told my story. I did not even have to reflect on the telling of the tale. I just listened to myself. When I then had to leave the room, since my case was to be discussed and deliberated upon, as is the custom, I literally felt like a lost sheep "far away in the mountains, wild and raw."

After a brief while I was asked to return. While I was walking into the room, then to the very front, the congregation sang the song, "Once I was far from the Saviour, as far as a *Mensch* can well be."

The Elder extended a friendly hand. The congregation had gladly forgiven me. Everything transpired most cordially. After the service was over, women came up to me, kissing and embracing me. "Lost and found again," it is said, and so it is held to be, although I have never been closer to the faith as in this barren time.

Hans and Luise came over that evening. Obviously they knew what had transpired; everyone knew, the entire colony knew. Both wanted to show me, with their friendliness, that no breach existed between us, not the slightest. We again walked to Luise's yard. All the friends of our group were assembled there and all greeted me with matter-of-fact-ness, as if nothing had transpired.

One of the teachers has bought a gramophone from a refugee who brought it along from Germany. It is a small box, no longer such a huge apparatus with a giant horn as on Neufeld's yard, many years ago. It is wound up with a crank. The teacher brought along records, both big and small.

"Well, Lizzie," said the teacher, "the first piece is for you. *Eine kleine Nachtmusik* by Mozart." We sat in a circle and listened devotedly to the two large records.

"Isn't that a song of the heart's jubilation?" asked Hans and looked at me when the music had died down. Everyone agreed: a song of jubilation, a rejoicing of the heart. Only I, I alone, heard something totally different.

"To me it is a scream of loneliness," I said softly, "only loneliness in the night, at night."

Should I rather have kept quiet? Had I not now exposed myself after everything that happened today? Luise immediately came up to me and sat down beside me and placed her arm around my shoulder. "How well I understand you," she whispered into my ear.

"Indeed," Hans stated very matter-of-factly. "Music is invariably also resonance; it always is that which it evokes in the listener. Music is multi-facetted, just as are the listeners." Then he directed the conversation to a factual level, and I was spared the embarrassment of my critical remark.

Then one record followed the next, classical pieces as well as folk songs and followed by—I was slightly startled—a song by Löns:

"The red fire's brightly burning, the sparks fly high above
Then they fall disintegrating, just like my ardent love;
My love is gone and missing, from my heart and from my sight
And I am left so lonesome, in the middle of the night."

A poem from my collection, and now I hear it on a record.

In my mind's eye I suddenly saw myself on our cotton field, together with Jake, with me holding a hoe in my hand, and my young blood racing. I had to smile and I suddenly felt that memories can also tune you happily—and gratefully.

"The fire no longer burns, it has died down, glowed away," is how the song ends.

Elisabeth Unruh died two years after this entry. It is not the last entry, but it amounts to a break and a conclusion of this chapter. Her death came unexpectedly for all. She suffered from an internal condition of which she did not speak. It was her gall bladder, which she was operated on, and which at the time was more serious than nowadays. However, according to her doctor, her chances of a recovery were most positive. Her heart was probably weakened from the quinine taken during the malaria epidemic. It may also be that her long and demanding missions to the pampas and Patagonia took a higher toll on her than she was prepared to admit.

In retrospect, though, her doctor stated that the main reason for her premature death was her lack of will to live.

The diary was in my possession for many years. Her entries continue, but they become sparse as if the inspiration source had dwindled, run dry. It is as if she mustered sufficient enthusiasm for a space, only to be followed by a falter. She works in her church for limited periods, but then suggests it is time for the younger generation to step up to fill the breach.

There is one entry in her diary which hit me very hard, since I believed that Elisabeth was too young to engage such thoughts. "I do not fear death," she writes. "Death has no terror for me. It is a friend who comes to me. The thought of life after death makes me happy and serene. What was the question at baptism? 'Do you believe with all your heart that Jesus Christ is the Son of God and that He has forgiven you all your sins'? Your answer! My 'Yes' applies to this day. And yet I have to look backwards on my short life and I cannot suppress the question: was that all there was? Was I born for that? I always thought that there is something yet to come. But nothing came and nothing will come."

Could one have approached such a Mensch and helped her?

Elisabeth, thereafter, it appears to me, dedicated more time and effort to her collection of poems and verses than to her diary. It is in poetry where she looked for consolation and answers for the meaning of life.

"O Lord, correct me—but with measure and not according to your anger so that you do not render me to nothing," Jeremiah 10:24. This entry was made prior to her decisive appearance before the church assembly.

Obviously the recorded poems are conversations with herself and reveal to me, that in spite of our close relationship, a human soul cannot provide the definitive security, the HALT as the German has it, the proverbial anchor, the rock of ages. In her search for consolation and balance in matters of transcendental questions, Elisabeth invariably reaches out to the hereafter.

"My hands in harmful nights I painfully extended and felt a weight placed on it by the Right," by Konrad Ferdinand Meyer. Emmanuel Geibel, Edward Mörike and invariably Hermann Hesse come to her aid with their profound verses. No one knew of this collection or of her diary before her death.

On the last page of her collection an anonymous verse reads, "And now I will think no more and suffer no grief as to what the future holds. I will allow your hands to turn me and revolve me, knowing that you are my all and everything."

Is this death, longed for? I had not anticipated this in our conversations and also not in the happy, indeed exuberant, hours in the company of friends. And yet, in retrospect, I have to accept it as such. A candle flickering, then gone.

It was heavy weather, in November, at that time. An exceptional humidity with low air pressure oppressed our souls. We knew that Elisabeth's end was near. And so we, her friends, walked over to the hospital at a very late hour and sang her favourite song at her window, "No blade grows on this earth, which heaven has not be-dewed…" whether she still heard us, I do not know.

The wind changed that night, blowing from the south. The morning was cool with a light drizzle—most unusual for the time of year—enveloping everything in a welcome grey, like a fog.

While reading her diary and the poems, I asked myself whether her life for her and her world was only what she may have believed in one of her dark hours: a disappointment.

This certainly was not the case. The length and breadth of a life are not decisive, the depth of it is. This holds true of many poets and artists. A human life is also its effect and I, and many others, have perceived this deeply and over time.

Other fiction available from Evertype

Kwaidan: Stories and Studies of Strange Things (Lafcadio Hearne 2015)

Pride and Prejudice (Jane Austen 2015)

Strange Case of Dr Jekyll and Mr Hyde
(Robert Louis Stevenson, illus. Mathew Staunton 2014)

The Book of Poison (Panu Höglund & S. Albert Kivinen,
tr. Colin Parmar & Tino Warinowski 2014)

Three Men in a Boat (To Say Nothing of the Dog) (Jerome K. Jerome 2013)

Treasure Island (Robert Louis Stevenson 2010)

Sealed with a Kiss (Rachael Lucas 2013; out of print)

The Hound of the Baskervilles (Arthur Conan Doyle 2012)

Snarkmaster: A Destiny in Eight Fits (Byron W. Sewell 2012)

The Haunting of the Snarkasbord (Byron W. Sewell et al. 2012)

The Burning Woman and Other Stories (Frank Roger 2012)

The Carrollian Tales of Inspector Spectre (Byron W. Sewell 2011)

The Cult of Relics: Devocyon dhe Greryow (Alan M. Kent, tr. Nicholas Williams 2010)

Nautilus: A Sequel to Verne's 20000 Leagues Under the Seas (Craig Weatherhill 2009)

Twenty Thousand Leagues Under the Seas (Jules Verne, tr. F. P. Walter 2009)

Through the Looking-Glass and What Alice Found There (Lewis Carroll 2009)

Alice's Adventures in Wonderland (Lewis Carroll; 2nd edition, 2015)

Lightning Source UK Ltd.
Milton Keynes UK
UKOW04f0843141017
310952UK00001B/54/P